THE CRITICS LOVE
DEBRA DIER!

SAINT'S TEMPTATION

"Ms. Dier, with deft turn of phrase and insight into human nature, wrings an emotionally charged tale from her characters which engages both the interest and empathy of her readers!"

—*The Literary Times*

DEVIL'S HONOR

"An 'I couldn't put it down!' novel."

—Lisa Ramaglia for America Online

"Devil's Honor is a quick-paced, fun-filled story full of vivid, strong-willed characters . . . a wonderful read."

—*The Literary Times*

"Devil's Honor is a wonderful regency romance that brilliantly borrows elements from the suspense sub-genre."

—*Affaire de Coeur*

"Debra Dier will keep you turning the pages in this entertaining, fast-paced tale . . . it both charms and delights with a little mystery, passion and even a bit of humor."

—*Romantic Times*

MORE PRAISE FOR DEBRA DIER!

MacLAREN'S BRIDE

"Debra Dier will delight readers with her delicious love story. Meg and Alec are a passionate pair and the Scottish setting is truly romantic! Ms. Dier has written a thoroughly enjoyable novel that readers will love!"

—*The Literary Times*

"Debra Dier's delightful drama is definitely a historical romance reader's dream."

—*Affaire de Coeur*

"The talented Ms. Dier captures the English/Scottish animosity to perfection and weaves an exhilarating tale that will touch your heart and fire the emotions. Great reading!"

—*Rendezvous*

LORD SAVAGE

"Exhilarating and fascinating!"

—*Affaire de Coeur*

"Kudos to Ms. Dier for an unforgettable reading adventure. Superb!"

—*Rendezvous*

"Sensual, involving and well-written, this is another winner from the talented pen of Ms. Dier."

—*The Paperback Forum*

LUSTFUL SAINT

She turned her head and looked up into his devastatingly handsome face. At the moment a frown marred his brow. He looked for all the world like a man in pain. She had seen that look in the eyes of other men. She recognized it for what it was: hunger. Pure, undiluted, masculine hunger. In other words, Lord Prim and Proper was suffering from a wicked bout of lust. How wonderful! "Are you certain I didn't hurt you?"

"Yes. Quite."

"I'm so glad." She shifted on his lap, turning to face him more fully, ruthlessly sliding her bottom against his most private region. His eyes widened. Through the layers of their clothes she felt an intriguing ridge rise against her. Her mother had informed her about the mating of humans. She recognized precisely what that bulge represented. Apparently the Saint was not completely immune to his more primitive instincts or her more feminine charms. Thank goodness!

SAINT'S Temptation

DEBRA DIER

Marlow
bk. 2

LEISURE BOOKS NEW YORK CITY

For my brother Tom and his family, Tom, Tim, Jennifer,
and Christopher.

A LEISURE BOOK®

December 1998

Published by

Dorchester Publishing Co., Inc.
276 Fifth Avenue
New York, NY 10001

If you purchased this book without a cover you should be aware
that this book is stolen property. It was reported as "unsold and
destroyed" to the publisher and neither the author nor the publisher has received any payment for this "stripped book."

Copyright © 1998 by Debra Dier Goldacker

All rights reserved. No part of this book may be reproduced or
transmitted in any form or by any electronic or mechanical means,
including photocopying, recording or by any information storage
and retrieval system, without the written permission of the
Publisher, except where permitted by law.

ISBN 0-8439-4459-5

The name "Leisure Books" and the stylized "L" with design are
trademarks of Dorchester Publishing Co., Inc.

Printed in the United States of America.

SAINT'S
Temptation

A Promise Remembered

Forget thee . . . Never—
Till Nature, high and low, and great and small
Forgets herself, and all her loves and hates
Sink again into Chaos.

—Alfred, Lord Tennyson

Chapter One

London
May 1816

She was the last person in the world he wanted to see. That realization pounded against her skull as Marisa Grantham paced the length of Clayton Trevelyan's library on Grosvenor Square. Although it was foolish to dwell on the past, the decision she had made seven years ago still lingered inside of her, as did the doubts. They hovered like ghosts who refused to depart to their proper place.

She ran her fingers over the arm of a leather wingback chair nestled near the hearth. Did Clay sit here often? Did he ever stare into the fire and think of a foolish young woman he once knew? Would he think it amusing to know she had never stopped thinking of him?

Marisa turned away from his chair, resuming her

restless prowl about the room. It was strange to be so near his things and yet so apart from it all. A tightness gripped her chest when she thought of things that might have been. The door opened. She pivoted, then froze beside the large claw-footed desk when she saw Clayton. Excitement flared through her like a flame through dry kindling. Any illusion she might have had of ignoring the appalling attraction she felt for him crumbled each time she saw him.

"I'm sorry to keep you waiting." Clayton moved toward her in long strides filled with the easy grace born of power. "It was unavoidable, I'm afraid."

"Greensley said you were being fitted for a new coat," she said, pleased with the composure in her voice.

"It took a few minutes to change."

Although she was considered tall for a female, the top of her head barely reached his breastbone. Marisa offered him her hand when he drew near. She wore gloves, yet she felt it all the same as his hand touched hers—a spark, as though she had touched flame. A startled look flickered in his eyes. Had he felt it too?

His long, elegantly tapered fingers embraced her hand with polite pressure. A clean scent of citrus and herbs curled around her with the warmth of his skin. She was grateful for her glove. It disguised the dampness of her palm.

Although she could conjure his face in her mind at will, memories did not compare to reality. Gray and green blended in his eyes, the color of spring leaves viewed through a silvery mist. Those beautiful eyes regarded her with a cool detachment that was somehow worse than the scorn she so well deserved. There was none of their history in that look. None of the secrets they had shared in their youth.

"You are looking well," he said.

"I can say the same of you." She hadn't caught more than a few glimpses of him since she had arrived in London for the Season. His black hair was brushed back from his brow. Sunlight spilled through the windows, mining sapphire highlights in the thick, luxurious waves. A master had carved his face, wielding a chisel with bold strokes, molding sharply defined cheekbones, a fine, straight nose, and a strong jaw that hinted at a stubborn streak. "You are completely recovered from your wounds?"

He released her hand. "Completely."

The undercurrent in his voice spoke of more than visible wounds. She had no doubt the wounds she had inflicted had healed. She wished she could say the same of her own. "I read about you in the *Times* after the battle. They called you one of the heroes of Waterloo."

"I did no more than many others."

Marisa knew better. Since he had purchased his commission seven years ago, she had gleaned every detail about him from every source she could safely employ, including his grandmother Sophia. Countless tales of his reckless bravery had chilled her. Every day she had expected to hear of his death on the battlefield. Every year since he had left, she had suffered in silence, her life suspended until the day she knew he was safe.

She squeezed the cords of her reticule as polite conversation dwindled into a restless silence. "I suppose you are wondering why I have come here this afternoon."

"I will admit I am curious." He frowned, his gaze traveling over the sofas and chairs in the room. "You didn't actually come here unattended, did you?"

"Of course not. I came with my Aunt Cecilia."

"Apparently your aunt has added invisibility to her

list of accomplishments.'' Clayton glanced up at the brass balustrade encircling the second-floor gallery. ''Or perhaps she is hiding in the gallery.''

His sarcasm plucked nerves already stretched taut. ''She is waiting in the carriage. I'm afraid Aunt Cecilia doesn't care for the company of men.''

''A chaperon who hides in the carriage. Quite an interesting choice you've made.'' Although his voice remained light, his eyes betrayed his disapproval. ''Most ladies tend to be very protective of their reputations.''

Although she hated to admit it, he was right. Any unmarried woman under the age of thirty required a chaperon while in London. ''I am well aware of the danger of coming here. My parents are spending a few weeks with my sister in the country. That left Aunt Cecilia. I apologize if I have offended your sense of propriety, but I would not have come here if it were not urgent.''

He frowned. ''What has happened?''

Marisa drew in her breath before plunging into the depths of the matter that had brought her here. She parried his questions, deflected his sarcasm, and related all the pertinent information she had gained in the Merrivales' maze garden during a ball at their home the previous evening. Still, she could see the tale had not moved him in the least. ''You aren't taking this seriously, are you?'' she concluded.

''I see little reason to take it seriously.''

''I know what I heard.'' She gestured with her hand as she spoke. Her reticule bumped a brass figure of a unicorn on the desk, toppling it over the edge. ''Oh, dear . . .''

She snatched for the figure. It slipped past her fingers. Brass glinted in the sunlight slanting through the windows as the unicorn tumbled. It landed with a thud—on the tip of Clayton's black boot. Marisa cringed at the sound of his soft gasp. She glanced from the scuff mark on the finely-buffed black leather to his face. His eyes were closed, his lips pursed, as though he had just had a tooth extracted against his will.

"I'm sorry."

He drew in his breath before he opened his eyes. "It's all right. I think only one toe is broken."

In spite of her embarrassment, his light tone made her smile. "I suppose we should be glad for small miracles."

"I suppose."

She bent to retrieve the unicorn. So did he. They collided, her brow whacking his jaw. The impact tossed her backward. Her bottom thumped the floor. Her teeth clicked together. When the pinpoints of light cleared from her eyes, his shiny black boots came into focus. She tilted her gaze upward, along the length of buff-colored cloth molded lovingly to his muscular legs, his dark gray coat, silvery green waistcoat, the white linen at his neck, and finally to the devastating male beauty of his face.

Clayton was rubbing his jaw, staring down at her as though she had just descended from the far side of the moon. Not for the first time in her life, she wished she could snap her fingers and disappear. Change into a wisp of smoke. Slide through the cracks in the floor. Escape her own foolishness. Yet she had learned long ago there was no such thing as magic, and floors seldom did what she asked of them. "I'm terribly sorry. I hope I didn't hurt you."

He frowned. "Not at all. A few loose teeth, nothing to worry about. How about you?"

"I'm fine." Except that her dignity lay in a thousand bits and pieces scattered across the floor.

He offered her his hand and helped her to her feet. As she stood, the toe of her shoe caught in the hem of her gown. She pitched forward. "Oh!"

"Careful!" He slid his arms around her, a reflex that brought her flush against the solid wall of his chest. The impact vibrated through her, shaking her to the core. His arms tightened around her in what might have been an embrace straight out of her dreams. His warmth surrounded her, soaking through her clothes, sinking beneath her skin, heating her in the most surprising places.

She glanced up at him and wished she hadn't. In that moment he seemed completely unguarded, as vulnerable and lonely as she was. Pain and need, a horrible confusion, all shimmered there in those beautiful eyes. For a heart-stopping moment she felt connected to him again, as she had once in a distant, idyllic dream. Yet the wall of indifference soon slammed down between them, leaving her to wonder if she had only imagined the turmoil in his eyes.

Clayton released her, breaking the delicate threads wrapping them together. He stepped back, as though he were afraid she might contaminate him with her touch. She stared at the intricate folds of the pristine white linen of his neckcloth, where an emerald winked at her, teasing her with a reminder of the past.

A chill settled around her, replacing the warmth she had felt in his arms. After all these years, the man could still set her heart racing with a touch. It wasn't supposed to be this way. This attraction was supposed to fade. She caught herself on the edge of a deep pool of regret, snatching for balance. Nothing could be gained by wishing for things beyond her reach.

He retrieved the unicorn and turned it over in his hands. "He managed to survive his fall without a scratch."

She couldn't say the same for herself. She felt bruised inside, battered in places she had hoped were safe from him. She slid the silk cord of her reticule through her fingers as she spoke. "I know you find it difficult to believe, but I heard the tone of their voices. I know those two men were serious about their intent."

He stared down at the unicorn in his hand. "I don't doubt you heard precisely what you say you heard. I do doubt they were serious about it."

"What do you suppose they meant?"

He set the unicorn on the desk. "People often mention things they would like to happen. Few have any intention of actually taking action to make those things come about."

Frustration rose inside of her until her hands trembled. "You must do something about this."

"I suspect you are taking this far too seriously."

She stepped back, wanting in that moment to grab those broad shoulders and shake him until his teeth rattled. "I don't recall your being this stubborn."

One black brow lifted. "I do recall your allowing your imagination to get the best of you."

"I'm sorry to have burdened you with my fanciful concern." She pivoted and marched toward the door with all the dignity she could manage. "Good-bye, Lord Huntingdon."

"Good-bye, Lady Marisa."

She left the room and closed the door behind her. Infuriating man! She took one indignant step, then jerked to a halt. She glanced behind her to find the blue muslin of her gown stretched to the limit, the hem trapped by the closed door. "Oh, no."

15

She reached for the brass door handle, hoping Clayton hadn't noticed. Her fingers brushed the cool brass just as the door opened. Her skirt swayed around her. There was no mistaking the humor in Clayton's eyes. "I caught my gown."

He nodded. "I noticed."

Heat prickled along her neck. She pivoted to leave. "Good-bye."

"Marisa."

She paused in the hall without turning to look at him. "What?"

"Thank you for your concern."

The dark current in his deep voice wrapped around her, tugging on her in unseen ways. She glanced over her shoulder and found him smiling at her, a warm, generous smile that sent her heart colliding into the wall of her chest. "You should take care. They sounded serious."

"I shall consider the possibility."

She managed a smile, while inside a vise squeezed her heart. "Good-bye, Clay."

"Good-bye, Mari."

She turned, her footsteps tapping against the parquet as she walked toward the stairs leading to the main hall. Regret was useless. Still, she couldn't prevent it, any more than she could prevent the bitter ache pounding deep inside her, or the sting of tears in her eyes. She would not contemplate the past. It was useless. Wishing, hoping, praying could not change the past. No matter how much she wanted to slip back and alter what had happened seven years ago, it was impossible. She could only make the most of each day as it came.

If Clayton Trevelyan thought for one moment that she would allow anything to happen to him, he had a great deal to learn. She intended to help him, even if she had to knock him down to do it.

16

Prelude

When first we met we did not guess,
That Love would prove so hard a master.

—Robert Bridges

Chapter Two

Devon, England
July 1809

Clayton Emory William Trevelyan, Earl of Huntingdon, Baron of Wendover, youngest son of the Duke of Marlow, had contemplated rebellion for a full thirty-nine seconds before accepting the invitation. He shifted on the black velvet squabs of his traveling coach and frowned at the moonlight streaming across the meadow the coach was passing. The summons from his father had arrived at Huntingdon House three days ago. True, the missive had arrived in the form of an invitation for him to visit Chatswyck, the duke's country seat and the place Clayton and his brother had been born and bred. Yet the only time their father remembered his two sons was when he wanted something of them. The trouble was, Clayton had no idea what his father might have in mind.

If he were more like his brother Justin, who was his elder by eleven minutes, Clayton would have allowed his noble sire to stew for a month before answering the summons. Yet, unlike his brother, Clayton had not been born with a streak of rebellion. Instead, he had been saddled with a sense of responsibility.

By the time he stopped for the evening, most of the guests at the Red Lion Inn had retired for the evening. A few gentlemen lingered in the taproom and were scattered about the public rooms. Clayton ordered a light supper; then, with a book tucked under his arm, he proceeded down a hallway to the private parlor he had procured. He opened the third door on the left and froze. In the dim light of two wall sconces, Clayton clearly saw a tall, slender young woman brandishing a poker at a tall, fair-haired gentleman. He recognized the man as one of his former schoolmates from Oxford, Viscount Ferndown.

"Stand back, or I shall be forced to murder you," the woman said, keeping her voice low.

"Come now, my lovely. Don't play games." Ferndown lunged for her. She poked his chest. He staggered back a step, then stood glaring at her. "Here now, that hurt."

"I shall be forced to do more than hurt you if you don't let me pass."

Clayton entered the room and closed the door behind him. "It's obvious the lady is not anxious for your attentions, Ferndown."

The woman glanced in his direction, fixing him with a direct look from a pair of golden brown eyes. The wary look in those beautiful eyes made it clear she wasn't certain if Clayton had come to her rescue or to reinforce her enemy. It didn't take more than a glance to realize she was a gently bred young woman of quality. Then again, he was not laboring under the weight of several bottles imbibed over the course of the evening, as he suspected the viscount was.

Ferndown frowned at him. "Which one are you? The Devil or the Saint?"

Clayton crossed the room, declining to answer the question. "I suggest you leave, Ferndown."

Ferndown lifted his fists. "I don't bloody well care which one you are, I can knock you down."

Clayton dodged a fist aimed for his nose. "Ferndown, you—"

"Stand still, blast you," Ferndown said, swinging with his right fist.

Clayton blocked the blow with his arm. The impact knocked the book from his grasp. Before it hit the floor, he rammed his own well-trained fist into Ferndown's jaw. The viscount's head snapped back. His red-rimmed eyes widened, and then he slowly sank to the floor at Clayton's feet.

Clayton studied his handiwork with a critical eye. Perhaps all those afternoons at Gentleman Jackson's boxing establishment were not entirely wasted. He doubted even Justin could have managed the situation with more alacrity. "Ferndown always did have trouble holding his liquor."

"If you have any thoughts of picking up where your friend left off, I would suggest you dispose of them."

He turned to face the young woman, stunned by the accusation in her voice. Yet the words he intended to speak caught in his throat at the sight of her. He hadn't truly realized what a prize Ferndown was fighting for until now. In spite of her ordeal, she did not appear on the verge of a swoon or hysterics. In fact she looked determined to bash his brains in should he make a wrong move. "I assure you, I have never acquired the practice of accosting young ladies."

She kept the poker poised for attack while she subjected him to a scrutiny so intense, his cheeks grew warm. A small, enigmatic smile touched her lips. "No, I don't suppose you have."

Glossy black curls framed the perfect oval of her face. Several long locks had tumbled free of their anchoring pins to fall in a lush, waving cascade over her shoulder. A blue satin ribbon dangled precariously near the end of one long curl. Her skin glowed in the candlelight, smooth and pale as ivory satin. Beneath slanting black brows, large golden brown eyes regarded him with an open honesty uncommon in most of the women he knew. There was no guile in those eyes, not a hint of the coquette, but a clear intelligence she hadn't learned to disguise.

"Thank you for saving me from the gallows."

It took a moment to find his voice; his attention had been snagged by a dimple at the right corner of her generous smile. "Gallows?"

"I was afraid I would have to hit him over the head. In which case, I very likely would have murdered him. Still, the gallows was a much preferred alternative to what he had in mind." She plucked at the ragged blue muslin at her shoulder.

The torn flap of material revealed a tiny wedge of innocent white lawn beneath. Nothing more. Far less than women revealed in ball gowns. Yet that illicit glimpse stirred ugly visions of what might have happened in this room. "Are you all right?"

"Yes. I'm fine."

He stared at the tear in the muslin, trying not to notice the white lawn of her chemise or the heat shimmering through his blood. He took the stick pin from

22

the folds of his neckcloth. "Perhaps this will help repair the damage."

An emerald winked in the candlelight as he handed her the pin. She fussed with the muslin a moment, then slipped the pin into the fabric, hitching the ragged edges together. "What do you think?"

A delicate scent wafted toward him, a fragrance that reminded him of white lilies after a spring rain. That scent reached deep inside of him, where it tugged gently on his vitals. "I think you would be wise not to roam about public inns unattended in the future."

"A woman shouldn't need a chaperon strapped to her side to keep from being set upon by drunkards."

"True, but we do not live in an ideal world, and a lady should take care."

"You are quite right; I should have realized it wasn't at all safe. I wasn't thinking. You see, I forgot my book. Instead of awakening my maid—Tillie does not travel at all well—or disturbing my parents, I came down to fetch it. That's when this man followed me." Her eyes narrowed as she glanced down at the viscount, who lay snoring near her feet. "I should have brought my pistol."

Clayton blinked. "Your pistol?"

She nodded. "When we were traveling the Mediterranean, Papa insisted I carry one at all times. I didn't realize England was just as uncivilized."

"I didn't realize young ladies had taken to carrying pistols."

She laughed softly, a husky sound that did something altogether wicked to his insides. "I'm afraid I have a great deal to learn about being a proper English lady. We have been out of the country for the past three years. And, as my Aunt Cecilia is fond of saying, I have been allowed to run wild."

"You have been traveling the Mediterranean?"

She smiled at him. His heart lurched against the wall of his chest. "Greece, Italy, Egypt. We actually traveled down the Nile."

In spite of his love of history, Clayton's travels had been only through books. "It must have been fascinating."

"It was marvelous. Unfortunately, after three years abroad, Mama wonders if she will ever be able to pound all the intricacies of proper English behavior into my head. Still, she is intent on managing that feat before we attend the Little Season at the end of summer. I have to admit, I'm a bit apprehensive about it myself."

"I cannot imagine you having a difficult time in London."

"You are being kind, but facts betray the truth. A proper lady would not have gone roaming about a public inn alone."

"You were perhaps a trifle naive."

"Another kind way of saying I was a proper henwit. Mama is hoping I shall learn how to swim before I take the plunge into the great pool of the haut ton. I turned twenty last month, and she is afraid I shall end a spinster if she doesn't get me to London." She glanced away from him, color rising on her cheeks. "And here I am rattling away. Another of my many faults, I'm afraid."

Clayton thought it unlikely this dazzling creature would end a spinster. "It must be the light. I cannot perceive any faults."

She smiled up at him. "You are indeed very kind."

The uncertainty in her beautiful eyes urged him to calm her every concern. Still, he had never been good at gallantries. Instead of assuring her of her exquisite beauty, her undeniable allure, her devastating charm, he retrieved a brown leather book from the floor near the hearth. He turned the book over to read the title. Books were a particular passion of his. As Justin was found of saying, Clayton was in danger of becoming a determined scholar. "*The Lady of Ravenwood Castle.*"

She laughed, a dark, sultry sound that made him think of sirens beckoning lovesick sailors to watery graves. "My secret is revealed; I am addicted to dreadfully romantic novels. I had them shipped to me all the while we were away."

He could imagine her curled up in bed, reading Gothic romances, falling asleep with visions of wicked dukes and dashing heros roaming about in her head. Unfortunately, with that image came another: this woman lying against white silk sheets, the light of a single candle flickering against her skin, all that black hair spilled across his bare chest. He stared at her, his cheeks growing warm from the wayward turn of his thoughts. "Your secret is safe with me," he said, handing her the book.

She held the book close against her chest and smiled up at him, curiosity glimmering in her expressive eyes. "Why did he ask if you were 'the Devil' or 'the Saint'?"

"I'm afraid the ton have contrived to saddle my brother and me with those peculiar epithets. Since we are identical twins, I suppose they felt it necessary to label us in some fashion."

She tilted her head, studying him with a look so candid, he wondered if she could peek into his soul with those intoxicating eyes. "I suspect you are not the Devil."

"No, I am not the Devil." He hadn't the dash of his brother, the bravado to tell all of Society to go straight to blazes. He was the sensible brother, cast in Justin's shade, a bore compared to his wild twin. "Since I would prefer not to propagate unduly high expectations, I shall introduce myself. Clayton Trevelyan."

She extended her hand. "Marisa Grantham."

He closed his fingers around her bare hand. Although her hand was slim, her fingers long and well formed, hers was not a delicate-as-a-flower hand. There was strength in this elegant hand, capability and assurance. "It is a pleasure."

"Yes, it is a pleasure to meet you. I suspect we would have met tomorrow, under different circumstances."

"Tomorrow?"

"You are one of the duke's sons, aren't you?"

"The younger."

"Earl Huntingdon."

He stared at her, astonished this dazzling creature would know anything about him. "Do you know my father?"

"Yes. My father and the duke are old friends. In fact, we are headed for Chatswyck. Father mentioned that you and your brother might be visiting as well. Perhaps you remember my father, Edgar Grantham, Marquess Westbury."

"Yes. I met him several times at my father's hunting lodge. He and my father often hunted together."

She tilted her head, her eyes glinting with mischief. "Odd, I would never have taken you for a man who would terrorize poor, defenseless birds."

"They need have no worry on my account. I am more fond of observing than of shooting anything except a target."

She was quiet a moment, looking up at him in that

candid way that made him feel he was made of glass. "I'm surprised we never met."

Clayton's chest tightened with the stirring of memories best forgotten. "My brother and I spent a great deal of time away at school," he said, distantly aware of a soft rap on the door. "We seldom—"

His words ended in a gasp as she threw her arm around his waist and spun him around until his back was to the door. "Lady Marisa?"

She hushed him with a soft whisper. Behind him he heard the door open, the sound followed by a soft feminine gasp. Still, he couldn't pry his gaze from the woman hugging him close. He stared down at Marisa, his body instantly aware of the feminine curves pressed close against him. The warmth of her body radiated through the layers of cloth separating his flesh from hers. That warmth stole into his blood, heating him until his skin tingled and his mind turned to mush.

"Please don't let her see me," Marisa whispered.

Her meaning pierced his befuddled brain. He glanced over his shoulder and found a plump serving maid standing just inside the room clutching a tray laden with his supper. He swallowed hard and snatched for his scattered wits. "I've changed my mind. You can take it back to the kitchen."

"Beggin' yer pardon, milord." The maid lowered her gaze, her brown eyes as round as pennies as she stared at Ferndown, who lay snoring on the floor.

"My friend just had a little too much to drink, I'm afraid." When the maid still made no move to leave, Clayton continued in a voice colored with a note of command that might have pleased his father. "We won't be needing anything more."

The maid looked at him then, sly understanding filling her expression. "Yes, milord," she said, backing

27

through the doorway. "I'll make sure ye aren't bothered."

After the door closed, Marisa released her hold on Clayton and stepped back. "Lud—I mean, my goodness, that was close. I certainly wouldn't want to compromise you."

Clayton moistened his dry lips. "Compromise me?"

"Alone with a lady who is dreadfully disheveled." She smiled up at him. "Before either one of us knew what was happening, we would find ourselves engaged to be married to prevent a possible scandal."

With her hair spilling from her pins, her gown ripped, her cheeks pink, she looked as though she had just been thoroughly tumbled. If anyone saw her like this, she would be ruined. And he would pay the price. Men had been forced to the altar for far less. "I hadn't thought of that possibility."

She tilted her head and studied him, as though she were trying to fit together the scattered pieces of a puzzle. "I'd better go back to my chamber."

"Perhaps it would be best if I escorted you back to your door to make certain you have no more adventures this evening."

"I don't wish to put you to any more trouble," she said, backing away from him. "Thank you again. I really—"

Her words ended in a gasp as her foot collided with Ferndown. The book slipped from her hand. It plopped on Ferndown's head, eliciting a low grumble from that quarter. She wobbled and tipped backward as her balance deserted her. Clayton grabbed her arms, catching her before she fell. She pitched forward, colliding with his chest. He absorbed the impact, and a tingling current rippled along his nerves.

She pressed her hands against his chest and looked

up at him, a sheepish grin curving her lips. "And now you will think me clumsy as well as brazen and hen-witted."

"No. Not at all." The intriguing scent of damp lilies curled around him, and with it came a slow trickle of heat into his blood. Her eyes reminded him of brandy held over a flame, golden brown, more intoxicating than the aged spirit. Distantly he realized he should release her. Yet his hands refused the command.

He should set her away from him. Release her. Now. It was certainly the proper thing to do. Yet his hands tightened on her arms and he found himself drawing her closer, confounding every sensible order his brain dictated. Her breasts brushed his chest, his muscles quivered in response. Her breath escaped on a startled sigh.

A curious expression filled her eyes. She stared up at him for a short eternity before she spoke. "I'm steady now," she said, her voice sounding breathless.

He flinched with the sudden realization of his improper behavior. He dropped his hands and stepped back from her. "I beg your pardon."

"There is no need, I assure you." She retrieved her book and stepped around Ferndown. "Thank you again for coming to my rescue."

"I shall accompany you. At a discreet distance."

She backed toward the door. "You really don't need to trouble yourself."

"It's no trouble. Really." Clayton could no more ignore the responsibility of seeing her safely to her door than he could deny the impact she had on his senses.

He followed her, staying far enough back to avoid any suggestion of impropriety, yet close enough to come to her aid should she need it. She turned at the door to her chamber and lifted her hand. The light of a wall sconce near her door illuminated her smile before she disappeared into the safety of her chamber.

"Lud!" Marisa leaned back against the door and cringed. She had made a complete fool of herself. Running about like a hoyden. Babbling like a fool. One glance at him and she had taken Lord Huntingdon's measure. He was a quiet, scholarly type, conventional, perfectly mannered. No doubt he found her a complete wet goose, shabby, an absolute disgrace to English womanhood. She clenched her eyes shut, but she couldn't hide from the memory of her own unladylike behavior.

Perhaps Aunt Cecilia was right. Marisa was hopeless. She would never fit into the English mold of feminine perfection. She would make a complete fool of herself in London, disgrace her family, send polite English gentlemen fleeing into the night with her brazen ways. Witness Clayton Trevelyan and the stunned look in his beautiful eyes.

Good heavens, he had stared at her as though she had just tumbled from the far side of the moon. Still, he hadn't seemed the least bit judgmental. In fact, he had been exceptionally kind. And the way he had held her—for one heart-stopping moment she had actually thought he might kiss her. Perhaps he hadn't completely disapproved of her. Still, the fact that she had placed herself in a position where a gentleman might think to take advantage of her was hardly proper. Oh, dear, she *was* hopeless, because she had actually enjoyed those few moments in his arms. How odd.

She hugged her book to her chest, astonished at her own reaction to the man. She had never so much as allowed a gentleman the liberty of holding her hand,

and yet she had come within a whisper of allowing a stranger to kiss her. What the devil had gotten into her? What was this odd, agitated feeling inside of her? Animal attraction? For a quiet, scholarly gentleman? Impossible.

Although she had to admit he was a handsome young man, remarkably so—tall, splendidly proportioned, with sharply chiseled features, not to mention those eyes, those glorious silvery green eyes—he was not at all in the style she preferred. She admired dash and excitement, blatant male power, a passionate nature. She wanted a man who could make her tremble with a glance. A man who would love her to the depths of his soul. A man who could accept a woman who had a few flaws. All right, more than a few when it came to adhering to all the sticky little rules of proper English behavior.

Certainly she could not be attracted to Lord Huntingdon. He was not the type of man she would marry. Unless she had lost all ability to judge men, he was the type of gentleman who devoured books, not life. The thought of passion would send him flying to a quiet corner of his library. A woman like Marisa would send him to an early grave. She released her breath on a long sigh. No, the gentleman certainly was not right for her.

It must have been the excitement of the situation. That was all. All this turmoil inside of her would be gone by morning. She was quite certain of it. Still, warmth flickered deep inside her when she recalled the way Clayton had held her. She had sensed heat smoldering beneath the cool surface of the man, like flames glowing beneath ice. He made her curious.

*   *   *

Clayton lingered in the hallway for a few moments after Marisa closed the door of her chamber, frowning at the turmoil inside of him. This irritating coil in the pit of his stomach couldn't possibly be what he thought it was. He turned and found a blue satin ribbon lying on the floor. Her ribbon. He lifted the strip of satin, slid the length of it through his fingers, thinking of the glossy waves that had tempted his touch. An uneasy heat flickered across his skin, startling him.

He slipped the ribbon into his pocket, then made his way to the large room he had procured for the evening. He sat on his bed and stared at the moonlight that spilled across the carpet, exploring the situation as though it were a particularly interesting mathematical equation.

Lust.

He recognized the feeling when he stared it straight in the eye. It was an appetite. At the age of fourteen he had learned how to appease that particular appetite when his brother had dragged him to a brothel for the first time. Although he was a healthy man of three and twenty with all the natural male urges for physical gratification, he had never felt anything remotely close to lust for any female who had not chosen to cater to that male affliction. He had always confined his primitive displays to the more genteel prostitutes of London. The truth was, most females of his own class made him uneasy.

He had no illusions about his own inadequacies. He was a dull fellow, more comfortable with a book of Greek philosophy than he was with a woman. Still, his title—coupled with the respectable fortune he had already acquired—made him the target of every ambitious chit on the prowl for a husband.

Each Season females flocked around him, each anxious to pry him away from his books. His natural shyness toward women did not deter them. His inability to flirt or engage in insipid small talk only made them more determined. Still, in spite of the best efforts of any number of perfectly lovely young ladies, he had never found a female who met his ideal.

When he contemplated marriage, which was not often, he knew precisely what type of woman would suit him. She would be a sensible lady, a quiet intellectual. They would share mutual respect, quiet esteem, and a gentle affection.

Marisa Grantham certainly did not fit his ideal. Unless he had lost all ability to judge human nature, her emotions ruled her. He released his breath on a long sigh. No, the lady certainly was not right for him. They were not at all well suited. It would be a grave error to think of Marisa Grantham in any terms other than as a friend. He had no intention of making that error in judgment.

Unfortunately the sensible side of his brain went off duty when he fell asleep. Marisa Grantham wandered into his unguarded dreams, filling his head with images of black tresses tumbled across his pillow, of brandy-colored eyes filled with mischief, eyes that could intoxicate a saint. She beckoned to the primitive male hidden deep in his soul, coaxing him into her arms with a smile. Pale skin as smooth as warm satin sliding against his skin, slender arms slipping around his neck, soft lips opening in welcome, breath mingling, limbs entwining, two indulging in one long, languorous joining. In various ways she enticed him through the long hours of the night.

Near dawn, Clayton awoke in a tangle of bedclothes, his skin drenched in perspiration, his breath coming in ragged gasps, his brain in a muddle. He fell back against his pillow and stared at the beamed ceiling, stunned by his wayward dreams, startled by the violent desire gnawing at his belly. Desire? Passion! For a gently bred female. Good lord, what a tangle.

Marisa Grantham was dangerous. If these insidious feelings were any indication of what the woman was capable of inflicting upon him, he would have to keep his distance from the dark-haired temptress. If he hadn't already told his father he would come for a visit, he would turn around and run back to the safety of Huntingdon House.

Still, he could not find it within himself to disappoint his father. He drew in a shaky breath. Certainly he could manage to survive a few days at Chatswyck. If he was good at anything, it was self-discipline. He reassured himself that Marisa Grantham would quickly realize he was a boring companion, completely ill equipped to deal with a spirited young woman.

He rose, bathed hastily, and dressed without the aid of his valet. He wanted to get out of this place before breakfast. He wasn't taking any chances of running into Marisa Grantham. He didn't think he could face her this morning. Not after those dreams.

Chapter Three

The dreams had been so vivid. So startlingly wicked. Marisa had never experienced anything like them before. She twisted Clayton's emerald stick pin in the sunlight streaming through the window of her father's traveling coach. Sparks of light shimmered in the stone—secrets revealed, fire hidden deep beneath the surface. What secrets lay beneath the surface of Clayton Trevelyan?

Clayton had the appearance of a harmless scholar, his black hair tumbled in disheveled waves over his brow, his beautiful eyes dazed and dreamy, his manner shy and retiring. Not at all the type of man who could command her dreams. Yet that was precisely what he had done, invaded her dreams.

Through the hours of the night Clayton had held her, kissed her, caressed her in the most astonishing ways. She had awakened this morning hugging her pillow, heated and restless. She supposed it was due to lingering excitement from the night before. It couldn't be anything more. Certainly she was not attracted to him, not in any romantic fashion. Still, she had caught herself searching for Clayton in the dining room this morning. And she had to admit a certain disappointment when he had not shown himself. It meant nothing, she assured herself. Yet, for some strange reason, she couldn't stop thinking about him.

"You should have pressed the advantage last night, Mari," Edgar Grantham said referring once again to her encounter with Clayton. "It would have saved you a trip to London, and me the pain of dealing with every blasted suitor sniffing after your skirts."

Marisa glanced at her father, who was sitting beside her mother on the seat across from her. He regarded her with dark blue eyes brimming with mischief. Tall and darkly handsome, at four and fifty, her father still managed to convey power and the roguish charm that had won her beautiful mother so many years ago. "Papa, you know how much I enjoy a challenge, and there is no challenge in shooting a fox in a cage."

"From what George tells me, his sons have avoided every trap laid for them. The elder is fast on his way to becoming the most notorious libertine England has ever seen. Justin has no intention of marrying in this lifetime. The younger is so shy of females, George is convinced a girl will have to strike him over the head to catch his attention. You had a poker last night. Clayton's head was within range."

"I suppose I should have, but I was afraid it might become a nasty habit."

Edgar grinned. "True, you could easily become a menace to the nobility."

"I expect her to become a menace, my darling."

36

Audrey patted her husband's broad chest. "In a much more subtle way."

Edgar nodded. "Still, if Mari had allowed the maid to get a look at her, the matter would have been settled. Since it was the younger son, I have no doubt he would have done the right thing. George says the boy knows the meaning of responsibility."

"I am not at all certain I want this particular fox, Papa. And if I did, I certainly would not resort to traps. One must play fair in these matters."

Edgar shrugged his broad shoulders. "It would have saved a great deal of bother. George is hoping you will drag one of his sons to the altar, although I believe he hopes you will snag the elder. Shame to have let such a golden opportunity pass you by."

Audrey Grantham crinkled her slim nose at her husband. Although Marisa had inherited her mother's golden brown eyes, and a similar cast to her features, Audrey's hair was a rich, dark auburn color. "Ignore your father's teasing, Mari. There is no need to rush. You will meet plenty of eligible young men in London. It would be foolish to single out any one of them before you take a look at the herd."

Edgar cringed. "Do you remember the debacle we endured when her sister made her come-out? Gad, we had every fortune hunter in all of Christendom camped at our door. It will be worse with Mari. She isn't a quiet, practical girl like Eleanor. She'll have them rioting in the streets."

Audrey rubbed her husband's arm. "We will alert the home guard."

"And you shall be there to protect me, Papa."

"I would say we've done a pretty good job of teaching you how to protect yourself." Edgar grinned at his daughter. "Still, I cannot imagine why you didn't allow me to put Ferndown's head through a wall this morning.''

''I thought it would upset my digestion. And I doubt he even realized who I was last night. I prefer to keep it that way. Besides, I am certain Ferndown had some difficulty eating his breakfast. Lord Huntingdon landed a prodigious right squarely on the viscount's jaw.'' In spite of his demeanor, there was strength beneath that gentlemanly exterior, Marisa thought. She couldn't deny that there was something about Clayton Trevelyan that intrigued her.

''Handled himself well, did he?'' Edgar asked.

''I suspect he has been well trained.'' Marisa also suspected there was a great deal more to Clayton Trevelyan than he revealed upon first inspection.

''Are you sure you don't regret not pressing the advantage?'' Edgar asked.

''Papa, the man is a quiet scholar. Can you imagine how quickly I might drive him to distraction?'' It was silly to think a man like Clayton could ever fall in love with a female who had a propensity for ignoring all the subtleties of propriety. No, he would never lose his heart to a headstrong, impetuous, dreadfully flawed young woman. Would he?

Edgar wiggled his black brows. ''Who is to say what hides in deep waters, Mari? The lad might have depths worth exploring.''

Marisa glanced down at the emerald, admiring its subtle fire. Perhaps they weren't well suited. Yet, for some strange reason, she couldn't get Clayton Trevelyan out of her thoughts. ''I wonder if Lord Huntingdon will be staying at Chatswyck for the rest of the summer?''

''George told me he had invited both of his sons to visit for the remainder of the summer. To provide some companionship for my daughter.'' Edgar slipped his fingers under Marisa's chin and tilted her head back. When she met his gaze, she saw a keen understanding in her father's blue eyes. ''It looks as though you will have the rest of the summer to see just what both young men are made of.''

A startling excitement rippled through her when she thought of seeing Clayton again. She frowned at the stick pin, confused by her reaction. It must be from the dreams, she assured herself. It could not be attraction. They were far too ill suited for her to think of Clayton Trevelyan in any terms other than friendship. She only hoped her behavior the previous evening had not poisoned Clayton against her. For some reason, it suddenly seemed very important for him to like her.

''Marisa, dear, I do hate to be a scold, but I hope you will refrain from putting yourself in situations where you need to defend your honor,'' Audrey said. ''If you had taken Tillie with you last night, or sent her after your book, you could have avoided a great deal of unpleasantness.''

''I know.'' Heat prickled her neck when Marisa thought of what Clayton must think of her. ''I shall do better in the future, Mama.''

Audrey smiled, a glitter of pride filling her eyes. ''I am certain you will.''

Marisa's chest tightened when she realized how soon she would be placed on display. In London everyone she met would judge her every move. She refused to embarrass her parents. They were far too dear to her to hurt them in any way. No matter how difficult it might be, she intended to turn herself into the perfect English lady, or die trying.

* * *

"I should have known it." George William Justin Trevelyan, the Duke of Marlow, paced the length of his sitting room. He paused near one of the long mullioned windows overlooking the east gardens. "Apparently your brother has chosen not to join us at Chatswyck."

Clayton sat in an upholstered armchair near the white marble hearth. "He may still come, sir."

George glanced at his son. Aside from the vein throbbing in his temple, he gave no other indication of his displeasure. "After he allows me to stew a while?"

"I am certain he means no disrespect."

"Are you? I, on the other hand, am quite certain that is precisely what he means to show." George rested his clenched fist against the window frame and stared out at the gardens. "Your brother has never forgiven me for what happened when you were boys. He still blames me for Wormsley."

Wormsley, the tutor who had taken over their lives after their mother's death and their father's desertion. Clayton tensed, while deep inside of him a shaking commenced in that place where his childhood memories lay buried in shallow graves. After all of these years, the mere mention of the blackguard's name could twist his insides.

"Wormsley is the reason he defies me. That's it, isn't it?"

Clayton knew the problem went deeper than Wormsley. Although Clayton understood the reasons the duke had altered so dramatically after their mother's death, Justin was not as forgiving. Justin saw only their father's desertion at a time when they needed him desperately. "Perhaps you should talk about this with Justin."

George shook his head. "I admit, Wormsley was an

error in judgment. I have told Justin so. What happened to you and Justin was regrettable. Still, regardless of what happened, Justin should have learned to control his emotions.''

Emotions must be controlled, or they shall control us. The words his father had spoken long ago rang in Clayton's memory. Time and time again the duke had repeated the lecture, as though he could erase all the emotion in his sons.

"That young man has spirit, I will say that." George smiled, pride filling his eyes. "Justin could topple empires if he put his mind to it. Bold. Daring. With a will of iron. He is the type of man who could make any father proud."

Unlike a quiet bookworm, Clayton thought. Still, he didn't need his father's words to confirm a truth he already knew. Over the years he had come to realize he could not win his father's approval, no matter how hard he tried.

. "And I *would* be proud of him, if Justin weren't so blasted intent on making me angry all the time."

"It might help to speak with him about your concerns, sir."

"I have spoken to him. I have lectured him on his role in society. I have cut off his funds, hoping to bring him to heel. And still he defies me."

A strong sense of protectiveness toward his brother rose inside of Clayton. "Justin has done well on his own, sir. His accomplishment is admirable."

"Under other circumstances, I would agree. The young man has managed to make a fortune without my help. Still, Justin is my heir. It's time he accepted that and stopped defying me."

"Perhaps he needs more time to settle down."

"And perhaps he never will." George flicked his

fingers against the heavy blue velvet draping the window. "If Justin refuses to produce a legitimate heir, I'm afraid the responsibility will fall to you."

Clayton shifted uneasily in his chair. "I am three and twenty, sir. I hardly think it is necessary to marry now."

The duke glanced at him, his gray eyes narrowing. "You and Justin were already two by the time I was your age."

"Not everyone marries young, sir."

"We never know what is waiting around the next bend, Clayton. Your life could be cut short. You could depart this world without leaving behind an heir."

Clayton smiled. "I prefer to take my chances rather than make an unfortunate match. It could very well mean my life would last a great deal longer than I wish."

George turned back toward the window. "Lady Marisa is a charming child. You remember Edgar Grantham? As I recall, you were along with us on several hunting trips."

"Yes, sir, I remember the gentleman."

The duke nodded his golden head. "Excellent man. Tall and fit, handsome as a devil. His title goes back to Charles I. There are rumors he is even wealthier than I am. And his wife, Audrey, has managed to make time stop. She is still as handsome as she was when she made her come-out. As you can see, the girl comes from excellent stock."

Clayton squeezed the arms of his chair as a noose settled around his neck. The duke had examined Marisa's bloodline the way he would any mare he intended to use for breeding. "From what I could gather last night, Lady Marisa is one of those females who has definite ideas of affection and romance in connection with marriage.''

George looked at him. ''You think so, do you?''

''She is passionate about Gothic romances.''

A muscle in the duke's cheek bunched with the clenching of his jaw. ''Affection is highly overrated.''

Affection is for the weak, remember that. His father had first spoken those words on a cold December night fourteen years before, when two frightened nine-year-old boys had come to their father for reassurance. Their mother had died that night. Yet Clayton hadn't realized until later that the father he had known had also died, struck down by a passionate affection for the woman he had married.

Gone was the warmth George had always shown his sons. There would be no more embraces, no more stories told at bedtime, no shred of affection. Their father became a stranger that night, a man who shunned them as well as emotion.

''I suppose I don't have to warn you about the danger of caring too much.'' George's voice grew low and bitter as he continued. ''You have seen what passion can do to a man. You understand the danger.''

''Yes, sir.'' Clayton clamped down hard on the lid of the tomb where he had buried his memories. Still, they crept through the cracks of his defenses. No matter how hard he tried, he would never forget that night. ''I suspect a lady fascinated with Gothic romances expects a great deal from marriage, sir.''

George turned to face him. Harsh lines carved his features. He had been handsome in his youth, but his face was hard now, ages older than his years. It was the face of a man who had glimpsed his own demons. ''I am not surprised Marisa has such foolish notions in her lovely head, considering the way her parents are with one another.''

''Under the circumstances, I doubt Lady Marisa would be interested in me in any romantic sense.''

The duke's golden brows lifted in surprise. ''You and Marisa?''

''I thought that was what you were implying, sir.''

George laughed softly. ''You and that spirited young woman! Good gad, Clayton, I cannot imagine Marisa would find you the least bit interesting.''

Heat prickled Clayton's neck. Although he knew his own inadequacies, it was still uncomfortable having them lifted to the light by one's parent. ''No, sir, I doubt she would.''

''Justin, on the other hand, now there is a man who could *inspire* a Gothic romance. No matter how dangerous it might be, nothing but unbridled passion will suit him. And, from what I have seen of Marisa, she just might be the girl to reform him. As you may have noticed when you met her last night, the child is a dazzling beauty.''

''Yes, sir, she is exquisitely beautiful.''

''From what I was able to gather from my fortnight at Westbury last month, she is also impetuous and willful, completely unpredictable. Everything Justin would find intriguing.'' George rocked back on his heels, smiling at the carpet. ''I have hopes in that corner, Clayton. If I can ever get Justin to meet her, I might actually see my blasted heir married.''

Justin married to Marisa. Although Clayton could see how the two might suit, the thought coiled around his chest, squeezing like a vise. His reaction startled him. Why the devil should the idea of Marisa married to his brother disturb him?

George cast him an amused look. "Obviously Marisa is not the girl for you."

"Obviously not." Still, even as Clayton spoke the words, a strange, proprietary instinct sank sharp talons into his belly. Proprietary notions about that passionate, headstrong, heartbreakingly beautiful woman? Was he losing his mind? Marisa Grantham would never lose her heart to a dull bookworm.

"Still, I hope you will entertain her while she is here. Take her riding, keep her amused until your brother arrives."

Clayton forced air past his tight throat as he thought of the passionate dreams Marisa Grantham had evoked the night before. Without much encouragement, he could fall under her spell. Lose his head. Make a fool of himself. "I had thought to stay only a few days, sir."

"A few days? Nonsense." He rested his hand on Clayton's shoulder. "I expect you to stay the rest of the summer. It has been too long since you have visited with me."

Clayton stared up into his father's smiling face while inside he weighed the danger in the temptress called Marisa against his responsibility to his sire.

"I am counting on you, son. I know I can depend on you."

The scales tipped. Clayton swallowed hard, pushing back the tight knot in his throat. "I shall do my best, sir."

Clayton left his father and took refuge in the library. He sat in a wing-back chair near the cold hearth and stared at a page in the volume of Ovid on his lap. In some corner of his mind he realized he had been staring at the same page for nearly an hour, but that distant realization had no impact on him. He couldn't stir himself to absorb the meaning of the words on the printed page. His mind was too busy grappling with the dilemma of Marisa Grantham.

It wouldn't take long for her to grow tired of his company, he assured himself. Truly, there would be little danger of committing some grave error in judgment, such as allowing lust to muddle his brain. Lady Marisa would find other amusements at Chatswyck. She certainly would not seek his company.

"I thought I would find you here."

Clayton flinched at the sound of his grandmother's voice. He glanced up and found Sophia, the dowager duchess, standing near the entrance to the room. Tall and slender, with golden blond hair and classically carved features, Sophia shared a resemblance with her son. Although in some strange way, she seemed years younger than the duke. Perhaps it was her vivacity, the way she savored every day of her life.

Clayton closed his book. "Have Lord Grantham and his family arrived?"

"They have." Sophia smiled, her blue eyes filled with humor. "Our guests are in the green drawing room. I thought you might like to join us."

"Of course." Clayton rose and set his book on a round table near his chair. He drew in a deep, steadying breath as he crossed the room. He would not hide from Marisa Grantham. He might be many things, but he was not a coward. He would face her and the ugliness inside of him. He could control this disturbing desire she stirred in him. Lust was an emotion, like any other. He could deal with it.

Marisa sipped her tea and tried not to stare at the young man sitting nearby in the elegant green drawing room of Chatswyck. What was it about Clayton Trevelyan that kept drawing her attention? Certainly he was handsome, but she was not one to be knocked off her feet by a handsome face and splendid physique. And it wasn't his sparkling wit. Clayton had contributed little to the conversation. Instead, he sat quietly beside his grandmother, stiff and uneasy, as though he were waiting to be called before his maker on Judgment Day.

No, Clayton Trevelyan certainly was not her style. Yet, for all her worth, she couldn't quell an insidious urge to smooth the rumpled black waves back from his brow. He looked so vulnerable, so utterly disarming. Marisa mentally shook herself. Clayton was definitely not the type of man who should attract her attention. Yet she had thought of little else since she had met him.

Sophia touched Clayton's arm. "Why don't you take Marisa for a stroll through the gardens, while we elders catch up on what we've been doing the past three years?"

Clayton looked at Marisa, his beautiful eyes betraying his utter dread at the proposition. Annoyance scraped her insides. Although she had been abroad these past three years, she had not lived cloistered in a nunnery. Marisa had met any number of gentlemen, none of whom had ever looked as though the thought of spending time in her company was the equivalent of having a tooth extracted. Still, Clayton did his duty. He offered her his arm and escorted her out of the house and into the south gardens.

The late July air was balmy. The sun played hide-and-seek with the earth, ducking behind thick puffs of white clouds, peeking out, casting golden rays upon the vast expanse of the gardens of Chatswyck. Still, her companion seemed oblivious to the beauty of the day or his surroundings. She studied Clayton's stiff profile, her pride sorely pricked. "I realize you must think me a brazen hen-wit, but must you look as though you are headed for the tooth-drawer?"

He glanced at her, his gray-green eyes wide with surprise. "The tooth-drawer?"

"You are frowning as though walking with me is the most disagreeable task you could be assigned."

He considered her a moment, as though he were solving a particularly interesting mathematical equation. "You are certainly in the habit of speaking your mind."

Marisa paused beside a large stone fountain where water spewed from a pair of playful sea horses. Twin plumes shot upward, reaching for the sky, only to tumble in silvery streams into a wide stone basin. "Speaking my mind is only one of my many bad habits."

"One of many?"

"One might add wandering about inns unattended, revealing my interest in Gothic romances, using 'lud' instead of 'Oh, dear,' and . . . oh, there are really too many to mention. By the way, here is your stick pin." She pulled the emerald pin from the bodice of her gown. "Thank you once more for helping me."

Instead of using the excuse to touch her hand, as many gentlemen of her acquaintance might, Clayton held out his hand palm up. She dropped the emerald stick pin into his palm and quashed the irritation building inside of her. A lady could not fault a gentleman for behaving in a gentlemanly fashion. Still, she bristled all the same.

Clayton stared at the pin as though viewing secrets in the emerald. He lifted his gaze and looked at her. He smiled, a wide, boyish grin that warmed the cool depths of his eyes and transformed a handsome face into something far more devastating. That smile hit her squarely in the chest, stealing the air from her lungs.

"My brother is fond of saying that anyone without a bad habit must be a dead bore."

With an effort, she recovered her breath. "Then I suppose your brother would approve of me."

He glanced away from her. "My brother generally approves of every beautiful woman he meets. I'm certain he would find you beguiling, as any man would who has ever met you."

The words were not spoken as a pleasant gallantry. Instead, he spoke with an honesty that knocked her off her axis. A warm breeze stirred the leaves of an elm standing along the side of the path. The rustling sound mingled with the splash of water, colliding with the pounding of her own pulse in her ears. She drew her hand through the sparkling stream of water spilling from a sea horse. "And how about you? What are your bad habits, Lord Huntingdon?"

He twisted the stick pin between his thumb and forefinger. "I suppose I have my nose in a book far more often than I should."

"Can't you think of anything more dreadful? Here I have admitted to being a brazen hen-wit with little regard for proper ladylike behavior, and your only sin is that you like to read." She flicked her damp fingers at him, flinging drops of water into his handsome face. His lips parted with surprise. "You are being shamefully ungallant."

A drop of water slid down his cheek and touched one corner of his shy smile. "I suppose you have uncovered another of my many faults. I am not at all good at . . . flirtation. You are flirting with me, aren't you?"

She stared at him a moment, stunned by her own behavior. It wasn't the fact that she was flirting. Over the past three years she had become adept at harmless flirtation. It was a skill her mother insisted she learn. Yet she had never expected to find herself flirting with a shy, bookish gentleman. "I do believe I am."

"And I am making a muddle of it."

"That, Lord Huntingdon, is a matter of opinion."

Curiosity glimmered in the depths of his stunning eyes. "I don't believe I have ever met anyone quite like you, Lady Marisa."

She could say the same of him. Instead, she tilted her head and smiled up at him. "I shall take that as a compliment."

"It was meant as one."

"I'm glad. I was afraid my behavior last night might have made you dislike me in some way."

"Not at all."

Her heart pounded against the wall of her chest. "Are you certain you don't think I am vulgar or fast?"

"If that were true, I would be a horrible prig. I may be conventional and terribly dull, but I am not a prig."

"No, I suppose you aren't." She had to disagree on a few other points. Although by all accounts she should have found him so, she certainly did not find him dull. As startling as it might be, the opposite was true. Perhaps it was the challenge of drawing him out of his shell. For some reason—she really must decipher this mystery—she found him utterly appealing, so confounded attractive she had trouble keeping her head. "Then I shall assume you really do not mind spending time in my company."

"What man could not wish to be in your company? Your astonishing beauty would be enough to delight any gentleman. Your candor and wit are joyfully refreshing." He glanced away from her, fixing his gaze on the fountain. "Yet I fear in time you will grow

50

weary of a gentleman who is not adept at witty gallantries.''

Did he have any idea how devastating his own candor could be? She had been paid pretty compliments by men from Italy to Egypt and all points in between. Yet never before had a gentleman been able to set her pulse racing with little more than a shy statement of his feelings. ''Does this mean you will not be composing odes to the lobes of my ears?''

He looked at her, his expression shifting from surprise to humor. ''They are quite lovely ears. I can see that they might inspire a poet. If I were more inclined to verse, I might compare them to . . . lily petals.''

''Lily petals? How nice. Although it might be difficult to find a rhyme.''

He nodded. ''You see, I am hopeless.''

She laughed softly. ''I suspect you are not as hopeless as you profess. Since I know you will be called upon to keep me company while we are here, I hope we may find a way to enjoy each other's company.''

''I shall do my best to be an entertaining host, Lady Marisa.''

''You make it sound a daunting prospect, as troubling as studying for a first in mathematics at Oxford.''

''I have always found mathematics less daunting than conversing with young ladies.''

The sun peeked out from behind a cloud. Golden sunlight tangled in his thick black lashes and painted the clean, sharply defined angles of his face. She found it rather hard to breathe once more. Still, she managed to keep her voice light as she spoke. ''It seems to me you have been doing quite well conversing with me. But then, perhaps you don't consider me a lady.''

His eyes widened while the color deepened in his lean cheeks. ''Of course I think of you as a lady.''

51

"Then I think you must reevaluate your rather odd opinion of your abilities. And perhaps you would do me a favor as well."

"A favor?"

"Since Mama is certain I need a great deal of polishing before I show my face in London, and I know she is quite right, do you suppose you could correct me if I misstep? Point out any slips in proper decorum? I would dislike making a complete cake of myself in London."

"I doubt I should make a very good tutor. I seldom pay a great deal of attention to the subtleties of social interaction."

"I suspect you shall make an excellent tutor."

His full lips tipped into a shy smile. "I shall try my best to be of some value."

She caught herself tracing the curve of his smile with her gaze. How odd. She had never suffered improper attentions from any man. And here she was wishing this shy young man might kiss her. Later, she would have to sort through the odd sensations he evoked in her. For now, she intended to delve deeper into the rather intriguing depths of Clayton Trevelyan.

Chapter Four

Clayton had never met a woman who was easier to be near than Marisa. He had known her little more than a month. Yet in ways he felt he had always known her. This afternoon, she rode beside him along one of the many paths winding through the vast estate of Chatswyck. Sunlight spilled across the brim of her straw hat, casting her eyes in shadow, illuminating the curve of her smile. She was looking at the copse of trees they were passing, as though the simple English countryside was the most enchanting place on earth. Somehow it became enchanting when she was near.

Although he had ridden every pathway, explored every copse, roamed each rolling hill, field, and meadow on the expanse of land that composed what might be called the kingdom of Chatswyck, when he was with Marisa it all seemed new to him, fresh and exciting. She cast a glow on everything she touched.

Not only was she delightful to look at, but he had

discovered she also had a lively mind. She had actually beaten him at chess, not once, but three times. Still, more than anything there was a warmth in her that beckoned to all the icy places deep inside of him. When he was with her, he felt like a traveler who had wandered miles through a winter storm to find shelter in her warmth.

In spite of his better instincts, he couldn't stop wanting her. The desire that had slammed into him the first day he had met her had only grown more virulent over the intervening days and nights. She haunted his dreams, leaving him heated and restless in the morning. He couldn't look at her without wanting her in his arms. Her beauty could steal the breath from him, even when her hair tumbled from its pins—especially when her hair tumbled from its pins. And her hair tumbled free of its pins with alarming frequency.

His wayward gaze followed the sinuous sway of a long ebony curl as it brushed the curve of her breast. Heat flickered deep within him as he imagined the slow slide of her unbound hair across his bare chest. Those thick black waves were as unruly as his poor threatened heart.

She halted her chestnut mare near the base of an ancient oak tree standing near the edge of the path. "Clay, look at that."

The informal use of his given name would have startled him a month ago. Yet Marisa had managed to dispense with formalities in the same direct manner she did everything. Clayton pulled up beside her, his gray stallion tossing its head and neighing softly. He followed the direction she indicated and saw the tattered walls of an old tree house peeking out from the leaves of the tree. "I haven't seen that in a long time."

She turned her smile on him. His heart bumped against his ribs. "Did you build it?"

"My brother and I built it a very long time ago. It was our sanctuary. I'm surprised there is still any of it left."

"Sanctuary? What an odd way to describe a tree house."

"At the time we needed . . ." He hesitated, reluctant to speak of a time better forgotten. He glanced back to where Harold, Marisa's groom, had stopped beneath an elm tree, far enough away to allow private conversation, close enough to serve propriety. Still, some topics of conversation were better avoided. "I suppose it is strange."

"Tell me about it," she said, her husky voice a soft caress. "Why was it a sanctuary?"

A bead of perspiration trickled down his spine. The day was warm, growing warmer. In spite of the warmth, a chill crawled over his skin as memories crept from their crypt—the sting of a strap against his back, the sharp blow of a hand across his cheek. "There is really nothing much to tell."

"A sanctuary is a place to hide. I suppose all children need a place away from their elders."

"I suppose." A voice screamed from his memory, spoken by the tutor who had controlled his life. *You are worthless, Clayton. I try and try to help you, but you shall never be good enough.* The fragrance of meadow grass and wildflowers drifted around them with the soft summer breeze. Still, the sweet fragrance could not erase the musty scent of a cold cellar from his memory.

"I used to play in a room of the tower of our home in Hampshire." She looked up at the tree house, a wistful smile curving her lips. "I would pretend I was a princess and my kingdom spread as far as I could see. I confess I was a little lonely. I am the youngest in my family. I have two brothers and a sister. The youngest boy is six years my senior. You can imagine what he thought of a little sister tagging after him. You are fortunate to have a brother your own age.''

"I cannot imagine life without my brother." Something in her candor turned a key deep inside him. He found himself wanting to share himself with her in a way he would have thought impossible a few weeks before.

"You and your brother both took sanctuary here?"

"After my mother died, my father went through a difficult time. He left Chatswyck and hired a tutor named Wormsley to watch over us. Unfortunately the man believed he could instill discipline with a strap.''

Her expression revealed her shock. "He beat you?"

"My brother had it far worse than I did. He was rebellious. Nothing more than a normal boy. Yet Wormsley was determined to break his spirit. After the beatings he would toss Justin in a cellar room and leave him there for days. I would slip away at night, and sleep on the floor outside the cellar door with a candle. I didn't want him to be alone." Clayton stared up at the tree house, his memories as vivid as the weathered planks nestled in that old tree. "Still, there was so little I could do to help."

"Was the man ever punished for what he did?"

"Father turned him off without a reference."

Marisa stared at him, her eyes wide. "That's all?"

"Father didn't want to cause a scandal."

"I cannot imagine why your father would have left you in a tutor's care after your mother died."

Clayton managed a smile. "It was a difficult time for my father. I don't think he could tolerate staying here then. There were too many memories of my mother.''

Marisa considered this a moment, a frown marring her brow. "I am surprised he didn't take you and your brother with him."

Clayton smoothed the reins across his gloved hand. "I suppose he needed time to himself."

"I cannot imagine anything worse in life than to lose a loved one. How old were you and your brother when your mother died?"

"Nine."

"So young." Marisa stroked her gloved hand over the neck of her horse. "At least you were old enough to know her. You must cherish your memories of her."

"Every night she would read to us. Her voice was always very soft, soothing. I remember fighting sleep, trying my best to stay awake, just to listen to her." He thought of his life before that cold December night. His mother had always smelled like spring flowers when she hugged him, and there had been lots of hugs. "At times, my memories seem to be of a time that didn't really exist. Things changed so much after she died."

"Your father must have loved her very deeply."

"I believe he did." Too deeply. His mother's death had nearly destroyed his father as well as her sons.

Clayton lifted his gaze to the tree house, his thoughts going back thirteen years, to a bleak November day when Wormsley had found their sanctuary. The beating that day had been worse than the others; it had left him bleeding and weak. Still, it was Justin who provoked Wormsley most. Justin who had been tossed into the cellar.

Clayton hadn't known what would happen when he wrote the letter. He hadn't realized it would bring his father as well as his grandmother back to Chatswyck.

He had known only that his brother would die if he couldn't get help. Wormsley would kill Justin. He would kill Clayton as well if he found out about the letter Clayton had written. Yet Clayton had taken the risk. He had smuggled the letter out of the house and into the mail. And help had come in time to save Justin.

For the first time in almost a year, his father had crossed the threshold of Chatswyck. He had dealt with Wormsley, then retreated to his study, as though he wanted to see nothing more of his sons. Still, Clayton had gone to his father that night, a frightened little boy seeking the security of his parent.

Memories taunted him with the events of that quiet moonlit evening. Clayton's skin grew damp and cold beneath his clothes. In his mind he could see it—silver glinting in the moonlight—a pistol in his father's hand.

I don't want to live without her, Clayton. I can't live without her. Nothing else matters. Nothing. His father's words echoed in his memory.

Somehow Clayton had broken through the thick wall of despair that had surrounded his father that night. Somehow he had managed to drag his father back from the brink. Yet it had come at a cost—the remaining shreds of his innocence.

Clayton glanced at Marisa, and found her studying him, a soft, pitying look in her beautiful amber eyes. He stiffened, feeling exposed suddenly, as though she had stripped him bare, uncovered all his inadequacies. His horse sidled nervously, sensing the change in his master.

Marisa glanced away from him. She stared out across the meadow for several moments before she spoke. "My Lord Huntingdon, I do believe I shall race you to that fence across the meadow."

She caught him off guard, as she usually did. It took

him a moment to digest her words, while she set off at a gallop across the meadow.

Marisa urged her mount faster across the thick meadow grass. Horse hooves pounded the soft ground. The wind whipped at her, yanking her hat back from her head. The burgundy satin ribbons settled around her neck, as the hat bounced against her shoulder blades.

She glanced over her shoulder. Clayton rode close behind her. Although her mount carried a lighter weight, the stallion was a larger beast, more powerful. Her short head start would not hold up against him. Still, she was not so much interested in winning the race, as she was in restoring a smile to Clayton's handsome face.

A dark sadness had settled around him while he spoke of the past. He had looked so somber and sad, his beautiful eyes clouded with remembered tragedy. It had taken all her will to keep from touching him. She wanted to throw her arms around him and hold him close, chase away all the ugliness that might touch him. She smiled as she imagined his expression if she had hugged him.

Instead she had done the first thing that had come to mind in an attempt to pull him from the dark memories.

They took the fence side by side, clearing the low stone barrier as if the horses might leave the bounds of the earth and soar toward the heavens. She pulled up in the adjoining meadow, laughing from the sheer exhilaration of the race. Clayton eased his mount into a walk and turned back to join her.

"I won," she said, grinning at him. His smile was her victory; it glowed like a bright ray of sunlight breaking through the darkness that had shrouded him.

"Won?" His stallion pranced about, anxious for another run. Clayton steadied it with a subtle movement of the reins and a soft word. With his horse under control he looked at Marisa, one black brow lifted in question. "We cleared the fence together. How do you consider that a victory for you?"

"You were riding astride, which gave you an advantage."

"And you had a head start, which eliminated my advantage."

"I suppose, in that case, we should call it a draw."

He grinned at her. "I accept those terms."

Oh, my, he had such a nice smile. "Would you like to rest here a while? It looks wonderfully cool."

Clayton glanced back across the lush green expanse of meadow they had just crossed. "I'm afraid we left Harold behind."

"We can wait for him by the stream. Will you help me down?"

Clayton hesitated, as though he were weighing the propriety of spending even a few moments alone in her company.

"Harold will be with us directly. I seriously doubt I shall be in any danger until then. Shall I?"

He grinned at her. "I think I can manage not to assault you."

She crushed a nagging twitch of irritation. He could at the very least tease her about finding her unbearably attractive. He could tell her how much she threatened his gentlemanly decorum. He certainly managed to threaten her tenuous hold on propriety. The other night in the rose garden she had stumbled, on purpose, and conveniently fallen against his chest. She had thought it might provoke him. It hadn't. Oh, there were times

60

when she wanted to shake the man until his teeth rattled.

He dismounted, the movement filled with fluid grace and potent power. He strode to her mount and gripped her waist. Although he wore gloves, the warmth of his palms seeped through the burgundy cloth of her riding habit. She rested her hands on the broad width of his shoulders. Thick muscles shifted beneath her palms as he lifted her from the saddle. Even though she was considered tall for a female, she felt like a delicate figurine in his grasp. When her feet touched the ground, her legs wobbled.

She gripped his shoulders, startled by the excitement tingling through her limbs. A clean scent swirled around her, the fragrance of herbs and citrus rising with the heat of his skin, mingling with the aroma of leather. That intriguing scent stole past her senses, setting her head reeling, her heart sprinting.

A curious look entered his stunning eyes. "Are you all right, Mari? You look a little flushed."

"I'm fine," she said, stepping back from him. Good heavens, the man could set her trembling like a leaf in a storm with nothing more than a touch. "It's just the heat."

"You'd better sit for a while." He took her arm and led her to the shade cast by a tall chestnut tree growing beside the stream. He shrugged out of his close-fitting dark gray coat and spread it on the grass for her to sit upon. After she was seated he stripped off his light gray gloves, tossed them to the ground beside her, then knelt on a broad, smooth rock on the bank of the stream.

Marisa pulled the ribbons beneath her chin, staring at him, following his every move, as though the simple act of dipping a handkerchief into the stream was the most fascinating thing she had ever seen. In some part of her brain she recognized she was acting like a love-sick schoolgirl. For some unforgivable reason, she couldn't help herself. In spite of her best intentions, these feelings he provoked in her had escalated past a safe point.

She laid her hat on the ground beside her. Without his coat it was clear that the breadth of his shoulders had been fashioned by nature. His green silk waistcoat hugged his narrow waist as closely as those buff-colored breeches molded the thick muscles of his long legs. Heat swirled inside her, collecting low in her belly, startling her. What the devil was she going to do about the man?

It wasn't that she wished to be ravished, exactly. Still, as humbling as it might be, she caught herself wishing he might actually try to steal a kiss. More than wishing, she had actually tried tempting him on more than one occasion. Yet the man had all the restraint of a saint. What would topple his reserve?

She peeled the tan kid gloves from her hands, ignoring propriety for the sake of comfort. For the hundredth time since meeting him, she reminded herself of all the reasons Clayton was not right for her. He was a quiet man, a reserved intellectual. She was forever looking for some new distraction in life. She would drive him to Bedlam.

Still, they had shared each other's company for more than a month and he didn't seem ready to pull out his hair. Instead of becoming bored with him, as she had anticipated, she found him more fascinating with each passing day. He was like an intriguing book. With each page turned, she found something new, something interesting, something irresistible, so compelling she wanted to keep reading forever.

Unlike most of the men she had met, Clayton treated

her as though she actually had a fully functioning brain. She could discuss Greek philosophy with him and not fear she would terrify him. She had discovered that nothing terrified most men more than an intelligent woman. Except Clayton wasn't at all like most men. He actually seemed to enjoy exploring her mind. She only wished he would take a little more interest in the rest of her. The man treated her like a sister. Blast him!

He rose and strode to her side. "Perhaps this will help," he said, handing her his damp handkerchief.

She pressed the cool linen to her warm cheek and smiled up at him. "Thank you."

He sat on the ground beside her, keeping a full fourteen inches between them. Propriety would be proud. She, on the other hand, was piqued. She sighed, resisting the urge to grab those broad shoulders and shake him. He was being a proper gentleman. She should be pleased. She shouldn't want to slap him for not assaulting her.

Even though she often found the rules of propriety somewhat constricting, she was not fast. She had never even been kissed before. She had never allowed a gentleman to so much as hold her hand. Still, this man awakened a part of her closely related to Eve.

She leaned back against the tree trunk and noticed that her groom had caught up to them and settled himself some distance away. She turned to gaze at the stream. Gray stones lined both sides of the bank, shaping a channel for the swiftly flowing water. Water tumbled over rocks, splashing softly, shimmering in the sunlight. A tall willow rose on the opposite bank, drooping long, slender branches toward the stream.

She glanced at Clayton, her gaze taking in the wind-tossed black hair tumbling over his wide brow, the clean angles of his sharply chiseled features, the shy curve of his lips. She couldn't imagine sitting here with any other man. "I wish I could paint. I would capture this day on canvas so I could look at it in the depths of winter and imagine myself here."

"I don't think I shall need a painting. All I need do is close my eyes and I shall see you here, with sunlight dripping through the leaves, sprinkling gold upon your face and hair." He lifted a thick curl from her shoulder. Slowly he rubbed the ebony strands between his fingers, as though he savored the silky slide against his skin. "And your hair all tumbled from its pins."

She watched the slow slide of her hair through his fingers, the soft caress echoing deep inside her, as though his hands brushed against her skin. "My pins never seem to be strong enough to withstand the wayward wishes of my hair."

"It's a pity you have to pin it up at all. It's very beautiful flowing in undisciplined waves."

Oh, my, she could scarcely breathe. Flattery from most men was simply a game they played. Compliments from Clayton always seemed a statement of fact. "Little girls may run about with their hair hanging free, but ladies must not. Unfortunately, my hair still hasn't learned that lesson."

"I wish it never had to learn that particular lesson."

There were moments when she sensed he cared for her, felt something more heated than friendship. Yet she couldn't seem to budge him in the right direction. "I have enjoyed the past few weeks. In many ways I wish the summer would never end."

He allowed her hair to tumble from his hand. "Wait until you arrive in London. You will be so occupied, you will never have time to think about this summer."

He spoke with dreadful finality, as though he intended to allow the past few weeks to fade into hazy memories. She would never forget this summer. And she had no intention of allowing this man to walk out of her life. Not if she could prevent it. "Are you going to London this September?"

"Yes."

"And shall you dance with me at my first ball?" she asked, managing to keep her voice light.

He clasped his raised knee and stared at his knuckles. "I shall try."

"That's an odd thing to say."

He flexed his fingers against his knee. "Only because you don't know the ton. You will be called a diamond of the first water, an original, so beautiful you will cause accidents when you walk down the street, from gentlemen watching you instead of the road."

She smiled at the warm humor in his voice. "I shall be a menace, is that it?"

"To every gentleman who has a notion to guard his heart."

Did he wish to guard his heart? "Perhaps I should be kept under lock and key."

"There would be rioting in the streets if you were kept under lock and key."

"And what does my penchant for causing anarchy have to do with your refusing to dance with me?"

"I shall not refuse. I shall try to get near you. But you will have so many gentlemen vying for your attention, you may not notice me. Gentlemen will trip over each other to win a place near you. Believe me, you shall have no lack of dance partners."

To her astonishment, she realized she didn't want another partner—in anything. "Do you imagine I am so shallow I shall forget my friends?"

He glanced at her, his eyes wide with surprise. "No. Of course not. I certainly did not mean to insult you."

"What did you mean?"

"All I meant to say is, you shall be surrounded by far more interesting men than one you met in the country."

Did that explain his reluctance to take notice of her shockingly blatant attempts to capture his affection? Did he feel unworthy in some way? "How odd. For some time now, I have thought you one of the most interesting gentlemen I have ever met."

Clayton's lips parted, then closed. He glanced away from her, the color rising in his cheeks. "Apparently you haven't met many gentlemen."

"Apparently you shamefully underestimate yourself."

He rubbed a speck of dirt on his knee. "You have a way about you, Mari. You can make even a dull bookworm feel he is a dashing fellow. You must be careful. A man's heart is a fragile thing, almost as fragile as his pride. You shall go about breaking a great many hearts if you aren't very careful."

What the devil was she going to do with him? She had already thrown herself into his arms, and still she couldn't break through his blasted defenses. Clayton wanted her. Marisa could sense it. Yet for some reason he didn't think she wanted him.

How could a man so incredibly intelligent be that blind to what was under his nose? Although she usually preferred the direct approach, in this case the risk of humiliation was far too great. What if she was wrong about judging his feelings toward her? She certainly could not march up to him and say, "I love you. Marry me." Could she? No, of course not.

A man liked to think he decided these issues. As Mama was fond of saying, a woman eluded a man until she allowed him to catch her. Marisa would simply have to find a way to put the appropriate words into Clayton's delightfully shy mouth. Still, she had very little time left. They were leaving for London in three days. She had a dreadful feeling that once they reached London, her chances of winning Clayton's heart would drift away, like dandelion seeds in a breeze. She had to do something. Soon.

She rose and mentally shook off her frustration. "I would love a cool drink."

"I'm afraid I don't have anything to hold water."

"I can use my hands."

"The bank may be a little too steep for you to do that." He rose and strolled with her the few feet to the stream.

She paused at the edge of the stream and gazed down at the swiftly flowing water. "It looks so cool. Should we go wading?"

"Unless I'm mistaken, that would mean exposing your ankles."

"And that would topple the empire?"

He grinned at her. "It would be a breach of proper decorum. And, as I recall, you asked for my help in that direction."

"There is no one here, except Harold. And he won't tell anyone. He is accustomed to my fits of fancy." She smiled up at him, tempting him to put a small chink in propriety. "What harm could it cause?"

He glanced at the water. "The current is fairly swift here. It would knock you off your feet and you would end up looking like a retriever who has just taken a plunge after a duck."

A ride back in sodden clothes and wet hair was not an appealing idea. "Are you always sensible?"

He laughed softly. "It is one of my many faults."

She smiled up at him. "I think your faults balance mine nicely."

"Strange, I never noticed you had any faults." He brushed his fingertips over the curve of her jaw, a beguiling warmth in his eyes.

The soft touch rippled through her, stealing the breath from her lungs. "I never realized you were so shortsighted."

He laughed softly. "Since I usually have my nose in a book, I have often been accused of not noticing anything around me. But you, my lady, are impossible to ignore."

"I am glad to hear it." Perhaps she was making progress. She knelt on a wide, smooth rock.

"Be careful," Clayton said, kneeling beside her. "It's steep."

"I can manage," she said, reaching for the cool-looking water. It was a great deal farther than she thought. Her fingers brushed the water. Her balance shifted. She gasped as her body commenced a slow tumble, headfirst into the stream.

Clayton grabbed her, his strong hands gripping her waist, jerking her back from danger. In the next instant her back collided with the solid wall of his chest. He sat back on the stone, his arms sliding around her waist, cradling her on his lap. She leaned back, her heart pounding from her narrow escape.

As the panic faded from her brain, her senses came alive with entirely new sensations. She was suddenly aware of every place their bodies touched—the firm saddle of his loins beneath her bottom, the powerful arms cinched around her waist, the solid wall of his chest against her back. He enveloped her, surrounding her with potent masculinity. His scent spilled into her every breath. His warmth radiated through her clothes, seeping into her pores. An electric current coiled through her, arcing along her nerves, heating her blood.

"Are you all right?" he asked, his chest vibrating with the deep tone of a voice that seemed strangely strained.

She turned her head and looked up into his devastatingly handsome face. At the moment a frown marred his brow. His lean cheeks were taut, as though he were clenching his teeth. He looked for all the world like a man in pain. "Did I hurt you?"

His Adam's apple bobbed as he swallowed hard. "No. I'm fine."

He didn't look fine. He looked as though he were suffering, dreadfully. Yet, even as the thought formed, another overruled it. She had seen that look in the eyes of other men. She recognized it for what it was: hunger. Pure, undiluted masculine hunger. In other words, Lord Prim and Proper was suffering from a wicked bout of lust. How wonderful! "Are you certain I didn't hurt you?"

"Yes. Quite."

"I'm so glad." She shifted on his lap, turning to face him more fully, ruthlessly sliding her bottom against his most private region. His eyes widened. Through the layers of their clothes she felt an intriguing ridge rise against her. Her mother had informed her about the mating of humans. She recognized precisely what that bulge represented. Apparently the Saint was not completely immune to his more primitive instincts or her more feminine charms. Thank goodness. "I was afraid I might have injured you in some way."

"You didn't." He moistened his lips with a quick slide of his tongue. "I think you should . . ." He nudged her arm. "I think you should move off my lap."

"Oh." She smiled at him. "Yes, I suppose I should. It isn't at all proper. Is it?"

"You know very well it isn't proper." He glanced over his shoulder in the direction of Harold. The groom was lying under a tree near the stone fence, his hat pulled over his eyes, apparently dozing.

She slid her fingertip over a fold in Clayton's starched white cravat, where an emerald stick pin winked at her in the sunlight. "You are always so very proper."

One black brow lifted as he pinned her in a disapproving glare. "And you are always looking for some mischief to get into."

She opened her eyes wide in pretended shock. "Me?"

"You." He clasped her waist and lifted her off his lap, depositing her gently on the smooth stone beside him.

She thrust out her lower lip. "I was much more comfortable on your lap."

He shook his head. "You shouldn't tease a gentleman, Mari. Even a bookworm. You never know when he may bite."

She grinned at him. Apparently he didn't realize she wanted very much to feel his bite. "I think I might be able to cup some water into my hands if you would hold my waist while I reach over the edge."

"Hold your waist?"

"Yes."

His gaze lowered to her waist. "I don't think that is a good idea."

Perhaps the castle defenses were not nearly as impenetrable as she had imagined. "I am dreadfully thirsty. Do you mean to say you won't help me?"

He shook his head, his lips tipping into a smile. "I

will gather some water in my hands, then pour it into yours. How does that sound?''

"Fine," she said, an alternate plan forming in her quick mind.

He watched her, suspicion entering his eyes as he removed the studs from his cuffs. "What are you about?''

"Me?" she asked, pressing her hand to her heart. "Nothing."

He slipped the gold studs into a small pocket of his waistcoat, then rolled his shirtsleeves up to his elbows, treating her to a glimpse of strong, tanned forearms shaded with black hair. "You look like a cat about to pounce on a plump mouse.''

She crinkled her nose at him. "How very flattering."

After scooping water into his cupped hands, he turned to face her. "Put out your hands."

Instead of doing as he requested, she slid her hands beneath both of his. Hands normally protected by gloves touched, male to female. The warm slide of flesh tingled along her nerves. Her fingertips touched the dark shading of hair on the backs of his hands, so very masculine. His lips parted on a sharp sigh. Her insides tightened like the string of a bow drawn back by an expert marksman. How odd; this seemed more intimate than the kisses he had given her in her dreams.

"Mari," he said, his voice holding a stern tone of rebuke. "What the devil are you doing?"

"It will be easier this way." She pressed her lips to the tips of his fingers. Slowly she tipped his hands, until the water poured across his long, elegantly tapered fingers. Without taking her gaze from his eyes, she sipped the cool water, tasting a faint trace of salt from his skin while droplets of water fell from the seam of his clasped hands to dribble against her warm neck.

His silvery green eyes darkened as he watched her sip from his hands. He looked in that moment as though he wished to crush her against him and kiss her until she moaned with pleasure. Perhaps she was borrowing overly much from one of the romantic novels she so enjoyed. Yet she was quite certain he wanted to—at the very least—kiss her. And she wanted nothing more than to experience her first kiss with this man.

Surrender to me, Clay. She licked a final drop from his fingertips. Never in her life had she indulged in such a sensual display. She felt a temptress, luring him from the shores of his carefully structured, all too confining world. She liked the feeling. Excitement simmered through her, making her feel naughty and deliciously feminine.

"It's lovely," she said, sliding her hand over her neck, spreading the cool water across her skin. "So cool. You should take a sip."

He lowered his eyes, his gaze resting on her lips. Without hesitation, she slid the tip of her tongue over her lips, licking away the water, tempting him. Her heart pounded against the wall of her chest. Her breath tangled in her throat, as she waited and hoped and silently beckoned to him: *Kiss me.*

Chapter Five

Kiss me. The words sang like a siren's call in Clayton's head. Even though he tried, he couldn't drag his gaze from Marisa. Sunlight spilled over her, tracing the sensual curve of her bewitching smile. His blood pulsed hard and fast through his veins, surging with each thud of his poor threatened heart. *Get away from her*, a sane portion of his brain shouted. Yet that sane voice couldn't overpower her siren's song.

Clayton leaned toward her, as though she drew him by a tether. Marisa lifted upward, her lips parting, reaching for his kiss. Her breath touched his cheek, warm, soft, sweet as a meadow after a spring rain. His lips brushed hers, as gently as a warm breeze against the petals of a rose. Her lips tasted sweeter than he had imagined. Excitement flickered through him, tingling his skin, spilling heat into his blood. Flesh she had tortured earlier stirred with a desire he couldn't prevent. His hunger for this tempting siren pulsed with every beat of his heart.

He felt a slow melting of her muscles against him, soft feminine curves snuggling against his hardened frame. Her arms slid around his neck, holding him, as though she would still be holding him this way when the world dissolved into dust. He deepened the kiss, parting his lips over hers, drawing her close against his chest. Her lips moved beneath his, following his lead, clumsy and eager and utterly beguiling. She was so warm and supple in his arms, sweetly curved, as though fashioned for his touch. And he wanted to touch her. All of her. He wanted to strip away the barriers, lay her back against the warm meadow grass, taste and touch and savor every luscious curve and valley of her sleek body.

Blood pounded in his ears, and he heard a low groan. His own. His brain registered the danger and this time his body obeyed. He pulled back from her and stared down into her upturned face. Her lips, damp from his kiss, were parted, as though awaiting the touch of his own. Slowly the thick black lashes lifted, revealing the drowsy look in her big eyes. She might have been a child, awakening from a delicious dream. Marisa was in fact a keg of black powder waiting to go off in his face. Passionate. Expressive. Explosive. What the blazes was he doing?

The splash of water and the soft rustle of leaves in the breeze filled up the silence stretching between them. She was a flame, beautiful to behold, beguiling in her warmth and light. He craved her warmth. It beckoned to him, tempting him nearer. Yet the sane portion of his brain knew that in the end this flame would consume him. Devour him. Leave nothing of him behind but a heap of ashes.

She leaned toward him, her warmth reaching for him. "Kiss me, Clay," she whispered, sliding her hand against the nape of his neck. "Kiss me."

Pull back, get away. Sensible words screamed in his brain, while his reckless body leaned into her warmth. "Mari, we shouldn't. . . ." His words dissolved in the heat of her sigh as her lips touched his.

A shimmering heat suffused his limbs, carried by blood turned to flame at this siren's touch. He devoured her sweet mouth, plunging his tongue past her startled lips, tasting her, dipping against her tongue until she followed him in this mating of lips and tongues and breath. She slid her hands into the waves at the nape of his neck, her fingertips gliding against his skin. He wrapped his arms around her, pulled her close, until her breasts snuggled against his chest, until he couldn't distinguish the beating of her heart from his own. Still she wasn't close enough. Not nearly close enough.

He slid his hands over her back, clutched her hips, drew her upward, pressing hungry male flesh against unsuspecting femininity. She stiffened in his arms, her lips parting on a gasp beneath his. He tasted her startled sigh. Yet he couldn't release her. Not yet. He spread kisses over her cheek, down the slender column of her neck. He tasted the faint trace of salt on her warm skin, breathed in the scent of lilies in the rain, and fought to keep some small shred of control.

He held her close, his lips pressed to her neck, while he waited for her to push him away, to stop him, for he certainly had no power to resist this spell of hers. Yet she made no move to escape him. Instead, she pressed her lips against the lobe of his ear, her breath sultry against his skin.

He moaned low in his throat. His body suffered the tortures of the damned while the sensible part of him attempted to keep the heated, primitive male she had unleashed from ravishing her—right here, right now. "Do you have your pistol with you?"

She pulled back to look at him, her eyes wide with surprise. "No. Why do you ask?"

He swallowed hard. "I had hoped you might shoot me, put me out of this misery."

"Misery?" A lovely smile curved the corners of lips made dusky and damp from his kisses. She smoothed her hand over his cheek. "Is that what this is, Clay? Misery? I had rather thought it closer to bliss."

Her words touched him deep inside, where hopes were hidden for safekeeping. "Foolish girl. You've gone and tempted me into compromising you."

Her eyes glittered with mischief. "Have I?"

His heart pulsed with equal measures of fear, anxiety, and hope. "I can see only one way out of this tangle."

She kissed his chin. "Can you?"

He pulled back hard on his runaway emotions. "I suppose you must . . . marry me."

She looped her arms around his neck. "Well, I suppose if I must, I must."

Hope soared within him. She actually didn't seem to mind the idea of being married to a dull bookworm for the rest of her life. "You do realize I am serious."

"You had better be. I certainly would dislike having to use my pistol to persuade you to do the proper thing."

He slid his hands upward along her slender back. "I have a rather strong propensity for propriety."

"I have noticed. I think at this moment there is only one proper course of action." She leaned forward until her breasts brushed his chest. "Kiss me, Clay."

It was always polite to comply with a lady's wishes.

And since he was ever an exceedingly polite gentleman, he pressed his lips to her soft, welcoming mouth. It was a mistake, of course. His sensible, unerringly honorable side recognized it at once. Yet it wasn't until he was lying flat on his back with Marisa cradled in his arms, her slender body stretched out on top of him, that he heeded the sensible warnings ringing like church bells in his head. He gripped her arms and lifted her from his chest.

She smiled down at him, the curve of her mouth sly and innocent at once. Her eyes held an intriguing blend—the wonder of a child mingling with the knowledge of a temptress. "I never realized kissing would be so very enjoyable. I could go on kissing you forever."

Clayton clenched his teeth and eased her off his poor, abused body. "I think we'd better go," he said, rising to a sitting position. "I must speak with your father."

She gripped his cravat, crushing the intricate folds he had so carefully crafted that morning. "I do hope you don't want a long engagement," she said, drawing him toward her. "There is a great deal I would like to explore with you, concerning what actually happens between a man and his wife."

He was falling, the ground slipping out from beneath him. His lips brushed hers before he found the will to pull away from his gorgeous siren. "Why do I have the feeling you shall be the death of me?"

She laughed, the husky sound tugging on his vitals. "I have the feeling you shall survive nicely."

"Enough." He scrambled to his feet and glared down at her, fully aware his grin spoiled the stern expression. Still, he couldn't prevent his smile. The most beautiful, tempting, exciting woman in all the world was going to be his wife. Something about that thought rested uneasily on his mind. Yet, at the moment, with her smiling at him, he couldn't decipher what it might be.

Two hours later Clayton sat in the green drawing room with Edgar and Audrey Grantham. Although Marisa's father had accepted his suit, her mother had a few things to say about the match. None of which were bringing any comfort to his mind.

"You have to understand, Clayton, I have no quarrel with you. You are a fine young gentleman." Audrey folded her hands on her lap and took an excruciatingly long moment before she continued. "But Marisa has a propensity for plunging into things without thinking."

Clayton managed a smile, though his stomach was drawn into a tight ball. He had never made a habit of plunging into anything without practical consideration, until he had met Marisa. "She is a bit impetuous."

"And headstrong. I am not saying she isn't serious about marrying you. I simply think it would be wise to allow both of you a little time to make certain this is what you truly want. Marriage is for a lifetime."

Clayton heard the words left unspoken. "You believe we aren't well suited."

"You and Marisa are very different in temperament." Audrey slowly rubbed her palms together. "I am not certain you have been acquainted long enough really to know if you can make a successful match. I want both of you to have time to think about this decision."

As much as he wanted to deny her words, Clayton could not ignore the simple truth in them. He also could not ignore the responsibility he had to abide by Audrey's wishes. "I understand."

"I cannot agree to a wedding before Marisa has had a full Season. I think it would be unwise. If you both find your sentiments are unchanged, we will announce the engagement in April and have the wedding in June, after her birthday. I hope you understand."

A year! Lord in heaven, how would he survive a year before making Marisa his own? Reckless notions plowed through his sensible brain, thoughts of elopement and rebellion.

Audrey frowned. "You do understand?"

He snagged those wayward thoughts. "Of course I understand."

The tension drained from Audrey's features with her smile. "I trust I can count on you, Clayton. I have little doubt Marisa will try to coax you into an elopement. When she sets her mind on something, she can be quite stubborn and clever in getting it."

"You have my word."

Audrey smiled. "I knew I could count on you, Clayton. I know you don't wish for Marisa to do something that could jeopardize her future happiness as well as your own."

"I would never intentionally do anything to make her unhappy."

"I shall trust you to mind the proprieties once you are in London. Marisa will do her best to ignore them. I think it is best if we do not allow anyone to know about your situation. I realize it will be difficult to maintain a proper distance, but I feel it is for the best."

"I shall not fail you." Clayton knew his sentiments would never change. Still, he wanted Marisa to be happy. And if that meant one day he would have to let her go, he would do it, even though it would tear him into pieces so ragged and small, no one would ever fit them all back together again. Nothing was more important than Marisa's happiness. He would give her a chance to see London, to meet all the exciting young gentlemen who would try to steal her heart, to be certain of her choice. And he would pray she would come back to him.

"Wait until after my next birthday!" Marisa stared at her mother. "You cannot be serious. That is almost an entire year from now."

Audrey sat on a sofa in her sitting room at Chatswyck, regarding her daughter, a solemn expression in her eyes. "I know it sounds a lifetime, but marriage *is* for a lifetime."

Marisa sank to the pale blue damask cushion beside her mother. "Did Clay agree to wait that long?"

"Clayton is a sensible young man. He understands my concerns and he has agreed to postpone your engagement for a few months." Audrey touched her daughter's cheek. "You just turned twenty. You haven't even had a Season."

"I don't need a Season. I've found the man I want."

Audrey smiled. "I know you think you have. And don't misunderstand me; I think Clayton is a fine young man."

"Still, you object to him."

Audrey sat back. "Marisa, I simply do not think you and Clayton are well suited."

"I am sorry you feel that way, Mama. And you know I have never gone against your wishes before. But I know Clayton and I will make a successful match."

"Mari, you have a habit of jumping into things without looking."

"I love him." Marisa looked past her mother to the evening sunlight streaming across the blue-and-yellow carpet. "I've never met anyone like him."

"Yes, dear. Clayton is very different from the gentlemen you usually prefer. I suspect that is one of the reasons he captured your attention."

"It isn't simply that he is different. He is kind and gentle. He talks to me as though I have a brain. And when he touches me . . ." Warmth coiled through her at the memory of his kisses. "Mama, I cannot possibly wait a year."

Although Audrey smiled, a serious look remained in her eyes. "I can see it will not be wise to allow you any time alone with him. You are quite likely to pounce on the poor, unsuspecting gentleman. I'm afraid Clayton is far too polite to prevent you from ravishing him, should you take the notion."

Marisa clasped her hands tightly in her lap. "You are making light of me."

Audrey shook her head. "No, darling. I know precisely how you feel. You are curious and anxious to explore the feelings awakening inside of you. It's only natural."

"I want to be his wife. I don't see why we must wait a year."

"Have you considered how very different you and Clayton are? He is quiet and reserved. You breathe excitement."

"I agree, we are different. But we balance each other." Marisa gripped her mother's hand. "I love him. I'm not going to change my mind. I don't need a London Season."

"It's important for you to enter Society. You must meet the appropriate people if you are to become Clayton's countess. And I want you to have a chance to enjoy balls, parties, musicales, all that is pleasurable about London during the Season."

"I don't see why I couldn't go to balls and parties and all the rest as Clayton's wife."

"It's very different once you are married." Audrey tucked a wayward curl behind Marisa's ear. "What if you were to marry Clay, then met another man, a man who seemed even more perfect for you?"

Marisa fixed her mother with a steady gaze. "That shall not happen, Mama."

Audrey nodded. "I know you do not believe it will. And if you both feel as you do today, we will announce the engagement in April. The wedding will take place in June."

"Mama, I—"

Audrey lifted her hand to silence her daughter. "Marisa, I feel very strongly about this."

"It's such a long time to wait."

"Your father and I have agreed. We shall not give permission for your marriage."

Marisa lifted her chin. "I am not a child. I know what I want and I shall not change my mind."

Audrey cupped Marisa's cheek in her warm palm. "If you truly care for Clayton, and if he truly cares for you, the two of you will have a lifetime together. This short time of waiting will be nothing more than the blink of an eye."

It was unsettling to wait. Particularly when Marisa thought of how she had thrown herself at Clayton. In a very real sense she had coaxed him into that proposal. "I am not happy with your decision."

"I know."

"I believe you and Papa are being very unfair."

Audrey slipped her arms around Marisa and held her close, rocking her gently as though she were a child. "One day you will understand why this is important."

Marisa understood her mother's concerns, but they

were not truly justified. She would never change her mind about Clayton. Never! Still, in a small corner of her mind a nagging little doubt dwelled, like a troll hidden in the shadows. What if Clayton changed his mind about her? What if he suddenly saw all of her faults and found them intolerable? What if he grew tired of her? She tried to send those doubts packing. If Clayton loved her the way she loved him, there was no basis for these doubts, she assured herself. Still, she couldn't banish that little troll lurking inside of her.

A short while later, as she left her mother's sitting room, all the dreadful possibilities pressed against her heart. She needed to see Clayton. She needed to hold him close. She needed to banish all of these terrible doubts.

She hurried down the long corridors of Chatswyck, rushing to the one place she thought he might be. She paused on the threshold of the library, her heart pounding with the same thrilling excitement she felt each time Clayton was near. He stood near one of the long, mullioned windows, staring out into the gardens.

The black wool of his coat hugged the wide breadth of his shoulders, the narrow line of his waist, his slim hips. A warm, tingling sensation spread across her skin with the excitement rippling along her nerves. Memories of the kisses they had shared this afternoon shimmered in her mind. His mouth had been so tender, so confident, so utterly intoxicating. She had never really expected a kiss to be so completely debilitating.

It truly was amazing what could hide beneath quiet waters—something as unexpected as passion. Anyone looking at Clayton would certainly never expect that such a quiet, serious young man could make a woman tremble with a touch. Yet he could. Oh, my, yes, he could set her pulse racing with a mere glance from his beautiful eyes.

Without a thought for propriety, she ran across the library. Clayton turned as she drew near. She caught a glimpse of his stunned expression before she threw herself against him. She coiled her arms around his neck and kissed him, slanting her lips over his startled mouth. He stood frozen in shock for a heartbeat before he plunged into the kiss with unbridled enthusiasm. He wrapped his arms around her and pulled her close, crushing her breasts against his hard chest.

He took her mouth in a brazen, openmouthed kiss that had no room for gentleness. There was no chivalry in this kiss, no tenderness. He plunged his tongue into her mouth, startling her with wild, untamed hunger. Lust in its unadulterated state, that was what she tasted in this kiss. None of the sweetness of affection. Not a trace of the connection she always felt when she was with Clayton. Instead of the warmth she had felt this afternoon in his arms, this kiss left her strangely unmoved. Had her mother been right? Had the spark that burned between them already died?

She pulled back and stared up at him, her heart pounding with anxiety. His lips tipped into a lazy, self-assured grin, the smile of a man certain of his own potent masculinity. Realization plowed into her with the force of a charging hunter. Although his eyes were the same startling gray-green as Clayton's, they regarded her with the blatant appreciation of a man who could strip a woman bare with a glance.

The smoldering scent of sandalwood drifted past her senses, so different from the crisp scent of herbs and citrus she associated with his brother. She smiled up into a face that might have been Clayton's, except for the expression, which was far too predatory. And instead of the keen intelligence or warm affection she often saw in Clayton's eyes, these eyes held pure mischief. "You must be Justin."

A glimmer of surprise touched his features. "You know the difference between us."

In a glance she took this man's measure. He was all dash and excitement, wild, untamed, more than a little dangerous—precisely the type of man she had always imagined would steal her heart. Yet, for some reason, he didn't conjure a single tingle. "Yes, I do know the difference."

He flexed his hands against her waist. "It would seem my brother has been enjoying himself this summer."

"Your brother has been busy this summer." She pushed against his arms, trying to break free of his embrace. He held her in his powerful arms, against all the rules of propriety. She suspected this man made his own rules. "If you release me, I shall tell you all about it."

Justin lifted one black brow. "And if I don't release you? If I should decide to kiss you instead?"

Marisa smiled up at him. "Then I shall be forced to hurt you."

George William sat on the edge of the desk in his study, glaring at his youngest son. "I don't understand this at all."

Clayton sat in a leather armchair in front of his father. "I have asked Lady Marisa to be my wife. And she has accepted me. Lord Westbury has approved the match."

George waved his hand impatiently. "I understand *that*. I'm not addled. What I don't understand is how you could have asked her to marry you."

Clayton squeezed the arms of the chair. "It all happened rather quickly."

"Good heavens, Clayton, I thought you had more sense than this."

"I thought you might be pleased, sir. You were concerned about the succession."

"I am concerned about your choice."

"Certainly you don't have objections to Lady Marisa."

"Oh, I don't have any problems with the girl. She is beautiful, spirited, comes from a fine family. Unfortunately, from what I have observed, she is also willful and impetuous. I think she would make an excellent wife. For your brother." George tapped the edge of his fist against his thigh. "I invited Edgar and his family here so Justin could meet the girl. I thought I was clear on the matter."

"Yes, sir, you were."

"Confound it. For once I thought there might be a chance to see Justin wed. The girl is perfect for him. Couldn't you see that? Don't you want to see your brother happy?"

"Of course I would like to see Justin happy."

"Yet you go behind his back and make off with one of the few women on the face of the earth who might very well make him a suitable bride. If Justin isn't saved from his wild ways soon, it might very well be too late for him. He will sink so low in his life of depravity, no one will be able to pull him out of it." George pinned his son with a cold glare. "What were you thinking?"

When he was near Marisa, his thought processes didn't function properly. "I certainly had no intention of harming Justin in any way. In all honesty, sir, we have no reason to be certain Marisa and Justin would have made a match.''

"She is certainly better suited to him than she is to you. You're a quiet man, reserved, conventional. How do you ever expect to keep that willful, headstrong beauty satisfied?''

Clayton flinched inwardly at the harsh assessment. "I shall do everything in my power to make her happy, sir.''

"She will make your life miserable. How could you allow your head to be turned by that beautiful face?''

"It's more than her beauty. Although hers is a beauty that touches the soul. So pure and unaffected.'' Clayton stared at one corner of his father's desk, where a brass unicorn glinted in the sunlight. "Yet her beauty alone would make her only an ornament if not for the beauty inside of her. She has a way about her, a way of making the most ordinary of days extraordinary. When I am with her, I feel I'm in some exotic place where it is always summer, and I am always warm.''

"Bloody hell," George said, his voice filled with disgust. "You've fallen in love with her.''

Clayton kept his gaze fixed on the unicorn, while inside he fought the shaking that gripped his vitals. "Yes. I'm afraid I have.''

"Damnation! I thought you knew better than to tumble into that trap. This is the most foolish thing you have ever done in your life. Do you realize that?''

Clayton glanced up at his father. "I didn't plan to become so entangled, sir. Yet I discovered there are some emotions that do not ask for permission.''

George shook his head. "I'm afraid you will both live to regret this. Still, there is nothing to be done now. You have asked, the girl has accepted, and your fate is sealed. The only hope you might have is if the girl cries off. You would be wise to give her every opportunity to end the engagement.''

Clayton would give everything he had to make Marisa happy. Yet in a dark corner of his heart, doubt sank sharp claws into his flesh. What if he couldn't make her happy? What if she opened her beautiful eyes one day and saw him for what he was, a dull bookworm who suddenly bored her to death?

Clayton left his father's study by the door adjoining the library, all the horrible possibilities pounding against his head. He entered the library and froze. Marisa stood near the windows, with his brother. Justin was bent at the waist, rubbing his shin.

Chapter Six

"Clay." Marisa hurried across the room toward him, pale blue muslin floating around her. She slipped her arm though his and smiled up at him. "I was looking for you, and found your brother instead."

Clayton covered her hand with his, welcoming the sweet radiance of her warmth against his side. "I suppose there is a good reason Justin is rubbing his shin?"

A dimple peeked out at the corner of her mouth. "It is his stubborn streak acting up, I'm afraid."

Clayton looked at his brother. "Stubborn streak?"

Justin straightened, his lips curving into a crooked grin. "It happens every time a beautiful woman throws herself into my arms."

"Into your arms?"

Marisa squeezed Clayton's arm. "I thought he was you. Once I kissed him—"

"You kissed him?"

"Yes." She smiled up at him. "Of course, I immediately realized my mistake. But your brother seemed intent on exploring the situation further.''

A certain uneasiness curled in his stomach as he looked from his intended's smile to his brother's grin. ''I suppose it's a little late for an introduction.''

Justin crossed the room, his gaze fixed on Marisa. He paused in front of her, closer than Clayton deemed proper. ''Actually, we never got around to formal introductions.''

The duke stepped out of his study and pinned his eldest son with a cold glare. ''If you had come when I invited you, you would have had your introduction weeks ago.''

Justin stiffened, all the humor in his expression freezing into a mask of cold arrogance. ''I assumed the invitation was still open.''

A muscle flickered in the duke's cheek. He glanced at Marisa. ''Lady Marisa Grantham, this is my eldest son, Justin, Marquess of Angelstone. Justin, may I present Lady Marisa, daughter of Lord Edgar Grantham, Marquess Westbury.''

Marisa offered Justin her hand. ''It is a pleasure.''

Justin held her hand longer than propriety allowed. Still, he had long ago turned his back on propriety. ''The pleasure is mine.''

''Indeed it is. Pity it comes so late.'' George pivoted and closed the door, leaving the library in silence.

Justin looked at his brother, a wry smile curving his lips. ''Welcome home.''

''I suspect Father is a little piqued you didn't come earlier.''

Justin looked at Marisa and smiled in a way that shouted, *the lady intrigues me*. ''I am beginning to regret waiting so long to visit Chatswyck.''

Dread curled around Clayton's heart like icy fingers

of frost. His brother was attracted to Marisa. Of course he was. What man could meet her and not think her the most fascinating creature on the face of the earth? Still, it was seldom that his brother showed any real interest in a lady of quality. Justin generally preferred the company of widows or prostitutes over that of innocent maidens. In fact, ladies of quality were generally listed under the headings of *plague* and *pestilence* in Justin's book of life. Yet it was clear Justin had slipped Marisa into an entirely new category.

Justin glanced from Marisa to his brother, a glint of curiosity in his gray-green eyes. "From what I gather, the two of you have become well acquainted."

Marisa looked up at Clayton, the warmth of her smile soothing his ragged nerves. "I'm afraid Clayton has been charged with entertaining me during our visit."

Justin looked at his brother. *What have you been up to, little brother?* Clayton could almost hear the question behind his brother's smile. "A difficult task, entertaining a beautiful female for the summer. I only wish I had been here to assist him."

Marisa patted Clayton's arm. "He managed quite well without any assistance. I didn't think you were coming to Chatswyck at all this summer."

Justin winked at her. "Once you get to know me better, you will find I'm a most unpredictable fellow. No one can ever be certain precisely what I shall do next."

"I see, you like to keep people guessing. Or is it that you like to shock them?"

"Both, I think." Justin lifted one black brow. "Why is it I have a feeling you would not be easily shocked?"

Marisa laughed, the husky sound far too seductive for Clayton's comfort. "I'm afraid I am a dreadful harridan at times. Mama has hopes I might reform before she exposes the poor unsuspecting ton to me. Your brother has been helping me with my lessons in propriety.''

''My father has been trying to reform me for years. He thinks I am a hopeless case, you know.'' Justin touched the tip of her nose with the tip of his forefinger. ''Of course, a beautiful woman might actually work a miracle.''

Clayton curled his hands into tight balls at his sides. For the first time in his life, he wanted to slam his fist into his brother's chiseled jaw.

Marisa tilted her head and smiled up at Justin. ''It would seem you are not always unpredictable, Lord Angelstone. I wager you would flirt with any female you happen to meet.''

Justin laughed softly. ''Only the ones who intrigue me.''

Clayton forced his hands open with an effort that shocked him almost as much as his own violent inclinations. He wanted to knock down his own brother. Good lord, was this what happened when one allowed passion to get a grip on one?

Marisa glanced up at Clayton, mischief glinting in her eyes. ''I'm certain you and your brother have a great deal to say to one another. I should give you some time alone.''

''Did you speak with your mother?'' Clayton asked.

Marisa crinkled her nose. ''A year seems a long time to wait.''

Clayton touched her cheek, her skin warm satin beneath his palm. ''You will be so busy, you will hardly notice the passing of the time.''

She lifted onto her toes and brushed her lips against his. The soft caress lasted an instant. Only an instant, but it was enough to set his blood pounding through his veins. "It will be a lifetime."

Clayton turned, watching her leave. Was that heated look he had glimpsed in her eyes actually for him? Lord, when she looked at him that way, he felt he could slay dragons in her name.

"I came because I sensed you were in trouble, brother. Now that I see the trouble, I wish I had come earlier."

Clayton turned to look at his brother. In spite of the grin on Justin's face, he saw a flicker of concern in his eyes. "There are a few things I need to tell you."

Justin nodded. "I can scarcely wait."

Marisa stood by a window in her bedchamber, watching Clayton and Justin stroll through the south gardens. Even from a distance, she could perceive the difference in the two men. Strange, how they could be cast from the identical mold, yet be so very different. She had met a hundred men like Justin, arrogant and bold, the type of man who could send a weak-minded female into a swoon with one smoldering glance. In her entire life she had met only one man like Clayton.

She watched as Clayton and his brother sat on the bench near the sea horse fountain. Clayton was the one man on earth fashioned for her. They belonged to one another. She felt it. Yet she couldn't suppress the doubts lingering deep inside her. What if he opened his beautiful eyes one day and saw her for the reckless, impetuous, all too passionate female she was? What if he grew weary of her? She rubbed her arms, chilled suddenly when she thought of how ruthlessly she had pursued her quiet scholar. She hadn't given him a chance to get away from her.

"May I come in?"

Marisa started at the sound of Sophia's voice. She turned and found the duchess standing near the door. "Yes, of course."

"I'm sorry. I didn't mean to startle you." Sophia crossed the room as she spoke. "I knocked. You must have been too deep in thought to hear me."

"Yes. I suppose I was."

"I came to wish you happy, my dear. And from the way you looked when I first came in, I sense you need those wishes." Sophia took Marisa's hands in her warm grasp. Over the past few weeks a bond had formed between the two women, an affection based on similarities of nature and mutual understanding. She treated Marisa as though she were her own grandchild. "Is something troubling you?"

"No. Nothing."

Sophia lifted one finely arched brow. "There are people who excel at concealing their emotions. You don't seem to have ever been one of them."

"I am afraid I have also never learned to excel in patience. A year seems a very long time to wait to be married." She gave Sophia a conspiratorial smile. "I don't suppose you could persuade Mama to relent?"

Sophia squeezed her hands before releasing her. "I feel we must respect her wishes."

"She is afraid I shall change my mind."

"Yes, she is."

"I will never change my mind about Clay." Marisa only hoped he would never change his mind about her.

Sophia turned her gaze to the two men sitting in the garden below. She observed them in silence for several moments before she spoke. "I have one great wish in this life. I want to see both of my grandsons settled happily. I'm afraid I tend to evaluate every young woman I meet in terms of Justin and Clayton. You see,

94

I am very determined to see my wish a reality. Before you and Clayton met, I wondered if you and he might suit."

Marisa's breath stilled. "And did you think we might?"

"I wasn't certain."

Marisa's stomach tightened. "You weren't?"

"You are so very different in temperament. One might have thought you and Justin would be better suited."

A scream of frustration rose inside of Marisa. It lodged in her throat, threatening to choke her. Did everyone think they were headed for disaster?

"I had doubts about you and Clayton." Sophia turned her head toward Marisa, a lovely smile curving her lips. "Until the first time I saw you together. There was a connection between you, a spark that was so brilliant it was nearly visible. I suspect your differences are what make you so well suited to one another."

"You do?"

"He needs your liveliness. And I daresay you need his reserve."

"Yes." Marisa pressed her hand to her pounding heart. "I know exactly what you mean. I feel that way, too."

Sophia patted Marisa's arm. "I know you and Clayton are perfect for one another."

"Thank you for believing in us."

"I feel you will make each other very happy."

"I intend to do my best." Marisa looked into the gardens below her window. "Nothing is more important to me than making Clay happy."

Clayton sat with Justin on a stone bench near the sea horse fountain in the south gardens. His brother remained quiet while Clayton told him of the events that had led to his recent engagement. "It all happened so quickly, I scarcely had time to realize what I was doing."

Justin broke a stem from the topiary figure of a rabbit growing beside the bench, releasing a tangy scent from the privet bush. "Did the duke badger you into offering for the lady?"

"You've seen Marisa. It should be obvious no one had to badger me into offering for her. I wanted her from the first moment I saw her."

"Lust?"

"At first; then I became acquainted with her. I'm afraid I managed to lose my heart."

Justin laughed. "I can see why. It would be easy to fall in love with her. Father must be in raptures."

Clayton rubbed at a crease in the wool covering his knee. "Actually, Father is against the match."

"Against it?" Justin twisted the green stem around the tip of his forefinger. "Why the devil would he be against a match between you and Westbury's daughter? The duke has been hungry for an heir since we were eighteen."

"He had hoped you and Marisa might make a match."

"One thing I can say for the duke: he has excellent taste. Your lady is exquisite."

"She is also impetuous, willful, and completely unpredictable."

Justin grinned. "I noticed."

"That is why Father thought she would be perfect for you."

Justin winked at his brother. "Pity I didn't meet her first."

Would it have made a difference? Clayton wondered. Would Marisa have noticed him if Justin had been in the vicinity? "Father certainly would have preferred a match between you and Marisa."

"The lady is getting a better bargain in you." Justin tossed the twisted privet stem to the thick grass at his feet. "I'm surprised George William hasn't completely given up on me by now. I told him what I thought of arranged marriages the last time he tried to find me a bride."

"I believe he is hoping you will change your mind."

"I have no illusions concerning my character, brother. Even though I am a scoundrel, I do maintain a few precious principles, honesty being among them. I have no intention of setting up a nursery for the sole sake of continuing the noble Trevelyan name. I won't live a lie. I've seen the ton's idea of marriage, men keeping mistresses, while their neglected wives take lovers to console them. I won't participate in that hypocrisy."

A warm breeze drifted across the garden, swaying the plumes of water in the fountain, spraying a soft mist against Clayton's face. "And if you met a woman who intrigued you, a woman who turned your blood to fire, a woman who never ceased to interest you? Do you think you might find yourself anxious for marriage?"

"Yes. I might." Justin laughed softly, a sound filled with bitterness. "Although I doubt I shall find one among all the hen-wits who keep throwing themselves in my path. To tell the truth, I'm beginning to doubt the Almighty has made a female who can hold my interest for more than a few weeks."

"It will take someone very special to win your heart. A woman of fire and passion. A woman so lovely, a man's heart aches just to look at her. A woman like Marisa.''

Justin rested his forearms on his thighs and leaned forward. "It's probably better if I never imagine myself in love. I have a feeling I would make a dreadful husband.''

"Strange, I have always thought you would make a better husband than I would.''

"Better than you?'' Justin stared at him, his lips parted, his eyes wide in surprise. "You're a bloody paragon. Why the devil do you think you would make a dreadful husband?''

"Oh, I always thought I would make a suitable husband for a certain type of female.'' Clayton stared at the fountain, watching the spouting plumes of water turn golden in the dying rays of the sun. "Someone who is quiet, reserved, conventional.''

"Dull as dirt?''

Clayton shifted on the bench. "In case you have forgotten, I am not exactly the most stimulating fellow in the kingdom.''

"You are hardly dull.''

He was hardly the type of man who could inspire a Gothic romance. Would Marisa see him for what he was one day? Would she regret her choice?

"What's wrong?'' Justin clasped his hands between his knees. "Something is bothering you.''

Clayton glanced at his brother. "Nothing is wrong.''

Justin lifted one thick black brow. *Who are you trying to fool?*

Clayton could hear the words behind his brother's perceptive gaze as clearly as if they had been spoken. He knew Justin could see through any facade he might try to erect. They had never been able to keep secrets from one another. They were joined in some way neither of them could explain but both understood. It was more than the identical cast of their features that bound them to each other. It went deeper, as deep as every thought, every emotion. "I suppose . . . I wonder if I shall make a fit husband for a woman who reads Gothic romances and expects her life to be just as exciting."

"Gothic romances? I should have guessed that beautiful head was filled with romantic notions."

"And I should have guessed she would want a man filled with dash and excitement. When I think of it, I find it mystifying. Why the devil would she agree to marry me?"

"Perhaps the lady wants someone who is steadfast and loyal. Someone dependable. A man who doesn't spend his time sniffing after every skirt in England. A man who will actually speak to her and not around her." Justin grinned at him. "You're a good man, Clay. She couldn't have made a better choice."

Clayton drew his fingertips over the rough stone bench near his thigh. "Her mother seems to think she could have. We aren't going to announce the engagement until April. That is, if Marisa doesn't change her mind before then."

"If she does change her mind, she is a fool and you are better off without her."

Lord, he didn't want to think of losing her. Yet he was a practical man who faced facts. "Marisa could have her choice of any man in England. Instead, she is settling for a dull, bookish fellow. I keep thinking one of these days she will open her eyes, see me clearly, and run screaming into the night." He looked at his brother and saw everything he was not. "I'm afraid she will regret not marrying someone more like you."

"Me?" Justin shook his head. "Good gad, Clay, don't wish someone like me on the girl. You might like books, but that hardly makes you dull. Just because you don't spend every night with a prostitute, or keep a ladybird, or go around trying to charm every female you meet, like some men, does not make you a bore. As for dash, you're a better whip than I am, a better shot, and you can match me any day with your fists."

Clayton thought of the blank mask that often descended over women's faces when he tried to converse with them, the glazed look in their eyes. "I bore women into a stupor. You don't have that problem."

"You mean you bore ambitious hen-wits who do not know Plato from Plutarch. I would wager Marisa knows the difference."

"She is remarkable."

"You deserve nothing less." Justin glanced at the fountain, a wistful smile curving his lips. "I have to admit, I'm a little envious of you. To confess, I have wondered what it might be like to fall in love. To want to see the same face every morning and every night. To lose oneself, body and soul, to a woman."

Body and soul. A complete union. A love so deep it sank into one's very bones. Clayton had never sought such a love. Now that he had found it, he wasn't sure he could ever live without it. "You just haven't met the right woman."

"I doubt she exists." Justin released his breath in a long sigh. "As much as I would like to meet a woman who could make my blood burn, I doubt any woman could redeem my black soul. I'm not capable of remaining loyal to any female. I am no doubt better off remaining a bachelor all of my days."

If there was any woman who could drag his brother from his life of debauchery, it was Marisa. She could redeem him. She could win his heart. She could give him children, make a home with him, love him as he needed love. "I don't want to think I have spoiled any chance you might have for happiness."

Justin studied his brother, understanding dawning in his eyes. "Do you plan to give Marisa up so I can have a try with her?"

"No." Although Clayton realized how selfish he was being, he knew the only way he would ever leave Marisa was if it was what she wanted.

Justin grinned. "Even if you did decide to be so foolishly noble, I doubt it would make a difference."

Clayton smiled, a weight lifting from his chest. "I would like to think it wouldn't."

"If Marisa wants to marry you, it proves she is far too intelligent ever to want to marry a man like me."

"You underestimate yourself."

"Apparently it is one of the traits we share." Justin loosened his cravat and unfastened the top of his shirt. He unhooked a gold chain from around his neck and slid a ring from the chain. "Take this."

Clayton opened his hand and Justin dropped the ring into his palm. "Mother's betrothal ring."

"You should have it."

The thick gold band, warm from his brother's skin, glinted in the slanting rays of the setting sun. A cabochon ruby glowed at him, so perfect it captured the light and turned it to smoldering fire. Blue-white diamonds surrounded the ruby, each round stone glittering in the sunlight. His throat tightened when he remembered this ring glittering on his mother's finger. "Father meant this for you," he said, offering it to Justin.

Justin raised his hand. "I doubt I shall ever find a woman I want to give it to. You, on the other hand, have found the ideal woman. Give it to Marisa."

"Are you certain?"

Justin clasped his brother's shoulder. "May she wear it for many long and happy years."

A warm breeze stirred the leaves of a weeping ash that stood near one corner of the terrace, the low rustle melding with the soft murmur of voices drifting from the drawing room. Marisa rested her hand on the stone balustrade and stared out across the pond in the center of the rose garden. The moon had turned the water to liquid silver.

Clayton stood beside her, so close her skirt brushed his leg. Yet not as close as she wished they could stand. She wanted his arms around her, now and always. She glanced up at him. Moonlight carved Clayton's features from the shadows, sculpting each chiseled line and curve. She wished she could paint; she wanted to capture the way he looked tonight, like a young prince who had stepped off the pages of a novel. Unfortunately, painting was only one of many feminine accomplishments she had never acquired.

"I want you to have this," she said, slipping a gold locket from the neckline of her bodice. She handed it to him. "Mama had the miniature of me painted in Italy last summer. I placed a lock of my hair on the other side of the locket this morning. I thought it might help you remember me when we are apart."

"Thank you." Clayton smiled down at the locket lying in his palm. "But I don't need anything to help me remember you. Your image is etched upon my heart."

Her own heart stumbled at his soft words. "Mama insists we leave for London tomorrow. I think she is afraid I shall do something foolish if you and I remain under the same roof."

He slipped the locket into his coat pocket. "Foolish?"

"I think she is afraid I might ravish you, and force you to marry me as soon as we can get a special license."

Moonlight traced the curve of his smile. "You could tempt a saint."

"I'm trying, but he isn't budging." She touched his arm, absorbing the warm strength of him through the soft wool. "Are you quite certain you don't want to elope with me?"

He cupped her cheek in his warm palm. "I gave your parents my word that we would abide by their wishes."

"A year." She rubbed her cheek against his palm. "It seems a lifetime. How shall I manage without seeing you?"

"You shall see me."

"But it won't be the same. I won't see you at breakfast every morning. We will not spend every afternoon together, every evening." She pressed her lips against his palm. "I shall miss you terribly."

He slipped his arms around her and drew her against his chest, enfolding her in his gentle strength. He pressed his lips against her hair. "You will be so busy in London, the time will pass quickly. There will be things to do every day, galleries and museums to visit, people to meet, shops to explore."

She pressed her cheek against his chest, feeling the solid thud of his heart. "You sound as though you won't miss me at all."

"I shall miss you the way the sky misses the sun after it slips away." He slid his hand over the curve of her back, warming her through the blue silk of her gown. "I shall miss you the way a desert misses the soft caress of rain. I shall miss you more than I can say in these simple, inadequate words."

Those simple words set her trembling deep inside. "You will come to see me every day."

"I wish I could." He held her closer, his arms tightening around her. "But I gave my word not to live in your pocket. People would start to gossip."

"I don't care what anyone might say."

"Your parents care."

She hugged him close. "I don't want to go to London. I want to stay with you."

He brushed his lips against her brow. "Your mother is right. You deserve a Season."

She pulled back in the powerful circle of his arms. "Why must I have a Season? I have the man I want. I don't see why we cannot announce it to the world."

He dropped a soft kiss on the tip of her nose. "Your mother wants you to be certain of your choice. And so do I."

She touched his cheek, her fingers gliding against the dark pinpoints of beard slumbering beneath his smooth skin. "I am certain."

"I hope you remain that way. Now and always." He slipped his hand into his coat pocket and withdrew a ring. "I know ours is supposed to be a secret engagement, but I would like you to have this. You need not wear it if you feel it will draw too much attention."

Diamonds glittered in the moonlight, embracing a huge oval ruby. "Oh," she whispered. "Oh, it's beautiful."

"It was my mother's betrothal ring."

Tears welled in her eyes as she held out her hand. "You must place it on my finger."

He slid the warm gold onto her finger, then cupped her palm in his. Slowly he lifted her hand to his lips. Warm breath brushed the back of her hand, soft lips caressed her fingers, heat spilled into her blood. "I love you, Mari. I always will."

"I love you, Clay." She threw her arms around his waist and held him close, the intriguing scent of citrus and herbs flooding her senses. Nothing would come between them, she assured herself. This connection she felt with him was real and honest and unshakable. It wouldn't matter if they waited ten years; they would still find one another. They belonged together. There was no reason for doubts or fears of losing him. Clayton loved her. She loved him. Nothing in London could jeopardize what they shared. "I will always love you."

Chapter Seven

Candlelight flickered against crystal in Lady Radbyrne's ballroom, casting a golden glow on the crowd crammed into the huge room. Clayton stood beside his grandmother in one corner of the room, watching Marisa glide gracefully through the steps of a country dance.

"I haven't seen such a fuss over a female since your mother made her come-out." Sophia slipped her arm through his.

Clayton smiled. "I never had any doubt Marisa would be a great success."

"You know, in some ways Marisa reminds me of Lisette. Although your mama's eyes were green, she had the same jet black hair and flawless complexion. She was also tall and graceful. And Lisette had the same vivacity Marisa does. A way of casting light everywhere she goes."

An uneasy mixture of anxiety and pride swelled in

his chest. "Marisa is like a brilliant star who has descended from the heavens to grace us with her radiance."

"This must be difficult for you." Sophia squeezed his arm. "Seeing all of these gentlemen vying for her attention."

Since arriving in London a little more than a fortnight ago, Marisa had captured the attention of every eligible gentleman in town. They swarmed around her at every event, salivating and panting like a pack of hounds. Ladies flocked to her, aware that they risked going completely unnoticed by the gentlemen if they strayed too far out of her orbit. A crowd inevitably formed around her at every event. Since Clayton had given his word to keep their engagement secret and allow Marisa to flit through the Season unencumbered, he was relegated to the position of one of the pack—a position that disturbed him more and more with each passing day.

"This is how it should be. I would never want her to have any regrets over something she might have missed." Although Clayton meant the words, the sentiment became increasingly difficult to uphold with each smile Marisa gave to another man.

"I am certain Marisa's head will not be turned by all of this attention. There isn't a better gentleman in all of England than you." Sophia patted his arm, then left him alone with his doubts.

Clayton waited through the next dance before he claimed Marisa for the only dance he would be permitted this evening. The scents of various sweet waters mingled uneasily with the musk of overly warm humans in the room. Yet the fragrance of white lilies after a rain filled Clayton's senses as he glided through the steps of a cotillion with Marisa, savoring every moment.

Marisa smiled up at him as they commenced a promenade. "I think I am finally feeling comfortable with this. I can even manage conversation while I dance."

He squeezed her hand, regretting the gloves that prevented him from touching the smooth warmth of her skin. "There isn't a lady in attendance who could match your natural grace."

She laughed softly, the husky sound tempting him to draw her into his arms. "As I recall, you have a few bruised toes that give the lie to that statement."

"What are a few bruises when compared to the pleasure of your company?"

"My gallant gentleman," she whispered, before she crossed to the opposite position.

Clayton clenched his jaw as she accepted the hand of her temporary partner, Lord Timothy Usherwood, Viscount Hanley. The predatory look in Hanley's eyes teased a primitive part of Clayton, a part he had not known existed before Marisa had plowed into his life. He masked his feelings well, Clayton assured himself. No one could see his heart pinned to his coatsleeve. No one could tell that Marisa had altered him in ways he was only beginning to understand.

When people looked at him, Clayton was quite certain they still saw the veneer of a civilized gentleman, even though that veneer had grown increasingly thin over the past two weeks. No one would suggest that instead of an elegant black coat and pristine white linen, he should be dressed in animal skins and carrying a club. Yet he knew the humbling truth. Marisa had unleashed a ravenous beast inside of him. Although he still looked a gentleman, inside he dragged his knuckles on the ground and growled each time another man touched her. After an eternity she returned to him.

"You haven't asked me to go in to supper with you," she said, as they addressed each other in the dance.

"I took you in to supper at the Langley ball two nights ago."

She took his hand. "And that means you cannot take me in to supper tonight?"

The oath Clayton had made haunted him. Audrey Grantham trusted him to adhere to propriety. "It would draw too much attention to us."

A crinkle appeared between her brows. "I don't really see why we need to be so careful. Since I came to London, I seldom see you at all."

"I gave your parents my word."

"Yes. I know." She glanced down at her feet as they commenced a promenade to the right. "I don't see how taking me in to supper would cause such a terrible scandal."

"I'm afraid I am obliged to take Miss Thurmond in to supper this evening."

"You asked Letitia?" Marisa missed a step, her foot coming down on his toes.

He winced at the sudden pain.

"I'm sorry."

He guided her into a promenade to the left. "Miss Thurmond is a friend, who is often uncomfortable at balls."

"I know." Marisa kept her gaze fixed elsewhere. "She is a very pleasant young lady. I am certain you will enjoy her company."

The hurt underlying her soft voice twisted like a wire around his heart. "You must know there is no one I would rather be with you than you. But I gave my word not to betray our situation. I hope you understand."

She glanced up at him. "Of course I understand."

The stiff curve of her smile said otherwise. There were times when he wished he could tell all of his honorable intentions to go straight to blazes. It took every ounce of his will to fulfil his obligations. With each passing day Clayton found it more and more difficult to fight the treacherous instincts whispering in his brain, instincts he hadn't realized he possessed until Marisa had entered his life. Instincts that urged him to toss Marisa over his shoulder and carry her to his lair.

Lord Braden Fitzwilliam, Viscount Shipley, heir to the Earl of Ashbourne, met them as they left the dance floor. Clayton's chest tightened as he relinquished Marisa to his old friend. Braden was eager, far too eager. Clayton could almost see the drool at the corner of Braden's mouth. He clamped down hard on his instincts as he watched the tall, dark-haired viscount take his place beside Marisa. It wouldn't do to strangle an old friend in the middle of a ball. Instead, Clayton stood on the edge of the dance floor, watching Marisa and Braden move through the steps of a country dance, feeling like a trapped barbarian straining at his chains.

"Do you think she will be the one to do it?" came a voice from behind him.

As Clayton turned, the owner of that voice—a tall, dark-haired man—moved to his side. Although they were not bosom friends, Gregory Stanwood had been an acquaintance since their days at Harrow. "Who and what do you mean?"

"There is only one female on the floor who commands attention." Gregory tilted his head toward the dance floor. "Lady Marisa Grantham."

His comment took Clayton by surprise. Although Gregory appreciated beauty, he had never singled out any female. Instead, he plied his cool charm liberally and impartially on them all. "She is lovely."

"Incomparable," Gregory said, as though admiring a piece of art.

"You must be discussing the Grantham chit," Harry Fitzwilliam said as he joined them. He paused beside Clayton and nodded at his cousin, Gregory.

Although he was not quite as tall as Braden, Harry bore a striking resemblance to his older brother. Both might have been cast from a mold of a Greek deity. Two years Braden's junior, Harry was forever looking for excitement. His latest pursuit was the army. A few weeks ago, against the wishes of his sire, the Earl of Ashbourne, Harry had purchased a commission. To the ultimate horror of his mother, he would soon be seeking glory on the bloody fields of the Peninsula.

"The lady is divine." Harry kept his gaze on Marisa as he spoke. "If I had known we would be graced with such an exquisite female this Season, I might have changed my mind about the army."

"I don't recall ever seeing Braden so infatuated with a female, that is one who wasn't an opera singer." Gregory glanced from Harry to Clayton, his keen blue eyes filled with speculation. "You know, I do believe Lady Marisa may be the one to do it."

Clayton suppressed his irritation. "Do what?"

Gregory grinned. "Clap my cousin in leg shackles."

With most of the gentlemen who swarmed around her, Marisa appeared cordial, friendly, nothing more. Yet she was smiling up at Braden in a way that teased the barbarian lurking just beneath the surface of Clayton's skin. He fixed his attention on Marisa's partner. Each time Braden touched Marisa's hand, Clayton's insides tightened. "Braden thinks it is his duty to win the affection of every attractive female he meets."

Gregory nodded. "True. Still, my cousin won't be

satisfied with anything less than the most dazzling creature as his bride."

"Lady Marisa certainly fits the mold," Harry said. "She is exactly the type of female who could sway my brother's course and direct him straight toward the altar."

Clayton had known Braden since their days at Harrow. They were close friends. At the moment, it was all he could do to keep from smashing his fist into Braden's proud nose.

"Pity I'm leaving soon," Harry said, grinning in the direction of Marisa. "I might give my brother a run for it."

Clayton clenched his jaw. Was every male in the city besotted with his fiancée? "I doubt Braden is interested in taking a wife. He is keeping a pair of ladybirds in Kensington."

Harry winked at him. "Sisters."

Gregory smiled. "Still, last night at White's, Braden said some interesting things about marriage. He seems to think a clever man can manage to keep his mistresses and his wife satisfied. And you know how clever Braden thinks he is. I believe he is considering offering for her."

It didn't matter, Clayton assured himself. Marisa was not a thoughtless jilt who pledged her heart to one man, then turned around and ensnared another. Still, what if she suddenly discovered she had made a dreadful mistake in accepting him? He couldn't dwell on that unfortunate thought. "I imagine Lady Marisa is clever enough to see through Braden's particular brand of charm."

"Perhaps." Gregory tapped his fingertip against his chin. "What of Justin?"

Clayton stared at him. "Justin?"

Gregory nodded. "Justin seems interested in the chit. He has actually danced with her on several occasions, and taken her for a drive through the park. Can you remember the last time your brother behaved in such a fashion?"

"My brother and Lady Marisa are friends."

"Justin *friends* with a beautiful female." Harry laughed, the sound a deep rumble against the soft lilt of the music. "That implies he doesn't want to bed her."

Gregory grinned. "Now, that *is* an aberration. You should take a look at the betting book at White's. More than a few wagers have been placed on Justin being the one to stand beside the lady at the altar."

A bead of perspiration trickled down Clayton's spine. "They are placing bets that my brother will marry Lady Marisa?"

Gregory nodded. "My money is on Braden. He has always said he would marry when the right female fell into his path. Justin, on the other hand, equates marriage with the pox. Although a woman as exquisite as Lady Marisa might change his mind."

Clayton doubted anyone would place a wager on him. No one would suspect that such a bookish fellow could win the lady's heart and hand.

Gregory studied the couple as they moved through the steps of the dance. "What do you think, gentlemen? Shall it be Braden or Justin?"

"Since I won't be in the race, I must adhere to fraternal loyalty and say the lady will choose Braden," Harry said. "What about you, Clay? Are you betting on your brother?"

"I think the lady may have her own ideas about marriage." Clayton resisted the startling urge to pound his chest. Marisa was *his*. He wanted to shout it to the world. Yet honor bound him. Honor kept him at a distance from the one thing he wanted more than anything in this life. Honor and the horrible realization that she might actually change her mind.

No matter how painful this purgatory became, deep inside himself, Clayton knew Marisa needed to enjoy the Season. She needed to meet other gentlemen. She needed to be certain when she spoke the vows that would bind them forever. Clayton watched Braden lead her through a promenade, a chill settling at the base of his spine. *If* she spoke her vows.

Marisa glanced across a field of small tables to where Clayton was supping with Miss Letitia Thurmond. There was no reason for jealousy, she assured herself. In the past few weeks she had come to know Letitia. She was one of the few females in town genuine in her friendship. Most of the other ladies, in spite of their smiles, viewed Marisa as a rival.

Letitia had never mentioned Clayton in any romantic terms. Still, Marisa couldn't stop thinking how well matched Clayton and Letitia were. Tall, with golden brown hair and large blue eyes, Letitia never seemed aware of her own beauty. She was quiet and reserved, an intellectual who would frighten men like the gentleman sitting with Marisa. Braden Fitzwilliam was not at all in the same mold as Clayton Trevelyan.

"You must have a great many stories to tell of your tour of the Mediterranean."

Braden Fitzwilliam's voice drew her attention from Clayton. She looked at the gentleman sitting across from her at the small table. She had to admit, Fitzwilliam was a beautiful specimen. His sleek black coat molded broad shoulders. His thick, dark brown hair gleamed in the candlelight, revealing a hint of chestnut hidden in the glossy waves. Carved with strong angles and curves, his face was guaranteed to please the feminine eye. Beneath dark brows, dark brown eyes regarded her with a warm admiration that might send a less sturdy female into a swoon. Yet Marisa saw that warmth for what it was: lust. She suspected Braden Fitzwilliam sought to conquer the heart of any agreeable-looking female he met. "I would think my tales would be far too tame to be of any interest."

"I doubt there is a gentleman alive who would not wish to hear you speak of your adventures. You could lecture on farming and it would sound the most fascinating subject in the world."

"Fortunately for you, we cannot test your theory. I know nothing of farming." She glanced at Clayton, her stomach crimping as she watched him laugh at something Letitia said. Jealousy was a silly, useless emotion. Clayton wanted to marry her, not Letitia, Marisa assured herself.

"I understand you spent several weeks this summer at Chatswyck."

"Yes. We had a lovely visit with the duke and his family."

Braden twisted the stem of his wineglass between his fingers. Candlelight rippled over the cut crystal, spraying sparks of color over his elegant hand. "I have been friends with Justin and Clayton since we were at Harrow. I hope Clayton was able to keep you amused. He usually finds entertaining females a rather difficult chore. There have been exceptions, of course. Notably Miss Thurmond."

Although he maintained a smile, there was a sly look in Braden's eyes. Marisa realized he must have noticed her staring at Clayton. She bristled when she realized she was wearing her heart pinned to her sleeve, while her fiancé managed to entertain another lady. "I understand Lord Huntingdon and Miss Thurmond are well acquainted."

"Yes." Braden sipped his wine. "Rumor is he has finally met his match."

Marisa stirred a piece of lobster through the butter sauce on her plate. "Really?"

"We all expected Clayton to offer for Miss Thurmond last Season."

Offer for her? Her stomach clenched at the thought. Good heavens, had Clayton been in love with another woman?

"Still, I suspect it will take him a little longer to get around to it. Clayton is a careful man. Practical in these matters."

Marisa forced her gaze to remain on Braden's handsome countenance, resisting the urge to look in Clayton's direction. It didn't matter what Braden said about Clayton and Letitia: Clayton hadn't asked Letitia to marry him. Still, those doubts deep inside of her pricked her with sharp little thorns. Would Clayton ever have offered for her if she hadn't thrown herself into his arms? She swallowed a nibble of lobster, but the tidbit caught in her throat.

Clayton had the uneasy feeling this was a mistake. The note had arrived the night before. *Meet me for breakfast. All my love, M.* As much as he knew he should, he could not find the will to resist the invitation. It had been nearly a fortnight since he had stolen a few moments alone with his fiancée. When he had arrived at the Westbury town house a few minutes ago, a footman had guided him to a table set for two in the walled gardens behind the house.

A cool breeze whispered through the leaves of chestnut and elm trees, rippling the white linen covering the round table that had been placed near a thick display of azalea bushes, all the blooms faded for the year. Sunlight spilled through the leaves of a nearby chestnut tree, glittering on crystal glasses, ivory china, and polished silver. A cart sat nearby, heavily laden with covered dishes. It all looked far too romantic.

"Clay."

Marisa's husky voice drifted to him on the breeze. He glanced at the house and found her waving to him from a window on the second floor. It took no effort to realize it was her bedchamber. Unfortunately it also took no effort to imagine her lying in her bed, with all that glorious hair spilled across her pillow, sunlight warm upon her naked skin. Desire twisted into a knot low in his belly. Once again he questioned the wisdom of coming here this morning. Each time he saw her, each time they shared a sweet stolen kiss, it became increasingly hard to keep his promise to her parents.

"I'll be right down." Marisa tossed him a kiss, then ducked her head back into the room.

Clayton drew a deep breath and summoned every ounce of his will. He could handle this, he assured himself. He could wait until next April before he told the world Marisa was his. A few moments later Marisa swept across the terrace. White muslin fluttered behind her as she ran along the garden path toward him. Pins tumbled from her hair, releasing two plump coils to tumble over her shoulder. She didn't seem to notice or care, her attention fixed on the man who stood bewitched beneath her spell.

"Clay," she whispered before throwing herself at him.

He staggered back with the impact, then surrendered to her innocent ardor. She coiled her arms around his neck, kissing him as though the world could come to an end and she would still remain locked in his arms. Heat flared and pumped with each quick thump of his heart. Need pounded like a fist in his loins. He fought the primal instinct to drag her down to the soft grass and make her his right here, right now. The scandalous thought stabbed his conscience.

He dragged his mouth from hers. It took a moment for her thick black lashes to flutter and lift. She looked up at him and smiled. "If we eloped, I could wish you good morning like this every morning."

He gently disengaged her arms from around his neck. "Marisa, I gave my word."

Her lips formed a beguiling pout. "It's such a long time to wait."

"We shall manage." He slid his fingertip under the suddenly tight creases of his neckcloth. "Somehow."

She brushed against his hip as he seated her at the table. The brief contact sizzled over his skin. He clenched his jaw. She smiled up at him. "I don't see why we must wait."

"For one thing, you are not of age." He took her plate and turned to the serving cart.

"We could go to Scotland."

"How scandalous of you, Lady Marisa." He lifted the cover from a plate of plump sausages.

"Not as scandalous as my other thoughts. Do you realize how often I imagine your hands on my skin, your body pressed close to mine?"

The cover slipped from his hand. It clattered onto the plate of sausages, scattering them across the cart. He grabbed for one plump link, trying to catch it before it rolled off the edge. Unfortunately he was still holding Marisa's plate in that hand. The plate whacked a basket of biscuits, sending one flying like a discus. It flew straight at Marisa's head.

Marisa caught it in midair. "Thank you."

Clayton met her satisfied little grin with a frown. "Marisa, you shouldn't tease me. My poor heart can stand only so much excitement."

She crinkled her nose. "I am not teasing. I am doing my best to coax you into what we both want."

He filled her plate, then set it in front of her. "We cannot run off to Scotland like a pair of hen-wits."

Marisa lifted the silver cover from a bowl of strawberry preserves. "It's not reasonable to ask us to wait nearly a year. And it certainly is not fair."

He took the seat across from her. "Reasonable or not, we have no other choice."

"Aren't you going to eat?"

"I have managed to lose my appetite."

She spooned a lump of strawberries onto a piece of biscuit. "I have been thinking."

He lifted his brows. "I was afraid of that."

She rose and came around to his side of the table. "Would you like a bite?"

The back of his neck prickled. He imagined this was how Adam felt when Eve first showed him the apple. "No. Thank you."

"Just a bite." She pressed the piece of biscuit to his lips. Besotted fool that he was, he opened for her. She popped the sweet morsel into his mouth, then slid her fingertip over his lips. The contact reverberated lower, in his loins.

She eased onto his lap. "Do you have any idea how much I want you to make love to me?"

He nearly choked on the biscuit. "Marisa, you are going to be the death of me. One day they will find my poor twisted body washed up on the banks of the Thames."

She slipped her arms around his neck. "I have an idea."

He released his pent-up breath. "I thought you might."

"If we were to become carried away, so to speak . . ." She brushed her lips over the tip of his nose. "I mean, if you actually did compromise me, then my parents would relent. There would be the possibility of a child, after all."

Her rounded bottom snuggled far too intimately against flesh screaming for a taste of her. He groaned, a man cast into hell by his own sense of honor. "Marisa, only a scoundrel would do what you are asking."

"Or two people desperate to be with one another." She brushed her lips over his. "Do you want me, Clay?"

There was nothing to hide his desire for her, except the layers of wool and muslin between them. "I want you more than I want my next breath."

She smiled, her eyes glowing with golden flames. "Come by for me this afternoon. We can say we are going for a ride in the park. You can take me to your house instead."

Hunger sang through his veins, drowning out the sane voice in his brain. "Marisa, we cannot do this."

"Yes, we can." She nipped the lobe of his ear, scattering tingles across his neck. "My parents will understand."

"No. They will not understand. What kind of man would I be if I didn't honor my word?"

"It was unreasonable to ask you to make that promise."

He looked into her beautiful face and understood all

the reasons her parents had asked him to wait. In spite of her beauty, her womanly allure, she was still a child—a child determined to get what she wanted. "Your parents had excellent reasons to ask us to wait. I want you to be certain when you speak your vows."

Her lips grew tight, her expression mulish. "I am certain. Perhaps you are the one with doubts."

He shook his head. "Never. I shall still be besotted with you when I take my last breath."

"Clay, I don't mean to be unreasonable. I really don't." She lowered her gaze. "I keep thinking something is going to happen to keep us from getting married."

"If our love is true, nothing will keep us from joining our lives." He slipped his fingers under her chin and tipped back her head until she met his gaze. "You do believe that, don't you?"

She smiled, yet doubt remained in her eyes. "Yes. Of course I do."

"Good." He gripped her waist, then lifted her off of his lap. "Now, my beautiful temptress, it's time to stop torturing your poor fiancé, or there shall be nothing left of me on our wedding night."

"I certainly would not want that to happen." She sauntered back to her side of the table.

He released his breath in a long sigh. His insides were so tightly wound, they threatened to snap. Somehow he had to find a way to resist the temptation of Marisa. He could not allow her to lure him into breaking his promise.

Chapter Eight

"I think this one would be very nice in a pale blue sarcenet." Audrey tapped the page of the pattern book she held on her lap. "Or do you think you would prefer a very pale yellow?"

"That's nice." Marisa sat beside her mother on a sofa in the morning room of Westbury House, staring at the rain dribbling down a nearby window.

Although her admirers still flooded Westbury House every day, and surrounded her at every social event, Marisa found little joy in the company of the dashing gentlemen pursuing her. One gentleman—the only gentleman she wanted—maintained a polite distance from her. With each passing day, more of the sparkle faded from the social events she attended. Although she tried to dismiss them, the doubts lurking inside of her set up camp and refused to be banished. *If our love is true, nothing will keep us from joining our lives.* Was Clayton having doubts? What was she going to do?

There must be some way to win his affection again.

"Of course, we could always have it done up in horsehair. I understand it is all the rage in Paris these days."

"That's nice." What if there was nothing at all she could do? What if she had lost Clayton's affection forever? She flinched when her mother touched her arm. She glanced at her, completely at a loss. "What?"

Audrey frowned. "Do you want to tell me what is bothering you?"

"Nothing."

"You have been wandering about in a fog for days. Even when you are surrounded by admirers, you seem alone. What is it? Have you and Clayton quarreled?"

"Quarreled? No. Clayton is far too polite to quarrel with me, even if he were angry about something."

"Do you think he is angry about something?" Audrey smiled. "I have noticed you flirting a bit lately."

"I have been flirting. In desperation."

"Flirting in desperation." Audrey tilted her head, as though giving this a great deal of thought. "I am not certain I have ever thought of flirting quite that way."

"I have been trying to draw Clayton closer to me. I thought if I flirted with a few of the more arrogant gentlemen in my acquaintance, like Lord Shipley, Clayton might feel the need to protect what was his. But he never seems to notice or care." Was she losing him? The dreadful thought had grown with each passing day, gaining weight until it felt like the Rock of Gibraltar pressing against her heart.

"Perhaps he simply doesn't show his jealousy," Audrey said, sounding less than convinced.

Marisa rose and moved to the windows. Across the street stretched the dark green expanse of Berkeley

Square. "I have this terrible feeling. I don't seem to be able to dismiss it."

"What is it, dear?"

Marisa rested her head against the window frame. She was not a woman who hid from the truth. She had to face the facts. Clayton never asked for more than one dance at any ball. He never hovered around her. At the theater, he would stop by the Westbury box for no more than a few minutes, spending most of that time conversing with her parents. Although Clayton avoided her, Marisa had noticed he always found time to spend with Letitia Thurmond. As much as she wanted to deny the possibility that she had lost Clayton, she could no longer avoid the truth. "I keep thinking Clayton has changed his mind about me."

"What makes you think that?"

Marisa stared through the rain streaming over the windowpane, watching a coach plow through a puddle in front of her house. "I seldom see him. And when I do, he is so . . . polite."

"You expect him to be anything less than a gentleman?"

"No. But he treats me as though I were a stranger."

"Your father and I asked Clayton to pay close attention to propriety. It certainly wouldn't be proper for him to live in your pocket. It would cause far too much speculation."

A chill seeped through the windows, brushing against her. "I don't care about speculation. We are engaged. We should be permitted to tell the world about it."

Audrey closed the pattern book. "Marisa, we have discussed this. I thought you understood why it was important for you to have a Season unencumbered by a formal engagement."

"I cannot stop thinking I am losing him." Marisa rubbed her arms, fighting a chill that came from within. "When I see Clay, he is so distant. So terribly polite. He treats me as though I were a friend he met in the country, nothing more. Except for an occasional drive through the park, I do not see him when there isn't a crowd about us. The truth is, I see more of Justin than I do Clay."

Audrey smoothed her hand over the cloth-covered book. "I have to admit I am surprised he has not tried to be alone with you. It would seem the natural thing for a man in love to do."

"Perhaps he doesn't want to be with me," Marisa said, forcing the words past her tight throat.

Audrey was quiet a moment, as though judging her words before she spoke. "I have noticed he seems to be very friendly with Miss Thurmond. I didn't want to mention it, but I have heard rumors that he might offer for her. Of course, one is always hearing rumors of that sort. Every week you hear different speculations."

A hard hand closed around Marisa's throat. "I cannot stop thinking that Clay regrets asking me to marry him."

"Clayton must have cared very deeply for you, or he never would have offered for you," Audrey said.

With the tip of her finger, Marisa traced the serpentine pattern of a rivulet of rain as it flowed down the cool windowpane, the heat of her skin radiating in steam across the glass. "I didn't give him much choice. I threw myself at him. I employed every feminine wile I possess. He said I had tempted him into compromising me. At the time I thought he was teasing me. Now I wonder. I have this feeling he felt compelled to ask me to marry him. Out of honor."

The sound of rain splattering against the windowpanes filled up the silence. "Compromised you?"

Marisa glanced at her mother. "He kissed me. After I threw myself into his arms."

Audrey released her breath. "Yes, he might very well feel obliged to offer for you. He takes honor and responsibility so seriously."

"Yes, he does." Marisa pulled her cashmere shawl close around her. Yet she couldn't ease the chill inside her. "What am I going to do? What if he has changed his mind? He would never tell me. He is far too kind to hurt me in any way, far too honorable to back away from a mistake he has made. He would marry me and make the best of the situation. Mama, I couldn't live knowing he had married me for the sake of honor and nothing more. I love him too much."

Audrey set the pattern book on the round pedestal table beside the sofa. "Marisa, you and Clayton shared a summer idyll. You could not have been more isolated had you been cast upon the shores of an enchanted island. It was natural to think you had fallen in love."

"I did fall in love. I haven't changed my mind. I shall never change my mind."

"You must consider Clayton. If you truly believe he has changed his mind, you must deal with it."

Marisa held her mother's steady gaze, seeing all of her fears solidified in her mother's practical look. "You think he has changed his mind, don't you?"

"You and Clayton are very different. I think it is very possible he has come to realize your marriage would not be a success."

Marisa fought the tears burning her eyes. "I would do my best to make him happy."

"I know you would. But sometimes that isn't enough." Audrey rose and moved to Marisa's side. "Clayton has no honorable way to alter this. Marisa, you are the only one who can end the engagement."

Marisa swallowed hard. "I don't want to end our engagement."

"I know." Audrey smoothed a tumbled lock of hair behind Marisa's shoulder. "Perhaps he isn't having any doubts. You need to speak with Clayton. You need to find out if he has changed his mind."

"I don't want to ask him." Marisa cringed at her own cowardice. "I'm afraid of what he might say."

"It is better to know now, rather than to find out after the vows have been spoken. You wouldn't want to see him made unhappy for the rest of his life. Would you?"

Marisa shook her head, her throat too tight to allow words to escape.

Audrey smiled. "Ask him, Mari. You shall regret it all of your life if you don't make certain this is what you both want."

"He is taking me for a carriage ride tomorrow afternoon. I shall ask him then." If she could find the courage. Still, Marisa knew there was no escape from this responsibility. She couldn't make Clayton unhappy, no matter how much it might hurt her.

"You are doing what is right."

"I know." Marisa just prayed all of her fears were based on her own foolish notions. She prayed she would never have to face the day when Clayton walked out of her life.

For Clayton, the only way to resist temptation was to avoid it. Although he wanted to see Marisa every day, his pledge to her parents kept him at a distance, far enough to keep his hands off of her, close enough to see every eligible male in London tripping over each other in an attempt to win her heart. And lately his beautiful fiancée seemed far too interested in several of the gentlemen paying her court.

At times it took every ounce of his will to maintain his composure. There were moments when he barely crushed the urge to toss her over his shoulder and carry her off to Scotland. He had contemplated leaving London and not returning until April. Yet he was afraid Marisa might forget he existed. As determined as he was for her to have the opportunity to see the possible error in her choice of a prospective groom, he wasn't philanthropic enough to abandon her completely to the pack sniffing after her skirts.

Clayton glanced at the lady who filled his dreams. Marisa sat beside him on the narrow seat of his curricle, staring straight ahead. The breeze rippled the gold satin ribbons tied beneath her chin. Beneath her hat, her thick black hair had been brushed into submission, allowing only a few wispy curls to flutter around her face. Lord, he wanted to pull the pins from her hair and smooth the silky strands down her back.

Heat pooled in his loins when he thought of other things he wanted to do. It had been a lifetime since he had held her in his arms. At times he wondered if he had ever really kissed those lovely lips, or if it had all been a beguiling dream.

He steered his pair of matched grays into Hyde Park. At this hour, the carriage paths were not crowded. Two hours from now, the horde would descend upon the park. "Did you enjoy the theater last night?"

She folded her hands in her lap. "Yes. It was quite enjoyable."

Clayton frowned, surprised by the chilly tone of her voice. Now that he thought of it, she had seemed distant from the moment he had arrived at her house. "Marisa, is something wrong?"

Marisa glanced at him. "No. Why do you ask?"

"You haven't smiled once since I arrived at your house."

Her lips tipped into a sad imitation of her smile. "I'm sorry. I don't mean to be poor company."

"You could never be poor company." Yet, as the drive continued, and every attempt he made at conversation earned a stilted response, he grew uneasy. The ice in her demeanor slipped beneath his skin, chilling his blood.

He stared over the heads of his horses and searched his brain for anything he might have done to anger Marisa. Nothing came to mind. Since he did not, in any way, count himself an expert in the workings of the feminine mind, he decided to ask her. "If there is something bothering you, I wish you would share it with me."

"Nothing is bothering me," she said, far too brightly.

He managed a smile, but anxiety pounded through him with each beat of his heart. "Nothing?"

She looked down at her tightly clasped hands. "I was just thinking of . . . things."

Something in the tone of her voice sent a shiver along his spine. He steered his team down a wide path winding along the Serpentine. "Anything in particular?"

She lifted her gaze, her eyes narrowing against the glare of sunlight on water as she stared across the Serpentine. The steady thump of horseshoes pounding the path and the soft jangle of the harnesses filled up the silence stretching between them. Marisa contemplated the view for so long, he wondered if she intended to respond to his question at all. When she spoke, her voice barely lifted above a whisper "Do you think two people who are very different can make a successful marriage?''

He shifted on the seat. "Are you thinking of us?"

She kept her gaze on the water. "We are very different, you and I. Do you still think we shall make a successful marriage?"

Clayton felt he stood on a narrow ledge high above a rocky shore. One wrong step and he would tumble. "We are different. Still, I hope we can make our marriage a success."

Marisa turned her head and fixed him with a direct stare. "But you have doubts?"

He looked into her beautiful eyes and saw his every doubt mirrored in the golden brown depths. Could she ever truly be happy with him? "Yes. I have doubts."

She glanced away from him. "I knew I could depend on your honesty."

Clayton felt as though his blood were slowly draining from his body. Marisa was slipping away from him; he could feel it as keenly as he could feel the tug of the ribbons in his hands. "Marisa, I didn't mean to upset you."

She smiled, her lips stiff and trembling. "You haven't."

"I just . . . we are very different."

"Yes. We are."

"I didn't mean to say I don't care for you."

"And I didn't mean to press you into an uncomfortable situation. I just needed to know." She glanced down at her hands. "Papa may actually take me to Tattersall's tomorrow. Mama is opposed, of course, but I think I can coax her into it. Do you think it would be terribly brazen of me?"

He had made a wrong step; he knew it. "I don't believe I have ever seen a lady at Tatt's."

She smiled far too widely, revealing a small portion of her upper gums. "Then I suppose I should defer to Mama's judgment. I did so want to see the yard and all that prime horseflesh."

A door had closed between them. He could sense it. Yet, as much as he wanted to open that door, he wasn't certain he could find a key. "Marisa, is everything all right?"

She glanced away from him. "Yes, of course."

Clayton touched her arm, hoping she would meet his gaze. She kept her eyes lowered, her thoughts hidden from him. "I hope you know, I care too much for you ever to intentionally cause you any harm, in any way."

"I know." She closed her eyes, her hands clenching in the strings of her reticule. "You are far too kind ever to cause me any harm."

He felt he had been drawn into deep water where dangerous currents lurked beneath the surface, waiting to drag him under. The look on her face awakened every doubt and fear lurking inside him. As much as he wanted to hide from the truth, he knew it had to be faced. He steered the carriage into a short, circular drive. The thick trees lining the drive shielded this area from the rest of the park. He sensed they needed some privacy. He pulled up on the reins and brought the horses to a stop. "There is something bothering you. Please tell me what it is."

"I keep thinking of the time we shared last summer," Marisa said to her clenched hands.

The weight of memories pressed against his heart. "I shall never forget last summer."

"It was an idyll, wasn't it? All golden and warm."

"I could not have asked for a more perfect moment in time."

She moistened her lips. "I suppose that is why we

rushed into a decision that required more care.''

Sunlight filtered through the trees, sprinkling golden light upon her face. She had never looked more delicate, more vulnerable, like a child lost in the woods. He wanted to touch her, to hold her in his arms, but he couldn't risk it. If he touched her he would lose his head, make this all the more difficult for her. "Was that what we did?"

She nodded. "We just got carried away with the romance of it all."

He had been carried away by a lovely creature of light and warmth. A woman who had made him believe in miracles, such as the miracle of a dazzling, exciting woman falling in love with a dull bookworm. "I suppose we did."

"I have given this a great deal of thought, and I feel it would be better for both of us . . ." She closed her eyes and a single tear slipped past her thick black lashes, glinting in the sunlight. "I think it would be best if we ended our engagement."

Although he had expected them, the words hit him so hard they drove the air from his lungs. Words clawed at his throat, pitiful pleas for salvation. *I love you. Please don't turn away from me.* Yet he sat mute beside her. If she wanted to end their engagement, he would not try to hold her with pity. He might be a dull bookworm, but he had his pride. He would never burden her with the knowledge of his poor, breaking heart.

She peeked at him from beneath her lashes. "Do you feel the same way? Would we be making a mistake if we were to marry?"

This was difficult enough for her, facing him with a truth she must know would pierce him like a blade. She was a sensitive young woman. He would not make it any worse by pouring out his own feelings on the subject. "It is as you said; we rushed into this."

"Yes." She tugged the glove from her left hand and slipped the betrothal ring from her finger. She stared at it for a long moment before handing it to him. "I wish you all the happiness in the world."

The bloodred ruby turned liquid in the sunlight. The diamonds sparkled in the light, sending sparks of color spilling across his palm. He closed his hand around the ring, the gold still warm from her skin. "I wish the same for you."

She wiped her damp cheek with the back of her fingers. "I am certain, in time, we will both look back upon this and . . . we will realize this was for the best."

He stared at her, an icy reality seeping through his veins. "Yes. I suppose we will."

Her soft exhalation of breath shuddered in the silence stretching between them. He searched for words that might ease the hurt he could see on her face. Yet there seemed nothing to say. Nothing except farewell. He pulled a handkerchief from his pocket and handed it to her.

She kept her eyes lowered while she dabbed at her cheeks with the soft white linen. "I apologize for turning into a watering pot."

An odd numbness crept through him, as though she had ripped all the emotion out of him. "You have no reason to apologize."

She smiled at the handkerchief she clenched in her hand. "You are very kind."

He swallowed hard, forcing back the bile in his throat. "Are you ready to go home?"

"Yes. I think that would be a good idea."

He eased the horses into a trot and found his way out of the park. He threaded his way through the crowded streets of the West End, making it to her house with only a vague awareness of the world around him. Once Marisa was safely in her home, Clayton headed for his own. The scene in the park played over and over again in his brain. Slowly the blessed oblivion of shock melted from him, like ice in the sunlight, and pain filled the spaces left behind. As he made his way toward his house, his mind replayed the scene in the park, over and over again. Marisa's voice whispered in his brain, each word unraveling the threads holding together the tapestry that was his life.

It was over. All the questions and doubts had ended in a few words. Only now did his body register the death of all his hopes and dreams as well. All the strength drained from his limbs. His heart pounded like a thoroughbred's after a race. He halted the carriage in the middle of the street, oblivious to the curious glances cast in his direction by several people strolling by.

Never again would he hold Marisa in his arms. Never again would he taste her lips, feel her hands slide through his hair, experience the singular thrill of hearing her say *I love you, Clay.* Lord help him, he wasn't sure how to face the prospect of a life without her.

Marisa hurried to a window overlooking Berkeley Square. Through a blur of tears she caught a glimpse of Clayton before he turned the corner and disappeared from sight. Her shoulders shook with the uncontrollable sobs gripping her body. Pain welled up inside her, so potent and bitter it stole the strength from her limbs. Her legs collapsed beneath her. She dissolved on the floor in a puddle of white muslin, her bottom thumping the carpet.

Until the end, until that last moment when he had accepted the ring, she had hoped he might turn it all around, fight the simple dissolution of their future together. Yet he had accepted it without a single attempt to alter her decision. Accepted it, because it was what he truly wanted.

It was over. All the hopes and dreams she had cherished these past few months had crumbled like dried rose petals crushed in a careless hand. Never again would she feel Clayton's strong arms around her. Never again would she melt beneath his kisses. Never again would she hear his soft voice whisper *I love you, Mari.* She hugged her arms close against her body and rocked back and forth while tears scalded her cheeks and sobs clenched her throat.

"Marisa."

Her mother's voice pierced the pounding of blood in her ears. Audrey knelt beside her and slipped her arms around her daughter's trembling shoulders. "It's all right, darling."

"No . . . it's . . . not." The words squeaked past Marisa's lips.

Audrey slid her hand over Marisa's hair. "I promise, it will be all right."

Marisa pressed her cheek against her mother's shoulder. The delicate scent of lavender surrounded her. She wept like a child, humiliated by the horrible retching sounds spilling from her lips, the miserable way her nose filled and dripped water. Still she couldn't prevent the display. All the while she sobbed, her mother rocked her gently in her arms, and hushed her softly. When the sobs slackened to a steady stream of tears, Marisa scrubbed her cheeks with Clayton's handkerchief.

"I'm sorry. I don't mean to act like such a hen-wit." Marisa forced the words past the tears strangling her throat. "I just don't seem to be able to stop weeping."

"Let the tears come, dear. They will help wash away the pain." Audrey tucked a wayward curl behind Marisa's ear. "In time, you will see that this was for the best."

Marisa blew her nose. "Was it for the best?"

"You wouldn't want to marry Clayton knowing it wasn't really what he wanted. You wouldn't want him to be unhappy."

Marisa closed her eyes. Still, the tears leaked past her lashes. "Maybe I could have changed his mind after we were married. I would have tried my best to make him happy."

"I know, dear. I know you would have tried. But it would only lead to unhappiness for both of you." Audrey hugged Marisa close. "You need a man who will love you with all of his heart and soul."

Marisa hiccoughed. "I want Clay."

"Marisa, I know you feel your heart is broken, but it will heal. One day you will find a man who will make you forget all about Clayton."

Marisa rested her head on her mother's shoulder. "I hope you are right, Mama. I have this horrible feeling I shall always be in love with him."

Chapter Nine

Five days later, Clayton sat in his library, watching his brother pace the length of the room. He realized he had upset Justin. Yet there was nothing he could do to prevent it.

"You cannot be serious." Justin paused in front of his brother's chair and stared down at him. "In case you didn't notice, we are fighting a war. You do remember a little empire builder by the name of Napoleon, don't you?"

Clayton propped his feet on the leather footstool in front of his chair. "I thought the army preferable to hanging myself."

"Bloody hell! There isn't a woman on the face of the earth worth getting killed over."

Clayton smoothed his fingers over the leather-clad arm of his chair. "It isn't simply Marisa. It's hard to explain, but I'm tired of who I am."

"There is nothing wrong with who you are."

Clayton glanced away from his brother's concerned countenance. He stared at the hearth, where fire consumed thick blocks of coal. "If I were different, if I were more like you, I never would have lost her."

"Damnation, Clay, you're twice the man I am. Who can say what flits through the mind of a female? Especially one as unpredictable as Marisa. You cannot blame yourself for her caprice."

"I just don't care much for the man I am."

"And so you want to march off and get yourself killed on some bloody battlefield?"

Clayton smiled up at his brother. "I don't plan to get myself killed."

"Then don't go."

Clayton couldn't remain in England. He didn't want to pick up the *Gazette* one day and see Marisa's engagement announced. He couldn't see Marisa, knowing she belonged to another man, knowing another man had earned the right to hold her and kiss her and live with her all the days of their lives. Not now. Not until he had found some way of putting together all the pieces of his heart. "I have thought about this. I think it's what I need."

Justin turned and threw himself into a matching chair across from Clayton. "You are damn stubborn, do you know that?"

Clayton shrugged. "It's one of the traits we share."

Justin stared down at the arm of his chair while he traced a pattern on the leather with the tip of his finger. "I wish I could have seen the duke's face when you told him you had purchased a commission."

Clayton grimaced as he recollected his father's reaction. For the first time in his life, Clayton had openly defied his father. Although distressing his father did not sit well with him, Clayton knew this was what he had to do. "I hope you try to reconcile with him, Justin. At the moment he feels both of his sons have deserted him."

"I'm amazed he even remembers he has two sons." Justin nudged the footstool in front of his chair with the tip of his boot. "When do you leave?"

"In three days."

"Then I suggest we make the most of the time we have." Justin gripped the arms of his chair. "You do realize I shall never forgive you if you get yourself killed?"

Clayton felt the strength of his brother's love, as well as the potent grip of his fear. "Then I suppose I shall have to do my best to come home in one piece."

Clayton would also do his best to heal. If fate was kind, time would erase Marisa's image from his mind. If he tried his best, the rigors of army life would alter him, strip away every last vestige of the man he was, this insipid, dull clod of a bookworm. If he trusted discipline, he would learn to live without Marisa. He had to fight his way through this horrible pain. If he didn't succeed, if he couldn't alter the man he was, then he hoped to heaven a bullet would end his life.

At White's that evening the news of Clayton's decision stunned the small group of his friends, Braden, Gregory, and Harry among them. No one had ever expected him to march off to war.

Gregory Stanwood sat back in his chair and fixed Clayton with a speculative glare. "What could possibly have convinced you to purchase a commission?"

Clayton twisted his glass on the table. "I thought I might enjoy the fresh air of the Peninsula."

Gregory lifted his brows. "First Harry. Now you.

Good heavens, you don't think it is something going around, do you? Like the pox?''

"Why not join us?" Harry asked. "Excitement and glory await."

Gregory lifted his hand. "I prefer to stay here and marry a wealthy woman."

"Marriage?" Harry winked at him, sly understanding in his eyes. "I thought you might consider that worse than battle, cousin."

Gregory shrugged. "I prefer my comfort. One must do what one must."

A short while later, Harry drew Clayton aside from the others. "I'm not sure why you decided to purchase a commission. But I am glad to know we will be in the same regiment."

Clayton smiled at his young friend. Although Harry was two years his junior, he obviously thought it his duty to protect his bookish friend. "There is no need to feel you have to watch over me. I shall be fine."

Harry squeezed Clayton's shoulder. "As much as I am looking forward to dispatching this nasty business with the French, I would like to come back in one piece. What do you say if we watch out for each other?"

"I think that sounds like an excellent idea."

"Clayton has purchased a commission." Marisa paced the length of her mother's drawing room. She paused at the windows and pivoted to face her mother, who sat on a sofa nearby. "It is my fault. I brought this about."

Audrey shook her head. "You had nothing at all to do with this."

"How can you say I had nothing at all to do with

this? Days after I ended our engagement, he decided to march off to war. To the Peninsula!''

''Killing is a natural instinct in men.'' Cecilia Grantham plunged her needle into the white linen stretched in her embroidery hoop. She sat in an upholstered armchair near the hearth, a slender, dark-haired spinster of six and forty. Although her face retained the finely molded features that had caused a stir with the male population in her youth, her expression managed to disguise that beauty behind a mask of bitterness. ''Beneath even the most elegantly tailored clothes, they are all wearing animal skins.''

''Clayton is different, Aunt. He is a scholar. He doesn't even enjoy hunting.''

Cecilia shook her head. ''You cannot trust any of them. It's in the blood, you know. A battlefield is the place for them.''

Marisa shuddered at the thought of Clayton on a battlefield. ''This is my fault.''

Audrey frowned. ''Marisa, you did speak with Clayton, didn't you? You did make certain he had changed his mind about your marriage?''

''He said he had doubts. He agreed it would be a mistake for us to marry.'' Marisa rubbed her throbbing temples. For the past few days she had relived every moment of that last conversation she had had with him, searching for something that could kill the doubts inside her. ''What if I was wrong? What if I have made a horrible mistake?''

Cecilia huffed. ''The only mistake you made is in trusting the male of the species.''

Audrey slowly rubbed her palms together. ''If Clayton had doubts, I am certain you did the right thing. You mustn't blame yourself.''

141

Marisa sank to the sofa beside her mother. "I have to do something. I have to stop him."

"There is nothing you can do," Audrey said.

"I gave him up so he could marry the woman he loved, not march off to some horrible battlefield." Marisa gripped her mother's hands. "He could be killed."

Audrey's lips pulled into a tight line. "Marisa, you have to face the fact that you may have had nothing to do with his decision to purchase a commission."

"But why would he do it?"

Cecilia waved her hand. "Never look for a logical reason behind a man's behavior. It will only land you in Bedlam."

"You have to let him go, Marisa," Audrey said. "Clayton has his life to live; you have yours."

"But I—"

"It is over, Marisa," Audrey said, her voice firm. "Clayton is no longer a part of your life."

"Thank heavens you found out before it was too late." Cecilia stabbed the linen with her needle. "He could have abandoned you after the engagement was announced. Made a fool of you."

Although Cecilia had learned her bitterness from experience, Marisa knew Clayton was not cast from the same mold as the man who had humiliated her aunt. "I want to speak with Clayton. I want to tell him . . ."

"What?" Audrey asked. "What do you want to tell him? Do you want to tell him you still love him? What do you suppose he would say?"

The cold reality in her mother's eyes penetrated Marisa's blood. "I don't know."

"He would laugh at you. That's what he would do. Don't allow him to make a fool of you, Marisa." Cecilia stared down at her embroidery hoop. "Keep your dignity."

"Or he may very well take pity on you," Audrey said.

Marisa closed her eyes. "Pity?"

"He may say anything to ease your distress." Audrey tucked a wayward curl behind Marisa's ear. "You must face this head-on. There is nothing more to say, Mari. You have made your decision. Clayton has made his."

Marisa sagged against the back of the sofa. "I shall die if anything happens to him."

"You are a strong girl. You will shake off this horrible despair. Tonight we will attend the Hanley party and you will take your first steps toward getting better." Audrey kissed Marisa's cheek. "Now smile, darling. Smile and face the world with the courage I know you possess."

Marisa forced her lips into a smile, while inside a horrible pain stabbed her with every breath. In spite of her mother's advice, Marisa knew she could not allow Clayton to march off to war without trying to prevent it. Her pride meant nothing compared to his life.

The note arrived late in the afternoon of his last day in London, a few lines scrawled on a piece of white parchment.

Please meet me in the gardens behind my house at eight. I shall leave the gate open for you. Please come. I must speak with you. M.

Astonishing the impact a few lines of ink could have on a man's soul. Even though a part of him shuddered with pain at the thought of seeing Marisa again, there was really no question about whether he would go. At eight that evening, Clayton opened the gate and walked into the gardens behind the Westbury town house.

Moonlight poured over the gardens, glinting on the damp grass, bathing the azalea bushes lining the path. The silvery light spilled through the leaves of the tall chestnut standing near the brick wall that separated the gardens from the rest of the world. Marisa stepped from beneath the branches of the chestnut, materializing like a wraith from a fantasy.

Her black hair was piled atop her head except for two long coils that had been allowed to fall over one slender shoulder. Black velvet wrapped her form, the cloak fastened at her neck. As she moved toward him her gown peeked from beneath the cloak, white muslin glowing like spun moonlight. His heart squeezed painfully at the beguiling sight of her. For one breathless moment he fought the urge to take her into his arms. He needed her warmth to fight the chill that had crept into his blood. But that time had come and past. She was no longer his to hold.

Marisa paused before him, allowing cold moonlight to fill the space between them. "Thank you for coming."

"I was curious. What is there left to say?"

She moistened her lips. "You purchased a commission."

He molded his lips into a smile. "It never ceases to amaze me how quickly gossip travels through this town."

"You cannot actually mean to march off to war?"

"I leave tomorrow."

"You could be killed," she said, her voice breaking with emotion.

"I realize I seem nothing more than a dull bookworm, but I can handle a saber and a pistol. I think I might actually manage to survive."

Moonlight revealed the guilt in her eyes. "You are doing this because of me. Because I ended our engagement."

"You must not think you carry any burden for this decision. It was completely my own. I have often considered the opportunities presented by the army. Adventure. Excitement. The chance to fight for the freedom of England." It was not a complete lie, he assured himself. He had considered the army often during the past few days.

She frowned, her expression revealing a flicker of uncertainty. "Clay, if there is anything I can do to change your mind about leaving, I will do it."

He would not have her pity or her sacrifice because of her guilt. "Thank you for the offer, but this is what I want to do."

She gripped his arm. "You cannot go to war."

He touched her cheek, his bare fingers sliding against the cool satin of her skin. "It is all right, Mari."

Tears glittered in her eyes. "No. It isn't all right. If you die in battle, I shall never forgive myself."

"It is time for you to continue with your life, and me to continue with mine." He pressed his fingertip to her lips when she would have spoken. "We had one glorious summer. I shall always treasure those memories. But we need to realize the warmth of summer does not always linger into autumn. There is nothing left for us. Nothing left to say. Except good-bye."

Her lips parted but nothing escaped except a soft breath. She looked so lost, so sad. It took everything he possessed to refrain from slipping his arms around her.

"Good-bye, Mari." He turned and walked toward the gate before he did something unforgivably foolish.

"May God keep you safe, Clay," she said, her voice soft with emotion.

He glanced over his shoulder and found her watching him, her beautiful face a portrait of regret. "May you find your happiness, Mari."

A single tear trickled down her cheek, glittering in the moonlight. "Good-bye."

"Good-bye." With that final word he left her.

After leaving Marisa, Clayton wandered the streets of the West End of London. He strolled past the Hanley town house, scarcely glancing at the brightly lit windows. He was supposed to have attended the Hanley party this evening, but he had no desire to spend his last night in London watching Marisa glitter amidst her legion of admirers.

The cool air brushed his cheeks with the smoky scent of the metropolis. Even here, in the fashionable part of the city, a gray haze hung on the evening air, visible in the glimmer from the street lamps. A few carriages rumbled along the streets. Yet most of the beau monde was already crowded into the drawing rooms and ballrooms of the houses he passed. The gaiety of the Season flickered into the streets from rooms where drapes had been thrown open to the world—beacons to the glittering butterflies of the ton. Occasionally a thread of music drifted to his ears, reminding him of evenings spent in those crowded rooms, watching a dark-haired temptress.

He strolled past the houses, set apart from the Society in which he had roamed since coming of age. At two in the morning he heard a watchman sing out the hour of the day and the comforting declaration that all was well with the world. Clayton smiled at the naive proclamation. He for one knew all was not right in this world.

A half hour later, he leaned against a tree in Berkeley Square, hidden from the dim light of the street lamps, waiting for one final glimpse of his temptress. Clayton watched and waited for what might have been an hour or two. Time had no hold on him now. Finally a carriage pulled up in front of the Westbury town house. Edgar and Audrey Grantham descended from the carriage, followed by Marisa.

The street lamp outside her house cast its feeble light upon her, glimmering on her midnight hair. The soft light brushed her cheek, gleaming white and smooth as polished alabaster. Yet he knew the warmth of that skin, the softness. He watched as she climbed the three wide stone stairs and disappeared into the house. He remained a few moments longer, waiting for the pain to ease from his chest before he turned toward his home.

Tomorrow he would begin his campaign for a different life. Tomorrow he would take his first step in putting the past behind him. Tonight he buried a dream.

Clayton plunged into war hoping to forge his character into steel. Yet he wasn't prepared for the brutalities and ironies of it all. The brutalities became constant companions. The ironies struck at odd times. The man who had never had a heart for hunting soon found himself on a battlefield facing the choice of killing a fellow man or allowing that man to kill him. The decision sprang from instinct. Survival proved far more powerful than compassion.

After their first battle, Harry sat with Clayton on the ground outside of their tent. They stared at the sky, both quiet, silently sharing the blood-soaked memories they had forged that day. The stench of battle clung to the warm evening air, a strange, sickly-sweet scent born of blood and gunpowder. The soft moans of the wounded drifted around them, stabbing Clayton in those places still raw from the killing he had done.

"They say it gets easier," Harry said, his voice a harsh whisper.

"I'm afraid it will." Clayton stared at the cluster of stars shaping Orion. He had always enjoyed stargazing. The stars were the same as they had always been. Yet he would never look at anything the same way again.

Harry wrapped his arms around his raised knees. "I never imagined battle quite this way."

"No one could explain it."

Harry released a shaky breath. "It is all for a higher cause. We must think of freedom, of England."

"Yes. I suppose we must, or we shall never be able to do it."

In the days that followed, Clayton learned the truth of war. With each slash of his saber the humanity spilled from his body, less conspicuous than the blood of the men he killed, yet every bit as real. The battles all blended one into another, the names of places such as Oporto, Talavera, Salamanca blurred in his memory, along with the faces of the men he killed. The missions he undertook in Paris as an operative for the ministry drained the remaining warmth from his blood.

In all the time Clayton was gone, his father never wrote. With each letter he received from his brother or his grandmother, Clayton expected to hear of Marisa's engagement. A part of him had thought Justin might find his happiness with the woman who still haunted Clayton's dreams. If Marisa did not choose Justin, she would certainly choose Braden. At first the letters

Harry received from Braden seemed to verify Clayton's dire thoughts; each one mentioned Marisa. In time, though, she disappeared from his correspondence. Apparently she had proved immune to Braden's charm.

As the years rolled past, Marisa continued to evade all of her suitors. Through the years, Clayton caught glimpses of her, on those rare occasions when he returned home for a few days of leave. As the years carved away the man he had been, she remained the same, lovely and bright, like a shining, all too distant star.

In January of 1815, a few months after Harry's father had been killed in a riding accident, Clayton returned home to see his own father one last time. Although he had always seemed so powerful, even George William could not command the course of the disease slowly eating him from within. Before he died, the duke pried a promise from his youngest son. Clayton agreed he would leave the army and return home to take a wife. The succession must be ensured. Yet Clayton was drawn back into war soon after, when Napoleon made his escape from Elba. One last campaign ended at Waterloo.

One last irony hit after the war had ended.

Several weeks after Waterloo, Clayton journeyed to Paris with Harry Fitzwilliam and several other officers, all recently recovered from the wounds of battle, all delirious with the heady brew of victory, all anxious to celebrate. On their last night in Paris, Clayton cast a critical glance in the mirror above the washstand in his hotel room. White braid slashed across the front of his dark blue coat; gold epaulets glinted in the candlelight. It would be one of the last times he would ever don this uniform. How long before the memories faded?

Clayton left his room and marched along the narrow hallway, headed for Harry's room. They were meeting the others at Le Chien Rouge for one final night of unbridled celebration, wallowing in the debauchery of prostitutes and wine. A door slammed around the corner ahead of him. A heartbeat later, a fair-haired man hurried around the corner and plowed into him. Caught unaware, Clayton was slammed back against the wall. The other man mumbled an apology in French, then hurried along the hallway.

Clayton rubbed the back of his head, grimaced at the sore spot left from the collision with the wall, then proceeded to Harry's room. He knocked and received no answer. Odd, Harry was always the last to get ready for anything. He knocked again, and this time he heard a soft sound from inside.

"Harry, are you there?" Clayton asked, trying the door handle. The brass handle turned in his grasp. He opened the door, stepped inside, then froze. "Harry!"

A low moan issued from the body lying facedown on the carpet. Clayton rushed to his friend's side. A dark red stain spread across the white linen of Harry's shirt, spilling from a rent between his shoulder blades.

Clayton eased Harry onto his back. "Harry," he whispered, touching his old friend's face.

Harry's lashes lifted. He stared up at Clayton, his dark eyes distant, unfocused. "Braden," he whispered, "must . . . tell him—" His words ended on a rattle of breath. Blood spilled from the corner of his mouth.

"Harry!" Clayton said, gripping his shoulder. Yet nothing could pull his friend back from the shadows of death. The last words Harry had wanted to say to his brother were forever lost.

Clayton closed his own eyes against the scalding burn of tears. They had fought side by side through every bloody battle of the war. And here it ended, on the dawn of peace.

Although Clayton spent a month searching for Harry's murderer, he never found a clue leading to the blackguard. Paris was bloated with English as well as citizens from the other allies, all anxious to celebrate victory in the city of the defeated. The authorities fared no better in their investigation.

When Clayton left Paris, instead of returning to England he went to Italy, where his brother was staying in self-imposed exile until the end of the mourning period for their father. Justin would not don black for his sire. The last traces of the wounds carved into Clayton's flesh healed beneath the warm Italian sun. Yet there were other wounds hidden deep within him, ghosts that rose when the sun set to stalk him with bloody memories. And, in spite of his every attempt to banish her, in unguarded moments, a dark-haired siren still slipped into his dreams: Some dreams died harder than others.

Clayton returned to London with Justin in March of 1816. He had accomplished what he had set out to do that first day he marched off to war. The sensitive, scholarly young man he had been had died in battle.

Temptation

Love is the tyrant of the heart; it darkens
Reason, confounds discretion; deaf to counsel,
It runs a headlong course to desperate madness.

—John Ford

Chapter Ten

London
May 1816

I need to speak with you on an urgent matter, M.

Clayton stared at the words scrawled in an elegant script across the back of Marisa's calling card. He tried to prevent the tightening that had commenced in his chest. Yet it was as unavoidable as the truth. Seven years, and the woman could still twist him in knots.

"Should I tell Lady Marisa you are not receiving callers this afternoon, my lord?" his butler asked.

Clayton dropped the card on his dresser, letting it fall upon a tray filled with jeweled stick pins, studs, watch chains, and seals. His first inclination was to send her packing. He had suffered enough at her dainty hands. Yet curiosity got the better of him. "No, Greensley. Tell her I am in the middle of a fitting for a new coat. I shall be with her directly."

"Aye, my lord."

Why the devil was she here? Questions whirled in his mind as Clayton forced his body to move with studied composure. Since coming to London for the Season he had caught only a few glimpses of Marisa. He had kept his distance; she had kept hers. Until today.

Clayton glanced at his reflection in a cheval mirror that stood in one corner of his bedchamber while the tailor fussed with the shoulder of the new riding coat. Little remained of the man Marisa had torn into ragged pieces. That shy young man had died in battle a long time ago, along with every shred of warmth or passion he had once possessed. The years had cured him. He no longer had a place in his life for women like Marisa.

After dispatching the tailor, Clayton proceeded to the library. He opened the door and froze, stunned by the sudden excitement rushing through him at the sight of her. Marisa pivoted near his desk, pale blue muslin rippling around her legs, giving him a glimpse of shapely ankles. Black curls framed a face that had haunted his dreams for more years than he wanted to remember. He noticed her shoulders rise with a deep inhalation just as he drew air into his tight lungs.

"I'm sorry to keep you waiting." Clayton forced his legs to move, crossing the distance between them in long strides. "It was unavoidable, I'm afraid."

"Greensley said you were being fitted for a new coat," she said, her voice cool and composed.

"It took a few minutes to change."

She offered him her hand, as though they were nothing more than old acquaintances meeting once more after a lifetime had passed. Even though she wore gloves, he felt it just the same, a spark of contact, as sharp and shimmering as a flash from flint. Her eyes widened, as though she had also felt it. In some twisted way he had hoped the years might alter her, strip her of the devastating beauty that had haunted him day and night. Yet she remained as she had been the first day he met her, as fresh and lovely as a dream. "You are looking well."

"I can say the same of you." She smiled, a dimple peeking at him from the corner of her lips. "You are completely recovered from your wounds?"

His body had recovered from the wounds of war. Yet there were others, more deeply inflicted, that still lingered like ghosts, haunting him with horrific memories. He released her hand, painfully aware of the fact that he had held it far longer than he should. "Completely."

"I read about you in the *Times* after the battle. They called you one of the heroes of Waterloo."

Only fools found glory in war. "I did no more than many others."

She looked up at him, her smile faltering as polite conversation dwindled. Silence stretched between them, in a space where only memories dared tread. "I suppose you are wondering why I have come here this afternoon."

"I will admit I am curious." He glanced around the room, for the first time noticing they were alone. "You didn't actually come here unattended, did you?"

"Of course not. I came with my Aunt Cecilia."

"Apparently your aunt has added invisibility to her list of accomplishments." Clayton glanced up at the brass balustrade encircling the second-floor gallery. "Or perhaps she is hiding in the gallery."

"She is waiting in the carriage. I'm afraid Aunt Cecilia doesn't care for the company of men."

Marisa hadn't changed. She was still the reckless, impetuous, willful female who had ravaged his poor heart all those years ago. "A chaperon who hides in the carriage. Quite an interesting choice you've made. Most ladies tend to be very protective of their reputations."

"I am well aware of the danger of coming here. My parents are spending a few weeks with my sister in the country. That left Aunt Cecilia. I apologize if I have offended your sense of propriety, but I would not have come here if it were not urgent."

The strain in her voice triggered instincts honed in battle. "What has happened?"

She studied him a moment. "Can you think of anyone who might want to murder you?"

The question hit him in the solar plexus. Considering their history, he should be accustomed to being knocked off his feet by this female. Yet she never ceased to amaze him. "Murder me?"

"Yes. Can you think of anyone?"

"Not offhand."

"No one at all?"

She looked so earnest, he couldn't prevent a smile. "You sound disappointed."

"I was hoping you might be able to identify someone, a man who would like to eliminate you."

"I suppose you have a reason for hoping I might know of someone who would like to murder me."

A tight knot formed in her cheek with the clenching of her jaw. "I was at the Merrivale ball last night. I noticed Lord Hanley leading one of my nieces into the gardens, so I followed."

"You followed. Where was her chaperon?"

"Actually, I am helping to chaperon Beatrice this Season. You see, my sister Eleanor has just recently given birth, so she and her husband remained in the country. They didn't want to cheat Beatrice of the Season, so I am helping as chaperon.''

He stared at her, stunned by the outrageous idea of Marisa acting as anyone's chaperon. "You are acting as chaperon?"

She lifted her chin, a militant gleam entering her eyes. "I am seven and twenty. I shouldn't think it would sound so extraordinary for me to act as chaperon."

He refrained from pointing out the obvious. "Since you were acting as chaperon, you took it upon yourself to follow your niece and Hanley."

"Exactly."

"That was when you saw something that made you think someone would like to murder me?"

She clutched the silk cords of her reticule. "I entered the maze, looking for Hanley and Beatrice. I reached the center without finding them. I had started back, when I heard a man mention your name. Something in his tone caught my attention. He was talking to someone on the other side of the shrubbery, so I had no trouble at all hearing them."

"What did you hear?"

"One of the men said, 'We shall have to get rid of Huntingdon; he could spoil it all.' The other man hesitated. He sounded nervous. He said a few things that weren't clear, but he finally agreed. The first man said they would have to be careful, that one wrong move could expose them. But he would arrange to have the threat *eliminated*. I heard them moving away, so I hurried through the maze, hoping to get a look at them."

"You followed two men you thought might be plotting a murder?"

"I wanted to see who they were. Unfortunately, by the time I found my way out of the maze, they were gone. But I'm certain I would recognize the one man if I ever heard him again. The one who seemed intent on eliminating you. His voice was very distinctive.''

A damnable sense of protectiveness stirred inside him. Marisa had no business roaming about, chasing after potentially dangerous men. ''Why the devil did your chaperon allow you to go roaming all over the gardens alone? No, wait, let me guess, your Aunt Cecilia was acting as *your* chaperon that night.''

She released her breath in a frustrated sigh. ''I am hardly in need of a chaperon.''

''That is a matter of opinion.''

''I didn't come here to discuss my need for a chaperon. I came here to warn you about a threat to your life.''

''I appreciate your concern.''

She tapped her toe against the thick wool carpet. ''You aren't taking this seriously, are you?''

''I see little reason to take it seriously.''

''I know what I heard.'' She gestured with her hand as she spoke. Her reticule bumped a brass figure of a unicorn on the desk, toppling it over the edge. ''Oh, dear . . .''

Brass glinted in the sunlight slanting through the windows as the unicorn tumbled. He snatched for it and missed. It landed with a thud on the tip of his black boot. He gasped at the sharp stab of pain. He closed his eyes with a silent oath. It shouldn't surprise him. From the first moment he had met Marisa, she had turned his carefully structured life into a shambles.

''I'm sorry,'' she said, her husky voice a soft caress.

He drew in his breath, gathered his patience, and opened his eyes. Then he wished he hadn't looked at her at all. She looked far too embarrassed, too fragile, too damned appealing. A lock of her hair had escaped its pins, tumbling over her shoulder in a shiny coil of ebony, reminding him of things best forgotten. "It's all right. I think only one toe is broken."

She smiled. "I suppose we should be glad for small miracles."

"I suppose."

He bent to retrieve the unicorn. So did she. They collided, her brow whacking his jaw. The impact knocked his teeth together. She careened backward. Her bottom thumped the floor. She sat staring at his boots for a long moment, tousled and dazed, and more beautiful than was safe. He rubbed his sore jaw, staring down at her, stunned.

She lifted her eyes and met his stare, revealing every shred of her humiliation. "I'm terribly sorry. I hope I didn't hurt you."

He frowned, appalled at the emotion slithering inside of him. He recognized it as something more than lust, something he had buried long ago. "Not at all. A few loose teeth, nothing to worry about. How about you?"

A soft blush painted the high crests of her cheeks, the dusky rose emphasizing the amber beauty of her eyes. "I'm fine."

He offered her his hand and helped her to her feet. As she stood, the toe of her shoe caught in the hem of her gown. She pitched forward. "Oh!"

"Careful!" He slid his arms around her, a reflex that brought her flush against the solid wall of his chest. The impact vibrated through him. Without thought, he tightened his arms around her, embracing her the way he had held her in countless dreams. Her warmth radiated through their clothes, teasing his skin, sending whorls of heat swirling through his loins.

She glanced up at him and his breath lodged in his lungs. Her eyes held a wealth of emotion, a turmoil that reflected his own horrible need. Did she ever think of him? Did she ever catch herself at night, lying in bed, contemplating the path her life might have taken? All of the defenses he had built against her over the years shuddered in one heart-wrenching moment. In that moment he imagined she had missed him as much as he had missed her. He imagined seeing regret and longing in those beautiful eyes. Time slipped away, drawing them back to a golden idyll, when a bookish young man had fallen helplessly under the spell of a dazzling temptress. He felt himself weakening, his body shifting toward hers. Lord, he must be insane!

Clayton released her. He took a step back, fighting the insidious attraction she held for him. After all these years, and his hard-fought battle to free himself from her web, he would not fall under her spell again. Never again. He retrieved the unicorn and turned it over in his hands. "He managed to survive his fall without a scratch." Clayton only wished he had been as lucky.

She looked away from him. She slid the silk cord of her reticule through her fingers as she spoke. "I know you find it difficult to believe, but I heard the tone of their voices. I know those two men were serious about their intent."

He stared down at the unicorn in his hand. It had been his father's, one of the few things he had left of his sire. "I don't doubt you heard precisely what you say you heard. I do doubt they were serious about it."

"What do you suppose they meant?"

He set the unicorn on the desk. "People often mention things they would like to happen. Few have any intention of actually taking action to make those things come about."

"You must do something about this."

The concern in her eyes mesmerized him. It took all

of his will to maintain an air of indifference. "I suspect you are taking this far too seriously."

She stepped back, her eyes glittering with fury. "I don't recall your being this stubborn."

He lifted one brow. "I do recall your allowing your imagination to get the best of you."

"I'm sorry to have burdened you with my fanciful concern." She pivoted and marched toward the door. "Good-bye, Lord Huntingdon."

"Good-bye, Lady Marisa."

Exasperating female! Why the hell couldn't she stay out of his life? He clenched his hands into fists at his sides, watching her leave, while a foolish, thoroughly insane portion of him wanted to draw her back into his arms.

She left the room and closed the door behind her. Yet she didn't completely make her escape. A strip of blue muslin peeked out at the side of the door. In spite of the turmoil she had ignited in him, he smiled. Only Marisa could turn a tragic ending into a farce. He crossed the room, opened the door, and found her reaching for the brass door handle.

Her skirt swayed around her. A sheepish smile curved her lips as she lowered her hand. "I caught my gown."

He nodded, doing his best to suppress his amusement. "I noticed."

Her color deepened. She pivoted to leave. "Good-bye."

"Marisa."

She paused in the hall without turning to look at him. "What?"

He suddenly realized there were a thousand things he wanted to say. He settled for the simplest of them all. "Thank you for your concern."

She glanced over her shoulder. The warmth in her eyes stirred something buried deep within him. Something dangerous. Something best forgotten. "You should take care. They sounded serious."

"I shall consider the possibility."

She smiled, a sad little twist of her lips that whispered of all the history they had shared. "Good-bye, Clay."

The husky tone of her voice stabbed him with far too many regrets. "Good-bye, Mari."

Marisa turned, her footsteps tapping against the parquet as she walked toward the stairs leading to the main hall. Clayton stood in the doorway, watching until she slipped from his view. Some perverse need led him across the library. He paused at a window overlooking Grosvenor Square, hungry for another glimpse of her. A few moments later, Marisa emerged from his front door. The breeze stirred the ebony curls peeking out from beneath her blue silk hat.

He rubbed the tender spot on his jaw. In some strange way it was as if time had never passed here in London. Marisa was still the same—beautiful, beguiling, utterly bewitching. Only time had not been so kind to him.

A curricle drawn by a pair of perfectly matched chestnuts pulled up in front of his house as Marisa crossed the sidewalk. Clayton recognized the driver in a beat of his heart. Justin tossed the ribbons to his tiger, then climbed from the carriage. He exchanged a few words with Marisa before helping her into her town coach.

Clayton was still at the window when Justin barged into the library and joined him at the window in time to see Marisa's carriage turn onto Brook Street. Clayton smiled at his brother. "Would you care for a whiskey?"

"What the devil was Marisa doing here?" Justin asked.

Clayton crossed the room and opened one of the cabinets built into the mahogany-paneled wall. He was appalled to find his hands shaking as he removed the stopper from a crystal decanter. "She had some information she thought I might find interesting."

Justin moved toward a pair of leather wing-back chairs near the fireplace. "And did you?"

"Not particularly." Clayton filled two glasses and joined Justin. He wished he had started a fire. He felt cold, as though he had been tossed naked into a winter storm.

"It must have been important for Marisa to come here," Justin said, accepting the glass of Irish whiskey.

"She thought it was." Clayton lifted his glass. Yet he didn't take time to enjoy the rich aroma. He drained his glass in three long swallows, welcoming the heat of the aged whiskey. He glanced at Justin and tried to answer the questions he saw in his eyes. "It was only some nonsense she heard at a party. Mari always had a fruitful imagination. I'm afraid it got the better of her this time."

Justin sipped his whiskey. "She is still as beautiful as ever."

"Yes, she is." Clayton turned away from him, hiding his expression. Still, he knew Justin could see through any facade he might try to erect as a shield.

Clayton sank into one of the chairs near the hearth and focused the conversation in another direction. He listened to his brother. He shaped sentences of his own. He spoke without stumbling. Yet, in spite of his best efforts, he couldn't relinquish thoughts of Marisa. After all this time, the woman could still knock the wind out of him with a glance from those beautiful golden brown eyes.

Justin twisted his empty glass in a stream of sunlight slanting through the windows behind him, sending shards of colored light flickering across the blue-and-ivory carpet. "Since I am getting married, there is no reason to continue with your plan to find a bride this Season."

Clayton leaned back in his chair. Two months ago Justin had met his match in the lovely form of a practical young woman named Isabel Darracott. "Before he died, I gave Father my word I would marry."

"Father wanted to make certain the succession was assured. Now there is no need to sacrifice yourself to some misbegotten sense of responsibility." Justin grinned at him. "I assure you, I shall do my best to produce an heir."

"I gave Father my word."

Justin shook his head. "Do you still intend to choose your bride from that list the duchess drew up for you?"

Clayton frowned when he thought of the list of potential brides their grandmother had made at his request. Although he trusted his grandmother to make a careful selection of the young ladies available this Season, something about the list made him uneasy. "The duchess has a discerning eye."

"What about your own eye?"

"From what I have observed, any one of the ladies she has selected would make an appropriate companion."

"Companion. Weren't you the one who told me that even a black-hearted scoundrel could change if he ran straight into something as unexpected as honest affection, a feeling so strong that it sank deep into his

166

bones?'' Justin grinned at him. ''I would think something like affection might be appropriate in the selection of your wife.''

Clayton shifted in his chair. ''It's different for you and Isabel. She loves you. She is a practical woman. Dependable. If you treat Isabel well, she will be there for you, for the rest of your life.''

Justin frowned. ''I've seen that blasted list. There isn't a female on it who wouldn't end up boring you after a few weeks, if she didn't freeze you to death first. Marry one of them and you'll find yourself longing to take a leap from the roof of Huntingdon House.''

Clayton twisted his glass against the top of a pedestal table beside his chair. ''I'm not looking for excitement in marriage. I've had enough excitement to last a lifetime.''

Justin's black brows lifted. ''From what Sophia said, you did have certain requirements of any lady she added to the list. As I recall, your prospective bride must be intelligent, serious-minded, practical, dignified, and dull.''

''Dull?'' Clayton frowned at his brother. ''I don't recall requesting that particular attribute.''

Justin shrugged. ''It comes with the rest of the package.''

Clayton laughed softly. ''And what type of female do you think I should consider?''

Justin winked at him. ''One who can make your blood burn.''

Clayton had known a woman who could make his blood burn. A woman so beautiful his heart ached to look at her. A dazzling creature. A woman who was so unpredictable he never knew from one moment to the next what she might do. ''I want my marriage based on something more solid than an incendiary agent in my blood.''

Justin rolled his glass between his palms. ''Sophia keeps reminding me she has never known a Trevelyan male to marry for anything other than true affection.''

Affection is for the weak, remember that. Emotions must be controlled. His father's words echoed in his memory. Clayton hadn't truly understood the reason behind those words until he made the fatal mistake of handing his heart into Marisa's keeping. He would not make the same mistake again. ''I prefer to keep emotion out of my marriage decision. You can take passion; I will take practicality.''

Justin stared into his empty glass, as though reading the future in the dregs of Irish whiskey. ''I wonder why Marisa never married.''

Clayton flinched. He met Justin's gaze and saw the clear understanding in his gray-green eyes. ''Who can say why a woman like Marisa does anything? I suppose she never found a man who fulfilled her ideal.''

''It certainly is not for lack of opportunities. She still has half the men in London sniffing after her skirts, like stallions after a mare in season.''

Clayton laughed, the sound bitter to his own ears. ''Mindless fools, those stallions. If they get a little too close to this particular mare, she will rear up and kick them straight between the eyes. Or somewhere considerably lower.''

Justin studied his brother for several moments before he spoke. ''Have you thought of adding Marisa to your list?''

Clayton squeezed the arms of his chair. ''I asked her to marry me once. Remember?''

''That was a long time ago.''

Clayton stared into the hearth, where streaks of black

against the bricks marked the passing of dead fires. "A lifetime."

Justin tipped his empty glass toward Clayton. "You might have a different result this time."

Clayton waved aside his brother's words. "I want peace, quiet, an orderly life with a sensible female."

"And so you intend to marry one of the ice maidens on Sophia's list."

"Mutual respect. Companionship. That is all I expect or want in a marriage."

Justin leaned forward and rested his forearms on his thighs. "All of this wedding nonsense makes a man think hard about the future. Take your time, Clay. You get leg-shackled to the wrong woman, you will regret it the rest of your very long and miserable life."

Clayton smiled. "Don't be concerned about me. I have my life well in hand. Discipline is the key. Discipline and a sound plan for how I intend to live my life."

Justin laughed, the sound rumbling from deep in his chest. "I had a sound plan. Isabel blew it to perdition the day she barged into my life. Until you meet a woman who can stir your blood, Clay, stay away from the altar."

"I intend to choose carefully."

Clayton knew what he wanted in a wife, and it certainly was not a flighty female who was more of an incendiary device than any bomb he had encountered during the war. He would never again give Marisa a chance to explode in his face. Their time had passed. Any chance they might have had for happiness had died a brutal death a long time ago. He intended to leave Marisa Grantham where she belonged—in his past.

* * *

Marisa sat on a sofa near the fireplace in her bed-chamber, staring down at the handkerchief she held. Slowly she slid her fingertip over the initials embroidered in white upon the white linen. She could almost feel the memories impressed upon the linen, the tears she had cried that last day with Clay, the day she had destroyed any chance she might have had to make a life with her one and only love.

This afternoon it had all been painfully clear. She meant nothing to him now. Over the past seven years Clayton had managed to push her out of his mind completely. Unfortunately she had never been able to pry him from her heart.

The door opened and her Aunt Cecilia entered the room. She frowned at her niece. "Are you feeling all right, Mari? You didn't eat much at dinner."

Marisa forced her lips into a smile. "I wasn't very hungry."

Cecilia pursed her lips. She crossed the room and took a place on the sofa beside Marisa. She stared into the lifeless hearth for a long while before she spoke. "Some women in this world are unfortunate enough to meet a man who continues to haunt them long after it is clear there is no hope for any happiness. Affection can be an affliction, Marisa, a disease that preys upon your vitals, devouring all the life from inside of you. If you are not very careful, you will look in the mirror one day and not recognize yourself, all because of a man. I do not want that to happen to you."

Marisa lowered her gaze to the handkerchief. "Neither do I."

"Then forget about Clayton Trevelyan." Cecilia gripped Marisa's arm. "Do not allow any man to get close enough to strike. They are like vipers. Their poison can kill you from within."

"Clay needs my help."

Cecilia fixed Marisa with a stern glare. "Apparently he does not take this threat seriously. I suggest you do the same."

Marisa shook her head. "I cannot ignore this. I heard those two men. I know they are going to try to hurt Clay."

Cecilia sighed. "He will make a fool of you, Marisa."

Marisa smiled. "I have to do anything I can to help him. If it means risking my pride, I shall."

Cecilia shook her head. "I do believe you have the sickness worse than I did."

Marisa smoothed the pad of her thumb over Clayton's initials. "I am afraid you are right, Aunt Cecilia. I doubt I shall ever recover from this particular affliction."

Chapter Eleven

Marisa stuffed her hair under the white turban she had borrowed from her mother's armoire for her mission. If Clay refused to take the threat to his life seriously, she would simply have to take steps to protect the stubborn oaf.

"Aunt Marisa, I do wish you would reconsider." Beatrice paced the length of Marisa's bedchamber, her green muslin gown flowing around her slender figure. She paused beside the vanity and looked down at her aunt. "Since you seem set on this, I feel you really must take Aunt Cecilia with you."

Marisa smiled at her sister Eleanor's eldest daughter. "Aunt Cecilia would rather hang by her thumbs than enter Justin's house."

"I can understand her sentiments." Beatrice stared at her. "Have you no concerns?"

Although she was only nineteen, Beatrice had a habit of trying to manage everyone in her orbit. Beatrice had inherited her beautiful mother's dark chestnut curls and large blue eyes, but Eleanor's shyness had not influenced her eldest daughter in any respect. "I shall be fine."

Beatrice pressed her hand to the base of her slender neck. "What if someone should recognize you? Your reputation would be utterly ruined."

"I am well aware of the danger of visiting a man with Justin's reputation." Marisa pulled the veil she had attached to the hat down over her face. She stared through the thick white silk, trying to distinguish her features in the mirror. Peering through the veil was like looking through a thick white fog. "I'm confident no one will recognize me. I only hope I don't walk into a wall while I am wearing this."

"Oh, I do wish you would wait until Grandmama returns. I am certain she could make you see reason."

Marisa lifted her veil. "I cannot wait. I suspect Clay has no intention of taking any precautions. I only hope Justin can talk some sense into his stubborn head."

Beatrice folded her hands at her waist and addressed her aunt the way a governess might a stubborn charge. "Aunt Marisa, it is quite possible that the men you overheard meant something entirely different from murder."

Marisa rose from the vanity. "I heard them, Bea. I know they had malice in mind."

Beatrice gripped Marisa's arm. "You cannot go to see the duke alone. He is far too dangerous."

Marisa crinkled her nose. "I have known Justin Trevelyan for many years. I realize he has acquired the reputation of being the most dangerous libertine in London, but I have always known him to be kind and generous."

"Kind and generous! He compromised Miss Darracott and forced her to agree to marry him. That sort of man is capable of anything.''

"Lud!" Marisa waved aside Beatrice's concerns. "I don't believe for a moment that Justin Trevelyan would force a woman into marriage. If anything, Justin has had to dodge all the women who have thrown themselves at him.''

"Aunt Marisa, you know Miss Darracott. She is hardly the type of female who would throw herself at any gentleman.'' Beatrice bent to look into the mirror above the vanity. She arranged the curls over her brow as she continued. "The truth is, she is so very conventional, I am utterly amazed at the stir she caused when she made her come-out. I cannot understand how gentlemen could become so interested in a woman of her years.''

The sublime arrogance of youth. It truly was an amazing thing to behold. "Since I am two years older than Miss Darracott, I suppose I really should don a cap.''

Beatrice straightened and addressed her aunt with all the authority of a magistrate passing judgment. "I don't believe it is necessary for you to don a cap this year.''

"I am glad to hear you say so.''

"Although I do think it would be wise to choose a husband this Season.'' Beatrice wagged her finger at Marisa. "You are getting on in years. And although you were once a great beauty, the bloom is fading. It is only a matter of time before the gentlemen lose interest.''

Although she knew the words had not been spoken with malice, Marisa still felt the sting of them. "I shall take your advice under consideration.''

Beatrice smiled, obviously pleased with herself. "I

am certain you can see why calling upon the Duke of Marlow would hardly be wise.''

"Beatrice, I need to speak with Justin this morning."

Beatrice pursed her lips. "After what happened to Miss Darracott, I cannot understand how you could even speak to that man."

From the few times Marisa had spoken with Miss Darracott, she had formed a positive opinion of the young woman. "Miss Darracott is intelligent, practical, and reserved. She is far too sensible to get herself into the type of tangle you seem to think she finds herself in."

Beatrice touched Marisa's arm, her lips tipping into a smug smile. "She didn't have a choice."

"Really, Bea, you have Justin painted as a barbarian who has dragged back a prize from a town he has pillaged."

Beatrice lifted her chin. "All of my friends agree, Miss Darracott is certainly better suited to Lord Huntingdon than she is to the duke. We are certain the duke forced her into accepting him."

Marisa bristled inwardly. For weeks she had watched from a distance while Clayton hovered about Miss Darracott. He had certainly behaved like a man who had lost his heart. Her own heart had suffered terribly, until the day she had heard of Justin's engagement to the lady. "Simply because two people are of the same temperament does not mean they are well suited. The same may be said of two people who appear very different in nature."

"Everyone thought Miss Darracott intended to marry Lord Huntingdon. Until that dreadful incident at the ball the duchess gave for her. You must have heard the rumors."

Marisa had heard the rumors, as she was certain all

175

of the ton had heard. "You were there, Bea. Did Miss Darracott look like a woman who had been forced into anything?"

Beatrice's eyes sparkled with the excitement of a young woman who had latched upon a particularly intriguing piece of fiction. "When I think of it, I am certain her countenance did reveal a certain amount of distress that evening."

"It isn't wise to believe gossip." Unfortunately, Beatrice counted in her circle of bosom friends several of the ton's most notorious young gossips. "I cannot believe Justin would ever have offered for Miss Darracott if he thought his brother intended to marry her. And I certainly do not believe Justin forced her into accepting him."

"From what I have heard of him, the duke stops at nothing when he wants something. They call him *Devil* Trevelyan. There must be a reason. That sort of man would not care if he crushed his brother's hopes. He certainly isn't the sort of man a lady should call upon under any circumstance."

"Justin would never do anything to purposely harm his brother." Still, what if both brothers had fallen in love with the same lady? It would not have been a matter of Justin crushing Clayton; it would have been a matter of the lady's choice. Oh, she really didn't want to think of that possibility. "And he certainly would not harm me."

"Aunt Marisa, you must reconsider."

Marisa patted her niece's arm. "There is no need for concern."

"If someone does recognize you, my reputation would be harmed as well as yours. The entire family would suffer. Have you taken that into consideration?"

"Of course I have. I have had the crests covered on

Papa's town coach. I am taking only Tomkin and Ralph, and they are both in black livery and are wearing wigs. So you see, I have taken great precautions. No one will recognize me.''

Beatrice released an exasperated sigh. ''Aunt Marisa, at times you are far too impetuous.''

Marisa laughed. ''It is one of my many faults. Now, you shall have to excuse me. I must see if I can convince Justin there is cause for alarm.''

Twenty minutes later, Marisa entered the Duke of Marlow's library. Through the heavy white silk of her veil she could see Justin standing near the fireplace. Unfortunately she could see little else. She bumped into the arm of a sofa as she attempted to cross the room.

''Do you intend to tell me who you are, or shall I guess?'' Justin asked, his deep voice colored with a trace of annoyance.

''It's dreadful looking through this,'' she said, lifting her veil. She smiled at him. ''Did you know me?''

''Marisa.'' He smiled. ''I thought it was you, but I wasn't certain.''

''You have such a wicked reputation, Justin. Even if I brought my mother as a chaperon, I would be the topic of gossip for weeks.''

Justin took her hands in a firm grasp. ''And did you give any thought to my reputation?''

''When did you start to worry about your reputation?''

''When I became guardian to three females.''

''Oh.'' She crinkled her nose, annoyed with herself for overlooking that small point. ''I hadn't thought of that.''

''And did you think of what my fiancée might think

177

if someone told her a mysterious woman was seen at my house?''

Marisa decided not to wander down that precarious path. She squeezed his hands. Any woman who truly loved a man would believe in him despite all the gossip in the world. "I'm certain you can set her straight."

He lifted one black brow, mischief glinting in his gray-green eyes. "You have such faith in my powers of persuasion."

She laughed. "Justin, you could charm a devoted man-hater like my Aunt Cecilia into running away with you, if you put your mind to it."

"Fortunately, I've never set my mind on that particular course."

"I must say, I'm glad to hear you care about what your fiancée might think. There are so many dreadful rumors about your engagement. I thought they were all a lot of humbug. No woman could ever trap you into anything, particularly marriage. And as for you forcing her—" She waved her hand to dismiss the idea. "Nonsense. You have never needed to force a female into doing anything, except perhaps to get her out of your house. By the way, have I wished you happy?"

Justin took her arm and led her toward one of the leather armchairs near the hearth. "I suspect you didn't come here this morning to wish me happy."

"No." Marisa sat on the chair and arranged her white silk gown around her. "I came here to ask you to talk some sense into your brother's stubborn head."

Justin rested his arm on the mantel and fixed her with a direct look. "This concerns the same thing you went to see him about yesterday?"

She nodded. "Did he tell you about it?"

"Only that you overheard something at a party."

She released her breath on an agitated sigh. "It is

178

like him to take such news with such dreadful composure. I suspected he would do nothing about it. That is why you simply must help me hammer some sense into his head.''

''I might do better if I knew what this was all about.''

''Murder.''

Justin blinked. ''Murder?''

She plaited the fringe of her white paisley shawl as she spoke. ''It was at the Merrivale ball the other night. Do you remember their maze?''

''Not as interesting as the one at Hampton Court. But suitable for an interesting rendezvous.''

''Precisely. Well, I noticed Lord Hanley leading my niece into the gardens, so I followed.''

Justin rubbed his chin. ''Acting as chaperon these days?''

Marisa smiled at his surprise. ''It shouldn't seem so strange for a woman of my years.''

''A woman who still has half the men in London dangling on a string.''

''Amazing what men will do for the sake of a fortune. Even dangle after a woman who is all of seven and twenty. I suppose I should have donned a cap years ago, but I enjoy parties far too much to put myself on the shelf.'' The truth was that she kept attending the Season each year because she was afraid of becoming the image of her Aunt Cecilia, so bitter and lonely she hated the world.

Justin rested his chin on his palm. ''I'm surprised you didn't choose a husband from your legion of suitors years ago.''

Marisa lowered her eyes, hiding her thoughts from his perceptive eyes. She had tried to fall in love again, she really had. But no one could take Clayton's place in her heart. She couldn't give her hand to one man while her heart belonged to another. "Some things don't turn out the way we plan. Life is funny that way."

From the corner of her eye she could see Justin studying her. She could feel the questions hovering in the silence, questions concerning the broken pieces of two lives. He released his breath on a soft sigh before he spoke. "You were saying that you had followed your niece and Hanley into the gardens, where you found what?"

She related the details of what she had overheard in the Merrivale maze. "Clay is certain it is all some misunderstanding on my part. He knows of no one who would like to murder him. I, on the other hand, can well imagine wanting to strangle the man."

Justin's eyes narrowed and she had the uncomfortable feeling he could see every wayward thought in her head. "You're worried about him."

"Of course I'm concerned. I heard them. I know they were serious." She rose from the chair. "You have to speak with Clay. He must take care. We have to look for these men. They have to be stopped."

He nodded. "I'll speak with him."

"If anyone can talk some sense into him, it's you."

He took her hand. "I'll do my best to resolve the problem."

"We have to find some way to keep him safe."

Justin slid his thumb over the back of her gloved hand. "If I didn't know better, I would think you still cared for him."

She slipped her hand from his grasp. "Of course I care for him, as I would for any old friend."

"I always wondered what happened to make you

180

change your mind about your engagement to my brother.''

''I thought I had good reasons, at the time.'' She stared at the figure of Zeus carved into the white marble fireplace as she spoke.

''I was expecting you to announce your engagement to another man.''

She kept her gaze on that raised figure of marble. ''There was never another man.''

He slipped his fingers beneath her chin and coaxed her to look at him. When she met his gaze, he smiled. ''There was never another woman for Clay. Isn't that interesting?''

The implication in his words stirred inside her, awakening the hope she had tucked away in her heart. It was dangerous, believing in all the possibilities inspired by that delicate seed of hope. Still, she couldn't force it back into the safe little niche within her heart. ''I have always wondered why Clay bought a commission days after I ended our engagement.''

Justin's lips tipped into a grin worthy of his epithet. ''Perhaps one day you should ask him.''

Marisa looked into eyes disturbingly similar to the ones that still haunted her dreams. In his own fashion Justin was offering her a slender thread of hope. ''Perhaps I should.''

A thousand questions whirled in her mind as she left Justin's house. Had she made a mistake seven years ago? That doubt had haunted her every day since the moment Clayton had walked out of her life. A part of her had never relinquished the hope that one day she might have a second chance with Clay. It was foolish to dwell on that dream, particularly when rumors abounded about Clayton and a certain list he had of prospective brides. She leaned her head against the black velvet squabs of her father's town coach. Still, wasn't it more foolish to stand aside and watch him choose another woman as his wife?

Gunfire cracked the air. Clayton handed his spent weapon to his footman and lifted a freshly loaded pistol from the shelf in front of him. It was the first time he had fired a pistol in nearly a year. Although many of his friends considered pistols and swords playthings, he had lost his taste for such games the first time he had killed a man. The crack of his brother's pistol ricocheted through his ears, an echo of distant battles.

A thin cloud of sulfurous smoke hung in the sunlight spilling through the open windows of the gallery, the acrid scent prying the lid from the tomb of memories buried inside of Clayton—voices lifted in desperate pleas, the horrible death cries of horses, artillery an infernal carillon pounding against him, the strange humming sound of a saber before it landed with a thud in human flesh. At times he couldn't escape the ghosts that lived inside him. And this afternoon, he couldn't escape his anger. "Marisa came to see you this morning? All dressed in white? With a veil over her face?"

Justin handed his pistol to one of his footmen for reloading. "She is concerned about you."

Clayton aimed his pistol and fired. He stared through the smoky air, noting the hole his bullet had plowed through the heart of the target. "You know how dramatic Marisa can be."

Justin lifted his other pistol. "She heard two men discussing the need to eliminate you."

Clayton handed his spent weapon to his footman. "How many times have you said you would like to murder someone? Yet I don't recall your ever having carried out the threat."

"She seemed to think it was serious."

"She has always had a lively imagination." Clayton picked up his other weapon and fired. The bullet slammed into the target a hairbreadth from the previous shot.

Justin smoothed his thumb over the handle of his pistol. "You can't think of anyone who might want to murder you?"

"No."

"Perhaps it is nothing. Still, it might pay to be careful."

Clayton grinned in spite of the anger boiling inside of him. Although he wasn't ready to believe there was a real threat in what Marisa had heard, he was practical enough to be cautious. "Why do you suppose I thought we should visit Manton's this afternoon?"

Justin cast a meaningful glance at his brother's target. "A blackguard who would plan a man's murder probably would not come at him straight on."

Clayton leaned against the wooden shelf separating the marksmen from the target area. "Aside from hiding for the rest of my life, there is nothing much I can do about it."

"Have you considered trying to find the men Marisa overheard?"

"What? Trail after Marisa at every function of the Season, eavesdropping on conversations, hoping she can identify the voices of two men she heard through a hedge?"

Justin smiled, the look in his eyes pure mischief. "She might be able to find them. And you may become acquainted with the lady again."

Clayton cringed. It had taken seven years to purge Marisa from his blood. He wasn't about to get close enough to the blasted female for another infection to grip him. "In less than a week Marisa and I would be at dagger point. Not to mention the gossip we would stir. Thank you, but I've already stuck my head under that particular guillotine."

Justin stared down at his pistol, his expression growing thoughtful. "Isabel sent me a note this afternoon. I received it just before I left to meet you here."

"A note. What did she want?"

"She wants to speak with me. A personal matter of some importance that must be resolved before our wedding day." Justin glanced at his brother. "It's probably nothing. I certainly haven't given her any reason to have second thoughts about the wedding. I'm certain it has nothing to do with that."

"Of course not." Still, in spite of his words, Clayton hadn't missed the uncertainty in his brother's voice. He knew his own disastrous engagement played heavily on Justin's mind. He frowned, an unsettling thought coiling in his brain. Rumors often spread through the ton with more speed and every bit as much destruction as the plague. It would be a minor miracle if half of London wasn't already discussing the mysterious veiled lady in white who had paid a morning visit to the Duke of Marlow. Marisa could have most of London thinking Justin had taken a mistress days before his wedding. And they would be quick to spread the news.

Since Justin had earned the title of the Devil of Dartmoor, his brother had never cared about gossip. Clayton knew his brother had cultivated the reputation of a black-hearted libertine mainly in self-defense. English huntresses could be ruthless in their pursuit of a title. A black reputation kept them at bay. Still, Justin had never before been engaged to be married.

Clayton squeezed the ebony handle of his pistol. If Marisa had caused any harm to his brother and Isabel, he would make the meddling little she-devil regret the day she was born.

The scent of burning beeswax mingled with the fragrance of various sweet waters and perfumes. The aromas drifted in the air with the musky scent of overly heated humans packed together in the crowded confines of the Dauntry ballroom. Marisa stood with Letitia Thurmond Dauntry near one corner of the dance floor, trying to catch the conversation of the gentlemen standing a few feet away from her. Could the blackguard she had overheard in the Merrivale maze be in attendance tonight?

"Beatrice is a tremendous success," Letitia said.

"I had no doubt she would do well in London." Marisa glanced at the dance floor, where Beatrice glided through the graceful steps of a cotillion with a slender, dark-haired gentleman Marisa recognized as the heir of the Earl of Hythe. "She has tremendous poise for a girl of her years."

"Confidence." Letitia laughed. "Something I usually lacked."

Marisa smiled at her old friend. At one time Marisa had thought the quiet, intellectual Letitia her rival. Two weeks after Clayton had left for the Peninsula, Letitia had confided her deep attraction to a terribly handsome and incredibly dashing gentleman. Tall and golden, Mr. Stanford Dauntry was a wealthy rogue who seemed to collect hearts the way some men collected watch fobs. Although Letitia feared a gentleman such as Mr. Dauntry would never notice her, before the Season ended, Stanford had lost his heart to the lovely bluestocking. "You had other qualities."

"And you had nearly every man in London at your feet." Letitia looked at the dance floor. "Beatrice is a great beauty, but I do not believe she has the following you did when you made your come-out.''

''It was only the Little Season when I made my come-out. The gentlemen did not have as many ladies to pursue.''

Letitia's blue eyes sparkled with humor. ''The gentlemen are still pursuing. If I am not mistaken, Lord Ashbourne is approaching with the purpose of asking you to dance.''

Marisa turned and smiled as Braden drew near. The earl had indeed come to claim Marisa for the next dance, a waltz. Although Braden's charm was no less polished this evening, Marisa's thoughts kept wandering to a blackguard she had overheard in a maze and the infuriating gentleman he intended to murder. Soon after the waltz, Braden drifted from her side, allowing Marisa the freedom to investigate a group of gentlemen standing near the entrance to the card room.

Marisa stood a few feet away from them, ostensibly watching the dancing, in reality straining to hear their voices over the collective din of noise in the large room. Conversation and laughter mingled with the music drifting from the orchestra at the far end of the room, conspiring against her.

''Aunt Marisa.''

Marisa started at the soft touch of her niece's hand upon her arm. ''Oh, dear, you startled me.''

''You have looked distracted the entire evening. I believe I have noticed you dance only a few times.'' Although she lowered her voice to a conspiratorial level, she still managed to sound like a strict governess when she continued. ''Standing about at balls will hardly find you a husband.''

''I suppose I should be on the hunt. But I have been occupied.''

Beatrice fixed her aunt with a disapproving glare. "Have you been trying to locate those two men you overheard in the garden?"

"If I hear that one man again, I will know his voice. I'm certain of it."

"Do you honestly imagine someone here might want to murder Lord Huntingdon?" Beatrice asked, her voice rising above the music.

Marisa took her niece's arm and led her a few feet away from the gentlemen, concerned someone might overhear them. "If the man I overheard is here, I shall find him."

Beatrice flicked her fan beneath her chin, fluttering the glossy chestnut curls falling over her smooth brow. "I was just speaking with Victoria Talbot about what you heard, and she agrees with me. We simply cannot imagine anyone who might want to murder Lord Huntingdon."

"You spoke to Victoria about what I heard?"

"Yes. And she agrees with me. They must have meant something other than murder. Or perhaps they meant the duke. We could think of several reasons someone might want to murder the duke."

"They said Huntingdon." Marisa hadn't expected to become a topic of conversation, but she supposed it was inevitable. Just as it was inevitable that no one would take her seriously. "I hope I am mistaken. I hope this is all a horrible misunderstanding on my part. Still, I feel I must do all I can to make certain Clayton is safe. Otherwise, if something should happen to him, I would always feel responsible in some way."

"Aunt Marisa, this is really none of your concern. Lord Huntingdon can certainly take care of himself. For heaven's sake, he is a war hero."

"I must do what I can to help."

187

Beatrice closed her fan, the corners of her lips dipping into a disapproving scowl. "Have you heard the horrible rumor?"

"What rumor?"

"Apparently it's spreading all over London. Victoria just arrived from the Ripley party, and she told me it was circulating there as well." Beatrice's eyes sparkled with excitement. "It's dreadful."

The ton devoured gossip and rumors like hungry dragons inhaling hapless peasants. Although Marisa did not care to perpetuate any gossip, she admitted to some curiosity. "What have you heard?"

"Aunt Marisa, everyone is talking about—" Something behind Marisa snagged Beatrice's attention. She stared, her eyes wide, her lips parted as though a ghost had just asked her to dance.

"Good evening, ladies."

Marisa's heart stopped at the sound of that deep, masculine purr, only to start again in a headlong rush. After all this time, she should be over this unfortunate affliction known as Clayton Trevelyan. Still, there was something elemental about him that drew her to him, as it always had. And to her utter chagrin, she suspected it always would.

She gathered her defenses, preparing herself for his indifference. He would bestow upon her a polite good evening, then stride past her. She molded her lips into a gracious smile. She certainly would not allow anyone to realize she was still hopelessly besotted with the man she had jilted years ago. She was not one to wear her heart pinned to her sleeve, not anymore.

She turned to find Clayton standing no more than a foot away. The look in his eyes sent a shiver down her spine. That look was hardly polite. The cool detachment she had seen yesterday in those gray-green depths had solidified into ice.

"I was hoping you would be here," Clayton said.

She stared at him, her breath suspended. "You were hoping to see me?"

He leaned toward her, his voice dropping to a husky whisper. "Meet me on the terrace in five minutes. I need to speak with you." With those few words he proceeded to stride past her, apparently unaware of the storm of emotion he had unleashed inside her.

Marisa stared after him, thoughts whirling like dried leaves in her befuddled brain. He moved with such utter assurance, coldly elegant, serenely powerful. He was no longer the charming, distracted, shy young man she had known. The ton had called him Saint Trevelyan, a man who could never be tempted by vice. Still, his years in the army had altered him, transformed every bit of softness that had existed in him to cold, glittering steel.

There was something altogether dangerous about him now. A warrior forged in battle. A man who had killed. A man who had faced death and lived to remember it. His choice of apparel only served to enhance the dark, predatory image he conveyed. Aside from a bit of snowy white linen at his neck, chest, and cuffs, he wore stark black. Although women cast him admiring glances as he strode past them, he returned nothing more than polite smiles, as though he held the entire world at a distance. What did he want from her?

"Aunt Marisa, I don't think it would be wise to meet with Lord Huntingdon."

Marisa managed a smile. "I really don't think I need a chaperon. Not with Clay. I suppose he wants to discuss something about the blackguards who want to murder him. Perhaps Justin was able to convince him to take the threat seriously.''

Beatrice moistened her lips. ''You may want to reconsider. I suspect he may not be in good humor.''

Marisa frowned. ''Why do you say that?''

Beatrice held her closed fan against her neck, the gilt trim glittering in the candlelight. ''He has probably heard the rumor about his brother.''

''The dreadful rumor you heard, it's about Justin?''

Beatrice lowered her voice to a harsh whisper. ''People are saying he has taken a mistress. And it's only days before his wedding.''

Marisa stared at her niece. ''I don't believe it. Justin would never do anything so vile.''

Beatrice twisted her fan. ''Aunt Marisa, they say she was seen entering his house. This morning.''

''This morning? There, you see, the rumor is a lot of rubbish. I was there this morning; I would have seen her.''

Beatrice lifted one dark brow, a look of triumph filling her eyes. ''According to rumor, his mistress dresses all in white and wears a veil over her face.''

''A veil . . .'' Understanding of Beatrice's words hit Marisa like a runaway carriage. ''Oh, no. I didn't think anyone had noticed me.''

Beatrice shook her head. ''Someone did.''

The blood slowly drained from Marisa's limbs. She gripped Beatrice's arm to steady herself. She should have taken more care. ''If you find my dead body tossed behind a shrub tonight, please do not mention to anyone that I went to meet with Clay. I most certainly deserve to be strangled. And I wouldn't want him to hang for it.''

Chapter Twelve

A cool breeze brushed Clayton's face as he stepped from the crowded ballroom. A few guests had ventured onto the terrace. Most of them hovered in the light spilling from the open doors. A few couples were scattered in the shadows, stretching the bounds of propriety. Yet he couldn't see Marisa. He searched for her and found her waiting for him at the far end of the terrace, a slender figure captured in the moonlight. Silvery light cascaded over her, caressing the smooth skin of her shoulders, the lush swell of her breasts, bared by the low neckline of her gown.

It was a respectable garment, gauzy gold silk covering an ivory-colored satin slip. Elegant. Fashionable. On any other female he would not have taken exception. But, with Marisa he had the insane urge to throw his coat over that creamy expanse of white. For some misbegotten reason the thought of half the rakes and roués in London salivating over that smooth skin drove a spike into his gut. The realization of how easily the woman could tease his emotions only darkened his already black mood.

He stalked her. In his entire life he had never once lifted a hand against a female. No matter how tempted, he would not start tonight. Only a coward used brute force against the defenseless.

Her eyes widened as he drew near. For one moment she looked as though she might turn and run. Yet she held her ground. He halted in front of her, resisting the urge to slip his hands around her slim neck and strangle the life out of her.

She gave him a sheepish smile. "You look angry enough to strangle me."

"Very perceptive of you." Clayton curled his hands into tight fists at his sides. He prided himself on his control. Discipline was the key. A cool head won the day. "I met with my brother at Manton's this afternoon," he said, keeping his voice level when he wanted to shout.

"Manton's?" She looked surprised. "You were practicing your shooting?"

"You never know when you might want to put a bullet through something."

A sudden wariness entered her eyes. "I assume Justin told you I went to see him this morning."

He leaned toward her until his nose nearly touched hers. "Of all the cork-brained antics. Did you even consider what people might think if they saw you going into his house?"

"I wore a veil over my face. I was careful no one would recognize me. I thought no one had noticed me."

"Oh, you managed to protect your reputation. Unfortunately half of London is gossiping about the mysterious woman in white, and her visit to the Duke of Marlow. They think you are his blasted mistress.''

''I know. Beatrice told me just before I came out here. I swear, it never even occurred to me anyone would think such nonsense.''

''I'm certain it didn't.''

''I only meant for Justin to talk some sense into your stubborn head.''

''My stubborn head? Never in my life have I met a more stubborn female than you.''

She pursed her lips. ''I didn't mean any harm.''

The scent of lilies in the rain drifted with the heat of her skin, coiling around him, dragging age-old imaginings from their carefully tended tomb. Clayton had never held this woman through the night. He had never felt her ebony waves slide in a silken caress across his bare chest. He had never tasted her skin, breathed in the scent of her, explored every inch of her slender body. At least not in reality. Still, the realm of dreams had betrayed him. His dreams had given him all the bittersweet pleasures the lady had denied him. Confounded, meddling little she-devil.

''I'm not accustomed to thinking of Justin as a man who guards his reputation. A month ago, no one would have thought anything if a hundred females had gone into Justin's house in the morning and not come out for a month.''

''Things have changed.''

She released her breath on a sigh that brushed his face with warmth. ''I know they have. I just wasn't thinking of the consequences.''

''What do you suppose Isabel will do when she hears her fiancé has taken a mistress days before their wedding?''

"I'm certain she will understand when Justin explains the circumstances to her."

"You are certain of that, are you?"

"If she loves him, she will believe him," she said, her voice filled with the conviction of a woman who would stand with her man.

He had once thought this woman loved him. He had once believed she would stand at his side for the rest of his life. With one carefully directed blow, she had managed to knock those sweet illusions out of his demented head. "And what do you suppose will happen if Isabel doesn't believe him?"

Marisa rested her hand on his coat above his heart, so lightly he could scarcely feel her touch. Still, his muscles quivered beneath her hand. "I promise, I shall find some way to set this right. I shall pay a call on Miss Darracott tomorrow and explain everything."

"And I suppose that will make everything right. I suppose that will stop the blasted gossip."

"What more do you want me to do?"

"I want you to stay out of my life."

She flinched as though he had struck her. Tears welled and reflected the moonlight in her eyes. "I only meant to help. I never thought I would make such a mess of things."

His chest tightened as he looked down into those liquid eyes. He had the uncomfortable sensation of having just kicked a kitten. He regretted the harsh words, yet not nearly as much as he regretted the infuriating urge to take her in his arms and hold her close against the wounds she had carved upon his heart. He lowered his eyes, tracing the curve of her lips with his gaze. Were those lips as sweet as he remembered? As soft? He couldn't touch her. He knew that as surely as he knew he had to keep drawing air into his lungs to live.

"There is no need to turn into a watering pot," he said, his voice harsher than he intended. "The damage is done."

"I'm certainly not going to cry," she said, a single tear rolling down her cheek.

Moonlight glittered in that single teardrop, spreading silver down her cheek. He touched her cheek; he couldn't prevent it. He slid his fingertips over the warm satin of her skin, wiping away the tear. The heat of that tear penetrated his skin, seeping into his blood. "I should not have been so harsh."

"And I should not have been such a hen-wit. If there were some way I could stop the gossip, I would."

"I know." He lowered his hand, the evening air cool against his damp fingertips. "Marisa, I know you mean well. But you really must stop trying to save me from disaster. Someone is liable to get hurt."

She lifted her chin. "If something happened to you and I didn't try to prevent it, I would forever feel responsible."

Her warmth radiated through his clothes, slipping past his defenses, stirring embers from the ashes she had left of his heart. Warmth flickered in his blood. He clenched his jaw against the insidious desire this woman had always provoked in him.

He would not fall prey to her nefarious charm. He would jump into a vat of boiling oil before he allowed the little tigress to sink her claws into him again. He stepped back, putting three feet of cool moonlight between him and her treacherous warmth. "I have been taking care of myself for a long time. I don't need a guardian angel."

"I can help you find the man I heard in the maze.

195

Once you know who he is, you can determine why he spoke of eliminating you.''

''I don't need—'' Clayton gasped at a sudden searing pain in his side.

''Clay!''

Marisa threw her arms around him as his knees buckled beneath him. Still, her strength was no match for his weight. She crumpled with him, collapsing to her knees on the stone terrace, cradling him in her arms. He leaned against her slender form, allowing her to impose balance in a world knocked off its axis. He turned his head against her shoulder, his lips brushing the smooth column of her neck.

''Clay.'' His name was a soft endearment as she slid her hand gently through his hair. ''Are you all right?''

Her scent swirled through his senses, lilies and spices and a fragrance he would always know as Marisa. Her warmth radiated through his clothes, teasing all the frozen places deep inside of him, taunting him with all he couldn't have. He would give the world to stay here, in her arms. Yet he had long ago realized the folly of broken dreams. He pulled away from her, a cutting remark rising in his defense. Yet his words evaporated when he saw the concern in her eyes.

She cupped his cheek in her hand, her warmth radiating through the softness of her glove. ''What happened?''

He swallowed hard, pushing back the knot in his throat. The pain in his side had dulled to a searing ache. He recognized it for what it was: the echo of his brother's pain. ''I don't know what happened. But I need to find out.''

Marisa watched Clayton march across the terrace. What had brought him to his knees? She took some solace in his powerful strides. He wasn't injured. Yet something had struck him as sharply as a blow. She watched until he disappeared into the house; then she turned back to face the gardens. She wasn't ready to return to the ballroom. Not yet. Not until she had regained her composure.

She had been prepared for Clayton's cool indifference, but the white-hot stream of his anger had completely taken her off guard. Hatred, raw and plain. Bitterness. His emotions had struck like clenched fists.

I want you to stay out of my life. The words ricocheted through her, ripping at the hope she had coddled in her heart. She leaned against the balustrade, fighting the sting of tears. She would not cry. Tears did nothing to ease the pain. They could not repair a shattered life. They could only humiliate her. She had been a fool to imagine she could try again with Clayton. He had left her in his past, and that was where he wanted to keep her. She forced air past the tightness in her throat. Very well. She would not hope for his love. But she would do everything in her power to keep him safe.

She straightened her spine, returned to the ballroom, and continued her search for a murderer. Although she meandered the entire ballroom, time and time again, listening for the man she had overheard in the Merrivale maze, she heard no one who sounded anything like him. It was only a matter of time, she assured herself. She would find that man. She only prayed it was in time to save Clay.

After returning home from the ball, Marisa spent a restless evening, finding sleep only after hours of worried imaginings. What the devil could have brought Clayton to his knees? She had a dreadful feeling about this. Although she had thought sleep impossible, she must have drifted into slumber sometime near dawn. She had enjoyed only a few hours of rest before her maid awakened her early the next morning. Marisa awoke with a start at the soft touch on her shoulder. She sat up in bed and stared at Tillie, her mind a sleepy jumble.

Tillie clasped her hands beneath her plump chin, her brown eyes wide. "I'm sorry, milady, but his lordship will not leave until he speaks with you."

Marisa pushed her tumbled waves back from her face. "His lordship?"

"Lord Huntingdon."

Marisa flinched as though Tillie had dumped cold water over her head. "Lord Huntingdon is here?"

"Aye, milady. In the drawing room. He said if you wouldn't come down he would come up. I think he means it."

Marisa tossed aside the covers and scrambled from the bed. "Clothes. I need clothes."

"Aye, milady. Should I have hot water drawn for your bath?"

"No. There isn't time. Tell Lord Huntingdon I shall be down directly." Marisa stripped off her nightgown as she ran into her dressing room. She threw the white muslin on the floor, then sloshed water from a pitcher into the porcelain basin on the washstand. The cold water raised gooseflesh as she bathed. Yet she scarcely noticed her own shivering.

After throwing on a chemise and petticoat she donned a pale green muslin gown, threw pins into her hastily coiled hair, and dashed out of her bedchamber. When she entered the drawing room she found Clayton standing near one of the windows. She paused a few feet from the threshold, taking a moment to calm the rush of her heart.

He turned from his contemplation of the square and fixed her with an icy gray-green gaze.

"What's happened?" She rushed across the room, oblivious of the fact that she had forgotten her stockings and shoes, or that her hairpins trailed along the floor behind her, releasing coils of hair to tumble down her back.

Clayton stared at her, an odd expression crossing his features, as though someone had just hit him squarely in the jaw. Thick black waves spilled over his brow in disheveled splendor. He looked as though he had dressed hastily, forgetting his cravat. His white linen shirt fell open at the collar, revealing a dark shadow of masculine curls.

"Are you all right?" Marisa paused in front of him, fighting an almost uncontrollable urge to touch him.

A muscle flickered in his cheek with the clenching of his jaw. "Yes, I'm fine."

Morning sunlight streamed through the window glass, touching his face, revealing the evidence that time had etched upon his face. Subtle traces of past frowns were revealed in the shallow creases carved between his thick black brows. Were the faint lines flaring at the corners of his beautiful eyes remainders of smiles? Or were they also forged by distant frowns?

She wished she had been with him through the years. She wished she knew the secret behind every line carved upon his face, a face still devastatingly handsome, even now when the expression he wore was hard and unyielding. "Last night . . . did you discover what happened?"

Clayton closed his eyes as though he were suddenly weary. "Justin was shot last night."

"Shot!" A hard hand closed around her heart. "Is he all right?"

Chapter Thirteen

Clayton looked into Marisa's eyes and immediately regretted it. In that moment he felt connected to her, as he had from the first day he had met her. In that instant he saw his own pain reflected in her eyes, his own fear, his own desperate hope. All the years he had spent away from her, all his efforts to distance himself from the foolish boy who had loved her, contracted, collapsing one upon the other, until he was once again that boy who had shared a golden idyll with a dazzling creature of warmth and fire.

Marisa gripped his arm. "Clay, please tell me Justin will be all right."

He dragged himself from his foolish musing. "He will be fine. The injuries aren't serious. A few days' rest and he should be up and about again."

"Thank heaven." She bowed her head for a moment, then looked up at him, her golden eyes glimmering with unshed tears. "What happened? Do you know who did it?"

"No. The blackguard got away."

"Why would someone want to shoot Justin?"

He had been asking himself the same question all night. The answer he kept tripping over was far from comforting. "Justin was shot in front of my house."

"In front of . . ." Her eyes grew wide with sudden understanding. "Oh my. The man who did this must have thought Justin was you."

"So it would seem."

"The men I overheard were serious. I knew it." She turned away from him, scattering hairpins in her wake. The remaining coils of her hair plummeted free, heavy ebony waves tumbling down her back as she paced to the fireplace.

He imagined this was how it would have been if they had actually spoken their vows all those years ago. He would have often seen her this way, with her hair tumbling in luxurious abandon, her feet bare. It was strange, but in a very real sense, being here with her this way seemed more intimate than all the times he had slept with a woman in his arms. Perhaps because none of those women had ever driven Marisa from his thoughts.

"They will try again." Marisa pivoted at the fireplace and marched back to him. "We have to find a way to stop them."

"I have every intention of preventing them from harming anyone again." If his brother had been killed because of him . . . lord, he couldn't think of that. "What do you remember about the men you overheard? I want to know every detail."

"I told you everything I heard."

201

"You said the one man was distinct. What made him so?"

Marisa shook her head. "I don't know. I'm not sure I can explain it."

"Try."

She lifted her hands. "He was just very . . . unique."

"Think about that evening; imagine yourself back in the maze." He had to know everything he could about the blackguards. "Close your eyes."

She stared up at him. "Close my eyes?"

"Close your eyes. It might help you concentrate."

She smiled, a glint of mischief entering her eyes. "We are all alone and you want me to close my eyes. Really, Lord Huntingdon, it hardly sounds proper. Even if it does sound terribly interesting."

He felt his lips tipping into a smile and quickly pulled them into a scowl. "Flirtatious as ever, I see. It's little wonder you still have every eligible male in London sniffing after your skirts. I'm surprised there hasn't been rioting in the streets."

"The odd thing about flirting is that it is meaningless unless it is with the right gentleman."

Although she maintained her smile, there was a gentle, wistful quality in her voice, a note of sadness that tugged at his vitals. Looking into her eyes he could almost believe she had as many regrets as he. Still, he was no longer foolish enough to fall under her spell. "Close your eyes. I want you to think back to that night in the Merrivales' garden."

"I'll try." She closed her eyes, a frown marring her brow.

"Imagine the garden that evening. Did the moonlight guide you through the maze?"

"No. There were lanterns placed at each bend in the maze."

"What about the men you overheard? Try to hear them again in your mind."

She drew her lower lip between her teeth. "It was as I told you. They were on the other side of the hedge."

"Take a deep breath, Mari. Try to relax."

Her shoulders lifted with a deep inhalation. Beneath the pale green muslin of her gown, her breasts lifted as well. As he watched their gentle fall with her soft exhale, an insidious traitor in his mind imagined unfastening, unhooking, untying every tape, hook, and lacing of her clothes. He employed every ounce of will to keep his breathing steady. "Relax," he whispered.

She rested her brow against his shoulder, as though she needed support, as though leaning upon him was the most natural thing to do. Her warmth penetrated the bottle green wool of his coat, the white linen beneath, radiating against his skin. Her gown brushed his legs. He felt like a beggar drawn in from a cold night to glimpse the warmth of a hearth. The muscles in his arms tightened, anxious to close around her. He resisted the insidious temptation. He could not succumb to this weakness. He could not draw her into his arms. He would not be pulled into her vortex again. "Imagine yourself back in the maze. Feel the brush of evening air upon your face. Can you feel it?"

"It was cool that evening."

He closed his eyes and tried not to think of pressing his face against the softness of her unbound hair. "Imagine the scent of boxwood."

She inhaled deeply, her breasts brushing his chest. His blood sprinted through his veins. He looked up at the ceiling, stared at the carved laurel wreaths, and silently wished he were anywhere but here. He could not believe this was happening. Becoming so heated and excited over nothing more than standing close to this woman was utterly ridiculous.

Since joining the army he had indulged in carnal acts that would rival his brother's salacious past. Yet here he was, heart pounding, blood racing, breath catching, all because he had touched one beguiling spinster. "Hear the men on the other side of the hedge," he said, appalled at the husky timbre of his voice. "Can you hear them in your mind?"

Marisa nodded. "The one man, I remember his voice was deep, though not as deep as yours. Yet resonant."

"What else?"

She tilted her head, brushing her cheek against his coat. He tried not to notice the way the sunlight gilded the tips of her lashes. "He spoke slowly, as if he savored the sound of his own voice. I got the impression he thought his every word was a gem to be treasured."

"Did he have an accent?"

"English. Upper class."

"And the other man?"

Marisa shook her head. "He spoke softly and quickly, as though he were anxious about what they were discussing, frightened of it. Now that I recall, he said they should walk away from this. The other man reassured him—'I shall take care of everything,' he said. 'Now, don't you worry. Leave it all to me.' The other man, the nervous one, replied, but I could scarcely hear him. I got the impression he might have been pacing."

"Would you recognize his voice if you heard him again?"

She shook her head.

"Could you tell if he also sounded upper class?"

"I believe he did." She released a frustrated sigh. "But I'm not certain. He wasn't at all distinct."

"Anything else? Anything at all?"

"Yes." Marisa looked up into his eyes, her expression solemn as she spoke. "The one man, the pompous one, he sounded as though he would enjoy eliminating you. That's what made me think he was very serious in his intent."

He resisted the urge to moisten his dry lips. "Yes, well, it appears as though you were right."

She smiled, a gentle curve of her lips that held none of the triumph he might have expected. "I'm certain I would recognize that one man if I ever heard him again."

"If you have some cork-brained idea of chasing all over London for this man, I suggest you forget it."

Marisa stiffened at his stern tone. "How do you expect to find him without my help?"

"I can manage."

"I don't understand why you are being so stubborn about this. You have a better chance of finding these men with my help."

"This isn't a game, Mari."

She pursed her lips. "I never once imagined it was a game."

"If they found out you could identify one of them, they might very well decide to eliminate you. You don't understand how dangerous this is."

"I know they want to murder you."

"Stay out of it. That's an order."

Marisa stared at him, her mouth open, her eyes wide and furious. "An order? In case you didn't notice, *Major*, I am not under your command."

"You don't understand." He gripped her arms. In spite of everything, he would give his life to protect her. He knew this with the same certainty that he knew

205

the sun would rise each morning. "I might not be able to protect you."

"*You* don't understand. I cannot stand by and allow someone to murder you!"

A dusky rose colored her cheeks. Her eyes glimmered like brandy over a flame. Her hair tumbled around her shoulders in thick, silken waves. It took everything he had to keep from crushing her against his chest. "I expect you to do as I say," he said, keeping his voice deliberately harsh.

Her eyes flashed golden fire. "I will not be treated like one of your soldiers. You have my help, whether you like it or not."

He flexed his hands on her arms. "Confounded, stubborn female."

"Arrogant, overbearing brute!" She thumped her fist against his chest. "I am not a child. I have every right to help you. And I am going to. You cannot stop me. I shall find that man, if I have to go around eavesdropping at every—"

Reason fled with the rush of emotions from carefully tended graves. He pulled her against him and clamped his mouth over hers. He cinched his arms around her, holding her close against the heart she had savaged so many years ago.

She struggled in his arms, turning her head, trying to escape the raw hunger he could not suppress. He gripped the back of her head, his fingers sinking into the softness of her hair, holding her for his assault. He slanted his lips over hers, kissing her with all the desire he had kept buried these past years, all the pain, all the need. This was what she had made of him. This was what was left of him. Raw. Primitive. All the sweetness had been ripped from his soul. All the gentleness had been bled from his heart.

He wanted her to face the truth, know him for the monster he had become. If she truly knew him, she wouldn't look at him with that beguiling glimmer in her eyes. She wouldn't flirt with him. She wouldn't make him crave things beyond his reach. If she realized the true nature of the man he had become, she would shun him for the animal he was. Maybe then he would be safe from her.

Without warning she stopped struggling. Against reason she looped her arms around his neck. Flouting sanity, she opened her tightly compressed lips, welcoming him with a warmth so sudden, he staggered back and hit the window frame. The sudden thump did not dislodge her. Marisa clung to him, kissing him as though she drew her life from him, holding him as though she would still have her arms around him when the world came to an end.

She pressed against him, soft and feminine, delicate curves caressing his brutal hardness. She molded her lips to his, sweet and innocent, eager and determined. He tasted sunshine on her lips, a warmth so beguiling he wanted to drink her in, fill all the frozen places deep within him.

He slid his hands along her back, discovering the shape of her beneath the soft cloth. Her hair brushed the back of his hands, a cool whisper of silk against his skin. His blood pounded hard and fast into his loins. He wanted her, as he had wanted her from the first moment he had ever glimpsed her. Wanted her with all the foolish ardor of a shy young scholar. Yet there was no denying the past, all that had shaped him from the day she had cast him aside.

He knew all too well what he had become. Beneath the thin veneer of civilization resided a cold-blooded animal. Even a light as bright as hers could not brighten the darkness shrouding his soul. He was long past redemption.

He broke the kiss and looked down into her face, his chest aching for what might have been. Her lashes fluttered, then lifted. She looked bewildered, like someone who had imbibed too much brandy for the first time. He wished he could draw her back into his arms, hold her for the rest of his days. He slipped his hands around her waist and forced his arms to push her away from him. He had to get away from her.

She wobbled and leaned back against the window frame. "You look angry enough to strangle me."

He swallowed hard. "Don't worry; I have remarkable restraint."

She stared at him as though she were trying to pierce his defenses, discover his darkest secrets. He had learned long ago to shield himself. "Why did you kiss me?"

He forced his lips into what he hoped would be a cold mockery of a smile. "I thought it was a good way to end the argument."

Her soft lips pulled into a tight line. "You were wrong. I intend to find that man I heard in the maze."

"Listen to me, and listen carefully." He leaned forward until his nose nearly brushed the tip of hers. "Stay out of this."

"You need my help."

"I don't need your help. I don't need or want anything from you. Now stay out of my life."

Before she could reply, he turned and marched out of the room. He should have known better than to come within a mile of her. He should have realized the power she could still wield over his senses. He had underestimated the danger. It was a mistake he could not afford to make again.

* * *

Marisa watched Clayton leave the room. She felt the way she had the first time she had been thrown from a horse: dazed, bewildered, bruised, and angry at herself for allowing the beast to toss her. "Infuriating brute!"

She leaned back against the window frame and stared out into the street. A few moments later, Clayton emerged from the house. Sunlight slipped into thick black waves made tousled and untidy by her own fingers. He had such lovely, soft hair. Pity his head was as hard as marble.

Had that kiss meant nothing at all to him? There was a time when a kiss had meant the world. Yet he had changed. She suspected he had kissed her in that brutal manner to teach her a lesson. He wanted nothing to do with her. Still, she was not a weak-kneed female. She would not fall to pieces over a setback, even one as disturbing as this.

"You are still breathing," Beatrice said, as she entered the room. "I caught a glimpse of Lord Huntingdon as he stormed out of the house. From the fierce look on his face, I thought he must have murdered you."

Marisa managed a smile. "No need to worry. I understand Lord Huntingdon has remarkable restraint."

Beatrice paused beside her aunt. She stared at Marisa with wide eyes. "Is he still angry about your visit to the duke?"

Marisa watched Clayton turn the corner. "I suspect that is only one of the things he is still angry about. Fortunately, I am every bit as stubborn as he is."

"I'm not certain I understand."

"He wants me to stay out of this business of chasing

after the men who want to murder him. He obviously knows nothing at all about me.''

Beatrice clasped her hands at her waist. ''Aunt Marisa, if he wants you to refrain from looking for these men, I believe it is only proper to comply with his wishes.''

Marisa waved aside her niece's words. ''Let him try to prevent me from searching for the blackguards. He will soon discover I am not a woman to be cowed, or ordered about like a young recruit. I am made of stronger stuff. I am no longer a foolish child. I am a sophisticated, intelligent woman, quite capable of making my own decisions.''

Beatrice lifted her dark brows. ''Aunt Marisa, do you realize you aren't wearing any shoes?''

Marisa frowned at her bare toes. ''So it would seem.''

''I suspect Lord Huntingdon noticed.''

Marisa cringed. ''I suppose he did.''

Beatrice shook her head. ''You hardly present the image of a sophisticated lady.''

Marisa shoved her unbound hair over her shoulder. ''No, I suppose not.''

Beatrice released an agitated sigh. ''I really don't think it is wise to go running about looking like a lost waif, Aunt Marisa.''

''I was distracted this morning.''

''You are thinking of all of this murder nonsense when you should be concentrating on the important issue of making an appropriate match.''

Marisa smiled. ''You will have to pardon me, Bea; every now and then I place the matter of murder above that of finding a husband.''

Beatrice nodded, apparently blind to her aunt's sarcasm. ''It is precisely that type of thinking that threatens to keep you a spinster. You must remain focused on your objective."

"I had rather thought I might try to keep Lord Huntingdon alive."

"Lord Huntingdon is hardly in need of your protection. The man saved his regiment at Waterloo. Although you and the earl are not precisely well suited, it is well known that Lord Huntingdon intends to choose a bride this Season. You certainly should try to attract his regard. A woman of your years must consider every possibility. In your youth you might have considered marrying for *affection*. Now you really must be more practical."

Would Beatrice still be pushing her to make a match with Clayton if she knew of their unfortunate engagement seven years ago? Marisa had the uncomfortable feeling she might. Beatrice was apparently of the opinion her aunt was on her last legs. Perhaps she was right. "I am afraid the earl is a bit irritated with me at the moment."

Beatrice patted Marisa'a arm. "I am certain you could smooth his feathers, if you had a mind to. You can be quite charming when you try. Perhaps you will see him when you pay a call on the duchess and Miss Darracott this afternoon."

"Since the duke was wounded last night, I don't believe visiting the ladies today would be appropriate."

Beatrice's eyes widened. "The duke was wounded last night?"

"Yes. He was shot. Luckily, the injuries are not serious. Unfortunately, it appears as though the men I overheard were serious."

"The men you overheard were serious?" Beatrice looked confused for a moment before her usual confidence took control again. "Isn't it possible someone wanted to shoot the duke?"

Marisa frowned as she considered the possibility. "Justin was shot in front of Clayton's town house. It would seem too much of a coincidence for someone to want to murder both brothers at the same time."

"I suppose. Although, when I mentioned what you'd heard to several of my friends last night, they were all quite certain the duke was a more likely murder victim. A discarded mistress or a jealous husband might have shot him."

"Beatrice, dear, it really isn't wise to listen to rumors. And I think it would be best if you did not discuss this situation with anyone from this moment on."

Beatrice looked at her aunt as though Marisa had asked her to lay an egg for breakfast. "I do not see the point of not discussing it with my friends. They will certainly be discussing it."

"I suppose they will." Marisa suspected it was already too late to keep her own involvement a secret. Gossip had a way of spreading through London the way fire flashed along a dry twig.

If they found out you could identify one of them, they might very well decide to eliminate you. Clayton's words sounded in her memory. It didn't matter. Nothing mattered except keeping Clayton alive. No matter how dangerous it might be, she intended to do everything possible to keep him safe.

When Marisa called at Marlow House on Park Lane two days later, she was ushered into the green drawing room. The scent of rose potpourri welcomed her as she entered the large room. Sunlight spilled through the long, mullioned windows, filling the room with a golden warmth. The duchess sat on a gilt-trimmed sofa near the hearth, slender and youthful, as beautiful as a painting of a celestial guardian. Marisa started when she noticed the huge cat stretched out on the sofa beside her, his regal head resting on Sophia's lap. "A leopard?"

Sophia slid her hand over the big cat's head. "He is an ocelot actually. Hempstead brought him back from South America last September."

"Have you been keeping him in the country?"

"I brought him to town with me at the beginning of the Season. The other times you have called I had him tucked away in my bedchamber. Although I felt confident Audrey would appreciate him, I thought he might send Cecilia into a fit."

"He would probably have sent her screaming into the street." Marisa grinned. "But then, most males can do that."

Sophia laughed. "Come, dear. I shall introduce you properly."

Marisa tugged off her gloves as she crossed the room. She knelt beside the sofa, oblivious to the creases she made in the raspberry-colored muslin of her gown. She slid her fingers through the cat's silky spotted fur, earning a deep-throated purr in response. "You're not a bit shy, are you?"

"Perceval is like most males; he will allow any lovely lady to stroke him." Sophia spoke with all the confidence of a woman who knew the male of the species in great detail.

"There are some males who would prefer to keep a distance from me these days, I'm afraid."

"Anyone in particular?"

Marisa looked up into Sophia's gentle blue eyes. A broken engagement had not altered Sophia's affection for Marisa. All of these years she had remained a kind and caring friend to the woman who might have become her granddaughter through marriage. "Did Clayton tell you about the men I overheard in the Merrivales' maze?"

"Not until after Justin had been shot."

"He didn't take me seriously until then. I am not certain I ever noticed how stubborn that man can be."

"As stubborn as an untamed thoroughbred. It's one of the qualities I always thought you and he had in common." Sophia nudged Perceval. "How many times must I tell you to rise when a lady enters? Now get down and allow Marisa to sit beside me."

The big cat protested with a deep-throated growl. Yet he leaped from the sofa and curled into a ball at Sophia's feet. Sophia patted the pale green silk damask. "Sit, child. And tell me everything you know about this dreadful business."

Marisa settled on the stiff cushion. Sophia's expression grew pensive as Marisa related everything that had happened concerning the murder plot she had overheard. "I'm certain you must have heard about the little disguise I wore when I visited Justin."

Sophia nodded. "A wise woman would certainly not be seen entering Justin's town house without a disguise."

"I never would have gone to see him if I hadn't thought it was serious. I hope I didn't cause Miss Darracott any distress. I was hoping to apologize to her this afternoon."

"I'm afraid she is not at home." Sophia smoothed her hand over her lap, brushing cat hair from the skirt of her India muslin gown. "Isabel and Justin had a few matters to settle with her family today. I am expecting her back at any moment. You must stay. I am certain she will be glad to see you."

"I can imagine she might like to box my ears. I never anticipated the gossip I would stir. I should have given it more thought before I descended upon Justin's home in that silly disguise."

"Don't concern yourself, dear. Justin is accustomed to gossip. And Isabel is a very practical young woman. She understood completely when Justin explained what had happened."

"I had hoped she would. I wish Clay had a better understanding. He insists that I must have nothing at all to do with this."

"From what Clayton told me, this could become very dangerous for you. It would be wise to stay clear of the entire business."

"I can help identify at least one of the men involved. I hope you understand why I cannot stay clear of the situation."

Sophia studied her a moment before she spoke. "I have suspected something about you for a long time. Now I am certain of it."

Marisa sat back, uneasy beneath Sophia's critical gaze. "What have you suspected about me?"

Sophia lifted one golden brow. "You still care very deeply for my grandson."

With the tip of her forefinger Marisa traced a green leaf etched into the silk covering the gilt-trimmed arm of the sofa. "I suppose there are some things in life one simply cannot control. No matter how much one tries."

"I am not certain why you wanted to try. You and Clayton seemed so perfect for one another."

"I thought so, until we came to London that September." Marisa rose and moved to the window. She stared across Park Lane, where the green depths of Hyde Park commenced. In the distance, the smooth water of the Serpentine glowed golden in the sunlight, reminding her of the last carriage ride she had taken with Clayton. "So many things changed after we came to town."

"Seven years ago, when I asked you what had happened to cause you to end your engagement, you said you had come to realize that you and Clayton would not suit. Although I couldn't understand how you could come to that conclusion, I accepted it on the basis of your youth. A girl who is scarcely twenty does not always see the consequences of her every action."

Marisa closed her eyes, fighting the horrible memories gripping her vitals like sharp talons. "It is true. We are not always terribly wise at the tender age of twenty."

"I assumed you were too dazzled by all the stir you had caused to realize what you were throwing away. I thought perhaps Braden Fitzwilliam, or one of the other dashing young bucks, had turned your head."

Regrets twisted around her, squeezing her chest until Marisa could scarcely breathe. "No matter how hard I have tried, there has never been another man for me."

"Over the years, when you neglected to choose from your beaux, I suspected as much. Still, I confess, I would like to know what actually happened to change your mind."

"Clayton changed my mind."

"Clayton?"

Marisa stared at the distant glitter of the Serpentine while in her mind she relived every moment of that last carriage ride with Clayton. "He told me he had doubts about our marriage. I thought perhaps he was in love with someone else, that he had only offered for me because I had thrown myself so shamelessly at him. And so I cried off. I thought it was the right thing to do at the time. I wanted nothing more than to see him happy.''

''Clayton told you he was having doubts? How odd. I cannot imagine what doubts he might have been having, but I am quite certain he adored you. Only you.''

''It didn't seem so at the time. He seemed more like a man who regretted he had ever become involved with me.'' Marisa turned to face Sophia. ''You cannot imagine how many times I have wondered if I made a mistake. If I somehow twisted everything in my mind. I spoke to him the night before he left for the army, but the damage was done. There didn't seem to be anything I could do to repair the breach.''

''I suppose not. If you thought Clayton had doubts, then I can understand why you would cry off.'' Perceval leaped onto the sofa beside Sophia. He stretched out on the silk cushion and rested his head on Sophia's lap. She stroked his side, keeping her gaze on Marisa as she spoke. ''I think you should know that before all of this trouble erupted, Clayton planned to choose a bride before the end of the Season.''

Marisa's heart squeezed painfully. ''Yes. I have heard the rumors. For a while I thought he might offer for Miss Darracott.''

''Isabel is far too practical for Clayton. They are far too much alike. She is perfect for Justin. Where he is as combustible as dried kindling, she is as calming as chamomile tea.'' Sophia slid her hand through Perceval's fur. ''Clayton, on the other hand, needs a woman who will ignite a fire in him, a woman who is impetuous and exciting, someone who will constantly keep him off balance.''

Marisa smoothed her fingers along the edge of a

green silk drape. "Did Clayton actually ask you to make a list of potential brides for him?"

Sophia rolled her eyes. "I am afraid he did."

"I don't understand. The man I knew never would have been so cold about something that should involve all of his heart and soul."

"He intends to marry to satisfy a promise he made to my son. Nothing more. Clayton didn't want any female placed on the list who preferred to marry for affection."

It all sounded so cold, so calculated, so contrary to the man Marisa had known. "I cannot imagine that he would actually want to live his life that way."

"Clayton has changed a great deal since he took the foolish notion of joining the army. There is a darkness about him now, as though all the warmth and light in him has been extinguished."

Marisa had sensed it as well, the darkness in him, the ice where there had once been hidden fire. "I could never understand why he bought that horrible commission. He was a man who didn't even enjoy hunting."

"He refused to explain why he had decided to do it. I didn't think he would survive the war. He was far too gentle a spirit." Sophia glanced down at her cat. "In some way, Clayton has closed himself off from everyone. He maintains a distance, even from me. I believe Justin has felt it, too, even with the bond they share. It's as though he has buried all of his emotions. I wonder if he had to bury them to survive in battle."

The weight of that decision she had made so long ago pressed upon her chest like a solid slab of marble. "All of these years, I kept wondering if it was entirely my fault. If I hadn't cried off, he never would have gone away."

"You can't blame yourself. You and Clayton both

had a hand in shaping what happened. He chose to march off to war. If he had stayed, the two of you might have found a way to reconcile."

"You don't know how much I wish I could turn back time, set things back to where they were before that dreadful day I ended any chance Clay and I might have had for a life together."

"We cannot alter the past. But we can shape the future. You cannot realize how much I keep hoping something—or someone—will break through the barrier Clayton has erected to keep the world at a distance. I keep hoping someone can bring back the man he was." Sophia tilted her head, a smile curving her lips. "I have a feeling you are exactly what Clayton needs."

Marisa only wished it were true. "Clayton has made it very clear he doesn't want me in his life. Whatever he might have felt for me in the past, it can be tucked into a volume of ancient history now."

"My dear, if we allowed men to make up their own minds, we would all still be living in caves." Sophia slid her hand through Perceval's fur, receiving a deep-throated purr in response.

Marisa rubbed her arms, feeling chilled. "He despises me."

"Nonsense."

"You didn't hear him. You didn't see the anger in his eyes."

"A wise woman can find a way to change a man's mind and make him think it was his idea in the first place." Sophia stroked her cat. "I suspect you are a great deal wiser now than you were seven years ago."

Marisa smiled, allowing hope to wiggle free of the restraints she had clapped upon it. "I have learned a few things in seven years."

Sophia winked at her. "Then put it all to good use, my dear."

Chapter Fourteen

The soft strains of a waltz swirled around Marisa as she glided with her partner on the Sotherbys' dance floor. Aside from her first disastrous Season, all the others Marisa had attended blended together. Over the years she had watched as her friends made suitable matches and embarked on new lives. They became wives and mothers, while—in spite of her best efforts—Marisa remained locked in time, trapped in a role that grew increasingly difficult to maintain with each passing year. In time the small joys she took in the Season would no longer be available to her. She teetered on the precipice of spinsterhood. If she did not marry soon, she would be expected to don a cap and take a place on the shelf. Two alternatives presented themselves to her: spinsterhood or a loveless marriage. One thing was obvious: she needed to find a third alternative.

She glanced past her partner's shoulder to where

Clayton was dancing with Lady Penelope Cuthberth, one of the candidates on his list. Heat prickled the nape of her neck each time she thought of that blasted list. Penelope possessed the type of beauty usually reserved for porcelain figurines; she was small and fair, with large blue eyes. According to Sophia, the girl also possessed a heart made of porcelain. The main qualities Penelope sought in a husband included wealth and a title. Couldn't Clayton see he would be perfectly miserable with any of the women on that dreadful list?

"You are an intriguing woman."

Her partner's voice dragged her attention back to him. Gregory Stanwood was certainly a handsome man—his features finely molded, his figure built along athletic lines. Yet the dark waves tumbling over his brow looked as though they had been strategically positioned. Everything about him always seemed too perfect, as though he stepped out of a mold each morning.

"In what ways do you find me intriguing?" she queried.

"You are one of London's most beautiful women, with a legion of admirers. And yet you have never chosen a husband." He lifted one dark brow, his blue eyes alight with humor. "Such behavior inspires all manner of romantic speculation."

Marisa parried with her usual response to an inquiry she had heard countless times. "I should think such behavior would signify only a woman who cannot make up her mind."

"Or does it signify a woman who has lost her only love?" He swept her into a graceful turn while he maintained the proper distance between them. "Stories abound about the tragic Lady Marisa."

Marisa kept her lips molded into a smile. "Stories abound about many people, as well you know. I am certain you have good reason not to believe them.''

He laughed. ''Touché, dear lady.''

''I suppose the fiction people have created of my life is more interesting than the reality.''

''They say you fell in love with a soldier in your first Season, but your parents would not allow the match. And so he marched off to war and never returned.''

She was surprised at how close to the mark they had struck. ''I have always thought the ton were far too bored. Now I am certain of it.''

He laughed, the soft sound a dark counterpoint to the violins. ''I suppose the rumors are something gentlemen have contrived to mend their wounded pride after you have declined their offers of marriage. I believe you are the only woman my cousin has ever offered for. Of course, Braden was certain you would agree, or he never would have announced it to the family.''

''Fortunately, Braden has a strong constitution.''

''He still has hopes.'' Gregory lifted his brows. ''This evening I heard a most astonishing rumor about you.''

Marisa stared up into his blue eyes, a cold sensation brushing against the base of her spine like icy fingers. ''People love to gossip.''

''Did you actually hear someone plotting to murder Clayton Trevelyan?''

Marisa missed a step, her foot coming down on Gregory's. ''I'm sorry.''

''It's my fault.'' Gregory eased her back into the rhythm of the dance. ''I shouldn't have startled you.''

All the consequences of the rumor pounded against her skull as she forced her feet to carry her through the steps of the waltz. "Who told you that particular rumor?"

Gregory frowned. "Let's see, I was in the refreshment room with Braden and several others. I believe it was Victoria Talbot who mentioned it."

Realization trickled like ice into her blood, chilling her straight to the bone. All of London must know about her little episode in the Merrivales' garden.

"According to the rumor, you are certain you can identify one of the men if you ever hear him again. Do you actually believe you can?"

Marisa had no intention of verifying anything about this particular *rumor*. She laughed, the sound hollow to her own ears. "Astonishing the stories one hears these days."

He smiled. "Indeed. I cannot imagine anyone wanting to murder Clayton. Can you?"

"No. I certainly cannot." She glanced away from Gregory, her gaze resting on Clayton. If he heard the rumor, he would be furious with her. She must do her best to quell it.

"The men you overheard did not give any indication of their motives?"

"No." If the men she had overheard realized she could identify one of them, they might try to murder her. Fear settled around her like an icy shroud. It didn't matter if the blackguard knew about her, she thought, shaking off the fear. She intended to stop him before he had a chance to harm Clayton.

Clayton led his partner through the sweeping steps of the waltz. In the past few months, all the parties and balls had blended one into the other. After his seven years in the army, everything seemed so artificial, as though everyone were floating about on their little clouds, oblivious of the world around them. Even when he was in the midst of it all, he stood apart from the others, as though he peered at the glittering array from behind a thick pane of glass. Nothing had come close to penetrating that isolation, except one infuriating spinster.

Clayton stared over his partner's fair head, watching Marisa as she glided gracefully in the embrace of her partner. Gregory had lost his wife in a riding accident nearly two years before. It was no secret he was on the prowl for another. And Clayton knew the man considered wealth and beauty the two primary requirements in any female he might choose. Marisa satisfied both. Still, Clayton doubted Marisa would succumb to Gregory's polished charm. Would she? The question made him uneasy, but not as uneasy as the tight knot that formed in his belly each time he thought of her with another man.

"They say Mr. Stanwood shall have a new wife by Michaelmas."

Clayton glanced down at his partner, Lady Penelope Cuthberth. From the turn of her conversation, he assumed she had noticed the direction his attention had wandered. Penelope never cared for any gentleman's attention to wander far from her lovely face. He had found certain similarities in all of the women Sophia had placed on his list of potential brides. Although each one was beautiful, every one of the nine females on that list possessed a wide vein of ambition. Each woman's ambition to marry a title rivaled Napoleon's for ruling the world. "People enjoy gossip."

Penelope smiled, candlelight glittering in her blue eyes. "I suspect in this case the gossip is true."

Although Lady Penelope's features were flawless, her beauty was the type better observed from a dis-

tance. The closer one drew to her, the colder one felt.
He had discovered she was the same as the others Sophia had chosen for him: a piece of ice resided where
her heart should be. Considering his own requirements
for a potential bride, he supposed that fact shouldn't
surprise. Still, he hadn't expected the ice to disturb him
as much as it did.

"I wonder if Lady Marisa is the one he has chosen
for his new bride? I do not recall seeing him pay so
much attention to any lady before."

Apparently Penelope was perceptive as well as ambitious. The smallest whiff of a possible rival brought
out her claws. "If he has chosen her, I'm certain Lady
Marisa will have her own ideas about the subject."

"You are right, of course. An heiress does not remain a spinster without having definite ideas of the sort
of gentleman she wishes to marry. And of course she
must be very careful about men seeking her fortune.
Mama is forever telling me about the importance of
making a wise match. I am certain a man in your position must be equally as careful."

Why had Marisa never married? The question had
hounded him for years, but never as much as it had
these past few days. "When one notices Lady Marisa
has never chosen one of her legion of admirers, it becomes obvious she is very particular indeed."

The corners of Penelope's smile tightened. "It is
amazing to see so many gentlemen interested in a
woman of her advanced years."

"I would find it amazing if gentlemen were not
drawn to a woman of such beauty and grace."

Penelope's delicate nostrils flared. "Yes, I suppose
it would be."

Clayton glanced to where Marisa was dancing with

Gregory. Why the devil did he find it necessary to leap to the woman's defense?

"You must have exciting stories to tell of your many campaigns in the army."

"I am afraid war hardly makes entertaining conversation."

Penelope's smile widened but her eyes remained cool, like a commander planning strategy. "I can think of nothing more fascinating than hearing every detail of your triumph at Waterloo."

Memories stirred within him, scraping along his vitals like the bony fingers of a skeleton's hand. "I was only one of many in battle that day."

"I have read every account of the battle. I am quite certain you have many thrilling tales."

Voices screamed in his head, the sobs of men in their last moments on earth. Beneath his elegantly tailored clothes, his skin grew cold, as though he stood naked in a brisk December wind. "I did only what was necessary."

"You are too modest. You were a hero."

"I appreciate your kind words, but I—"

"Tell me what it was like to fight for England," she said, clinging to the subject like a pug with a favorite bone. "You must share every detail. I insist."

He molded his lips into a smile while inside he fought to push the memories back into their carefully tended graves. "I never realized you were so bloodthirsty, Lady Penelope."

Some of the confidence slipped from her expression. "Bloodthirsty?"

He swept her into a graceful turn. "Would you like to hear in detail how a saber slices through a man's chest?"

Her eyes widened. "A saber?"

"You would be surprised at how easily a well-honed blade passes through flesh and bone. Of course you can feel a thud when you hit bone, but the resistance lasts only a heartbeat."

Penelope moistened her lips. "I see."

"The look in your enemy's eyes when you have hit a death blow—it's often surprise, as though the pain had caught him completely unaware."

She stared at him. "Lord Huntingdon, perhaps—"

"There is an odd sound when you hit a lung, a wheezing, gurgling blend of breath and voice. Then there is a dribble of blood from the lips. The eyes take on a glazed look." Similar to the look in Penelope's eyes. "And he is done."

She swallowed hard. "Perhaps you are right, Lord Huntingdon. Perhaps war doesn't make entertaining conversation."

"Perhaps not." And perhaps he wasn't fit for gentle company. Although he was not fond of the lady, he regretted the terrified look he had placed in Penelope's lovely eyes. She remained quiet and grim for the rest of the dance. After he returned her to her chaperon, he prowled the room, feeling like a tiger trapped in a cage. He no longer fit in this glittering world that had once been his domain. The problem was, he didn't seem to fit anywhere. At times he wondered if it wouldn't have been better if he had never returned from the war.

He glanced around at the faces of the guests, looking for one beautiful face in particular. He frowned when he spotted her. Marisa was hurrying toward one of the doors leading to the terrace, like a hound with the scent of a fox in her nostrils. What the devil was she about?

The cool evening air brushed her warm cheeks as Marisa stepped onto the terrace. She glanced around, searching the shadows for the man she had glimpsed leaving the ballroom. She had heard his voice drift from a group of men standing in one corner of the ballroom, just a few words caught above the din of conversation and music. Still, she was certain the voice belonged to the same man she had overheard in the Merrivale garden. She had trailed him through the crowded room without getting a good look at his face. To be of any help, she had to get a better look at him.

She hurried along the length of the terrace. Several couples had taken refuge in the moonlight, each guarded by a chaperon. Yet a slender, fair-haired man was not among them. Where was he? She paused on the top of the two stone steps leading down into the gardens. She studied her surroundings, searching for the blackguard.

The walled expanse behind the house had been divided into several different areas by a series of hedges and walkways leading off a winding, gravel-lined path. Lanterns dangled from cords strung along the pathways, casting soft golden light against the shrubs and statuary placed about the gardens. A man stepped into view near the first bend of the path. It was the same man she had followed from the ballroom.

"Did you need a little air, Lady Marisa?"

Marisa's heart plowed into the wall of her chest at the rumble of that deep masculine voice. She pivoted and found Clayton stalking her. He paused a foot in front of her, so close that the crisp scent of citrus and herbs brushed her senses, sending heat swirling through her blood. Although the moon showed only half its face this evening, it was enough to illuminate the sharp lines and angles of Clayton's fierce expression. His mood apparently had not improved in the two days since she had last seen him in her drawing room. Still, she didn't have time to indulge his anger. "Follow me."

He frowned. "What the devil—"

"I'll explain later." She hurried down the stairs. If Clayton wanted to stand around being angry with her for some misbegotten reason, he could. She had a potential murderer to catch.

Clayton caught up with her a few feet along the path. "I assume you are not hurrying to meet one of your lovers, since you invited me to accompany you."

His words hit her with the force of a clenched fist. She froze on the gravel path and fixed him with a stunned stare. "One of my lovers?"

His lips tipped into a cold imitation of the smile she had loved. "What are you doing, Mari?"

"What did you mean by saying I had lovers?"

He shrugged. "You are hardly a chit straight out of the schoolroom. Given your propensity for flirtation, it seems only logical that you have indulged your more passionate side from time to time."

"You think I have . . ." She stared up at the only man she had ever wanted in her arms, the injustice of his words flooding her. "You have no right to say such vile things to me."

One corner of his mouth tightened. "No, I don't. I apologize."

Marisa turned away from him and forced her legs to carry her deeper into the gardens. How could he think she would do something so vulgar? Yet she knew the answer. He thought so little of her. Tears burned her eyes. She clenched her jaw and refused to let them fall.

"What are we looking for?"

The man they were following disappeared around a bend in the path, shielded from her view by a tall row of hedges. "I heard him, the man from the Merrivales' maze."

229

Clayton gripped her arm, dragging her to a halt. "He was here?"

"I followed him out here." She broke free of his grasp and marched along the path. "He is just ahead of us."

Clayton joined her, his footsteps crunching with hers against the gravel. "You followed him out here? Alone?" he asked, his voice a harsh whisper. "I thought I told you to stay out of this."

She glared into his furious eyes. "I don't take orders, remember?"

"What the bloody hell would you have done if—"

"Could we discuss this later?" she asked, keeping her voice low. "At the moment I have other things to do."

He stayed close beside her as she hurried along the path. As they approached the far end of the gardens, she heard the creak of hinges. The main path ended in a perennial garden sheltered on two sides by tall yews, and on the third by an ivy-covered brick wall. Marisa paused on the edge of a small round reflecting pool and glanced around. She saw no one, except the angry man standing beside her.

She hurried toward a wooden gate in the brick wall. "He must have slipped out this way."

Hinges creaked as Clayton pulled open the gate. "Stay here," he growled in a tone that held no room for disobedience.

Marisa curled her hands into fists at her sides as he stepped into the alley behind the gardens. The man had no right to give her orders. Still, she hesitated a moment before following Clayton into the alley.

A single street lamp burned at the far end of the alley, shedding a faint glow in the darkness. She caught a glimpse of Clayton as he ran through that light before he turned the corner leading to Audley Street. She ran after him. When she reached the street she paused near a lamppost, breathing hard to catch her breath.

Street lamps lined the sidewalk, each carving a circular glow in the darkness, but the accumulated glow failed to illuminate the crowded street. Carriages inched along Audley Street, carrying people from one party to the next. Guests were leaving the Sotherbys' party as others arrived. Clayton emerged from a crowd of people milling about the front of the Sotherby house, and headed back in Marisa's direction.

Clayton gripped her arm and ushered her back toward the alley. "I thought I told you to stay in the garden."

"I believe I told you I don't take orders." She smiled in defiance of his angry glare. "What happened?"

Clayton frowned. "I lost him."

She hurried to keep up with his long strides. "Did you get a good look at him?"

"It was too dark." Clayton turned into the alley.

"At least we have some idea of what he looks like. We are looking for a slender, fair-haired man, a little above medium height."

"How old?"

"I would guess he could be anywhere between five and twenty and forty."

Clayton ushered her through the open gate. "You have just described half of the men in England."

"That is why I followed him. I wanted to get a better look at him."

Hinges creaked as Clayton closed the gate. He pivoted to face her. "Who was he with in the ballroom?"

She frowned, trying to recall the faces in the group of men where he had been standing. "I'm not certain."

"You didn't see his face and you don't know who he was with." He lifted his hands. "Well, you have managed to narrow the search considerably."

She bristled at his sarcasm. "It was crowded. I heard this voice say 'It's stifling in here, I need some air.' I turned. There was a crowd of gentlemen standing nearby. I saw a man wending his way toward one of the doors leading to the terrace, so I followed him."

"You cannot even be certain it was the same man you overheard at the Merrivales' party."

"It *was* the same man. The next time I shall make certain to get a look at his face."

"There will not be a next time." Clayton fixed her with a cold glare. "I don't want you running after men who might be potentially dangerous."

"I see no other way to discover who he is."

"Infuriating, stubborn . . ." His words dissolved in a muttered oath. "Stay out of this."

"You have no authority over me." She pivoted to leave, the skirt of her gown smacking his legs.

He blocked her way when she tried to return to the main path. "Tell me something. What would you have done if you had come upon him alone?"

He towered above her, his broad shoulders shutting out the rest of the world. Moonlight spilled over him, slipping silver into his midnight hair, as though worshiping him. He seemed a dark angel tossed from heaven—beautiful, dangerous, bitter in his exile. Flirtation and social banter had long ago become part of her feminine arsenal. But his presence so overwhelmed her, it took every shred of concentration to form a coherent thought. "I only wanted to get a better look at him. I didn't plan to confront him."

Clayton leaned toward her, his breath brushing her

face with damp heat as he spoke. "What if he had decided to confront you?"

Marisa caught an intoxicating trace of champagne on his breath. "He doesn't know anything about me."

"I wouldn't be so certain." His eyes narrowed into dark slits. "Rumors have a way of traveling quickly through London."

A sick feeling curled in the pit of her stomach when she thought of the rumors circulating about her. "It doesn't matter. I still intend to find him."

"It does matter. You could be hurt."

"I am your best chance of finding him before he finds you."

"I want you to leave town. Tomorrow morning. I want you to stay at Westbury until this business is finished."

She forced starch into her back and tried to ignore the heat simmering through her veins. "In case you didn't notice, I am not one of your servants. I do not take orders from you."

"It isn't safe for you here."

"How do you suppose I would feel if I left town and they succeeded in murdering you? I have to do everything I can to help."

"I won't have your death on my conscience."

"Then work with me, Clay. Help me find these men before they can hurt anyone again."

"You are the most stubborn, infuriating female." He glanced toward heaven, a man seeking control. When he looked at her, his eyes held all the anger simmering beneath the quiet tones of his voice. "I don't want you involved with this."

She brushed past him. "I don't intend to argue with you."

He grabbed her arm, halting her when she tried to

march back to the path. In the next instant he whipped his arm around her waist and hauled her back against his chest and off the ground. The sudden impact against that hard plane of masculinity shivered through her. Excitement sprinted through her veins. "What are—"

He pressed his gloved hand against her throat, cutting off her words. "What if I had a knife, Mari?" he asked, his voice a harsh whisper against her hair. "What chance would you have?"

She gripped his wrist, trying to pry his hand away from her neck. Even though it was Clayton holding her, she couldn't prevent the fear bolting through her, fear born of an overwhelming sense of helplessness. "Clay—"

"I wouldn't need a knife."

There was something about him, a horrible, icy calm beneath the anger, that chilled her. She fought the instincts screaming in panic. She forced her body to remain still in his hold. This was Clayton. He wouldn't hurt her, she assured herself.

He stroked his fingers along the column of her neck. "I could break your neck with a twist of my hand."

She closed her eyes. An odd, tingling sensation rippled through her body, an uneasy blend of fear, excitement and a longing too potent to deny. "You're trying to frighten me."

"You should be frightened. I've done it, Mari. I've snapped a man's neck like a twig," he whispered, his lips brushing the top of her ear. "I know how easily you could die."

He had killed in the past. Yet a death in battle was hardly a murder in cold blood. No matter what had happened in war, no matter what he had done, he would not harm her. "He doesn't know anything about me, so he wouldn't have a reason to break my neck."

"Unlike me." He brushed his lips against her temple. "You are the most maddening creature on the face of the earth."

She had ruffled his composure. In spite of everything, she latched onto that tiny shred of encouragement. "You cannot change my mind by trying to frighten me. I will help you find that blackguard."

"You're trembling, Mari. I can feel it. Like a bird held in a hunter's hand." He opened his hand against her neck, forcing her head back against his shoulder. His heat soaked through the amber silk of her gown, an odd contrast to the chill in his voice. Still, in spite of his anger, his touch was gentle. "Perhaps you realize how easily I could murder you."

If he only realized how easily he could set her trembling, with a glance, a touch, a whisper. "I'm not frightened of you, Clay."

He cupped her cheek in his palm. "One swift twist and I could snap your neck as easily as I could the stem of a crystal wineglass."

She smiled up into his hooded eyes. "Could you?"

He stroked her neck with one long finger, scattering shivers across her skin, none of which had anything at all to do with fear. "Such a slender neck. Your bones would shatter easily."

She slid her arm along the powerful arm he held cinched around her waist, hugging him to her, delivering herself completely into his hold. The thick muscles of his chest tightened against her back. The warmth of his breath stirred the curls at her temple. "Your hands were always so strong. Yet so very gentle. No matter how angry you are, you won't hurt me."

Slowly he allowed her to slide along his body, until her feet touched the ground. When he might have released her, she held his arm against her. He seemed to

235

sense her need to be held by him. Or was it his own need he indulged by holding her? He held her close against his chest, one strong arm wrapped around her waist, the other curved loosely around her neck, his hand gripping her shoulder. She leaned against him, trembling with the heady excitement of just being near him.

"People change, Mari," he whispered, his voice strained with what might have been pain. "You don't know me anymore."

"In ways we change." His warmth curled around her, like a lover's embrace. For too many nights she had hugged her pillow and longed for the warmth of this man. She sensed the tension in him, heard it in the quick breath that warmed her temple with each sharp exhalation. "We learn. We grow. We look back at the choices we have made and realize the different paths we might have taken. But deep inside, we remain the same."

She felt the soft brush of his lips against her hair. "Do you honestly believe that?"

"Yes." She tilted her head to look up at him. The wall of indifference he presented to the world lay shattered on the ground between them. He seemed utterly vulnerable in that moment, as lost and lonely as she was. "Deep inside you are still the same man I knew, even though a lifetime has passed."

He slipped his arm from beneath hers, then stepped away from her. "You certainly haven't changed. You are still as reckless and impetuous as ever."

The evening breeze touched her back, cooling the lingering warmth from his body. She turned to face him. "Is it really so impetuous for me to want to save you from a murderer?"

He stared at her, and she could almost see him rebuilding that wall between them, brick by brick. "You shouldn't be taking chances like this."

"No, I suppose I shouldn't. I shouldn't care if that blackguard murders you. But for some reason I do."

He turned away from her and stalked to the edge of the reflecting pool. "I don't want you involved in this."

She wished she could slip her arms around him and hold him close. Even if he didn't want to admit it, he needed that connection as much as she did; she could sense it. "I am involved in this. I am the only one who can identify him."

He turned to face her, his expression once again a carefully guarded mask of indifference. "I suppose the only way to make you stop meddling is to kidnap you and keep you prisoner in the country."

"Yes, it is. But it sounds a little severe. And think of the consequences. Papa would hold you responsible for my reputation. You see, he still thinks my reputation is worth defending."

An uneasy expression crossed his features as she drifted toward him. "I spoke out of anger. I am sorry."

"I understand." She sat on a stone bench near the pool. "I wonder if there are other people who think the same thing of me."

"Marisa, I was wrong to imply you had ever acted improperly." He sat on the bench beside her, maintaining an all too proper distance.

Marisa didn't need to close her eyes to imagine another time and place, a warm summer day when she had first tasted his kiss. In some ways it all seemed a dream. In other ways it seemed more real than the life she was living. She tilted her head and smiled at him. "I am much better at minding propriety now than I was when you first knew me. I have learned to disguise most of my many bad habits."

"Anyone without a bad habit must be a dead bore." He smiled, a warm, generous curve of his lips that filled his eyes with a light she had never forgotten. "Remember?"

She remembered. That was the problem: she remembered far too much of that precious time they had shared. She plucked a slender sprig of lily of the valley from a bed planted beside the bench. The sweet fragrance filled her senses as she twirled it between her fingers. "I still have more bad habits than I care to admit. But I have learned to keep them closely guarded when I am in society. For instance, I have refrained from throwing myself into the arms of any gentleman, the way I did with you."

The smile faded from his lips. He turned his attention to the pool, where moonlight reflected on the water. "I suppose it is safer that way. You refrain from making another mistake."

Marisa didn't want to make another mistake, not with this man. A breeze whispered across the garden, rustling the leaves of an elm tree that stood near one corner of the ivy-covered wall. The soft breath of wind stirred the waves that had tumbled over Clayton's brow, tempting her to smooth the silky strands back from his face. She lifted the lily and brushed the aromatic white flowers against her chin as she spoke. "I often think of how different both of our lives might have been, if we had actually managed to . . . marry one another."

Clayton gripped the edge of the bench. "I find it is wiser not to dwell on what might have been."

"I suppose it is. Still, there are times when I find it impossible not to wonder about the past and the decisions I have made. The decisions you have made. I never understood why you purchased a commission."

He rose and rubbed the back of his neck. "I thought it was a good idea at the time."

She hesitated a moment, aware of how precarious the ground was beneath her. "I often wondered if you did it because of me."

His shoulders rose with a deep inhalation of breath. "As surprising as it might seem, my world does not revolve around you."

Marisa flinched at the cruel words. "I never thought it did."

He turned to face her. Moonlight carved his features from the shadows. "I was interested in making a change in who I was. I succeeded."

She stared into his eyes, seeing ice where warmth had once burned. "Yes. I can see you did. The man I knew never would have uttered a cruel word to anyone."

A muscle bunched in his cheek with the clenching of his jaw. "The man you knew died a long time ago."

Had he? Dear heaven, she had to believe the Clayton she loved still survived, trapped in this angry man. "I am sorry to hear of his passing. He was a very special man."

Clayton smiled. "He was weak."

"No, he wasn't." She rose and found that her knees trembled beneath her. "He was warm and caring. The type of man who would sleep on a cold cellar floor just so his brother would not be alone. The type of man who was not afraid to converse with a woman as though she actually had a fully functioning brain."

He glanced away from her. "The type of man who couldn't fight for what he wanted."

With the moonlight against his skin, his profile

seemed carved from marble and as cold and unyielding. *Please, Clay. Please show me a glimpse of the man buried inside of you.* "What was it you wanted to fight for, Clay?"

He shook his head. "It doesn't matter."

"Doesn't it?"

He looked at her. Although his body remained rigid, emotions flickered across his features, pain and anger, regret and sorrow, all mirrored in the beautiful eyes she would never forget. "There is no going back. There is no way to alter the decisions we have made. There is no point in contemplating things we might have done."

"No, there isn't. We can only make the best of each day we are given." She held his icy glare, and took a single, shaky step toward facing the truth of the decision she had made seven years ago. "We can only try to amend the mistakes we have made in our lives."

He frowned, a wary look entering his eyes. "Some mistakes cannot be altered."

Dear heaven, she had to believe this one—the most important, glaring, tragic mistake she had ever made—could be altered. "How do we know until we try?"

He frowned. "I suppose we don't."

She smiled. "Then I suppose all we can do is our best."

He glanced away from her, but not before she saw the uncertainty in his eyes. "This man you overheard, I don't want you trailing after him unless you are with me."

She stared at him, her breath growing still in her throat as she recognized the opportunity he presented her. "Do you plan to live in my pocket?"

He shifted on his feet. "I suppose it's the only way to keep you from getting yourself hurt."

Oh, yes, she very much liked the way this was turning. "Aren't you afraid of what people will think?"

"Not particularly," he said, his voice unduly harsh.

She could not resist the temptation of broaching a particularly annoying subject. She needed to know exactly what obstacles were in her path. "It might discourage the ladies on your list."

Chapter Fifteen

"My list?" Clayton stared at her, his gut churning with a horrible certainty. "What the devil do you know about that blasted list?"

Marisa brushed the lily against her chin. "I know I was terribly surprised to discover you intended to choose a bride from a list of women you didn't even know."

He felt as he had the first time he had ridden into battle—naked and vulnerable, certain he would make a fool of himself. "I suppose Sophia told you about it when you called upon her yesterday."

"She didn't need to." Marisa opened her arms wide. "This is London. Nothing remains a secret."

"Apparently not." He shuddered inside when he thought of the ton dissecting the reasons behind that bloody list.

"When I first heard of your list, I couldn't imagine

why you would rely on your grandmother to choose a bride for you."

He clenched his jaw. "I decided Sophia might be able to narrow my search."

"Oh, I see. Then you really are taking more interest in your choice of a bride than it would appear."

Marisa was the last person on this green earth with whom he wanted to discuss his plans for marriage. "You seem to be taking a particular interest in *my* affairs."

"I have always been dreadfully curious. It's one of my many faults."

"Curiosity will get you into trouble one day."

She shrugged, her slender shoulders rising into the kiss of moonlight. "It might."

Clayton caught himself staring at the creamy expanse of pale skin exposed by her low neckline, his mind conjuring images he could not prevent—smooth skin naked in the glow of candlelight. She drifted toward him, a fairy spun of evening shadows, moonlight, and dreams. Her skirt rustled with her every step, igniting thoughts of long, slim legs sliding against white silk sheets, entangling with his. Heat swirled and eddied low in his belly. Lord help him, he wanted her. He wanted her more than he wanted his next breath. He wanted to lay her down in the grass, strip away every shred of her clothes, taste and caress and kiss every luscious inch of her.

Marisa paused beside him and directed her gaze toward the reflecting pool. "What criteria did you use?"

Her voice dragged him back from the dangerous path he had taken. He had to swallow hard before he could safely employ his voice. "Criteria?"

"You must have given Sophia some direction." She

tilted her head and looked up at him. "What do you require in a wife?"

He stared into the face of the only woman he had ever truly imagined as his wife, his chest tightening with the war raging inside—the battle to keep his emotions safely guarded. "This really isn't any of your concern."

His harsh tone bounced off of her like an arrow hitting steel. "I am certain you have some ideas about the woman with whom you intend to spend the rest of your life."

Confounded female! "Intelligence."

She nodded. "I suppose she should be able to discuss Plutarch and Plato?"

Memories of past conversations he had shared with this woman taunted him. "She need not be a scholar."

Marisa looked up at him, a portrait of wide-eyed innocence. "What must she be?"

"She must be serious-minded. Practical. Dignified." The litany sounded stilted and dull to his own ears.

"I may have a cousin who would fit your requirements perfectly. You don't mind if your future bride has just the smallest twitch in one eye, do you?"

Clayton fixed her with a cold stare, praying she would not see through his mask into his need. "I appreciate your concern, but I believe I have sufficient candidates to consider."

"What will you do if you settle on one particular *candidate*, and she isn't interested?"

He shrugged, knowing it didn't matter. "Choose another one."

"I see." One corner of her lips twitched. There was a glitter in her eyes. "So it would seem one woman is just as good as another when it comes to choosing a wife?"

"My choice of wife is none of your concern."

"Of course not. I was just curious." She brushed the tip of the lily against the side of her neck, drawing his attention to the smooth curve of her shoulder. "I am certain you will have no trouble at all obtaining a bride. You are, after all, young and handsome as well as wealthy."

He shook his head. "You cannot help it, can you? Flirtation is as natural to you as taking a breath."

She smiled. "I may flirt a little. But no more than what is expected of any female in society. It is an art we all learn."

"And you have mastered it."

"I thought all gentlemen, as well as ladies, were expected to be familiar with the intricate art of flirtation."

He inclined his head in a small bow. "You shall have to forgive me if I am not as adept at flirtation as Braden Fitzwilliam and the other men sniffing about your skirts. I have been distracted by other things these past few years."

"Yes, I can see you shall require a great deal of instruction. Particularly if you expect to win a bride by the end of the Season. You have very little time left. Obviously you need my assistance."

"And here I thought I was managing well enough on my own."

She shook her head. "Although it pains me to say this, you are shamefully rough around the edges when it comes to paying court to a lady."

Clayton drew in his breath, fighting to maintain the composure she threatened by her very existence. "I have a fair suspicion my title will tip the scales in my favor with or without my rough edges smoothed."

"True." Marisa smoothed the lily across her palm.

"Most females will overlook the most dreadful flaws for a title and wealth. You are fortunate in that regard."

He pressed his hand against his heart, appalled at the quick pounding beneath his palm. "I shall give thanks to my maker."

"Of course, I had thought you might be interested in contracting a match with a female who might want you for something other than social position and deep pockets."

"I prefer to base my marriage on practical needs."

She tilted her head and stared up into his eyes. He fought to maintain a mask of indifference, while inside his emotions pushed dangerously close to the surface of their tomb. "Do you truly require so little in a marriage?"

He glanced away from her, his gaze resting on a bed of lilies planted near the pond. "I require honesty, loyalty, mutual respect. I do not consider those trivial qualities."

"And what of affection?"

"I have found affection a highly overrated as well as an unreliable emotion." As much as he tried, he could not prevent the bitterness from seeping into his voice as he spoke.

Marisa glanced down at the delicate lily resting across the palm of her gloved hand. "Affection need not be either. It might in truth be constant, unshakable, so strong nothing on earth can damage it."

What did she know of constancy? What did she know of affection so strong it could rip a man into so many pieces he feared he could never fit them all together again? He had never been able to repair the damage done by affection. He had never been able to fit together all of the pieces. "I have found that your sex praises many romantic notions, but seldom remains constant to any.''

She lifted her eyes and met his gaze. In those golden depths he imagined he saw all the regret he had suffered all of these years, and all of the pain. ''I must suggest you do not know women as well as you may believe.''

''History stands as a testament to the perfidy of women. Authors have long ago chronicled the inconstant nature of a woman's heart. Poets have immortalized your fickleness. Troubadours have sung of your wicked betrayals. Still, with all of these warnings, my sex does not often believe how dangerous a female can be until we have passed through the fire of heartbreak. Only then, with flesh seared and hearts turned to ashes, do we realize the fools we have been for trusting in the constancy of a woman's *affection*.''

Clayton realized he had revealed too much. But there was no hope for it, no chance to deny what she must certainly see: the true extent of the wounds she had carved across his heart all those years ago. Still, there was no look of triumph in her eyes. Instead those beautiful golden eyes seemed a mirror, a reflection of all the years he had suffered since the day she had cast him aside.

''I cannot defend every female in history. I cannot deny every story told of a woman's fickleness. I can only speak from what I know. There are those of my sex who love long after all hope is gone, women who cannot stop loving a man even when it is clear the love she holds for him will cause her nothing but pain.''

Did she suffer regrets? He held her gaze, while his heart pounded against the wall of his chest and the air between them thickened until he could scarcely draw a breath. Broken dreams and shattered promises littered the space between them, sharp and dangerous as shards of glass. Still, in spite of everything he knew, all of their history, a part of him—a pitiful, weak shred of what he had been—wanted to cross the distance between them. He needed her in his arms; he needed her warmth her softness, her reality. He needed . . . to keep his distance. "I shall leave it to the other members of my sex to test your theory. I prefer to avoid the sentiment."

"And so you choose to marry a woman who will not complicate your life with affection."

The warmth of her body drifted to him on the evening breeze, tempting him. He crushed the rising heat of his desire for this woman. "Precisely."

She fixed him with a direct look. "If that is all you are looking for in marriage, I would imagine you will find it easily. There are many women who want nothing more than a title and wealth."

All the questions that had haunted him all these years swirled in his brain. Even though he knew they were better left unspoken, he couldn't resist. "After I left for the Peninsula, I thought for certain I would hear of your marriage. You surprised me."

She glanced away from him, hiding the expression in her eyes. "Half of the men who are interested in marrying me want to replenish the family fortune. The other half are interested in a pretty ornament to hang on their arms."

Clayton could not believe she had never met another man who had been captivated by her. Another man who would have given his last breath just to hold her in his arms. "There must have been men who fell desperately in love with you."

"It has been a very long time since I have encouraged a gentleman to lose his heart to me." Marisa stared at the flower in her hand a long moment before she lifted her gaze to his eyes. "The last time it was you."

The soft, wistful tone of her voice teased him. The regrets shimmering in her eyes beckoned to him. Did she mean to torment him? Did she intend to tempt him into thinking of all the things he had so desperately wanted in his youth? All the things that could never be. "I cannot imagine you thought much of what happened between us."

"How could I not think of it? We were to be married."

He forced his lips into a smile. "You need not seek to plump up my pride. I realize how easy I was to forget."

"I had never met anyone like you, not before or after you came into my life. You have no idea how often I wished I could forget you."

How easily she worked her magic, like a sorceress casting her spell. He hadn't realized the true potency of her charm, until now. Deep inside he felt a stirring in places he had thought hollow and empty. It had taken him seven years to free himself from the yoke of emotion. He should not pursue this conversation. It could lead nowhere. It would only leave him restless. Yet he couldn't stop himself. "What type of man will win your heart, Mari?"

She smiled. "He will be intelligent. Compassionate. Sincere. A man who will accept me for who I am, not merely because he thinks I am a fancy ornament. A man who believes in honor and loyalty. A man who is looking for the love of his life and believes he has found her in me."

He had been that type of man, a lifetime ago. Still, all that he had been had not been enough for her. "I should think after all of this time you would have imagined yourself in love with one of your beaux."

"I tried." She stared at the emerald nestled in the crisp white linen at his neck. "But I suppose love cannot be forced."

Marisa had never met her true love, whereas he had lost his a long time ago. The breeze stirred the scent of lilies around him. He lifted a curl from her shoulder, holding the ebony coil in his palm. For seven years he had kept a locket with a curl of her hair hidden inside. "What shall you do if the love of your life never crosses your path? Will you settle for something less? Or will you end your days alone?"

"I am still much too optimistic to relinquish my hopes for a love match."

"Nothing less will do?"

"I suppose in some ways I feel I would be cheating my husband of something very precious if I were to marry for convenience."

He allowed the curl to tumble from his hand. "Look around you, Mari. A great many successful marriages are based on something more practical than the illusion of love."

She lifted her gaze and looked straight into his eyes. "I suppose I want more from life. I believe love is more than an illusion."

It was more. It was a force that could rip a man into shreds. "I hope you find it, and when you do that it is all you dream it should be."

She touched his chest, resting her hand above the heart she had shattered. "Can you really settle for less?"

"I believe in taking only as much as I am capable of giving."

"You were once capable of giving a great deal."

He touched her cheek, regretting the glove that

shielded her skin from his touch. "I have changed."

"Have you?" She brushed the lily against his chin, releasing a subtle perfume. "I wonder."

What game was she playing with him? Did she think he was still the same foolish young man so easily caught in her web? "I think it's time we returned to the party, before someone decides you have been kidnapped." He gripped her arm and steered her back toward the path. "I suppose your Aunt Cecilia is your chaperon this evening."

"Yes. And I doubt she would ever suspect anyone might kidnap me."

Their footsteps crunched on the gravel path. "I suppose she would never suspect anyone might want to strangle you, either."

She brushed her fingertips along a sculpted yew as they strolled past it. "You do realize it would be wise for you to refrain from strangling me until after we catch the men who want to murder you?"

In spite of his turmoil, he smiled. "I only hope I can find the strength to resist temptation."

"I have every faith in you."

The lively notes of a country dance drifted from the ballroom as they approached the terrace. She paused at the steps and slipped the lily into the edge of his black silk waistcoat, allowing only the very tip of the flower to show. He glanced down at the small flower, then at her. What the devil was going through that dreadfully quick mind of hers?

She climbed the steps, then turned and smiled down at him. "Do you realize it has been seven years since you danced with me?"

Without another word Marisa turned and crossed the terrace. He watched her enter the house, as stunned and shaken as a soldier who had survived his first battle.

After all that had passed, their history, she had the temerity to flirt with him. Lord, he had thought himself safe from her. He had never imagined she might try to twist him around her dainty little finger again. Did she really need another conquest?

He pulled the lily from his waistcoat. The blasted female had a way of dredging things up that should remain buried and forgotten. Did she regret what had happened between them? His chest tightened with all the memories and regrets he could not deny.

Instead of entering the house, he turned back into the gardens. He would not dance to her tune. Yet he had the dreadful feeling that if he walked back into that house he would ask the beguiling witch to dance with him. Oh, lord, he really must be insane.

The confounded female had a way of turning everything upside down in his world. This evening, in the garden, he had meant to frighten her, to show her how dangerous it was to tangle with men who were not afraid to kill. Yet with a touch she had transformed all of his anger into something far more heated. He stared down at the lily, the breath tangling in his lungs. It was over. Any chance they might have had for a future ended a long time ago. He no longer possessed the capacity to give himself to anyone.

Still, in spite of his every conviction, when he returned home he withdrew a small chest from the bottom of his armoire. He laid the slender lily beside a gold locket that contained the face of an angel and an ebony curl. There were other mementos in the chest as well, things he had meant to burn but could never bring himself to toss into the flames: a blue satin ribbon from the first day he had met her, hairpins that had tumbled from her hair, letters written by a young girl who thought herself in love.

Clayton closed the small chest and drew air into his tight lungs. It was foolish to dwell on the past. Yet how did a man purge his soul of a temptress? He hadn't. That was clear. Just as it was clear that he needed to get on with his life. A life that had no place for Marisa.

The next morning Clayton sat in his library with one of the men who had served with him from the first day he had purchased his commission. "I have asked my grandmother to obtain the guest lists from both the Merrivale and Sotherby parties. She should be able to do it without stirring any gossip." Clayton smiled at Sgt. Maj. Adler Newberry. His former sergeant sat in a leather wing-back chair across from Clayton. "When I get them, I should have a good idea of where to begin."

Beneath bushy dark brows, Adler regarded Clayton with a pair of shrewd blue eyes. He was tall and broad, with a thick nose that recorded several past blows from his days in the boxing arena; his deliberate movements and unhurried speech belied his keen intelligence. Clayton had learned long ago to trust the man with his life. Since the end of the war, the sergeant major had found use for his talent at Bow Street. "Do you have any idea at all why the blackguards would want to murder you, Major?"

Clayton stared down into his cup of coffee. "They said I could spoil it all. I have been trying to think of anything I might be involved with that could cause someone so much trouble that they would want to eliminate me."

"And have you thought of anything?"

Clayton sipped his coffee. "No."

Adler's bushy brows lifted slightly. "We haven't much to go on, sir."

"I know. I think it would be a good idea for the Grantham household to acquire a new footman. I want someone to keep an eye on Lady Marisa. If these men find out she can identify them, she could be in danger."

"Aye. I'll see to it at once." Adler smiled, revealing a chipped front tooth. "Not to worry, Major; we've been through worse than this and survived. We'll find the bastards."

"I have confidence we will."

"I hope we can keep this quiet, sir. The less these men think you know of them, the better off we shall be."

Clayton nodded. "Marisa realizes how important it is to keep this contained. We shouldn't have a problem."

"I hope you're right, sir. This could get very messy if they know she can identify one of them."

Clayton's chest tightened when he thought of Marisa in danger. "It certainly could."

That evening Clayton strolled into White's, hoping for a little diversion from thoughts of a golden-eyed temptress and a murderer hidden in the shadows. He had scarcely entered the building before Roger Wormsley accosted him. Clayton suppressed the surge of anger he felt each time he saw his former tutor. Since Wormsley had wormed his way into the political arena, he often appeared at the club or the same social events that Clayton attended. Most of the time Clayton was able to avoid the man.

Wormsley had changed little in the twenty years since he had been tutor for the Duke of Marlow's sons. He was still so slender he looked as though he hadn't eaten in a month. The skin of his face was stretched so tautly over the bones, it looked as though it might crack if the man smiled. Yet he didn't seem as tall as he had when Clayton was a boy. And his light brown hair had thinned until it revealed glimpses of his scalp.

Wormsley smiled, the skin crinkling at the corners of his small brown eyes. "I heard a most peculiar rumor about you."

"I have found it wise not to believe rumors."

Wormsley touched his coat when Clayton started to leave. Clayton glanced down at the bony hand upon his dark gray sleeve, then glared at the man.

Wormsley snatched away his hand, an uneasy expression crossing his features. "I thought you might find this rumor interesting."

Clayton inclined his head. "Did you?"

Wormsley shifted on his feet. "I heard someone wants to murder you. Apparently Lady Marisa Grantham overheard two men in the Merrivale maze discussing ways to bring about your demise."

Clayton had long ago learned to hide his emotions. Tonight his discipline served him well. He held Wormsley's excited gaze without so much as blinking. "You shouldn't believe everything you hear."

Wormsley flicked his tongue over his thin lips. "I thought it was a great deal of rubbish. If it were your brother, I could understand."

"Could you?"

Wormsley's eyes grew wide at the icy tone of Clayton's voice. "I only meant, you were always far more responsible than your brother. Far less likely to get into trouble. That is all. I certainly never intended to insult His Grace."

"I am glad to hear that." Clayton lifted one brow. "My brother is an excellent shot."

"Yes. Yes, I am certain he is." Beads of moisture dotted Wormsley's high brow. "I understand you are advising Lord Hempstead on the ministry position vacated by the death of Mr. Stedman."

"He has asked my opinion of the candidates."

"I always said you had excellent judgment." Wormsley dabbed at his brow with his handkerchief. "I am certain you will look at the qualities of each candidate and choose the gentleman with the best qualifications. You would never allow some small incident in the past to influence your decision."

Clayton curved his lips into a smile designed to chill the man's blood. "I think I can manage to be fair."

Without another word, he left Wormsley standing in the hall. If Wormsley knew about Marisa, that meant half of London must know. By the time he made his way to one of the salons, three other gentlemen had stopped him with similar questions about Marisa, confirming his fears. Although he had deflected their questions, Clayton knew the damage had already been done. He ordered a bottle of Irish whiskey from one of the servants, then joined three of his friends, who sat at a table near the hearth.

"Just the man we were talking about," Gregory said, lifting his wineglass to Clayton.

Clayton cringed inwardly as he sank into a leather-upholstered armchair between Gregory and Miles Cranely. "It would seem a common enough activity this evening."

Miles lifted his quizzing glass and inspected Clayton's cravat. "I say, that is a particularly splendid waterfall."

Clayton smiled at the slim, fair-haired young man sitting beside him. Like Braden and Gregory, they had spent their days at Harrow together. If Miles had ever joined the army, he would have been one of those men who could ride through the heat of battle and still keep his cravat in perfect order. "I shall relay your compliments to my valet."

Braden rolled his brandy snifter between his palms. "I take it you have heard the rumors."

"I did walk through the door." A footman placed a glass on the table before Clayton, filled it, then placed the bottle of Irish whiskey beside the glass.

"You are just the man who can set us straight," Miles said, once the footman had left.

Clayton lifted his glass. "I believe you give me far too much credit."

Gregory grinned at Clayton over the rim of his wine-glass. "Perhaps, but you can tell us if there is any truth to the rumors."

The rich aroma flooded his senses as Clayton lifted his glass. He sipped his whiskey, the liquor warming his mouth and throat. Yet it did little to ease the tightening in the pit of his stomach. There was no way to quell a rumor once it took hold of the ton. The men who were behind this plot would soon know everything, including Marisa's involvement—if they didn't already know.

"When Justin was shot, we all assumed it was someone intent on sending him to his maker. A jealous husband, perhaps." Braden laughed softly. "Lord knows they can be nuisances."

"Now it seems someone was actually trying to murder you," Gregory said.

"I heard all about it at the Sotherbys' last night." Miles tapped the edge of his quizzing glass against his chin. "Rumor has it, Marisa Grantham overheard a gang of men discussing your murder at the Merrivales' ball."

Debra Dier

"Sounds like nonsense." Braden leaned back in his chair. "Is it?"

Clayton twisted his glass on the table. "Half of London must know by now."

"Then it is true." Gregory leaned forward and rested his forearm on the arm of his chair. "Why the devil would someone want to murder you?"

Clayton shook his head. "I have been asking myself that question for days."

"Now, if it were Justin, I could think of several men who might want to murder him." Miles grinned at Clayton. "All over one woman or another."

"I doubt it has anything to do with a woman." Although at the moment, Clayton could think of one female he would like to lock in the tower of Huntingdon House until this business was settled.

"You don't have any idea who it might be?" Braden asked.

"Two men who think I could spoil something for them. What that might be is still a mystery."

"You have no idea what this is all about?" Gregory asked.

"None at all."

"Why the devil does someone take a notion to murder a man?" Miles twisted the ribbon of his quizzing glass, setting the glass spinning, the lens scattering the spark of candlelight. "Jealousy. Greed. Anger."

"Fear." Braden looked up from his contemplation of the brandy in his glass. "They said you could spoil something for them. It sounds as though they are afraid of something you will do. Or something you know."

"Perhaps it was something from your days as a spy in France." Miles tapped his quizzing glass against his chin. "Perhaps there was a traitor you never caught. Perhaps he is afraid you will recognize him."

Clayton smiled. "I am afraid I cannot recall any traitor during the time I was in the army."

"Is there anything we can do to help?" Braden asked.

"Yes." Gregory smoothed his fingertip around the rim of his wineglass. "Perhaps we could commence an investigation of some kind."

"That's a capital idea." Miles rested his quizzing glass against his chin. "Of course, I haven't the slightest idea of where to begin. Anyone?"

"According to rumor, Marisa Grantham can recognize one of the men by his voice," Gregory said. "She should be a great help."

Clayton squeezed his glass. "It isn't wise to believe everything you hear."

Gregory lifted his brows. "Then Marisa isn't able to identify either man?"

Clayton intended to do everything he could to shield Marisa from this mess. "Their voices were muffled. She isn't even certain of everything they said."

Gregory frowned. "Pity."

"Where does that leave us?" Miles asked.

Fortunately Clayton had made more than a few investigations during his time in the army. "It is possible one of the men is average in height, slender, with fair hair."

Miles grinned. "You could be describing me."

"I could be describing half the men in London." Clayton swirled the whiskey in his glass. "I can only hope to find him before he finds a way to eliminate me." And he had to find a way to keep a certain infuriating, stubborn beauty from danger.

Chapter Sixteen

It was after midnight when Clayton left White's. Instead of taking his carriage home, he directed his driver to return without him. He needed to walk. He needed to decide upon the best course of action. Something had to be done about Marisa.

He prowled the West End, occasionally passing a house where candlelight and music flowed into the street. A few carriages clattered past him, kicking up dust from the stone pavement. It was too early for the ton to flutter home, too late for them to drift to another party. Without even realizing where he was headed, he found himself at his destination. He stood in Berkeley Square, across from the Westbury town house. The house was dark. Apparently the ladies had not ventured out for the evening.

How the devil could he convince Marisa to leave town until he could take care of this business? The beautiful hen-wit had no idea how dangerous it might be for her. Arguing with her would only make him frustrated enough to put his fist through a wall. As the watchman sang his ode to one o'clock, Clayton realized the only way to convince her would be to demonstrate precisely what she might be facing. The lady needed a lesson in life. And he was just the man to teach it to her.

He made his way to the back of the house. The gate was locked, but that didn't stop him. He climbed the brick wall encasing the gardens and dropped softly to the thick grass. Not a single light glowed in the darkness of the house. Still, there was enough moonlight to illuminate the windows on the second floor. He knew which windows looked out from Marisa's room. She had once, a lifetime ago, tossed him a kiss from a window of her bedchamber.

Clayton crossed the garden, and slipped his hand into the thick ivy covering the wall, seeking purchase. As he began to scale the wall, he thought of Marisa lying in her bed. Heat spilled into his blood as images crept into his mind. Her wayward black waves tumbled across the white linen of her pillow, pale moonlight brushing the smooth curve of her cheek, her lips parted with the soft rhythm of her breath, awaiting his touch. Countless times he had imagined holding her through the night. Countless mornings he had awakened with his arms wrapped around his pillow, aching and empty, humiliated by the longing he couldn't suppress.

With sheer force of will he crushed the images from his mind. He was not doing this for any romantic reason. He certainly had no intention of threatening her virtue. He was doing this only to make her see reason. Thick ivy vines clung to the bricks, allowing precarious footholds.

By the time he reached the first floor, he was beginning to doubt the wisdom of his actions. When he reached the second, he was certain of his own insanity. He gripped the sill of the open window, pulled himself up, and looked straight into the business end of a pistol.

"Lovely night for a climb," Marisa said, keeping the pistol aimed at a point between his brows.

A bead of perspiration trickled down his spine. "Put that thing away before it goes off in my face."

"Put it away? And leave myself defenseless?"

"That's like saying a tigress is defenseless without a club."

The pistol remained pointed at his head. "How do I know you haven't some nefarious reason for coming here tonight? I do recall your mentioning you would like to strangle me."

"Confound it, Mari. Put the blasted thing away before I lose my footing."

She lifted her brows in an expression filled with mock astonishment. "You want me to let you come in?"

He glanced over his shoulder, his stomach tightening as the ground seemed to stretch farther away from him. "Don't make a game of this."

"I wouldn't think of it. Not when it is so very improper." She pressed her fingertip to her lips. "You know, I am certain there is one, but I really cannot think of the proper response when a lady finds a gentleman about to climb uninvited into the window of her bedchamber."

"In this case, I suggest you let him come in. Otherwise, you must consider the mess my shattered body shall leave for your gardener."

Marisa glanced past him and stared down into the gardens below. "You would very likely land in the roses. Mama is very fond of those roses. She would not be pleased if you crushed them.''

''By all means, we must think of the roses.''

''Of course, you might miss the roses and smash into the perennial bed. In which case—''

At that point Clayton snapped. He yanked the pistol from her hand and tossed it to the floor. It thumped on the carpet.

''Do be careful,'' she said, her voice a harsh whisper. ''You'll have half the household up to investigate.''

He ignored her, concentrating instead on climbing into the room. When his feet touched the floor, he straightened and faced her, appalled to find his limbs trembling.

She smiled up at him. ''You know, you really must learn discretion if you are ever to become a proper burglar.''

''You are impossible.''

''Me?'' She waved her arm toward the window. ''I am not the one climbing about like a lunatic. Good heavens, you might have fallen and snapped your neck.''

''Now you consider that possibility.''

She tilted her head, fixing him with one of her direct looks. ''Why did you come here tonight?''

Heat prickled his neck as he thought of the fool he had made of himself. ''I had some foolish notion of showing you the danger you might be facing. I should have realized it would blow up in my face. I swear, if we had used you as an incendiary device during the war, Napoleon would have tucked his tail and fled in terror years ago.''

''You came to show me the danger I am in?'' Marisa leaned toward him, her voice lowering to a husky whisper. "Does that mean you have something wicked in mind?"

"No. I do not." Flirtation was as natural to the infuriating female as breathing. "I have never made a habit of seducing innocent females. I assume you still fall into that category."

"You need not be insulting." She brushed her fingertips over the pale blue ribbon that was threaded through the neckline of her nightgown and dangled just below the hollow of her collarbones. "You shall have to excuse me for asking your intention, but when a gentleman climbs into a lady's bedchamber, it does make that lady wonder what he has in mind."

"My only intent was to warn you." Clayton didn't mean to allow his gaze to wander from her gorgeous face, but he was a man, and blast it, he couldn't help himself. Especially not when she was wearing nothing except a filmy white nightgown, a bit of fine lawn that outlined every luscious curve of her body. His gaze traveled down to where her toes peeked out from beneath the hem of her gown, then made a slow ascent, devouring everything in its path.

The soft swell of her breasts rose and fell with her breath. He paused, his gaze snagging on the dark shading revealed by the thin material—twin, berry-shaped nipples pressed wantonly against the cloth. Blood pumped swift and hot into his loins. Heaven help him, her nipples were taut and high and so tempting he ached with the need to touch her.

"You came to warn me?"

Her soft voice dragged his wayward gaze back to her face. She was smiling in a way that told him she knew exactly what she was doing to him. Maddening female! "Why the devil didn't you put on a dressing gown?"

"I was too concerned with preventing an intruder from crashing into my bedchamber."

He only wished she were as concerned about her state of undress. "Where is it?"

She lifted her brows. "What?"

"Your dressing gown."

"Oh. It's on the chair by the bed."

Moonlight guided him across the room. He snatched the dressing gown from the chair, and cursed his luck. The blasted thing was a slip of silk. He would have preferred it to be along the same lines as a horse blanket. He marched back to the windows and thrust the flimsy garment at her. "Put it on."

She slipped into the wrapper but didn't fasten the gold loops to the buttons running down the front of the garment. "I don't see why you are getting so upset about my clothing. What did you think I would be wearing when you decided to climb into my bedchamber in the middle of the night?"

"I expected you to be in bed."

"Wearing my riding habit?"

Clayton clenched his teeth. "I thought you would be covered by the bedclothes. I expected to—Oh, confound it! Why can't you ever do what a man expects you to do? You were supposed to be sleeping."

She shrugged, her slender shoulders rising beneath sapphire blue silk. "It's just one of my many faults, I suppose."

In spite of the frustration churning in his gut, he couldn't prevent a smile. He had to admit that Marisa was never boring.

"You still haven't explained why you came here tonight."

"There is a rumor flying about London. Half of London knows about what you overheard in the Merrivales' garden. The other half will know by tomorrow."

A frown marred her brow as she fiddled with the ribbon exposed by her open wrapper. "You came here tonight to frighten me? To make me realize how dangerous it is for me to stay in town?"

He frowned, feeling like an idiot. "Something like that."

"I suppose you thought discussing the matter with me would be pointless."

"Do you mean to say you would see reason and leave London?"

"No. I have no intention of leaving town."

He rubbed the skin between his brows, his mind grappling with the problem known as Marisa. "You don't seem to realize that you might very well become a target."

"Perhaps. But I cannot imagine they would be overly concerned about me. Once you are dead, even if I were to identify the murderer, I could hardly prove anything."

He cringed at the easy way she discussed his murder. "Perhaps he won't wish to take the chance of being identified, before or after my demise."

She tilted her head at a defiant angle. "That is a chance I am willing to take."

"I'm not. I want you out of this mess."

"Be reasonable, Clay. I have the best chance of finding this man before he can murder anyone."

"I don't want you involved in this."

She folded her hands at her waist. "I believe we have had this discussion before, but just in case you don't remember, let me refresh your memory. I am already involved."

Clayton leaned toward her and gave her his best scowl, a look that had set seasoned soldiers trembling in their boots. Marisa held his steady gaze without flinching. "I can take care of myself. How do you suppose I would feel if I left town and they succeeded in murdering you?" she asked. "I have to do everything I can to help."

A tantalizing fragrance of lilies after rain swirled through his senses, ambushing his resolve. He fought to remain focused. "I won't have your death on my conscience."

"Then stop asking me to leave town, and help me find these men before they can hurt anyone else."

"You are the most stubborn, infuriating female." He muttered an oath under his breath. "What the devil am I going to do with you?"

Marisa smiled up at him, her eyes filled with a dangerous glint. "I will leave town, if you agree to come with me."

"I have to find these men."

"Precisely. Neither of us will truly be safe until they are caught. Who is to say what would happen to me if they managed to murder you? The best chance I have of staying alive is to help put these men in prison."

Although he hated to admit it, he could see some logic—twisted though it might be—in her thoughts. "Nothing short of kidnapping will get you out of town, will it?"

Her eyes narrowed. "I shall take it very badly if you decide to do something so high-handed."

Although he hadn't completely dismissed the tactic, he regarded kidnapping as a last, desperate measure. Such an action would only result in marriage to the infuriating witch, a fate that might prove worse than what they faced from a pair of murderers. "I don't want you taking any unnecessary risks. That means you

267

won't go around following strangers unless I am with you."

"I promise."

"If anyone asks you about what you heard that night, tell them you couldn't possibly identify either man. You could scarcely hear them. With any luck the blackguards will stop thinking you are a threat."

"That sounds reasonable."

He released his breath in a long sigh. "If it does, I'm surprised you recognize it."

She crinkled her nose. "I am often reasonable."

"I don't see how you manage to find time to be reasonable, with all the time you devote to being stubborn."

She smiled up at him, a cat who had just found her way into the cream pot. "I promise I shall not take any unnecessary risks."

The back of his neck prickled. "I warn you, if I think you are taking risks, I will see to it you spend a very long time in the country."

She stared up at him a long moment in that way she had of piercing any defense he might try to raise against her. He prepared himself for a battle that didn't come.

"I was thinking."

"I always get nervous when you try that."

She glared at him in mock anger. "We might get the lists from the Merrivale and Sotherby parties and compare them to see what men were at both."

"I've already arranged it."

She looked pleased with him, and in spite of his best intentions, that look of admiration warmed him. "I've been going over in my mind everything I heard in the garden that night. I keep wondering what they meant by 'he could spoil it all.' Can you think of anything you are currently involved with, perhaps a political or financial venture, that could make someone so desperate he might want to murder you?''

"I have been treading the same territory."

"And you still have no idea who might be behind this?''

"I'm involved in nothing out of the ordinary."

"What might seem ordinary may mean a great deal to these men.''

"Perhaps. But I still find nothing to enlighten me."

"Pity." She smiled up at him, mischief glinting in her eyes. "Are you certain you haven't any spurned ladybirds, a female who might enjoy seeing you draw your last breath?''

"I have been a little too preoccupied these past few years to keep a ladybird.''

"Yes. I suppose you have." She touched his arm. "We shall stop them, Clay. We have to."

Moonlight unveiled the beauty of her face—the artfully carved features, the slight upward tilt of her large eyes, the dimple at the corner of her smile—all combining to capture and hold a man's attention. Yet her beauty was a result not only of the delicate carving of her features, but of the glow that came from within. Warmth and light, when she smiled it was the sun breaking out of the clouds on a bleak and gray afternoon. When she smiled at him, it seemed she smiled only for him, as though all of her warmth, all of her light, were gathered and given for his pleasure alone.

He lowered his eyes, his gaze resting upon her lovely smile. She was so close he could feel her warmth. So close her fragrance drifted with that beguiling warmth, tempting him, luring him. Strands of longing wrapped around him, as gossamer as moonlight, as strong as steel, drawing him to her. His heart beat a rapid rhythm. He had to get away from her. Now. Before he made a complete fool of himself.

"I had better leave," he said, his voice husky to his own ears.

"Yes. I suppose you should."

In spite of her words, her fingers tightened around his arm. He gathered his will. Still, he could not find the strength to pull away from the gentle grasp of her hand.

"I have often wondered what it might be like to stand with you again in the moonlight. Just the two of us." Marisa lifted herself toward him. "It has been such a terribly long time."

Clayton heard the longing in her soft voice, saw the need in her beautiful eyes, and felt his will unravel. He couldn't allow this to happen. He had exorcised her from his soul. He would not . . .

She kissed him, a gentle brush of her lips against his. Soft and cool, a sip of water on a hot summer day. His will snapped like dry kindling beneath her gentle touch. She was the rain, sweet and cool, and he was the desert, parched and hungry for each blessed drop falling upon him.

He cinched his arms around her, like a man tumbling to his death snatching a lifeline. She came to him, linking her arms around his neck, pressing against him, as though she could not get close enough to him. Desire made more potent with each passing year pumped through his veins, more intoxicating than brandy. Longing surged within him, a flame searing reason into ashes. Too many regrets crammed his heart. Too many nights he had dreamed of holding her this way. Too many nights he had stared into the darkness and imagined her lying beside him. Sense had no chance.

"I love your mouth," she whispered against his lips.

"So warm and firm. I feel I'm melting in your arms."

Her soft voice caressed him, awakened the longing for her he could not deny. He dragged his hands over her back, learning the shape of her through the layers of silk and lawn. Yet it wasn't enough, not nearly enough to satisfy seven years of wanting her. He needed the smooth heat of her skin against his hands, his lips, his tongue.

He had held countless women since the day Marisa had banished him from her life. Yet with every kiss he had imagined Marisa in his arms. Still, his imagination paled in the face of reality. Her lips parted beneath his, as eager as in his dreams, made sweeter by an innocent maiden's ardor. She kissed him as though the years had never separated them. As though she still believed the promises they had made on a moonlit night a lifetime ago. As though she needed him as much as he needed her.

The part of his brain still functioning loudly recounted all the reasons he should not become involved with this woman. All the heartache. All the pain. This was madness. He didn't need or want the emotions plowing through him. It was too dangerous. He had fought too hard to free himself. This had to stop. Now.

She gripped his shoulders, wiggling against him, a lithe creature of the moonlight seeking to burrow her way straight into his skin. Her breasts brushed his chest. His muscles quivered and tensed in response, eager to plunge into the danger that was Marisa.

He dragged his lips over her cheek, down the slim column of her neck, while he slipped his restless hand between them. Cool silk slid beneath his palm. His fingers curved over her firm breast, and beneath the silk and fine lawn he felt her nipple. He wanted to brush his cheeks against the plush warmth of her bare breasts, taste her, inhale the scent of her deep into his lungs.

Marisa whimpered low in her throat as he rolled the taut tip between his fingers. "I want your hands on me, your skin against mine. I have wanted it for a lifetime," she blurted out.

So had he. Heaven help him, so had he. Yet a slender thread of reason kept him from the fall. The path she was leading him down ended in disaster. He recognized the stirring within him, acknowledged the danger of it. Over the last seven years he had managed to bury his emotions. It had been the only way to survive. Yet it was a shallow grave, and each rested in fitful slumber. It was better this way, empty and safe. Marisa would slice him open again. She would rip all of his emotions from their graves. She would force him to feel again.

Clayton lifted his head and stared down at her. She blinked, as though she had risen from a deep slumber. She stared at him, a thousand questions shimmering in her eyes. The answers were better not contemplated.

"Confound you!" He gripped her arms and tugged them from his neck. "You could tempt a blasted saint."

She frowned, looking as bewildered as he felt. "I must be doing something wrong. You certainly seem able to resist."

"I am not a saint. I never was." He sat on the windowsill and swung his legs over the ledge.

"You aren't going to climb back down? It's far too dangerous. You could break your neck."

It was more dangerous staying here. "I'll manage."

She touched his arm. "Let me show you to one of the doors leading to the gardens."

"No. Thank you." Clayton gently disengaged his arm. If he didn't get away from her now, the last shred of his will would crumble beneath her. He climbed out of the window and began his descent.

Marisa stood beside her window, watching as Clayton slowly climbed down the ivy-covered wall. The man had obviously lost his mind. She sucked in her breath as his foot slipped in the ivy. "Clayton, for heaven's sake, be careful."

"Go to bed," he growled in a harsh whisper, before he returned his attention to his task.

She held her ground, watching him, her breath lodged in her throat. After what seemed an eternity, he dropped safely to the ground. He jogged through the gardens, and climbed the wall enclosing them. He paused on the top of the thick brick wall and glanced back at the house. She waved to him. He frowned back at her before lowering himself down the opposite side of the wall. She stared into the gardens and replayed in her mind everything that had happened from the first moment she had heard someone scaling the wall beneath her bedchamber.

She prided herself on possessing a strong understanding of the male of the species. Most males, that was. At the moment she had to admit a certain bewilderment. Clayton wanted her, that at least she knew without a doubt. If she had been a dish of pudding, he would have devoured every morsel, then licked the dish.

Marisa leaned her shoulder against the window frame and contemplated the puzzle. Why would he leave without taking what she had so brazenly offered? She seriously doubted she had injured his delicate sense of propriety. But Clayton had escaped her room as though the hounds of hell had been nipping at his heels.

What had she done to startle him? Oh, well, the puzzle could wait until morning. She felt deliciously sleepy. Clayton wanted her, and where desire dwelled, hope prospered. ''My darling Clay, you may run if you wish, but you cannot escape me. I have no intention of letting you get away from me. Not this time.''

Chapter Seventeen

Although there were those in London who were certain the heavens would turn black, the sun shone in a clear sky on the morning of the eighteenth day of May in the year of our Lord eighteen hundred and sixteen, when Justin Hayward Peyton Trevelyan entered St. George's Hanover Square to speak his marriage vows. More than a few in attendance expected the bride to flee in terror at the last moment. Yet Isabel, eldest daughter of the Baron of Bramsleigh, stood beside the devilishly handsome Duke of Marlow and spoke her vows in a clear voice that held no hint of doubt.

After the ceremony a select group of guests, some two hundred and thirty-three strong, filed into Marlow House to partake of a wedding breakfast and celebrate a union that had set tongues wagging for weeks. The Devil of Dartmoor had actually taken a bride. Although it was a trifle eccentric, after a feast had been served, the guests were treated to dancing in the ballroom. The Duke of Marlow made his own rules.

Marisa sat on a gilt-trimmed chair in the ballroom, flanked by Braden Fitzwilliam and Gregory Stanwood, watching as Justin led his new bride through the graceful turns of a waltz. Tall and slender, her dark golden hair a mass of curls upon her head, her blue eyes fixed on her new husband, Isabel looked beautiful, and so happy no one could doubt she was precisely where she wanted to be. Never in her life had Marisa seen two people more obviously in love. The depth of their feelings for one another showed in every touch, every glance. Justin and Isabel might have been alone in the room, for all they noticed anyone around them.

Gregory watched the newly married couple as he spoke. "I would have wagered Clayton would be the first to speak his vows."

"I suppose he would have if he hadn't marched off to war." Braden sipped his champagne. "Still, I never could decipher that piece of business. He never mentioned anything about the army until that night at White's when he stunned us all."

"Harry actually tried to coax me into joining them in their insanity." Gregory glanced into his glass of champagne, his expression growing somber. "Poor Harry. I still find it hard to believe he won't be coming home."

"Unfortunately, my brother had a taste for glory." A muscle bunched in Braden's lean cheek with the clenching of his jaw. "I'm certain Clayton had another reason for going. He never had the same impetuous streak that cursed my brother."

Marisa glanced to where Clayton stood near the entrance to the adjoining music room. In spite of the elegant drape of his dark gray coat, the perfection of his linen, there was something dangerous about him, dark and primal, something that plunged her heart into a headlong tumble. His attention was focused on his brother and Isabel, a wistful smile on his lips. She hadn't seen him in the two days since he had climbed into her bedchamber and teased her with a glimpse of heaven. He was avoiding her. Why? What was he afraid of?

"I have always thought it was a woman who sent Clayton off to war," Braden said. "Harry had the same suspicion."

Marisa squeezed her glass of lemonade. "Your brother thought Clayton had purchased a commission because of a woman?"

"Although Clayton had never confided in him, Harry mentioned his suspicions more than once." Braden smiled at her. "Tell me, fair Psyche, have you ever heard any lady boasting of her conquest of Huntingdon's tender heart?"

Marisa slid her gloved fingertip over a droplet of water sliding down her glass. "I suspect any woman who would boast of such things would not be a lady."

Braden's black brows lifted, his dark eyes glinting pure mischief. "Does this mean you have never delighted in any of your conquests?"

"I am hardly a conqueror."

"Not true." Braden pressed his hand to his heart. "You conquered my heart long ago, dear lady."

Marisa tilted her head and smiled at him. "Strange, I thought you were one of the pack seeking Miss Darracott's hand."

"I fancied the idea for a brief moment. Only because you keep refusing me." Braden gave her one of his most beguiling smiles. "When shall you take pity on me and accept my suit?"

Gregory grinned at his cousin. "The lady has more sense than that."

Braden never took his gaze from Marisa. "So much sense she finds us all lacking, including you, cousin."

"It proves she has good sense." Gregory smiled at her over the rim of his glass. "Tell me, are you still trying to hunt down the men you overheard plotting to murder Clayton?"

Marisa managed a smile. "You have been listening to too many rumors. I certainly didn't hear them clearly enough to recognize either of them."

Gregory smiled. "Then there should be no reason for you to worry about trouble from these men."

"I am certain the lady has enough sense to stay away from them altogether." Braden smiled at her. "It is hardly the type of diversion fit for a beautiful woman."

"I told Clayton this morning, he might want to stay hidden awhile. Leave town." Gregory twisted the stem of his glass, swirling the golden liquid in the crystal. "Perhaps in time these men will change their minds, stop trying to murder him."

As much as Marisa would like to believe that was true, she thought it unlikely for a pair of murderers to give up without a good reason.

"And tell me, dear lady, when will you change your mind about marriage?" Braden asked, deftly guiding the conversation in a different direction, one he obviously felt was better suited for her delicate ears. He grinned at her. "You keep us all in suspense, wondering who will be the fortunate man to win your hand."

"If you want my cousin, better accept him soon. He is in a bad way," Gregory said, his voice dropping to a conspiratorial tone. "He has some notion of marrying to preserve the succession. Since poor Harry won't be doing his duty, it's left up to Braden. Must keep the title of Earl of Ashbourne in his bloodline. Won't have it fall to the cadet branch, you know. Before we know it, he'll be leg-shackled to the next female he meets.''

Marisa knew Braden had his choice of women. He was an earl, wealthy, and so handsome he could drop a female into a swoon with one generous smile.

Braden pinned his cousin with a chilly glare. ''Haven't you someone else you wish to speak to?''

''Very well. No need to hit me over the head.'' Gregory stood and tugged on the hem of his claret-colored coat. ''I shall spread my eloquence elsewhere.''

Braden took Marisa's hand once Gregory had left. ''Tell me, my darling, what will it take to win your heart?''

Marisa looked into his beautiful dark eyes and saw the sincerity of his question. ''I am obviously a hen-wit, or I would have succumbed to your charm long ago.''

''You are too wise to be fooled by a rogue's charm. Still, you may just be able to reform me.'' Braden squeezed her hand. ''Look at how Miss Darracott has changed Justin. She tamed the Devil.''

''Justin is in love with Isabel. It makes all the difference in the world.''

He looked down at her hand. ''I do adore you. There isn't another woman I would rather marry.''

Braden was the most persistent of the gentlemen who sought her hand. Over the years she had seriously considered marrying him each time he had offered for her. Several times she had come close to accepting him. He was an undeniably charming rogue, sinfully handsome, entertaining, generous. She had always enjoyed his company. He would make a charming husband, as long as she didn't mind his mistresses. Yet the very fact that she *didn't* mind his mistresses was enough to keep her from taking the final step in his direction. "I suppose I have rather foolish ideas about marriage that include fidelity."

Braden grimaced. "I would do my best."

"I know you would."

"And I might actually succeed in changing my wicked ways."

Marisa smiled. "Might you?"

"Yes." Braden squeezed her hand. "I once thought it wasn't possible for a man like me to change. But I have seen it happen. And I see how happy Justin is."

"Braden, I—"

"Don't give me your answer yet. You are a woman who should have a husband and children, my beautiful Psyche." Braden pressed his lips to the back of her gloved hand. "And I am a man who has decided it is time to marry. Promise only that you shall give my offer some thought."

She realized this would be the last time he would ever offer her marriage. It left her with a strange, hollow feeling, as though she had already made that tumble into spinsterhood. Which would truly be worse? Marriage to a man destined to wander? Or life alone, pining for a stubborn man who seemed intent on avoiding her? "I promise, Braden. I will consider all you have said."

"That is all I can ask." As the orchestra began the strains of another waltz, Braden smiled. "May I have the honor of this dance?"

"I am afraid the lady has already promised this dance to me."

The dark resonance of Clayton's lush baritone rippled through her. Marisa turned her head as Clayton paused in front of her. Her gaze traveled upward, over a silver waistcoat and white linen, to the devastating male beauty of his face. He smiled as she met his gaze, a cool curving of his lips that seemed at odds with the glitter in his eyes.

Clayton took the glass from her hand and gave it to Braden. "Look after this awhile."

Braden lifted his brows. "I don't suppose I could convince you to give her up to me."

"No." Clayton offered Marisa his hand. "Shall we?"

Clayton hadn't asked her. He had simply sauntered over and claimed her. If any other man had dared such tactics, she would have sent him straight to the devil. Yet this was not any other man. And poor bewildered, besotted bedlamite that she was, she could not prevent the excitement sprinting through her. She slipped her hand in his.

The simple barriers of propriety could not prevent the spark of contact. It penetrated the gloves they both wore. It darted along her nerves, bringing her senses into sharp focus. She glanced up and caught a glimpse of surprise in his eyes before it vanished beneath the cool surface of his composure.

"Do you know, it is strange, but I don't recall your having asked to dance with me," she said as he led her onto the dance floor.

"Didn't I?" He clasped her waist, the warmth of his gloved hand penetrating her gown, inching her temperature upward. "I am certain I meant to."

She was not a silly schoolgirl, she assured herself in a valiant attempt to slow her racing heart. She had danced with more gentlemen than she could remember. Yet this was the first time Clayton had ever held her in the embrace of the waltz. Power and grace filled his every move. Everything else in the room dissolved into a blur of color and light. Clayton remained the only solid substance in her world.

Marisa followed him through the intricate sweeping turns, without thought to the steps her feet must make. It seemed so wonderfully natural, as if her body responded to his on a level that required nothing more than instinct, which, under the circumstances, was a blessing. Her brain had stopped rational thought the moment he had touched her.

"Are you angry with me?"

She stared up into his eyes. "Angry?"

"For interrupting you and Braden. You looked as though you were in serious conversation."

"You were rather high-handed. I suppose I should be angry." She stared at the emerald winking at her from the elegant folds of his cravat. "Still, I find it impossible to manage any anger, when I have been hoping to dance with you for such a long time."

He flexed his fingers against her waist. "Always the coquette."

She lifted her gaze to his eyes, where a glint of wariness glowed in the silvery green depths. "Do you think I am flirting with you?"

His brows lifted. "Aren't you?"

She smiled. "I suppose I am."

"You should be careful of flirtation. It could win you more trouble than you want." The warm pressure of his hand on her waist drew her closer. He swept her into a turn, bringing her flush against his chest for a moment before once again allowing the proper amount of space between them.

The sudden contact stole the breath from her lungs. She looked up into his eyes and saw a glimmer of something dangerously close to anger lingering there. Yet she suspected anger was only a small part of what he was feeling. "Why do I get the impression you are trying to teach me another lesson?"

He shook his head. "I suspect any attempt to teach you a lesson would merely result in a great deal of frustration on my part."

"You are angry with me."

"I'm not angry with you."

She lifted her brows. "No?"

"No." He swept her into a graceful turn. "I want to apologize for what happened the other night."

"I should think you would. You did leave rather abruptly."

One corner of his mouth tightened. "I should have left a great deal earlier. In truth, I never should have come."

Just as she'd thought. He was angrier at himself for surrendering to temptation than he was at her for tempting him. "Would it help your conscience if I told you I enjoyed your visit?"

His lips flattened. "It would be better for both of us if we didn't explore that avenue of thought."

"And you find it so easy to put it from your mind?"

He studied the white rosebuds entwined in the intricately woven braids atop her head. "You are still one of the most beautiful women I have ever seen. What man would not be tempted to bend society's rules when he is near you?"

She tried to settle her heart. She needed to think clearly. "I have never been tempted with any other man. Only you."

He squeezed her hand, a haunted look crossing his features. "I am not the man you knew, Mari. And I am certainly not the man you need in your life."

She smiled up into his wary eyes. "Are you certain of that?"

"Yes."

Obviously the poor man had no idea what was best for her. Fortunately she knew what they both needed.

He swung her into a sweeping turn as the waltz ended. He held her until the last notes had faded from the air, then stepped back, leaving her craving his embrace. "Thank you for the honor."

"I have often wondered what it might be like to waltz with you," she said, looking up into the face that had haunted her dreams. "Now that I have, I realize everything I imagined was wrong."

He frowned. "Wrong?"

She smiled up at him, deliberately allowing the moment to stretch between them before she replied. "Waltzing with you was far more exciting than I imagined."

Clayton looked as though she had slammed her fist into his chest. His lips parted but not a single syllable escaped. He stood staring at her as though she were his worst nightmare come to life. She saw that look for what it was—the look of a man who realized his heart was not as safe as he thought it to be. "Flirtation with the wrong man will win you a great deal of trouble, Mari."

It was clear he thought he was the wrong man. Why? She wanted to ask him that and a hundred other questions. Unfortunately, Braden Fitzwilliam chose that moment to claim her for the next dance. Clayton turned away from her and marched across the room. Sophia's words echoed in her memory: *In some way, Clayton has closed himself off from everyone.* He wanted to keep her at a safe distance. Marisa could sense it. He didn't trust her. And she supposed he had good reason. She glided through the steps of a cotillion and contemplated ways to storm the barricade Clayton had erected around himself.

Clayton sat on a sofa in the library of Marlow House and stared into the fireplace. Sunlight slanted through the windows, glinting on the polished andirons. The woman was impossible. A future with Marisa was completely out of the realm of possibility. Yet something about her made him think that all things were possible. The distant strains of music drifting from the ballroom grew louder as the door opened and Justin entered the room.

"There you are." Justin closed the door and crossed the room. "Are you all right?"

Clayton molded his lips into a smile. "Fine. I was just sitting here thinking of how lucky you are."

"I am lucky. Luckier than I deserve." Justin sat on the burgundy velvet beside his brother. "More than once today I thought of how close I came to losing Isabel. I nearly allowed my blasted pride to deprive me of the most precious gift in this world."

"There were a few times in the past months when I thought you needed a good swift kick in your hindquarters."

Justin stared into the fireplace as though he were gathering his thoughts before he spoke. "I learned something recently, something I would have scoffed at before I met Isabel."

Clayton grinned at his twin. "That could be any of a thousand things."

Justin laughed softly. "True. I did tend to scoff at the world. If Isabel hadn't barged into my life, I imagine I would have gone on as I was, growing more cynical with each passing day, content with the various depravities I had cultivated, the loveless affairs, the meaningless attempts to ease my boredom. In the end I would have gone to my grave a shell. No more empty than I was in life.''

Clayton stared at the streaks of black etched against the bricks at the back of the fireplace. He was a shell. He might have survived the war, but all the life had been drained from him.

''With Isabel I have found more than I ever imagined possible,'' Justin said, his voice low and soft. ''Her love is more precious to me than my life.''

''She loves you very deeply.''

Justin smoothed a crease in his pearl gray breeches. ''Not every man finds the one woman who holds the missing half of his soul. If you have a chance, if you find her, you should grab her with both hands and never let her go.''

''Good advice.'' Clayton rested his forearms on his thighs and clasped his hands between his knees. ''Except it's a little late for me.''

''I don't think it is. Marisa still cares for you; I can sense it.''

''I doubt Marisa is capable of fixing her affection for very long. I suspect she enjoys collecting hearts the way some people like to pin butterflies to a board.''

Justin shook his head. ''I think you're wrong about her.''

Clayton shrugged. ''It doesn't matter if I am.''

''You're still in love with her.''

''No. I am over my madness.''

Justin lifted one black brow. ''Are you sure of that?''

''I will admit to a certain desire for her. What man can look at her and not feel the sting of lust?'' Clayton stared down at his tightly clenched hands. ''I still think of her. It's impossible not to think of her. I still want her, as any man with blood in his veins would want her. But I no longer love her."

"Are you so certain what you feel is merely lust? Perhaps you underestimate the attraction."

"I know what I am." Clayton stared into the lifeless hearth. It was cold, empty, with only the scars of past fires to claim a time when flames had burned and warmth had glowed. "My heart shriveled and hardened into a pebble a long time ago. It was the only way I could survive."

"The war? Or Marisa?"

Clayton released a dry laugh. "Both. I am not the same man who marched off to war. He died a long time ago."

Justin studied him, his expression troubled. "I don't believe he died. I think he needs more time to heal."

"You cannot continue to kill if you bleed each time you slice your saber through another man. Killing alters a man, Justin. It drains all of the life out of him, until there is nothing left inside. That is not the type of man Marisa needs or truly wants."

"You're numb inside. There is a difference." Justin winked at him. "Marisa just might be able to help you feel again."

"You don't understand. Even if I could pry open my heart, I don't want to feel again. I don't want to feel as though I might die if she turned away from me. I don't want to open myself to any female, ever again. Certainly not to an impetuous, unpredictable, flirtatious little temptress like Marisa. She wants nothing less than everything from a man. I cannot give her that."

"I do understand. I held Isabel at a distance, too. And I nearly lost her because of it." Justin rested his hand on Clayton's shoulder. "I can tell you this, brother. If I hadn't risked my heart and my pride, I never would have known the joy of Isabel's love."

"I have taken enough risks in this lifetime. I don't want a female who keeps exploding in my face." Clayton opened his hands, stretching his cramped fingers wide. "I want peace. A quiet existence. That's all."

"You feel that way now, but how will you feel in a few years, when the wounds are healed?"

Clayton shook his head. "There is nothing left inside of me. Certainly nothing for a woman like Marisa."

"I know you, the way I know the man I see each morning in the mirror. You may want to live your life without the warmth of affection, but one of these days the ice will crack and all of those emotions you have locked inside will pour through you." Justin paused a moment, holding his brother in a fierce look. "What will you do when that happens and you find yourself married to the wrong woman?"

"I once wondered if I could make Marisa happy. I now know there isn't a chance of it. Marisa needs more than I can ever give her."

"You mean more than you are willing to give."

Clayton smiled. "It doesn't really matter, does it?"

"You're even more stubborn than I am. I can only hope you see the truth before you ruin your life." Justin released his breath on a long sigh. "Has Newberry been able to turn up any information that could help find the men who want you dead?"

Clayton shook his head, grateful for the change in subject. "Nothing. Yesterday I asked him to have a man start following Wormsley."

Justin stiffened. "Wormsley?"

"Hempstead has asked for my advice concerning several of the candidates he is considering for a ministry position. Roger Wormsley is one of the men under consideration."

"A ministry position. That means money and power."

Clayton nodded, acknowledging the suspicion that had been working on his mind for days. "Wormsley always had great political aspirations."

"The bastard should be in prison."

"He is in politics instead."

Justin frowned. "Does he know you might hold his fate in your hands?"

"Yes. I am certain he does. He asked me about it the other night at White's."

Justin's eyes narrowed. "He might believe you would spoil his chances."

"He might."

"Except he doesn't fit the description. I suppose he could be the other one in the garden."

"We cannot be certain he is either one."

Justin stared down at his clenched hands. "No. I suppose we cannot."

"I reviewed the guest lists from both the Merrivale and Sotherby parties and made a list of the men I didn't know. Newberry is investigating the men on that list to identify anyone who is slender, fair haired, and about the right age. With any luck, the man Mari overheard is one of them."

"Then all you need to do is find a way for Marisa to hear each of the men on that list speak." Justin rubbed his palms together slowly. "And you can nail the blackguard's hide to a wall."

"If the man was on both guest lists, we have a chance. Unfortunately, hostesses never really mind if an extra bachelor shows up at a party. Our aspiring murderer might have come with someone else."

A muscle tightened in Justin's cheek as he clenched

his jaw. "Then we shall think of another way to find him."

"I would like to find a way to find this man without involving Marisa."

"She is your best chance of identifying them."

"I know. I just don't like putting her in any kind of danger."

"As long as they don't think she is a threat, she should be safe."

Clayton tried to ease the tightness in his chest. He would do everything in his power to keep her safe, even if it came down to tossing her over his shoulder and carrying her to Huntingdon House. Lord help them both, he hoped it didn't come to that. The consequences might kill both of them.

Chapter Eighteen

Marisa glanced at the gentleman sitting beside her on the narrow seat of the curricle. Although elegantly attired in a close-fitting coat of bottle green wool and pearl gray breeches, Clayton did not wear a hat. The morning breeze took advantage of the situation, sliding through his silky black hair in wanton abandon. She slid the strings of her reticule through her gloved fingers. "You have the list narrowed to fourteen men?"

"It was the best I could do." Clayton steered his team of grays into Hyde Park. "Unfortunately, fair-haired men are abundant in England."

She watched his hands, admiring the effortless way he handled the team. He had such gentle hands. Memory stirred within her, bringing with it a tingling across her breasts. "And you can think of no connection you might have with any of these men?"

"None."

The carriage swayed, throwing his thigh against hers.

He glanced at her, a startled expression flitting over his features before he once again donned his mask of indifference. The man was certainly determined to ignore the attraction simmering between them. "We must think of a way for me to meet them."

"I have been giving that some thought."

Marisa had been giving many things a great deal of thought. How could a woman dismantle defenses built over seven long years? "Have you come upon an idea?"

"I thought I might arrange for a party to be given at Marlow House, ostensibly by my grandmother. That would give you a chance to meet each of them."

The gentle rock of the carriage brushed his arm against hers. The last time she had driven with him through the park, she had been a foolish child blindly wandering down a path to disaster. She had no intention of taking that path again. "The man I overheard might suspect it is a trap."

"Any man who does not accept an invitation from the dowager Duchess of Marlow would certainly elevate himself on the suspect list."

She drew the tip of her tongue over her upper lip, slowly. His gaze dipped to her lips, as she had known it would. He was a man, defenses or no defenses. "Yes. I suppose it would call attention to him."

"Yes. It would." He dragged his gaze back to the carriage path.

The rain that had poured over the city that morning had washed the sooty scent from the air, leaving the breeze sweet and clean upon her face. At this hour the park was nearly deserted. They passed an occasional rider on horseback, and a few people strolling the paths, but most of the ton were still in their beds.

She shifted on the seat, just enough to close the small

gap between them. He glanced at her, a glint of suspicion filling his eyes. She smiled, certain she presented a portrait of innocence. "Have you decided when you will hold this party?"

He shifted restlessly on the seat, trying to edge away from her. The narrow confines of the carriage allowed no refuge from the contact of her hip against his. She had him trapped against the high padded leather on the side of the carriage. "The invitations will go out tomorrow."

Clayton's warmth seared through her ivory pelisse and the green muslin gown beneath. The subtle scent of herbs and citrus drifted to her senses, fueling the fires smoldering deep within her. "I suppose we can hunt these men down at other social events while we are waiting for the party."

He glanced down at her, an encouraging warmth kindling in the depths of his eyes. "Yes. I suppose we can."

She had another hunt in mind. Sunlight slanted through the trees, glinting golden on the misty air. It seemed a magical morning, a lovely beginning to a fresh new life. "Do you remember the last time we drove through the park?"

His hands tightened on the ribbons. The horses tossed their heads and whinnied in response, silvery manes fluttering in the breeze. "I am not likely to forget that day."

Neither would she. She clasped her hands in her lap, gathered her courage, and broached a subject neglected for far too long. "That day, I asked if you thought we could make our marriage a success."

Clayton released his breath in an irritated sigh. "Marisa, I don't see any point in—"

A loud crack shattered the morning air, cutting off

his words. Marisa gasped as the carriage pitched to Clayton's side.

"What the—" he mumbled.

"Clay!"

The violent surge tossed Marisa toward his side of the carriage. Clayton grabbed her, cinching one strong arm around her shoulders as her momentum threatened to toss her from the carriage. He braced one foot against the front of the carriage and tucked her close to his body. The startled horses plunged into a run, dragging the crippled carriage. Marisa pressed herself against Clayton's chest. Thick muscles flexed against her as he fought to control the team and hold her in the carriage. Marisa sucked in her breath as the team left the drive and headed straight for a stand of trees.

Clayton talked to his team, his voice firm and sure as he eased the terrified horses into a walk and finally halted them a few feet from the trees. Marisa clutched his coat, her side plastered against his chest, her head tucked beneath his chin, too stunned to move.

He squeezed her arm. "Are you all right?"

She nodded. "I'm fine."

"If you would move just a little. The feather in your bonnet is tickling my nose."

"Oh." She straightened and rammed his chin with her hat. She tilted her head and smiled up at him. "Sorry."

He shook his head. "It's all right. I'm getting accustomed to taking one on the chin when you're around."

She tried to draw away from him, but the slant was too severe. He grunted as she fell back against his chest. "Sorry."

"Marisa, stay where you are. Don't move."

"But I'm sure I can—"

"Yes, I'm sure you can. But let me." He dropped the reins, slipped his arm under her knees, and lifted her across his lap.

Her knees threatened to buckle as her feet touched the thick grass. Good heavens, she was trembling like a schoolgirl at her first ball. She stepped away, allowing Clayton room to climb out of the sharply tilting carriage. He climbed from the carriage and touched her arm.

"Are you sure you are all right?"

She forced her numb lips into a smile. "Yes. I'm fine."

He studied her, his gaze roaming over her as though he intended to make certain all of the pieces were still where they belonged. A smile touched his lips as he straightened her bonnet. "I would suspect most women would have fallen into a fit of the vapors after nearly being thrown from a carriage."

She forced starch into her sagging spine. "Oh, dear, I suppose I really never have learned how to behave as all proper ladies ought."

He cupped her cheek in his gloved palm, the soft kid leather warm against her skin. "This lady is behaving like a very brave young woman."

She didn't feel brave. She felt like curling up in his arms and hiding there for the rest of her life. Still, she refused to surrender to weakness, not when he seemed so pleased with her strength. She turned, watching his every move as he checked the horses. He spoke softly to each of his team, stroking their long necks, calming them as he had calmed her. After he checked the horses, he bent and examined the place where the wheel ought to have been.

Marisa leaned over his shoulder. "What happened?"

"Someone made certain the wheel would shear completely away from the shaft."

A chill crept across her skin. "It wasn't an accident?"

Clayton straightened. "No."

Until now, Marisa had harbored some small hope that the blackguard who wanted to murder Clay would give up, turn tail, and run after his first attempt had failed. Now she realized he had every intention of seeing his deadly task through to the end. When she acknowledged how close Clayton had come to being killed, the anxiety she had kept dammed up broke over her, like a wave crashing against the shore.

Clayton faced her, his expression growing concerned.

"Marisa," he whispered, gripping her arm. "You're as pale as milk."

She stared up at him, trembling. "You could have been killed."

"It's all right."

She shook her head. "No. It isn't all right. He will try again."

"Marisa . . ."

She clutched the lapels of his coat. "Clay, you could have died."

"I have been through a great deal worse."

She stared up into his eyes, honesty pouring from her with her fear. "If anything happened to you, I wouldn't want to live."

He stared at her, his lips parted without a word escaping. Yet his expression revealed more than any words. Surprise, disbelief, a haunting sadness all blended into a certain wariness. "You're upset. It's reasonable to be upset. You were nearly thrown from a carriage."

"I'm not worried about me." She pressed her cheek against his coat, above the comforting throb of his heart. "We have to keep you safe."

He hesitated a moment before he slid his arms around her. "Marisa," he whispered, his voice a tortured whisper as he held her close.

She drew in her breath, fighting the tremors ripping through her. He needed her strength, not her weakness. He slid his hands up and down her back, whispered softly to her, words to calm her, to reassure her. She felt so warm in his arms, so safe, protected, as though nothing in the world could harm her. Yet who would protect him? Who would keep him safe? She drew back in the circle of his arms and looked up into his beautiful eyes.

He tugged the glove from his right hand and touched her cheek. "We'd better get you home."

What game was Marisa playing? Clayton looped a starched length of white lawn around his neck, trying to concentrate on the intricacies of his cravat. Yet memories kept taunting him, dragging his mind back to a golden-eyed temptress.

If anything happened to you, I wouldn't want to live.
The words had been spoken with such heartfelt sincerity. They had wrapped around him, threatening the walls of his defenses. No matter how much he tried to dismiss them, a part of him, a pitiful, needy part of him, wanted desperately to believe she cared for him. Yet he knew her words meant nothing. They couldn't.

Marisa was a beautiful, feckless, flighty female. She was incapable of remaining constant for more than a fortnight. She flirted with every man who came within her orbit. She considered it her mission to enslave the heart of every male who met her. Certainly she did not still harbor any deep feelings for him, if she ever had. He had realized long ago he was but one in a long line of men she had conquered and abandoned.

Yet she had held him this morning as though she wanted to tuck him into her reticule and keep him safe. And the few times he had kissed her, she had responded with a warmth that had seared him to the core. She was also willing to stand beside him to find these blackguards who wanted him dead. He crushed the stirring inside of him. Only a fool would fall under her spell again. Everything she did had a purpose. It was all part of her game.

He frowned at his image in the mirror above his dressing table. It was hardly the face of the tender boy Marisa had torn to pieces. All the tenderness had been sliced away from him, leaving only a dark, sardonic mask that hid an even darker soul. No, he would not be taken in by her soft words and her melting looks. He would not become another of her besotted puppies.

Clayton glanced over his shoulder as his butler entered the dressing room. "What is it, Greensley?"

The slender old gentleman inclined his head, a slight smile curving his lips. "This was just delivered, my lord."

Clayton took the calling card from Greensley and frowned at the words written in an elegant hand. *I must speak with you. Tonight. M.* What the devil could have brought Marisa to his house at this time of the night? Lord help him, the woman would have tongues wagging from one end of London to the next.

He glanced at Greensley. "Is she in the library?"

Greensley shook his head. "No, my lord. She is waiting for you in a coach in the alley at the back of the house. This was delivered by one of her footmen."

Clayton released his breath on a long sigh. The less

he saw of the temptress, the better his chances of withstanding her nefarious charms. Still, it must be important, or she wouldn't have come to see him. He dismissed Greensley, finished tying his cravat, donned a black wool coat as though it were armor, and marched out of his house to face his golden-eyed temptress.

A burly footman opened the door to the large black coach waiting in the alley. Clayton climbed inside and cast Marisa a cool glance. "I trust this is important."

She smiled. "It is."

He took a seat on the black velvet squabs across from her and faced his opponent while the footman closed the door. The interior coach lamp spilled a golden light over her, caressing her smooth face, illuminating a portrait of feminine perfection in white and black.

White rosebuds entwined with the glossy black curls piled on top of her head. A black silk cape rested across her shoulders, unfastened, revealing a single strand of pearls glowing against her pale skin. The soft swell of her breasts rose above the small silk rosebuds adorning the neckline of her white silk gown. His gaze lowered to her hands, lying pale and bare against the white silk covering her lap. Although it was a cool evening, with the promise of rain hanging in the air, Clayton felt uncomfortably warm. "Am I to guess what it is that brought you here tonight?"

"No." She moistened her lips, the quick slide of her tongue leaving an inviting sheen there. "I think it would be best to show you."

He frowned as the coach lurched into motion. "Show me?"

She clasped her hands. "Yes."

"I suppose you have no intention of telling me where we are going."

"Not yet."

In war, he had learned how to judge an opponent, discern weakness, exploit it for his own purpose. Marisa looked as nervous as a cat cornered by a mastiff. "You are being very mysterious tonight."

"I suppose I am." Although she smiled, the warmth did not erase the uneasy look in her eyes. "But then, aren't women supposed to be mysterious?"

He had never been able to understand them. "I take it we will be missing the Elsberry musicale tonight?"

She cupped the back of her hand and rubbed her thumb over the palm of the opposite hand. "I suppose we shall."

He leaned forward and rested his forearms on his thighs, resisting an insidious urge to draw her into his arms. "Are you feeling all right?"

"Yes. I'm perfectly fine."

She looked so fragile, so utterly beguiling. He clenched his hands into fists to keep from touching her. "Marisa, you had quite a shock this morning. Are you certain you are recovered?"

"Completely." She lifted her chin. "I do apologize for losing my composure."

"It isn't every day one is nearly tossed from a moving carriage."

"No. It isn't." She glanced at her hands. "I never expected them to try something in daylight."

Clayton sensed this avenue of discussion would do nothing to alleviate the anxiety so obvious in her demeanor. He leaned back against the cushioned upholstery and snatched for an alternate topic, something that would take her mind off of catching two murderous blackguards, and his off of kissing one unpredictable beauty. "Is your niece enjoying her first Season?"

Marisa smiled, a glimmer of relief in her eyes. "Beatrice has been a tremendous success. I am afraid she will leave a trail of broken hearts when she finally decides on one of her beaux."

"It runs in the family."

She looked at him, her eyes wide and haunted. He immediately regretted his careless words. They revealed too much of his own pain. "Clay, I never meant to hurt you."

He lifted his hands in a sign of surrender. "Ancient history. Believe me, I harbor no ill will. I simply meant that your lovely niece has her choice of gentlemen. As does her beautiful aunt."

"Beatrice and I really aren't so much alike. She is much more practical than I am." Marisa clasped her hands, linking her fingers together. "She really cannot understand why I keep refusing to accept advantageous offers of marriage. She is convinced I must choose a husband this year, or I shall find myself a spinster the rest of my days."

Something dangerous coiled inside of him when he thought of Marisa married to another man, something primal, something he had fought long and hard to exorcise. "Perhaps you should explain to her your views on the perfect man."

She laughed, a husky sound that wrapped around him like warm strands of velvet. "I have. But, being a practical young lady, she thinks I am a silly fool. She has been trying to convince me to marry Braden Fitzwilliam."

That primal viper of jealousy coiling in his belly sank sharp fangs into his vitals. "I am a little surprised Braden hasn't convinced you by now. He has been after you for the past seven years."

She held his gaze. "I'm not in love with Braden."

Clayton tried to crush the warmth that admission conjured inside of him, and failed.

"And Braden isn't in love with me."

"Yet your niece still thinks you should marry him?"

"Beatrice is very practical. She believes a woman should search for her true love for only so long. After a certain age—and I am long past that age—a woman is wise simply to make a suitable match with an agreeable gentleman." She tilted her head and smiled. "There have been moments when I have wondered if she might not be right. Is it better to live alone, or marry an agreeable gentleman for companionship and children?"

"Do you really imagine you could be happy living with only part of the dream?"

"I suppose I could. If I lost all hope of ever having a life with my one and only love." She glanced down at her tightly clenched hands. "But I still have hope. And as long as that lives inside of me, I will wait for him."

What would it take to win her heart? More than he had to give. Still, the thought of Marisa in love with another man stabbed him close to the heart. "What if you never meet him?"

"Oh, I have met him." She looked at him, a wistful smile on her lips. "It is simply a matter of convincing him that he cannot possibly live without me."

Marisa was in love with someone, a man who somehow managed to resist her charm, while Clayton still had trouble keeping her out of his dreams. It shouldn't matter to him. It didn't matter. Yet he couldn't prevent the tightening in his chest. The air turned to stone in his lungs; he felt the weight of it pressing against his heart. "Have I met this paragon?"

She opened her hands and pressed her palms together. "Have you no idea who he might be?"

Clayton clenched his teeth together. "I prefer not to play a guessing game."

She nodded. "And I have a feeling this may not be a good time to tell you."

"Fine." If the infuriating wench didn't want to tell him who the poor, misbegotten fool was, then he certainly would not press her. He certainly pitied the man. If she could respond to his kisses while she was in love with another man then . . . His thoughts collided with an unexpected idea. He glanced at Marisa and found her studying him, as though she were waiting for him to fit together all the pieces of a puzzle.

It couldn't be, he assured himself. He would not tumble into that trap. Marisa certainly hadn't spent the last seven years pining over him. He refused to set foot down that particularly dangerous path.

He pushed aside the leather shade on the coach window and looked into the darkness. Marisa was playing a game with him, amusing herself, like a hawk toying with a hapless mouse. She certainly—His thoughts halted as his brain registered the fact that they were on a road outside of town. He glanced at her. "Just where the devil are we headed?"

She gave him a sheepish grin. "Westbury."

"Westbury. In Hampshire?"

She nodded. "I decided to kidnap you."

He stared at her, his befuddled brain trying to make sense of the facts laid out before him. "You are kidnapping me?"

"It is the only way to keep you safe."

"Marisa, I have to find these men. It's the only way I am going to be safe."

"I know. But I decided it would be wise for you to

303

leave town until I can identify at least one of the men who want to murder you."

"I have no intention of allowing you to search for these men on your own."

"But I have to return to town. I am the only one who can identify the fair-haired man. You can do nothing more than provide him a target."

"I have no intention of hiding from this black-guard."

"Be reasonable, Clay. I have the best chance of finding this man before he can murder anyone. If you stay out of the way, I am certain I—"

"Stay out of the way!"

"Yes. All you need do is stay at Westbury for a short while. No one will be there, except for a few servants. I doubt anyone would suspect you were hiding there."

He frowned. "I don't intend to *hide* anywhere."

"You really should try to be more reasonable. If you were to hide, just until I could find this man, then you could return. All you need do is stay out of sight until after the party."

"I am not going anywhere until this is finished."

She shrugged. "I knew I could not talk any sense into your stubborn head. That is why I am kidnapping you."

He swore under his breath. "Confound it, Marisa. You cannot just go about kidnapping people."

"I don't intend to make a habit of it."

"I'm glad to hear it." He rose and smacked his head on the low ceiling. "Blasted, meddling—"

"Do be careful," Marisa said sweetly.

He glared at her, then opened the trapdoor. One of the footmen peered at him with dark brown eyes. "Turn this blasted coach around."

"Sorry, my lord, we have orders to take you to Westbury."

The big man turned around, ignoring Clayton's sharp commands and dire threats. Clayton turned his furious gaze on Marisa. "Tell them to turn this blasted coach around."

"I cannot do that." She smoothed her hand over the skirt of her gown. "I told them to turn around under no circumstances."

Clayton slammed the small trapdoor shut and latched it. He closed the distance between them, swaying with the pitch and roll of the coach. He leaned toward her, employing his most sinister glare. "Tell them to turn this bloody coach around or I shall make you regret the day you were born."

She sighed. "I knew you would be upset."

"Upset!" He straightened and rapped his head against the ceiling.

"Do sit down, before you pummel yourself senseless."

He sank to the seat beside her, rubbing the sore spot on top of his head and glaring at her. "Of all the hen-witted things to do. You cannot actually think for one moment you can manage to keep me at Westbury once we arrive, can you?"

"I shall certainly do my best."

He gripped the door handle and found it locked. He reached across her. The other door could not be opened either.

"They are both bolted. From the outside. I wanted to make certain you didn't get hurt trying to jump from a moving coach."

"How very considerate of you."

"I know how impetuous you can be."

"Impetuous." The woman had obviously lost her mind. "Me?"

She rubbed her arms, as if she were cold. "You did run off to the army without any warning."

His muscles stiffened at her direct hit. "That was not an impetuous act."

She lifted her brows. "No?"

He crossed his arms and fixed her with a look he hoped would quell this line of conversation. "I gave it a great deal of thought."

"You purchased a commission five days after I ended our engagement."

"It had nothing at all to do with you."

"I think it did."

"You are mistaken."

"Am I?"

"Yes." He drew breath into his tight lungs. "There really isn't anything more to discuss about the subject."

For a moment she looked as though she intended to plunge into their past. Instead, she turned on the seat to face him, the cape slipping low across one slender shoulder. "Clay, I realize you are angry with me now, but this is the only way I could think to keep you safe."

His gaze traced the flicker of lamplight across the pale skin of her shoulder. "I didn't ask you to keep me safe."

"I know. But I have to do everything possible to keep you alive and well."

He leaned toward her, so close that the scent of lilies after rain spilled over him, tempting him to brush his lips against the silken skin at the joining of her neck and shoulder. "I—on the other hand—am finding it desperately difficult to keep from strangling you."

"If you do, you will spoil all the efforts I have made

to save your life. They will no doubt hang you."

He brushed his bare fingertips over the smooth column of her neck, smiling as her soft breath brushed his cheek. He was quite certain he revealed nothing more than a controlled mask of composure, even though his pulse had kicked into a gallop. "But think of the satisfaction I would get from watching your lovely face turn blue."

She moistened her lips. "Clay, if you stop being angry for a moment, you will see this is the most sensible thing to do."

"Sensible. When did kidnapping a man become a sensible thing to do?"

"When that man is the target of a killer." She folded her hands in her lap and addressed him like a prim governess lecturing a recalcitrant charge. "Once I identify the fair-haired man, then I shall send for you immediately."

"If you think for one moment you will succeed in keeping me prisoner, think again."

"Did you recognize the footman you spoke with? His name is Silas Trawley."

Clayton frowned. "Should I know him?"

"He was once quite a promising fighter. He actually came close to beating Tom Cribb in a mill near Aylesbury a few years ago."

"And so you intend to have your footman pound me to a pulp if I try to escape? Wouldn't that be defeating your purpose?"

"His brother Ralph is also traveling with us. Although he was never a boxer, he is every bit as large as Silas. I am hoping they won't need to pound you to a pulp. Just persuade you that it would be wise to refrain from trying to escape."

"So your idea of saving my life is to allow two burly footmen the chance to smash my jaw?"

She shook her head. "If you don't give them any trouble, they will not lay a hand on you."

"And if I do?"

"Then you are a complete addlepate." She released her breath in an irritated huff. "If you cause trouble, I have instructed them to subdue you as gently as possible, and tie you up until you are safely locked away at Westbury."

He stared at her. Despite his anger at her high-handed tactics, he admitted a certain awe at her bold concern for him. And no matter how much he wanted to deny it, he could not suppress the heat saturating his blood. "You do realize the consequences we could both face as a result of your little plan?"

She looked wary suddenly. "Consequences?"

He smiled at her, a smile he knew held an icy edge. He had intimidated more than a few soldiers with that smile. Marisa didn't flinch. "If anyone found out you and I had traveled to Westbury, alone in a coach, your reputation would be destroyed."

"Oh. Those consequences." She smiled, apparently immune to his attempts at intimidation. "I'm afraid your reputation would suffer as well. There wouldn't be a mama in London who would allow you near her daughter, not after you ruined me."

"There would be only one alternative."

She nodded, her solemn expression spoiled by the glimmer of triumph in her eyes. "You would have to marry me."

He had the uneasy feeling he had stumbled into another trap. "Better put, you would have to marry me."

She smiled, an all too satisfied look gracing her features. "Yes, I suppose I would."

He tried to swallow, but found his mouth as dry as parchment. "You realize I have nothing to lose. I intend to choose a bride by the end of the Season."

"And you don't really care who that bride might be."

He inclined his head and smiled at her. "While you are waiting for your one and only love to get around to asking for your hand."

"I am prepared to do what is necessary." She opened her hands at her sides. "If it means marriage to you to keep you safe, then marriage it shall be."

He leaned toward her. "You are bluffing, sweetheart."

Her brows lifted. "Am I?"

"We shall see." He cupped her breast in his hand.

She gasped, her eyes growing wide. "What are you doing?"

"Testing your conviction." Slowly he slid his thumb over the tip of her breast, watching the color rise in her cheeks, feeling the tantalizing tightening of her nipple beneath his touch.

"Oh." She swallowed hard. "You cannot mean to seduce me here. Now."

"That depends." He nuzzled his lips against her neck, inhaling the intoxicating scent of her skin into his lungs. Blood flooded his loins.

A sweet tremor rippled through her. "Depends?"

He flicked the tip of his tongue against the delicate hollow beneath her ear. "Tell them to turn the coach around."

She shook her head. "No."

"That sounded a great deal like a declaration of war."

Chapter Nineteen

Clayton eased the cape from her shoulders. The heavy silk tumbled to the seat behind her with a soft hiss. "Are you really prepared to do battle?"

Marisa's eyes narrowed. "You wouldn't seduce me. Not here."

He slid his arm around her waist and tugged her against him. "Wouldn't I?"

She pressed her hands against his chest. "In a coach?"

"It's very private." He brushed his lips against her brow. "You have seen to that."

She drew back in the circle of his arms and glared up at him. "I will not be seduced in a coach as if I were a common doxy."

"There is nothing common about you." He brushed his lips over her brow. "Tell them to turn the coach around."

She frowned. "Clay, be reasonable."

"I will be as reasonable as you are, my sweet."

"You cannot—"

He clamped his lips over hers, capturing her protest. She stiffened in his arms, holding herself as rigid as a marble statue. Yet the warmth of her radiated against him, betraying her humanity. He slid his lips over hers in a brazen, openmouthed, take-no-prisoners kiss. He wanted to punish her for everything she was and all that she had found lacking in him. Punish her for tearing his heart into shreds, while she protected her own. Punish her for making him want and need until he ached with a desire that defied all reason.

She pushed against his shoulders, twisting in his arms. He held her tighter, relentless in his assault, flicking his tongue against her tightly clenched lips. He was no longer the boy she had twisted and snapped. He was a man who had marched through hell. A man who would not be brought to his knees by any woman. A man free of her tyranny. This was what happened when a foolish little girl tried to control a man who would no longer be controlled.

He held her close, her breasts searing him through the layers of clothes keeping her skin from his. She made a sound low in her throat, a soft, startled whimper as he slipped his tongue across her tightly clenched lips. The heat she kindled in him flared and burned. Memories stirred in him, as vivid as oils splashed across a canvas: Marisa warm and supple in his arms. *I love you, Clay.* The words taunted him. Hunger sank sharp claws into his vitals.

All his need to punish melted into a far more potent desire. All of his anger melted in the heat she kindled within him. In spite of his best intentions, he could no longer deny the feelings creeping from deep within him. He had wanted her for too many years. He felt

311

himself softening, his lips gentling against hers.

Open to me, Mari.

He sensed the exact moment she stopped struggling, the instant of surrender. Her soft lips parted beneath his with a sudden sweetness that ripped though him like a gunshot. She cinched her arms around his neck, as though she were suddenly afraid he might find some way to escape her. Heaven help him, he had never tasted anything more potent than Marisa's kiss. He slid his tongue past her lips, dipping into the dark heat of her mouth, teasing her tongue until she followed him, until she dipped and plunged with an innocent ardor that threatened his every defense.

Somehow he had become turned around in this battle. He had lost track of his purpose. All that mattered was Marisa, and the incredible reality of having her in his arms. His fingers trembled like a boy's as he unfastened her gown, fumbling with tiny silk loops and silk-covered buttons. He had divested countless women of their clothes, yet all his finesse deserted him. He stumbled through the intricacies of her petticoat and chemise until he could smooth the garments away from her skin.

Golden light flickered from the lamp above her, sliding over the skin he bared, caressing the rounded softness of her breasts. He had known she would look this way, her nipples taut and high, the color of ripe raspberries, tempting him to savor their flavor. She tipped back her head, a soft moan slipping from her lips as he licked the lamplight from her skin, dragging his tongue down the column of her neck. He nibbled the taut skin over her delicate collarbones, flicked his tongue in the hollow between. Need clenched low in his belly as he brushed his cheeks over the velvety softness of her firm breasts.

"Clay," she whispered, tangling her hands in his hair. "I have dreamed of you holding me this way."

So had he. A lifetime of wanting. She held him close as he drew one taut nipple into his mouth. He teased the little bud with his tongue, all the while teasing his own blazing need for her. He caressed the sweet tip, then drew it deeper into his mouth, suckling like a hungry babe.

She squirmed in his arms, soft, inarticulate sobs escaping her lips, her hands roaming restlessly over his hair, down his neck, across his shoulders. Her fingers flexed against him, digging into his coat as he teased and suckled one luscious nipple, then the other.

He shifted her in his arms, tumbling her over his lap. She lay with her bare back across his arm, staring up at him, her eyes wide and bewildered, her breath coming in ragged gasps.

"I want to see you. All of you," he whispered, tugging the tangled mass of silk and linen down from her waist. "Lift your hips."

She obeyed, giving him free rein as he slid the garments from her hips and down the length of her legs. The garments fell to the floor of the coach with a soft whisper. She lay naked in his arms except for a single strand of pearls glowing against her pale neck, her white silk stockings, and white silk slippers. He touched an innocent white rosebud adorning one of the white garters that held her stockings above each knee. He stared at her, drinking in her beauty like a man who had wandered years through a desert might devour the sight of a lush oasis.

"I always knew you would be this beautiful," he said, drawing his hand down the center of her body, his fingers grazing the slope of her breast, his palm sliding over her ribs, her belly.

"I never cared to be beautiful for any man except you. Only you."

The sincerity in her eyes spread like a balm over the ragged wounds carved in his heart. He laid her back across the black velvet squab, leaning over her. He wanted her now. His arousal pressed against the barriers of his drawers and trousers, seeking a taste of her. Still, he refused the hungry demands. He slid his lips down her neck, flicking his tongue against her skin, forcing himself to proceed slowly, to savor and cherish when his hunger demanded he devour her. For years he had imagined touching her this way. It was too precious a gift to squander.

He explored her, discovering the realities of his dreams, tasting her, inhaling her, smoothing his hands over each lovely curve, every valley. He recalled the countless nights he had conjured her likeness before falling into a restless slumber. He remembered all the ways he had loved her in his dreams, and he proceeded to make those dreams come true. He dragged his tongue down the center of her body, dipping into her navel before slipping to his knees before her.

"Clay?" she whispered, as he draped her long legs over his shoulders.

"It's all right. Let me touch you." Her hands clutched his shoulders as he brushed his cheeks against her smooth belly.

"Let me taste you." He savored the smooth skin of her inner thigh, then kissed his way upward along the other until he reached the most tempting morsel of all. Crisp curls tickled his nose. A rich, womanly scent flooded his senses as he indulged in a kiss more intimate than any he had ever tasted.

"Oh!" She tossed back her head, her hair coming

undone upon the black velvet. "Oh, my . . . I never. . . ."

"I have wanted to do this for a very long time," he whispered, sliding one finger inside her tight passage.

She breathed a sound, half sigh, half moan. "Yes. Please don't stop."

"I couldn't. Not now." Not with the scent of her seeping into his blood. Not with the taste of her upon his tongue. Not with the tiny feminine contractions tugging at his skin.

Her soft sighs vibrated through him, playing against his heart like deft fingers stroking the strings of a harp. He knew deep in his soul that Marisa had never experienced the pleasures of her body before. She had never felt a man's hands on her skin, his lips and tongue conjuring the age-old magic. His throat tightened as he heard her startled cry, as he felt the tremors shake her, as he tasted the nectar of her feminine flower blossoming for the first time. His name burst from her lips and she stiffened against him, her fingers twisting in his hair as he felt the rapture tremble through her.

As the last tremor rippled through her slender form, he rose and scooped her up into his arms. She fell across his lap, her cheek pressed against his shoulder. He had never realized he could find such pleasure in nothing more than touching and kissing a woman. Still, his aroused flesh ached, demanding release.

"I love you, Clay," she whispered.

His hand paused upon the top button of his trousers. "Aren't you mistaking love for lust, Mari?"

"No, my darling." She snuggled against him and yawned. "I know the difference."

He smoothed his hand over her tumbled hair, several pins falling free. *I will always love you.* Her words echoed through the tangled threads of his memory, words spoken on a soft summer night a lifetime ago. His belief in those words had nearly cost him his life. He had vowed never to believe in that elusive, all too destructive emotion again. Yet, in spite of all his experience, all his wounds, he wanted to believe in her.

He looked down into her drowsy eyes and fought to rebuild the defenses around his poor threatened heart, only to find them badly battered. "You'd better get dressed before you fall asleep."

She kissed his chin. "Will you help me?"

He crushed the need clenched like a fist in his belly. He eased her off his lap and reached for her tangle of clothes. He was a man walking along a narrow ledge. One wrong move and he would tumble straight to the jagged rocks below. He handed Marisa her petticoat and chemise and prayed for a way to survive the coming storm.

Marisa stretched her arms wide and smiled up at the stars. They burned like pinpoints of fire through black velvet. Soon after getting dressed, she had fallen asleep in Clayton's arms. She would be there yet if they hadn't stopped to change horses and take care of nature's necessities.

She walked back to the coach, thinking of all that had transpired this evening. Clayton had taken a great deal of care to ensure that he pleasured her. And he had. Her mother had explained all about the peculiar, sometimes elusive whirlwind that could grip a woman. Clayton had conjured a storm within her. She also knew he had been left in a highly agitated state.

According to her mother, it was extremely uncomfortable for an aroused male to go about without finding his own release. Marisa climbed into the coach and sank against the padded squabs. At the time, Marisa had been too inebriated with pleasure to question Clayton's behavior. Now she couldn't quite understand why he had ended their encounter without taking his own pleasure. She leaned her head back against the thick black velvet and smiled. She would have to ask him about it when he returned to the coach. There were a few other things they needed to discuss as well. Although they had spoken of marriage as a consequence, she preferred to have that particular detail clarified.

A knock on the coach door broke her reverie. Silas stuck his head inside and glanced around. He looked at Marisa, his expression as close to sheepish as a man who had been battered in the ring could come. "I guess his lordship hasn't come back to the coach."

Marisa leaned forward, a dreadful anxiety gripping her stomach. "Lord Huntingdon was with you."

"Aye, he was." Silas lowered his dark eyes. "We seem to 'ave lost him, milady."

"Lost him! How the devil did you lose him?"

"Well, milady, he went into the privy, and we was waiting for him, Ralph and me, that is. Now, we never walked away from the front of it, no, milady, we didn't. After a bit—it seemed to be taking a long while—we knocked on the door. When his lordship didn't answer, we tried to open the door. Seemed the only thing to do, you see. But it was locked, so we thought maybe—"

"Silas, can I assume his lordship was not in the privy?"

"Aye. His lordship removed one of the boards on the back of it, and got away. I never would 'ave thought of anyone doing that, milady. Suppose with his lordship being a war hero and all, we should 'ave known he'd be full of tricks. A sly cove that one." Silas rocked back on his heels, a grin curving his lips.

1

"I'd wager he'd peel to advantage, too. Be a real challenge with his bunch of fives. I would 'ave liked a real turn-up with him, I would."

"You might still have your chance." Marisa smiled, visions of strangling a certain earl dancing through her brain. "Search for him, Silas. He cannot have gone far on foot."

Silas cleared his throat. "Well, that's the thing, milady. He ain't on foot."

"He isn't?"

Silas shook his head. "He has a horse."

"How did he get a horse?"

"Well, the innkeeper, he says his lordship took a horse and said you would be paying for it."

"Oh, he did, did he?" Marisa swore under her breath. "Oh, he is the most infuriating, stubborn . . . We shall go after him."

"As you wish, milady. But seeing as he is on horseback, and we have the coach, and how it is he has a head start on us, I'm thinking—"

"Now!"

Silas started at her sharp tone. "Aye, milady."

They managed to make it back to the Westbury town house without catching a glimpse of Clayton. She went to her bed, half expecting him to climb through her window in the middle of the night. But morning came without a visit from the earl.

Early in the afternoon she sent a note to his house. They needed to talk. The reply she received through her footman said only that the earl was not at home. Where was he? Later that afternoon, she stopped by Clayton's house, only to be told the earl was still not at home. Soon afterward, Marisa paid a call on the dowager Duchess of Marlow.

* * *

Sophia sat on a gilt-trimmed sofa in the green drawing room of Marlow House, her eyes wide as she watched Marisa pace the length of her green drawing room. "You kidnapped my grandson?"

Marisa pivoted at the windows. "It was the only way I could think of to keep him safe. It seemed the only sensible thing to do."

"Sensible." Sophia stroked her hand over the big cat lying beside her on the sofa. "Yes, of course. I don't know why I didn't think of it."

"He should have arrived in London sometime last night. But according to his butler, the earl is not at home."

"Marisa, dear, I do wish you would stop pacing. Perceval thinks you want to play. I suspect he is about to pounce on you."

Marisa sank to one of the gilt-trimmed armchairs across from the duchess. "If something has happened to Clay, it is my fault. I shall have no other alternative except to jump off of London Bridge."

Sophia smiled. "And the Thames is quite dreadfully dirty these days."

"I don't understand why he hasn't returned to London by now. Something must have happened to him on the way. Outlaws, perhaps." Marisa pressed her hand to the base of her neck. "He could be lying somewhere, hurt."

Sophia studied Marisa a moment, her expression growing thoughtful. "Marisa, you need not worry. Clayton had breakfast with me this morning."

"He did?" Marisa squeezed her hands together. "Did he mention what happened last night?"

"No."

A chill seeped into her blood as she sat captive under

319

Sophia's blue gaze. "I suppose he may be a little angry with me; that is why he refused to see me."

"He may have been out when you called upon him. He did say he had a few things he needed to do this afternoon."

"I suppose."

Sophia gave her a warm, encouraging smile. "I seriously doubt Clayton would remain angry with you. He must realize you only kidnapped him to save him from danger. It was the only sensible thing to do."

"Thank you. But I doubt Clayton sees things as clearly as you and I do."

Marisa left Marlow House with a hundred questions whirling in her brain and an uneasy feeling gripping her heart. Clayton was in London, and he hadn't made a single attempt to see her. Only two people knew what had happened in the coach last night. If Clayton chose to forget all about it, there was little Marisa could do. She certainly did not intend to force him to marry her. He might think the responsibility for what had happened lay squarely on her shoulders. He might see it all as a game. A game she had lost.

She fought the anxiety gnawing at her insides all through the day. By the time she entered Vauxhall Gardens that evening, with her Aunt Cecilia and Beatrice, Marisa had nearly convinced herself there was no reason at all to worry about Clayton asking for her hand in marriage. He must care for her. She simply refused to believe last night meant nothing at all to him.

Although moonlight spilled from a generous moon, the gardens were lit with lanterns burning in golden globes, the soft light flickering upon the trees lining the walkways. The quick notes of Mozart punctuated the warm evening air from the orchestra in the center of the grove. Dancing couples already crowded the nearby rotunda. Marisa led her small entourage through the crowd of fashionables to the supper booth she had reserved. At the back of the brightly lit booth, oils shimmered in the golden light, depicting ladies dancing gaily around a Maypole.

Gentlemen soon started stopping by their booth like moths alighting from a milling swarm. A few came to visit Marisa, though most came to worship at the temple of her niece; each received a chilly glare from Aunt Cecilia. Only the most stalwart lingered more than a few minutes.

"Aunt Cecilia, I do wish you would stop frightening all of my beaux away." Beatrice flicked her fan under her chin, fluttering the shiny curls framing her face. "At this rate, I shall end my days a spinster."

Cecilia smiled. "If they aren't brave enough to sustain a cold glare from me, they aren't anything to take home."

Their words buzzed in Marisa's ears, sounds that could not penetrate the pounding of her own blood. She stared at the people who occupied the booth across the way, her breath lodged in her throat. The well-lit booth revealed Lady Penelope Cuthberth, her parents, and the gentleman they were entertaining. Lord and Lady Cuthberth smiled in obvious approval as they watched their beautiful daughter converse with the tall, dark-haired gentleman seated beside Penelope. What the devil was Clayton doing?

Marisa jumped when Beatrice touched her arm. "What?"

Beatrice frowned. "Aunt Marisa, you are staring. I am afraid people may notice."

Heat crawled upward along Marisa's neck. "Thank you."

Beatrice squeezed Marisa's arm. "I think you should know, Victoria told me everyone is quite certain Penelope Cuthberth is the one Lord Huntingdon plans to choose from his list."

"I see." Marisa's wineglass trembled in her hand as she lifted it to her lips. She sipped the claret while the blood slowly drained from her limbs.

"You are all right, aren't you?" Beatrice asked.

"Of course. Clay and I are friends. Nothing more." Except her entire world.

Cecilia touched Marisa's arm. She smiled when Marisa met her intense gaze. "Smile, child. Maintain your dignity above all else."

Marisa forced her lips into a smile, while inside she was screaming. He couldn't do it. After all this time, all these years, Clayton couldn't marry that woman. Could he? She stared into her glass of wine. She had to stop him from doing this. Penelope could not make him happy. Yet if last night hadn't altered his decision, then there was nothing more Marisa could do. She had revealed her feelings and much more. Her cheeks heated when she thought of those moments in his arms.

Marisa noticed her aunt watching her, a pitying look in her eyes. She would not be pitied. Not by anyone. She squeezed her glass. No matter how much she wanted to ignore it, she had to face the truth. If Clayton had wanted her, he would be sitting beside her, not Penelope Cuthberth. Last night she had made a complete and utter fool of herself. All of the years, all of the hopes and dreams, were for nothing. Worse of all was the end of hope. How did one learn to live without hope? She would find a way. She had no other choice. She would face the rest of her life with dignity.

As the evening progressed, Marisa fought to hold together the pieces of her composure. She supped on wafer-thin pieces of ham, chicken, biscuits, and cheese-cakes without tasting a bite. She smiled without feeling. She fashioned small talk with their visitors without remembering what she said. When it came time for the fireworks, she followed Cecilia and Beatrice out of the booth to a better viewing area.

So this is what it feels like to be an automaton, Marisa thought. To move and function without feeling anything inside. She stared as the first rocket exploded, sending streamers of glittering light across the black sky. Wheels of exploding light spun on tall poles. The noise pounded upon her ears. Yet she didn't flinch. The light flickered upon her eyes. Yet she scarcely noticed the color and excitement.

Someone touched her arm. She turned and found Miles Cranely smiling at her. "I thought you should know I noticed your niece walking off toward Hermit's Walk with a gentleman."

"A gentleman?" Marisa tried to shake off the cotton wool shrouding her mind. "Who was he?"

Miles shook his head. "I didn't recognize him. He was about my height, slender and fair. I thought you would know him."

"Fair haired." Realization trickled through her befuddled brain, bringing with it a sudden fear. "Thank you."

Marisa glanced around, looking for Clayton. She couldn't find him in the crowd, and there was no time to look for him. She needed to find Beatrice. The crowd grew thinner as she approached the Grand Walk. Fireworks exploded overhead, illuminating the night. Beatrice was nowhere in sight.

Marisa hurried toward Hermit's Walk, her shoes crunching the gravel-lined path, her heart pounding against the wall of her chest. Once she crossed the

Grand Walk, the path became deserted. She glanced around her. The great expanse of wilderness stretched beyond the trees to her left, the downs to her right. The hair on her forearms prickled.

"Beatrice!" Her voice dissolved in an explosion of fireworks.

Marisa swallowed the bile in her throat and forced her feet to carry her along the pathway. Lanterns glowed along both sides of the tree-lined path, carving flickering shapes from the shadows. Any of a hundred men could have led Beatrice away from the crowd, Marisa assured herself. Fair-haired men were abundant in England. There was no need to fear—

What was that? A dark shape moved beneath the branches of the elm to her left. In the next heartbeat a hard hand grabbed her arm. She started to turn. A strong arm whipped around her waist, dragging her back against a rock-hard chest. She opened her mouth to scream. Her attacker clamped his hand over her mouth, capturing the sound against his gloved palm.

Fear speared through her. She struggled against her attacker, twisting in his powerful arms. He didn't seem to notice or care. With a stunning suddenness, he lifted his hand from her mouth. She sucked in air and screamed. The sound died inside the thick canvas sack he yanked over her head.

She swayed as he released his hold on her waist. The canvas sack settled around her hips. The thick scent of oats flooded her senses one moment; in the next the air whooshed from her lungs as a hard shoulder rammed her middle. Her world tilted as he lifted her from the ground. He jogged along the path, her screams cut off with each thud of his shoulder into her middle. She had a dreadful feeling she had just found the fair-haired man.

Chapter Twenty

Fear slammed through Marisa with each upward thrust of his shoulder into her belly. The blackguard would toss her into the Thames. That certainty pounded with the blood in her head. He lowered his shoulder. Her feet hit something solid. The next instant he pushed her shoulders. This was it. She sucked in her breath and fell . . . against a padded cushion. A door shut nearby. Harnesses jangled and the seat beneath her swayed. A coach? Where the devil was he taking her?

Marisa gripped the bottom edge of the sack and pulled it up over her head. She blinked, the coach lamp seeming as bright as sunlight after the darkness of the sack. Her vision cleared and she stared straight into Clayton's smiling face.

"You look surprised." Clayton leaned forward and plucked a dangling comb from her hair. "Were you perhaps expecting to see a fair-haired man?"

"What the devil . . . where is Beatrice?"

"When last I saw her she was dancing with Gregory Stanwood in the pavilion. But not to worry; your Aunt Cecilia is watching over her."

Marisa glared at him. "*You* had Miles tell me she had been taken away by a fair-haired man?"

He nodded. "I knew you couldn't resist the chance to get into trouble."

"What was I supposed to do? I had to look after Beatrice."

Clayton leaned closer, his eyes narrowing to silvery green slits. "You should have asked someone to go with you."

"There wasn't time."

"Miles would have obliged."

She frowned. "I didn't think to ask Miles."

He shook his head. "I didn't expect you to."

Marisa shoved her drooping hair back from her face. "So you did this to teach me a lesson."

He raised his hands in a sign of surrender. "Good heavens, no. I cannot think of a greater waste of time. What man short of Hercules could hope to tame your headstrong ways?"

"I see." She lifted the sack from the black velvet seat beside her. "So you tossed a sack over my head merely to amuse yourself, to pay me back for last night. By the way, you might have washed it first. I am certain to have every horse in London following me about looking for a nibble of oats."

He grinned. "You should be accustomed to it. You have always had stallions sniffing after your skirts looking for a nibble."

"How very amusing." She dropped the sack on the floor. "If you didn't intend to teach me a lesson, what were your intentions?"

Clayton leaned back against the squabs, stretching

his legs to the side to accommodate their length. "Do you mean to ask if my intentions are honorable?"

Her heart pounded furiously. "If you have any plans to ship me off to the country—"

"No. I realize you would find some way to come back to haunt me. And—as much as I hate to admit this—you are right. At least on one point."

"You have me breathless. What could I possibly have gotten right?"

He rolled his eyes to heaven. "If I am to have any hope of catching these blackguards, I shall need your help to do it."

Marisa tilted her head and smiled. "I am glad you finally decided to see reason. But that still doesn't explain the sack."

"Oh." He nudged the sack with the tip of his boot. "I am kidnapping you."

"Kidnapping me! But I thought you realized you needed my help."

"I do. I have also decided I shall never in my life be engaged to you again."

"Oh, I see." She straightened her back, though she felt like curling into a tight ball.

"No. You obviously do not see." Clayton slipped his hand into his coat, withdrew a folded piece of paper, and handed it to her. "I obtained that this afternoon."

Her hands trembled as Marisa opened the parchment. She read the words on the page twice, then managed to force a few words past the knot in her throat. "A special license."

"I warned you what would happen if you didn't turn that blasted coach around last night. Now it is time to face the consequences."

Consequences. As tempting as it was to hold him to

his strict code of honor, she could not do it.

"I realize I put you in a difficult situation last night." Tears blurred her eyes, joy and anxiety conspiring to turn her into a watering pot. "Still, I want you to know that if this isn't what you want . . . if you would rather marry Penelope Cuthberth, I shall not hold you to any code of honor."

She glanced up at him, her breath lodged in her chest. There, she had said what needed saying. Now all she could do was wait, and hope he wasn't foolish enough to imagine any other woman could make him happy.

His black brows lifted. "Penelope Cuthberth?"

"You seemed very attentive to her this evening."

"I guess you didn't see Penelope's mama drag me into the booth."

Hope surged with every quick beat of her heart. "No. I didn't."

Clayton studied her a moment, a lazy smile curving his lips. "You were jealous."

"I was." Marisa squared her shoulders, ignoring the screaming voice of her pride. "You would be making a mistake if you married any of those women on your list. But if that is what you want to do, if you are asking for my hand because of what happened last night, I think you should know I shall not hold you to any misbegotten sense of honor. I take full responsibility for what happened."

Clayton held her gaze, his expression revealing nothing of his emotions. "I intend to take a bride by the end of the Season. It might as well be you."

The words cracked like an open palm across her cheek. "Your choice of a wife really doesn't matter to you? You don't care if it is me or one of the women on your list?"

"You are one of the most beautiful women I have ever seen." He glanced out the window. "You may be a bit headstrong, but I see no reason why we should not manage well enough. Particularly if last night was any indication."

She bristled at his casual reference to what had been the most exciting moment of her entire life. "So you wouldn't care if I decided to turn down your offer."

Clayton kept his gaze fixed on a point in the street outside. "It is entirely your decision to make. You can marry me tonight or you can have me drop you off back at Vauxhall. But if you do decide to refuse my generous offer, remember that I shall not feel obliged to ask you again."

If she were still the foolish young woman she had been seven years ago, she might have missed the under-current in his voice. On the surface he was all ice, smooth and polished. But underneath that mask, she detected just a hint of uncertainty, enough to give her a slender thread of hope.

Although she had done it with only the best intentions, Marisa had no doubt she had shattered his pride seven years ago. She had since learned a great deal about the male of the species. Masculine pride was a particularly fragile, far too precious commodity. Men would fight wars to protect it. They would sequester themselves on a deserted island to keep anyone from threatening it. And woe to any woman who might bruise it just a bit. Clayton certainly would not be quick to place that delicate item within her reach again. Perhaps he wasn't as cool about the entire decision as he appeared.

"I suppose we do share a certain . . . lust for one another."

He shifted on his seat. "So it would appear."

"And I would hate to live my days as a spinster."

Clayton shot her a dark glance. "You could always marry Braden."

Marisa shook her head. "I doubt I would play the role of forgiving wife well. I would probably shoot him the first time I caught him with another woman. Even though I know the poor creature hasn't the ability to be loyal to any female."

He lifted his brows. "I shall keep that in mind."

She smiled at him. "It would be wise."

He drew in his breath. "Does this mean you intend to use that license this evening?"

"I suppose, under the circumstances, it is the only course of action." She leaned forward and rested her hand on his thigh. Thick muscles tensed beneath her palm. "You see, I would really like to discover how the rest of it turns out."

He frowned. "The rest of it?"

She smiled. "I am terribly curious. I know I shall not be content until I get the answers."

"To what?"

"You left things unfinished last night." Marisa drew a serpentine pattern against the inside of his thigh, smiling as his breathing turned ragged. "I want to know what happens when you actually carry everything through to a natural conclusion."

Flames flickered in his eyes. "You won't have long to wait for the answers."

She sat back, excitement tingling along her nerves. Although she wished her parents could attend her wedding, she was not about to risk another disaster for the sake of waiting for them to arrive in London. After all that had transpired over the past seven years, she was certain they would understand why she could not wait for them. Still, it would be nice to have some members of her family witness the most important event of her life. "I wonder if you might send someone for my Aunt Cecilia and Beatrice. I am certain they would like to attend the ceremony."

"I believe I can manage to have them in attendance." Clayton's shoulders rose with a deep inhalation. "I told Sophia and my brother they might have a wedding to attend this evening. They are awaiting my word."

"You were quite certain of yourself, it appears."

Clayton shrugged. "After last night, I thought you might agree to the marriage."

Marisa slipped off her shoe and drew her stockinged toes upward, over his polished boot. "After last night, I might agree to almost anything you propose."

Clayton shifted on the seat, drawing his foot away from her mischievous toes. "I have the feeling you will be the death of me yet."

Marisa laughed, her joy escaping in a husky sound. "I have a feeling you will manage nicely."

Marisa was his wife. Although his brain registered the reality of vows spoken, a part of him still could not believe that the woman standing before him was his bride. Clayton stood near the vanity in the bedchamber adjoining his, watching Marisa explore her surroundings. Last month the chamber had been decorated for the bride he had intended to take this Season. At the time, he had taken little interest in the project, allowing Sophia to make all the necessary selections. Now he wondered if Marisa approved of the chamber.

Candles burned behind the etched crystal globes of the wall sconces, casting a warm glow over the room. Pale blue silk flowed down the walls, from thick mahogany molding to polished mahogany wainscoting.

Shades of blue and ivory shaped an intricate pattern in the thick carpet beneath her feet. Marisa slid her fingertips over the pale blue silk brocade cascading from the canopy down a carved bedpost. The covers had been turned down, exposing the white silk sheets awaiting her. She hopped up on the bed, splashing the emerald silk of her gown over the sheet. "It's lovely."

Clayton released the breath he had been holding. "You can decorate it as you wish."

Marisa slid her hand over the embroidered lace trim of a pillowcase. "I see no reason to make any changes."

Although he had nearly taken her innocence last night, he couldn't shake an uneasy feeling gripping his stomach. He felt awkward and clumsy, like a boy with his first woman. It was ridiculous. He had bedded more women than he cared to remember at this moment. Yet, looking at Marisa sitting there, her hair falling over her shoulders, her smile making him feel as though he were the only man in the world, he couldn't stop thinking he might make a mess of this night.

It was a silly fear. Clayton knew it. If women remained virgins until the day they died, the entire human race would be extinguished. Yet all of his experience left him as green as grass when it came to an untouched maiden. "I realize you must regret your parents not being in attendance tonight."

"I am certain they will understand. I think my mother still regrets her decision to make us wait the first time we were engaged."

Clayton crushed the memories stirring within him. This was not a night to let memories litter his path. "I'm not sure why she should regret it. You needed time to see if marrying me was what you really wanted. And obviously it wasn't."

She slipped off the bed and moved toward him. "I never changed my mind about wanting to marry you, Clay."

"Marisa, there is no need to revise history."

Marisa paused before him. "I love you. I have never stopped loving you."

The light was playing tricks on him. He could almost believe he could see the truth of her heart in her eyes. "Do you make a habit of crying off engagements with men you love?"

She slid her fingertips down his cheek, spreading warmth over his skin. "Only when I think it is what he wants."

Clayton stared at her. "I should know better than to try to follow your logic. One of these days my mind will become so tangled I shall never be able to use it again."

"Clay, I was a girl barely twenty. Filled with passion and romance. I wanted so very much to know I was loved. By you. Only you." She opened her arms. "For the past seven years I have thought of what I might say if I ever had the chance to stand with you like this. And now I am at a loss as to how to begin."

"I don't see any point in dredging up the past. It cannot be altered."

"No, it cannot. But I think we should start our marriage with all of the questions answered."

Memories rose inside him, bitter and burning. "There is no need to plunge through events that happened a lifetime ago. We are not the same two people we were when we first met. No matter what happened then, it is in the past. Leave it there."

"But how can you expect to move forward if you never resolve something as important as a broken engagement? For heaven's sake, Clay. It changed both of our lives. I want you to understand what happened. And I need to know a few things as well.''

He cupped her face in his hands and kissed her, allowing her to taste the raw hunger gnawing at his vitals, the need for her he could no longer deny. She barely had time for a startled response before he lifted his head and stared down into her confused eyes. ''This is what matters. A fire burns between us, Mari. Don't question the flames.''

''Lust?''

He slid his hands over her shoulders. ''You should not underestimate the power of lust.''

Her finely arched brows lifted. ''While it burns I imagine it is very powerful. But shouldn't a marriage be based on more?''

Clayton drew her closer, until her breasts brushed his chest. Whorls of heat spiraled through him. Her lips parted on a soft sigh. ''Don't try to make something more of this than exists. I will be a good husband to you, Mari. I will be faithful and constant. I will see to your comfort. I will do my best to give you pleasure. But don't ask me for more than I am capable of giving.''

''Capable of giving? Or willing to give?''

He smoothed the tip of his finger down her neck. Her body brushed his, conjuring heat, like sunlight upon a frozen lake. The scent of lilies in the rain swirled through his senses. The warmth of her seeped into his pores. Her smile drew him like a beacon in the middle of a moonless winter. In spite of his every intention, he felt himself falling, tumbling into her web. ''They both result in the same thing,'' he said, forcing a harsh tone into his voice.

''Yes. I suppose they do.'' In spite of her smile, Clayton had an uneasy feeling when he looked into her eyes, as though a silent declaration of war had been issued between them. "You don't trust me. Do you?"

"I am not certain I understand what you mean."

She studied him a moment in that candid way she had of stripping away pretense. "There is a distance between us, a barrier. You are afraid I shall get too close to you."

He touched her cheek, her skin warm satin beneath his fingers. "I shall allow you to get very close to me. As close as a man and woman can come."

Marisa smiled, a wistful expression touching her features. "You mean you will share your body with me."

He lifted a lock of her hair, the curl lying like black silk across his palm. "It is all I have to give you, Mari. There is nothing left inside of me."

"Clay," she whispered, cupping his cheek in her warm palm. "My poor, wounded darling. If it takes the rest of my life, I shall find a way to make you trust me. One day you shall, you know. One day you will realize it is safe to open your heart to me. Because there is nothing more precious to me than your love."

He wasn't certain he could pry open his heart. "And if that day doesn't come?"

"It shall." She patted his chest. "I have faith in us, my darling."

Clayton looked into eyes that had haunted him through the years, eyes as intoxicating as the aged brandy they resembled. He saw hope in those beautiful eyes, conviction and faith. She would do her best to shatter every defense he had. He turned away from her, needing some distance. "I should give you a few moments to prepare."

Marisa gripped the hem of his coat, halting him like a stallion on a tether. "I have had seven years to prepare for this moment. All I need is you. Here and now.''

Her words rippled through him. Clayton glanced over his shoulder and wished he hadn't. The hunger in her eyes triggered an instant reply deep inside. Heat coiled though him with each surge of his heart. His coat brushed his hips as she released the soft gray wool.

She pulled the tape at the side of her bodice and peeled open the emerald silk, revealing the white muslin of her petticoat. ''Last night, when you touched me, I felt I was melting inside, turning all warm and liquid.''

He followed her elegant hands with his gaze as she tugged the tie inside her gown. The emerald silk spilled open. He intended this marriage to go forth under his terms. He was commander here. He would leave, and return when he had allowed her to stew awhile. That would show her she had no power over him.

Marisa shrugged her shoulders. Clayton watched the emerald silk fall around her. Slowly he turned toward her, when his brain shouted another command: *Leave!* Yet his body responded to a much more tempting order.

''The way you looked at me when I lay naked in your arms''—she unfastened her petticoat as she spoke—''made me feel so deliciously wicked. The way Eve must have felt when she coaxed Adam to take a bite of the apple.''

Clayton swallowed hard. He should get away from her. He must show her he would not be manipulated or controlled. He was in command here. No woman would lead him about by the nose. She peeled the petticoat and chemise from her shoulders. He watched, entranced, as the white muslin slid over her breasts, her belly, the length of her legs, falling with a soft sigh at her feet.

Marisa slid her hand over her belly in a slow caress. "When you look at me that way, I feel so warm inside. Like melted butter."

Last night she had felt like melted butter, slick and hot against his fingers. She had tasted like summer rain. She stepped away from the puddle of her clothes, but she did not approach him. Instead she walked to the bed. He tried to look away from her. Yet his gaze remained riveted on her slender body, watching each graceful move as she climbed onto the bed and settled against the pillows.

Marisa lifted one shapely leg, pointing the tip of her emerald slipper at him. "I wonder if you might help me remove my shoes and stockings?"

He should refuse. It was the sensible thing to do. Show her now he was made of stronger stuff. Yet his feet were already moving straight for her. He couldn't help himself. All the sense in the world couldn't stand against the power she wielded. He slid the shoe from her foot. It made a soft thump against the floor. He removed the other and let it drop. White lace adorned the white garters holding her stockings above her knees. His fingers trembled as he unfastened the ties. His arousal strained against the barriers of his clothes, desire pounding like pain through him.

"Your hands," she whispered, as he slid one silk stocking from her leg. "I love your hands. So strong, yet gentle. I want them on my skin. Everywhere."

His breath lodged in his throat. Clayton slid his hand down her leg, caressing the softness of her skin as he removed the other stocking.

She drew her fingers over the thick ridge of his

arousal, caressing him through the layers of his clothes. Clayton moaned with the sweet torture.

"This time, I want you just as bare as I am." She flicked open the top button of his trousers.

Clayton watched her work the buttons on his trousers, her pale fingers dismantling the last of his defenses. The flap fell open, revealing the solid proof of her power over him. There was no hope for it, no salvation from this fall. He had wanted her for too long. He needed her more than he needed his breath.

He stripped off his coat as Marisa unfastened his drawers. Silk and wool slid over his hips, exposing him fully to her gaze. The first touch of her warm fingers upon his heated flesh nearly brought him to his knees.

"Oh, my goodness," she whispered, exploring the length of him. "I suppose it is silly to wonder if we will fit."

He tossed his cravat to the floor and pulled the studs from his cuffs. "We will fit perfectly, my beautiful temptress."

She smiled up at him. "I know we will. I have always known it."

Clayton pulled the shirt over his head and tossed it to the floor. Marisa's fingers stilled upon his arousal. She stared at his chest, her expression revealing her shock. Clayton glanced down at the scars sliced across his skin, appalled that he had exposed her to such ugliness. *Clumsy oaf!* He would end up making a mess of this yet. "I'm sorry; I should have put out the candles."

Marisa drew her fingertips over the raised white scar slicing across his ribs. There were others, stark reminders of the brutalities of war. "So much pain," she whispered.

"I'm healed," Clayton said, his voice harsh in the

quiet room. "I sometimes forget about the scars. I shouldn't have exposed you to them."

"You need not hide anything from me." She leaned forward and pressed her lips against the ugliest of the scars, as though the puckered flesh were somehow precious to her. His muscles quivered beneath her touch. "You came home. Nothing else matters."

Marisa looked up at him, and in that moment he felt he could pluck every star from the sky, if she were beside him. "Come lie with me, Clay. Make me your wife in every way."

Enchantment

The man in arms 'gainst female charms,
Even he her willing slave is.

—Robert Burns

Chapter Twenty-one

Marisa watched as Clayton stripped away the rest of his clothes. When he was as bare as she was, he stood beside the bed, looking at her as though she were some rare creature from the far side of the world who had just tumbled into his bed.

Candlelight gleamed on smooth skin, caressing the width of his shoulders, spilling down his chest where a ring dangled from a gold chain to nestle against the black curls shading the thick, muscular planes. Rubies and diamonds glinted in the light, teasing her with memories of the few precious weeks she had worn that ring. He had not offered her the ring again. Would he ever feel she was worthy to wear it?

The scars of war did not steal from his blatant male beauty. They served only as reminders of mortality, of how precious each moment of this life should be, of how close she had come to losing him. If it took her the rest of her life, she would prove to him how much he meant, and had always meant to her. She brushed the backs of her fingers over the curve of his hip. "You're more splendid than I imagined."

Clayton shook his head, an enigmatic smile touching his lips. "Strange, I never realized you were so short-sighted."

"Then perhaps you should come closer." Marisa took his hand and tugged him toward her. "So I can see you better."

The soft mattress dipped as he climbed onto the bed beside her, rolling her toward him. Their bodies brushed, flesh against flesh, woman and man. Excitement rippled through her like pebbles tossed upon a quiet lake. She saw that same excitement mirrored in his beautiful eyes.

He slid his hand over her hip, drawing her close against him. The searing slide of his arousal pressed against her. She slipped her arms around his shoulders, snuggling against powerful muscles, the crisp curls on his chest teasing the sensitive tips of her breasts. Marisa moaned at the sudden stab of sensation that spiraled through her. His nostrils flared, like a stallion with the scent of a mare in season.

She had waited a lifetime to hold Clayton like this, to feel the brush of his skin against hers. He might try to keep those barriers against her in place, but she intended to drag the walls down, brick by brick. She nipped the smooth skin at the joining of his neck and shoulder, smiling as his breath escaped in a rush.

"I shall warn you, Clay. I have been dreaming about you for seven years. Now that I have you in my arms, I just might keep you trapped in this bed for a month."

He laughed, a dark rumble from deep in his throat. He slipped his arm around her and rolled with her until she lay pinned beneath him. The ring she had once worn dangled from the chain around his neck, brushing the valley between her breasts. The hard length of his arousal pressed against her inner thigh, searing her skin with a sweet promise. "I wonder if I could endure such torture."

"Torture?" She nuzzled his neck, flicked her tongue against his skin, tasting him, inhaling his scent deep into her lungs. "My darling, torture was lying in my bed at night wondering where you were. Torture was looking at the newspaper each day and praying your name was not among the casualties of war. Torture was not knowing if I might ever hold you in my arms."

He smoothed his hand over her hair, a glimmer of disbelief in his beautiful eyes. "You thought of me once in a while?"

"Every day." She turned her cheek and pressed her lips against his warm palm. "Every night."

He brushed his lips against her brow. "There is no need to feed my pride. No need to speak of the past."

She needed to speak of the past, to explain her own foolish actions, to understand why he had set her wandering down that path to disaster seven years ago. Still, she sensed this was not the time. She slid her hands over the broad width of his shoulders, his skin smooth and warm beneath her palms. "I love you so much. I only wish I could go back and claim every moment of your life that I have missed."

He closed his eyes, as though trying to block her from seeing into his soul. Yet she had glimpsed the doubts in his eyes, the need he couldn't conceal. He wanted to believe her as much as he wanted to hold her at a distance. Tonight she intended to pry the first brick from his defenses. "Clay, I—"

He clamped his mouth over hers as though he wanted to drive all thought from her mind. He touched the tip of his tongue to her lips, and she opened, welcoming the slick slide of his tongue into her mouth. He claimed her, feeding her hunger with a taste of his own, drugging her with his own potent brand of masculinity.

He slid his hands over her breasts, down her sides, and gripped her hips, lifting her against him. She wrapped her arms around his neck, holding him close. Yet she couldn't get close enough to him. He slid the heated length of his arousal over her nether lips, teasing her with a taste, a nibble, before he pulled away from her.

"Clay," she whispered. "I need . . . please."

"Easy. Some things are better if savored."

It soon became clear he intended to drive her as mad as he had the previous evening. He spread kisses down her neck and across her shoulder, all the while his hands roamed up and down her sides, her hips, her breasts, his long fingers flexing against her skin as though he couldn't get enough of her. The black silk of his hair brushed her chin as he lowered his head, his lips closing over her breast. She slipped her hands into his hair, held him close as he suckled her, sending sensations skittering in all directions.

Last night he had introduced her to this sensual world, where pleasure came from a touch, a brush of skin, a whisper of breath. She wanted more. She wanted to claim him completely, to give of herself and take all he had to give in return. She wanted the heat of him, the strength of him, his fears, his hopes, his dreams. She wanted to share all that she was and all that she could be with Clay, only Clay.

A sweet ache pulsed in the most private part of her. Instinct lifted her hips. Need prompted her to brush her flesh against him, seeking surcease from the ache centered there. He growled low in his chest, the primal sound rippling through her, whispering to a part of her she was only beginning to understand. He slid his mouth over the slope of her breast, nuzzled the valley between, then made a slow ascent of the other slope until he claimed her nipple. He suckled her, the sweet tug against her flesh sending sensation chasing sensation until inarticulate sobs slipped from her lips.

He slithered down her body like a sensuous flame, igniting fires in his wake. Her every nerve tingled, coming to life beneath his touch. He slipped his hands under her hips as he settled between her thighs. From the first day she had met him, Clayton had colored her every thought of desire and passion. Yet all of her innocent musings could not compare to the reality of Clayton.

"From the first day I saw you, all those years ago, I have dreamed of doing this," he whispered, brushing his lips against her inner thigh. "I had never thought I wanted passion until the day you barged into my carefully ordered life."

"I always knew I wanted fire and passion." She flexed her fingers on his shoulders. "With one special man. From the day I met you, I couldn't get you out of my mind."

He turned his cheek against her thigh, his nose brushing the curls at the joining of her legs. "A dull bookworm?"

"A warm and generous man who made me feel I was beautiful inside."

"Beautiful." He nibbled the inside of her thigh. "Intelligent. Unpredictable. A creature of fire and light."

Marisa sucked in her breath, tension drawing her vitals like the string of a bow, as he moved upward, spreading kisses along her inner thigh. He threaded his fingers through the dark curls at the joining of her legs, then touched her with his lips. She arched against him, seeking the same blinding pleasure he had given her last night.

She tossed her head back and forth against the pillows, snatched handfuls of the sheet, soft sobs spilling from her lips as he worked his wicked magic. Her body arched and quivered beneath his touch, a violoncello singing beneath the touch of a master.

"Clay!" She arched against him as the pleasure burst over her, exploding like the fireworks she had seen that evening. Her body shuddered beneath his, shaking with the pure power of it, the incredible joy he had given her.

As the last spasm shook her body, he entered her, plunging in one glorious thrust deep into her body. She gasped with the unexpected pain splintering through her. She gripped his shoulders, pressed her face against his neck, and sought to keep her wits.

"Mari." He brushed his lips against her ear. "I'm sorry. It's only the first time, sweetheart. I swear, it will be better next time."

She felt him sliding out of her and tightened her legs around his hips. "What are you doing?"

He smoothed his hand over her hair. "I think you have had enough of me for one night."

She swallowed hard. "I shall never in this lifetime have enough of you."

He smiled in spite of the tension she could feel vibrating through his body. "It's all right."

"No." She wrapped her arms around him and held him when he would have pulled away from her. "Finish it."

He frowned. "Mari, you're so small. I cannot avoid hurting you."

"Make love to me, Clay." She eased her hips upward, reclaiming the long length of him, pain a dull burn now. "I promise I won't break."

He smoothed his hand over her cheek. "Are you certain?"

"More certain than of anything else in my life."

The uncertainty in his eyes eased as he slowly began to move within her. He kissed one corner of her lips, slid his mouth over hers, until he claimed her completely. The sweet concern in his kiss spread like a gentle balm through her. With each slow, sure stroke of his body the pain drew away until only a distant memory of it remained.

He slipped his hand between their bodies, found the secret place where pleasure dwelled, and awoke that pleasure, coaxing it to take flight until it rose and shimmered inside of her. He was a sorcerer conjuring magic with his touch. He was her one and only love, coaxing pleasure with his gentleness. Joy bubbled within her, like the effervescence of champagne in crystal, until it filled her.

She arched against him, lifting to meet his downward thrusts, reaching for the summit hidden beneath a misty veil. She moved with him, matching his ever increasing rhythm, dashing for that summit, until she burst through the mist and claimed it as her own.

"Clay," she whispered, clutching him to her. His breath warmed her neck as he eased against her, his body pressing her down into the soft eiderdown. She had never in her life felt more complete.

Clayton resisted the urge to purr as Marisa slid her hand down his back. He had thought himself experienced with women. He was wrong. Never in his life had he experienced anything like this, a joining so complete he felt he had lost a part of himself, and found another, far more precious and rare. Pleasure. He had thought he had known what it was until now.

He eased away from her, just far enough to relieve the pressure of his chest upon her. Marisa was lying with her head turned on the pillow, her eyes closed, her lips tipped into a smile so beautiful she seemed an angel delivered to him from heaven. He smoothed the damp curls back from her cheek. "You seem to have survived."

Thick black lashes fluttered and lifted, revealing the expression in her eyes. The look in those golden depths drove all the breath from his lungs. Warmth, affection, a contentment so deep he could feel it curl around him. For years he had imagined joining his body with hers. Yet the satisfaction, the pleasure, the pride of knowing he had given her pleasure, were more than he had ever dreamed.

"Making love with you. It wasn't what I thought it would be."

Her words trickled like ice into his heated blood. "It wasn't?"

"No." Marisa drew her fingertips over his chest, pausing to explore a nipple hidden beneath the hair on his chest. Clayton sighed at the gentle sensation rippling across his skin. "Have you ever dreamed of something, thought about it, imagined it happening? And when it finally does happen, you discover you were wrong about it?"

"Wrong?" He held his breath, waiting for her to continue, all the while trying to convince himself it didn't really matter if she had been disappointed with his lovemaking.

"I have often wondered what it would be like truly to be your wife. To lie with you. To have your body joined with mine." She opened her hand on his chest, spreading her slender fingers beneath the betrothal ring dangling from the gold chain around his neck. "I never realized how powerful this could be. I underestimated it. Of course, I'm not sure anyone could truly describe it. And if you had never experienced it, you would never truly understand."

He breathed again. "I understand what you mean. It was more than I dreamed it could be, too."

The corners of her lips tipped into a shy smile. "You dreamed of making love with me?"

He looked away from those perceptive eyes. She had a way of stripping him bare, of finding all of his secrets. "It's fairly natural for a male to imagine making love to a beautiful woman."

"Oh, I see," she said, her soft voice revealing a trace of disappointment.

He eased from her body, feeling as though he had left a part of himself with her. She moaned softly as he left her body, and he glanced back. "Are you all right?"

She nodded. "Better than I have been in a long time."

He fell back against the pillows and stared up at the canopy above her bed. Candlelight flickered against the pale blue brocade, carving away the shadows. She snuggled against him, resting her head on his shoulder. He held her, savoring the reality of her pressed against his side, indulging in his own need until he felt her drifting off to sleep. Only then did he move away from her.

"What is it?" she asked, grabbing his arm when he tried to leave the bed.

He leaned back against the pillow, resisting the urge to stay with her. "I should leave and give you a chance to sleep."

"Leave?" She rolled to her side, propped herself up on her forearm, and leaned over him. "You intend to leave?"

Her hair spilled across his chest, the silken strands teasing his skin. He looked up into her wide eyes, fighting the desire rising once more within him. No matter how much she had enjoyed their first time together, she would be sore. He had no intention of hurting her again. "You're sleepy. I should return to my chamber."

She frowned. "I thought you might sleep here, with me."

He smoothed his fingertips over her cheek. "I am often restless at night. I would no doubt keep you awake."

Marisa folded her arms on his chest, rested her chin on her arms, and smiled at him. "For seven years I have been dreaming of sleeping in your arms. Please stay with me."

He thought of the nightmares that haunted him at night, the times he awakened in a cold sweat. He would not expose her to that ugliness. Still, a part of him longed to stay with her.

"Please, Clay," she whispered.

He could not deny that soft entreaty, not when it coincided with his own need. Perhaps he could stay awake all night, just holding her. He slipped out from beneath her and climbed from bed.

"Where are you going?"

Clayton glanced back. Marisa lay across the bed, her bottom lip pouting, her hair an undisciplined mass of glossy black waves. She was naked and gorgeous and his. "I'm going to get cleaned up a bit. I'll be back."

"That sounds like a good idea." She lowered her

gaze, a sultry smile touching her lips. "Do you need any help?"

He glanced down at his rising shaft and clenched his jaw. "I think I can manage."

"Yes. I am certain you can." She climbed out of bed and moved toward him.

"Marisa, it is too soon for you to think about ravishing me again. You'll end up too sore to walk."

She rested her hand on his chest. "Are you certain?"

"Quite."

"Oh, well, if you say so." She drew her fingertip in a lazy, wavy pattern down his chest. "Still, I wonder if you might help me clean up a bit."

He closed his eyes. "Is there any wonder Adam was tossed out of Eden on his ear?"

She laughed, a husky sound that rippled through him like music. "Come, my darling, let's get you ready for bed."

Sunlight played against his eyelids, dragging him from slumber. Still Clayton resisted. Something soft snuggled against his side, warm and lush. A woman. *Marisa.* He opened his eyes to the sight of a slender arm slung over his waist, thick black waves spilling across his chest. Her breasts brushed his side with each soft inhalation.

He turned his head and looked at her face, her cheek nestled against his shoulder. Thick black lashes lay against her pale skin, her soft lips were parted, her breath puffed warmly against his skin. Beneath the sheet her thigh smoldered against his loins, its smooth skin tempting him. He drew his hand down her arm. For the first time in a very long time he had slept through the night. The ghosts had not come to haunt him. The horror of the battlefield had not tortured him.

For the first time in a lifetime he felt a sense of peace.

A soft little moan escaped her lips. She stirred against him, her thigh brushing the rising heat of his arousal, her arm sliding over his waist. He smoothed the hair back from her cheek and watched her open her eyes to the new day. She smiled, warmth filling her sleepy eyes. "Good morning, husband."

Something stirred within him, something warm in a place that had been frozen for far too long. "Good morning, wife."

She sat up and curled her arms over her head, stretching, her breasts lifting, drawing his hungry gaze. "I had the most marvelous dream."

"Did you?" He touched her; he couldn't prevent himself. He brushed his fingertips down her arm, slid his fingers around her wrist, and lifted her hand to his lips.

She sighed as he touched her skin with his tongue. "I just realized something."

He smiled at her. "What?"

"No matter what I dream, these days reality is far more intriguing."

Laughter rose inside of him, soft, contented, a sound he hadn't heard in a very long time. Marisa was his dreams, all of them. He groaned with pure joy as she climbed on top of him. Her long legs settled between his, her smooth belly brushed his hair-roughened one. She stretched, slipping her arms around his neck, her breasts snuggling against his chest. His every nerve tingled in ways he had never suspected possible.

She kissed his chin. "Do you suppose we could stay in bed all day?"

He slid his hand down the sleek warmth of her back. "I have a meeting with Adler Newberry this afternoon."

She crinkled her nose. "That gives us only a few hours."

He tucked her hair behind her ear. "I suppose we shall have to make the best of them."

She wiggled her hips, brushing soft, feminine curls against his hardened flesh. "I suppose we shall."

Clayton stood by the fireplace in his library, listening to Adler Newberry's latest report, trying to pry his mind from the woman he had left sleeping in her bedchamber. *Marisa.* The thought of her alone could heat the blood in his veins. He glanced at Adler and realized the big man was waiting for a reply. "You found nothing suspicious."

Adler Newberry leaned forward in his chair, soft leather sighing beneath his weight. "Wormsley has made no contact with any man matching the description of the fair-haired man Lady Marisa overheard. It's possible they are staying clear of one another for now."

"It's possible." Clayton curled his hand into a fist against the white marble mantel. "And it is just as possible he had nothing at all to do with this."

"Aye, sir. It is." Adler rubbed his thick chin. "I've been thinking about the party you have planned. If the blackguard we're after does get an invitation to attend a party given by the dowager Duchess of Marlow, he might become suspicious. If he thinks you know who he is, he might come at you even harder than he has so far."

Clayton had already considered the risks. "We don't have many options."

"Aye." Adler tapped his palms together. "I'm thinking you could use a few more extra footmen."

Clayton grinned. "Greensley said he isn't at all pleased with the two new footmen I hired. He feels they are as likely to break a plate as they are to deliver it safely to the table. He assigned them both to scrubbing pots.''

Adler chuckled. ''Holcomb and Bikens told me as much last night, sir. I had to convince them it was a very bad idea to hang your butler up by his thumbs.''

''Thank you. I had a talk with Greensley. I think we have reached an understanding.''

Adler nodded. ''I'll see to it you have two more men by this evening. Still, I wish there were more we could do.''

''So do I.'' Clayton tapped the edge of his fist against the mantel. ''I hate this, not knowing who the enemy is.''

''And you have thought of nothing else, no one at all who might be behind this?''

Clayton clenched his jaw. ''I haven't been back in England for more than a few months.''

Adler rose from the chair. ''Could it be someone from before you joined the army, sir? Someone who perhaps was hoping you wouldn't be coming back from the war? Someone who might benefit from your death?''

''My brother would inherit everything should I die.'' Clayton grinned. ''I seriously doubt he plans to eliminate me.''

''Aye, sir. The duke is a fine man.''

Clayton released his breath in a frustrated sigh. ''We'll know more after the party.''

Adler nodded. ''We'll catch the bastard, sir.''

Clayton thought of Marisa. If he could, he would wrap her in cotton wool and hide her in the country until this was over. Yet even if he could manage to keep her locked away, he knew she would never forgive him for doing it. He would give her a chance to identify the man at the party; after that, they would talk about a strategic retreat, at least for her.

Chapter Twenty-two

Six days after his marriage, Clayton faced his new mama-and papa-in-law for the first time. They sat on the sofa across from Clayton in his drawing room, looking as comfortable as they might in their own home. Clayton could not share that sense of calm. He was not a callow youth, a boy who had to explain himself to his elders. It was ridiculous to think of promises he had made seven years ago or the fact that he had stolen their chance to share in their daughter's wedding. Still, Clayton couldn't shake his discomfort as he sat with Edgar and Audrey Grantham in the drawing room of his home.

"Marisa is still in bed?" Audrey settled her cup on the saucer she held. "How odd. She is usually one of the first to rise."

As Clayton sipped his coffee, steam brushed his face with the thick scent of the dark brew. Yet the warmth simmering through him had nothing at all to do with coffee and everything to do with the reason his wife was still asleep. He had made love to Marisa twice last night. Yet it hadn't cured him. He was still as randy as a buck in rut. This morning, as the first light of dawn touched her face, he had taken her once more. For some confounded reason he couldn't get enough of the woman he had married. "I expect she will join us directly."

Edgar chuckled softly, drawing his wife's attention. He winked at her. "As I recall, there are still mornings when we rise early and yet manage to sleep through breakfast."

Audrey turned wide eyes on Clayton, understanding dawning in the golden brown depths. A smile curved her lips. "I suppose it will take a while to think of Marisa as a married lady."

Heat crawled upward along his neck. As much as Clayton tried to dismiss it, he felt like a boy of twenty again, with all of his intimate secrets placed on display for his elders.

"Mari's letter took us by surprise." Edgar crossed his long legs. "As much as I wish we could have been here to share your wedding day, I can understand your haste—after what happened the last time you and Mari were engaged."

Clayton's stomach clenched at the reminder. "I thought it best not to have a long engagement."

Audrey set her cup and saucer on the pedestal table beside her. She folded her hands in her lap and addressed Clayton in a quiet tone. "I hope you can forgive me, Clayton. If not for my cautious desire to be sure that both you and Mari were certain of your decision, you and my daughter would have been married a long time ago."

Clayton managed a smile. "You only gave Marisa a

chance to change her mind. It was better she did it before we exchanged our vows.''

Audrey looked surprised. "Change her mind? How odd. I was under the impression you were the one who had changed his mind about the marriage."

Clayton held her steady gaze. "Marisa told you I was the one who wanted to end our engagement?"

"She told me you were having doubts," Audrey said. "I told her the only honorable thing to do was to cry off. A gentleman certainly couldn't do it. And she certainly didn't want to make you unhappy. She was very concerned about your happiness."

Clayton's throat tightened. "She cried off our engagement to make me happy?"

"I am certain you can understand why she could not go through with the marriage if you were having doubts." Audrey studied him for a moment. "You were having doubts?"

"The only doubt I had was whether or not I could make her happy."

Audrey nodded. "I see. I suspect you were both too young, and too concerned with making the other one happy, to see how miserable you were making each other."

Miserable? Had he made Marisa miserable?

"Well, at least the two of you have found your way back to one another." Edgar shook his head. "I was afraid my beautiful daughter would end her days a spinster, pining over you."

Pining over him? Beautiful, sought-after Marisa? Clayton's head whirled. Soft footsteps sounded in the hallway. Marisa hurried into the room, rose-colored muslin swishing softly around her legs. She smiled at Clayton, a warm, generous smile that whispered of shared intimacies and promises made. Clayton watched as she greeted her parents, all that Audrey and Edgar had revealed swirling in his brain. It was possible Marisa had concocted the nonsense to explain her own decision to send him packing. Yet that explanation rang with a hollow sound in his brain.

Later that evening, Clayton lay in Marisa's bed, waiting for his wife to leave her dressing room. After dinner, she had told him she had a surprise for him tonight. His blood had been simmering ever since she had led him into her chamber. Hell and damnation, his blood had been simmering from the first day he had found her waiting for him in his library. When that woman was near him, discipline went up in a puff of smoke.

He had to face facts. He could not control his primitive instincts when it came to Marisa. The thought of her sent the blood pumping hard into his loins. One look at her turned him into a ravenous barbarian who should be stalking about in animal skins. One touch led to complete madness. He still could not believe he had taken her on the desk in the library yesterday afternoon. But at the time the bedchambers had seemed ten thousand miles away.

"I hope you like this," Marisa said, as she stepped out of her dressing room. "My modiste had two girls working for the last three days to make it. She is quite proud of the result."

Clayton frowned at her dressing gown. It was black silk trimmed in scarlet. He was certain he had seen it before. "Make what?"

"This." She slipped off her dressing gown and tossed it over the back of a chair near her bed. A single candle burned beneath a crystal globe on the table beside the bed, but it was enough to illuminate the new negligee she wore. One look stole the breath from his lungs.

Burgundy red silk brushed the curves of her body, so sheer he could see the dark triangle of curls at the joining of her thighs. Black embroidered lace edged the deep U of the neckline, plunging to just above her nipples, revealing the pale swells of her breasts. As she walked toward him, he noticed that the same black embroidered lace edged a slit in the left side of the gown. Heat coiled low in his belly as he watched her move, the burgundy silk parting with each step, giving him a glimpse of a shapely leg from just below the curve of her hip.

Marisa paused beside the bed. "Well, do you like it?"

Clayton had to swallow hard to use his voice. "Yes."

She took the edge of the sheet covering the lower half of his body. She drew the sheet away from him, sliding white silk across his skin, exposing the flesh that rose to her siren's call. She lifted her brows, a mischievous glint filling her eyes. "Yes, I can see you do like it."

"The package is nice." He gripped her hand and pulled her onto the bed beside him. "But the real treasure is inside."

She lowered her lips to his, and Clayton abandoned himself to this woman. He caressed her, rubbing his hands over the sheer silk warm from her body, stroking her back, her sides, cupping her breasts, sliding his thumbs over the taut nipples. He drank the soft sighs from her lips, desire licking at his loins like hungry flames.

"I want to please you the way you please me." She wiggled free of his grasp and took his hands. "Let me touch you."

He frowned as she spread his arms wide and placed them on the bed on either side of him. "What do you have in mind?"

"I want to touch you the way you always touch me."

Erotic images blossomed in his mind. Blood pumped fast and hot, collecting low in his belly, until his loins throbbed with a heavy ache. "You want to touch me?"

"Yes. All of you." She pressed her lips to his nipple and stabbed the tiny nub with her tongue. Clayton gasped at the sharp sensation. "Will you let me?"

He brushed his fingertips over her breast, where black embroidered lace met smooth ivory satin. "You can do anything you want."

She took his hand from her breast and laid it once more on the bed beside him. "*I* am going to touch *you*. You must lie there and take it, or you will distract me before I get a chance to explore everything."

Never in his life had he been led in lovemaking. Yet she looked so earnest, as though she were very serious about this request.

"I know you pride yourself on your iron discipline." A challenge glittered in her eyes. "Do you think you can manage to lie there without touching me?"

He released his pent-up breath. "Go ahead. Touch me."

Her lips tipped into a smug little smile. "I have wanted to do this for quite some time. But you always manage to distract me."

He wasn't certain what she had in mind, or how far she would really take this game. But he knew he wanted very much to play.

She slid down the length of his body, kissing him, flicking her tongue against his skin as though she sa-

vored the taste of him. As he surrendered himself to
her will, he discovered a secret. Allowing her to feel
her way through this new territory held rewards he had
never suspected. She was like a child with a new toy,
an innocent discovering all the intricacies of making
love. She was a woman entrancing her man.

"Your body is so fascinating." She spread his legs
and knelt between his thighs, the warm silk of her
negligee brushing his skin. "The textures are so vi-
brant, smooth and rough, soft and hard. So incredibly
intriguing."

Her hair spilled over his hips as she leaned forward,
the sinuous slide sending sensation spiraling along his
skin. He pressed his palms down into the mattress to
keep from touching her. She drew one fingertip upward
over the length of his arousal, the hardened flesh bob-
bing toward her, seeking more of her touch. He tipped
back his head, a groan slipping past his lips as pleasure
darted along his nerves. She touched him in ways a
woman had never touched him, kissed him, tasted him,
until he feared he would come to pieces beneath her
touch.

He gripped the sheet in both hands, struggling to
keep from taking her until she was ready. Finally she
straddled his hips. He sucked in his breath at the exotic
brush of damp femininity against the tip of his arousal.

"I love you, Clay," she whispered, as she took him
into the warm haven of her body. "Only you. Always
you."

Her soft words thumped against the stone encrusting
his heart. He could feel stone splintering, tiny cracks
opening around his defenses. Still, there was nothing
he could do to prevent it. As much as he wanted to
protect himself, he wanted even more to believe her.

Clayton watched, helpless to look away as Marisa drew the negligee over her head and dropped it on the floor. She leaned toward him, touching her bare breasts to his chest. He slipped his arms around her and drew her upward. He brushed his face against the warmth of her breasts, and her soft sobs of pleasure spilled through him like sunlight. She was all the light and warmth in his life. And he wanted to bask in that light, savor her warmth. He licked the valley between her breasts, slid his tongue upward along the soft slope. The light of a single candle flickered upon her skin, beckoning him. He drank the golden light from one taut, pink nipple, suckling her as she moved her hips above him, riding him, controlling him as no woman had ever done in his life.

The first delicate contractions of feminine release tugged on his flesh. She grasped his shoulders, his name escaping on a sob. She rode him, thrusting her hips, meeting his every upward movement, until he felt the pleasure crest inside of her, until the tiny spasms grasped his aroused flesh, dragging him with her. A low growl shuddered from his chest as he surrendered to the pleasure, joining her in a realm where memories had no meaning.

Marisa sagged against him. She slipped her arms beneath his neck and pressed her lips to the hollow below his ear. The innocent fragrance of lilies after rain mingled with the lush scent of their lovemaking, swirling through his senses. She bathed him with warmth, filled him with light, touching him deep inside, where all of his dreams lay buried. He closed his arms around her, holding her close against his heart. He realized now that there never had been any hope of resisting the temptation of Marisa.

"That was very nice," she whispered against his skin.

He nipped her shoulder. "You have a talent for understatement, my sweet."

She lifted herself away from him, far enough to look down into his face. She traced the curve of his smile with her fingertip. "I had almost given up hope of ever finding this kind of happiness."

As much as he tried to ignore them, questions that had haunted him over the years pecked at his brain. He slid his hand upward, along the length of her back, beneath the heavy silk of her hair. "Why did you do it, Mari?"

"Why did I do what?"

He looked into her sleepy eyes and realized how much he wanted to believe she had always loved him. "Why did you cry off our engagement? Your mother has the impression I was the one who wanted to end our engagement."

He had expected her to stiffen in defense. Instead, she smiled. "You were."

He drew the sheet up over them, shielding her from the evening air. "Marisa, I never once said I wanted to end our engagement."

She folded her arms on his chest and rested her chin on her arms. "You couldn't. You were far too honorable, much too kind ever to do anything to hurt me."

He stared at her. "You honestly believe I wanted to end our engagement?"

"I actually had doubts you ever really wanted to marry me in the first place. I did throw myself at you shamelessly."

"I told you how I felt about you."

She nodded, her hair brushing his sides. "You told me how you felt before we came to London. After we

were here, you seemed so distant. Then Braden told
me you had intended to offer for Letitia Thurmond.''

"He what?" Clayton swore under his breath. He
should have realized Braden would use almost any tactic to cut him out. "I never intended to offer for Letitia."

"I didn't want to believe it, but you and Letitia did
seem so well matched. And then you started avoiding
me. I saw more of Justin than I did of you. As much
as I wanted to believe you loved me, it seemed more
and more likely that you had changed your mind."

"I had given my word to your parents to abide by
their wishes. Every time I got near you, I kept hearing
this soft voice tempting me to break my word, to run
off to Scotland, or make love to you. Good gad! The
only way I knew to resist the temptation was to stay
away."

"Truly?" She looked like a child who had just received the most lovely present in the world. "Did I
really tempt you?"

"You have been tempting me from the first moment
I saw you."

She released her breath in a long sigh. "I wish I had
looked at it from that perspective, but the evidence
seemed so clearly to be against me. And then when
you told me you were having doubts about our marriage, I knew there was only one thing I could do. I
had to release you from your obligation, even though
I thought I might die of a shattered heart."

Die from a shattered heart. He had felt that way, as
though all the light had been ripped from his life. "I
thought it was what you wanted."

"Never." She pressed her lips to his neck, her breath
a warm sigh against his skin. "That day in the park, I
kept hoping you would tell me I was making a mistake.

But you seemed so accepting of it. I thought it must be what you wanted.''

He shook his head, smiling at the foolish young man he had been. ''It made perfect sense to me. Why would a beautiful, exciting woman like you want to marry a dull bookworm?''

''There was nothing dull about you. You were the most interesting man I had ever met.'' She brushed her lips over his. ''I loved you so much. I never stopped loving you.''

Clayton knew the honesty in her eyes could not be counterfeited. ''Marisa, I am not the same man I was. I don't know if I am capable of giving you all you need.''

''I have all I need. I have you.''

In the quiet room he heard the sound of barriers crumbling. ''I couldn't get you out of my mind. For seven years you were the only woman who haunted me.''

She grinned. ''That's because we were destined for each other.''

''Destined?''

''Yes. Our souls have loved before, in countless lifetimes. We were destined to find each other in this lifetime.''

Clayton smiled at her innocence. ''Such romantic notions.''

She drew circles with her fingertip upon his chest. ''You will believe them one day.''

He had the strange feeling he already did believe them. He turned with her in his arms, spilling her back against her pillow. ''Did you have a good time torturing me this evening?''

Marisa crinkled her nose, her eyes sparkling with mischief. "Incredible."

He nibbled her shoulder. "It is your turn to lie there and take it, my sweet."

A Promise Fulfilled

True love's the gift which God has given
To man alone beneath the heaven. . . .
It is the secret sympathy,
The silver link, the silken tie,
Which heart to heart, and mind to mind,
In body and in soul can bind.

—Sir Walter Scott

Chapter Twenty-three

Marisa awoke with a start, a sudden wrenching from slumber that sent her heart slamming against her ribs and sucked the air from her lungs. She snapped open her eyes and found Clayton leaning over her.

"Get up," he said, tugging her arm. "Put these on."

She took the nightgown and dressing gown he thrust at her. He stood beside the bed, dressed in a shirt he hadn't fastened and a pair of dark gray trousers, his white shirttails dangling over his hips. "What is it?"

A muscle clenched in his cheek. "Fire."

"Fire!" Even as she spoke the word, the scent of burning wood slithered into her senses.

"Get dressed," he said, his voice low and filled with command. "Quickly."

Marisa scrambled out of bed. She tugged the white cotton nightgown over her head, while Clayton dragged the counterpane from the bed. "What happened?"

"I don't know."

She slipped her arms into the black-and-scarlet silk robe and shoved her feet into her slippers. "Is the fire in the hallway?"

"Yes." He threw the counterpane around her shoulders and grabbed her hand. "Come on."

They ran to the door leading to the hall. Clayton touched the wood, then swore under his breath. "It's hot."

She tried to moisten her lips, but her mouth had turned to parchment. "That isn't good."

"No. That isn't good." He pushed her behind him. "Pull the counterpane over your head and stay behind me. I'll see if there is a chance we can get out this way."

Marisa did as he ordered. She huddled against his back as Clayton opened the door. Protected as she was, she still felt the blast of heat. He slammed the heavy door shut, and drew her away from the door. "Come with me."

She let the counterpane sag around her shoulders as she ran with Clayton across the room. In the few seconds the door had been open, black smoke had filled the room. Her eyes watered; her nose burned. Marisa coughed, smoke searing her throat, fear tearing her vitals. Clayton paused beside the bed, coughing as he stripped off the sheets.

When Marisa could catch a breath she looked up at him. "What are you doing?"

He threw the sheets over his shoulder. "Since we cannot get though the hall, we'll have to find another way out."

Marisa dragged a corner of the counterpane over her watering eyes. "What are we going to do?"

"Use the window."

"The window?"

"It's the only way out." He grabbed her arm and dragged her with him. They ran into the sitting room between their chambers. Clayton slammed the door behind them. She let the counterpane fall from her shoulders as they ran across his chambers.

Clayton ran to his bed and tore off the counterpane. He stripped off the blanket and sheets as he spoke. "I'm going to lower you to the ground."

"What about you?"

He lashed the sheets together. "I'll climb down after you are safe."

Marisa glanced at the door leading to the hall. An orange light glowed at the cracks where the door met the frame. Black smoke crept from beneath the solid oak. "But Clay, there isn't much time. You should climb down and let me take my chances climbing down as well."

"I cannot risk it."

"But Clay—"

"Don't argue with me, Mari."

Marisa's chest tightened as she stared at the door. Smoke crept into the room. It coiled across the carpet, lifting, writhing like a serpent. Flames hissed at the door.

Clayton tied the makeshift rope under her arms, then kissed her. "Hold on tightly. I'll make sure you don't fall."

She gripped his arm. "You make sure you get out of here safely."

He smiled. "I will."

Marisa sat on the windowsill and glanced down to the ground below. "Good heavens," she whispered.

"Don't look down."

She swung her legs out the window, choking back her fear as Clayton began lowering her toward the ground. Time and time again she bumped against the ivy-covered wall, but she scarcely felt the pain. About six feet from the ground, her descent halted. She glanced up at Clayton and found him leaning out the window, his arms stretched as far as he could manage.

He frowned down at her. "I'll have to let you drop the rest of the way."

Marisa swallowed hard. "Drop?"

Smoke slithered out the window above him. "Bend your knees when you hit the ground. Ready?"

No. But she didn't have a choice. "Let go."

Clayton released the sheet. Marisa fell, her knees buckling as she hit the ground. She thumped her bottom on the thick grass. The silk-sheet rope tumbled beside her.

"Are you all right?" Clayton yelled from above.

"I'm fine." She struggled to her feet and wiggled her way out of the makeshift rope. She stumbled away from the house as Clayton climbed from the room. "Be careful."

Marisa watched, her heart lodged in her throat as Clayton slowly climbed down the ivy-covered bricks. A scream tore from her throat as he slipped. For one heart-pounding moment his legs dangled. Then he found his footing and continued his climb. His feet hit the ground and she threw herself at him. "Clay!"

Clayton caught her, tightening his arms around her, staggering with her away from the house. "It's all right, love."

She looked up into his face. His cheeks were streaked with soot, his hair a mass of wild black waves. He had never looked more beautiful. "I was terrified you were going to fall."

He smoothed his hand over her hair. "Are you all right?"

"I'm fine now. I don't know what I would have done if anything had happened to you."

He kissed her softly. "I want you to wait in the gardens. Stay back from the house."

"What are you going to do?"

"I have to warn the servants."

She gripped his arm. "Be careful."

"I won't be long."

Clayton turned back toward the house. He took two long strides before a loud crack shattered the quiet night. Marisa flinched at the sudden noise. Clayton stumbled back toward her, pivoting as he collapsed, drifting toward the ground in a slow spiral. Marisa stared, too stunned to move for what seemed an eternity.

"Clay!" His name tore from her throat in a tangled sob. She ran to him and sank to her knees on the thick grass beside him. He lay unmoving on his back, his shirt covered with blood. She stared at him, unable to breathe for the fear crowding her chest.

"Clay," she whispered, touching his cheek with her trembling hand. His lashes lay against his cheeks; his lips were parted. She could detect no sign of breath. Overwhelming grief clenched her heart. "Clay, please!"

"I do apologize for this."

Marisa started at the sound of that distinctive male voice. Through a blur of tears, she glanced up from Clayton's still face to the fair-haired man standing nearby. The voice—she had heard it once in a garden maze, once more at the Sotherby party. Now she could put a face to the nightmare. "You."

He smiled, a far too pleasant smile for the horror he had just inflicted upon her. "So it seems you can recognize me just by the sound of my voice."

"You killed him!" Her throat closed around the words she still could not truly accept.

"I am afraid I had no choice." He slipped a pistol into his coat pocket. "I could not take the chance he would recognize me."

He wasn't at all the way she had imagined. The evil of his soul did not reflect on his face. He was surprisingly handsome, if one preferred finely molded features, a delicate, slim nose, high, sculpted cheekbones, and a thin mouth. And he was young. He could not have been more than five and twenty. "Who are you? Why would it matter if Clay recognized you?"

"I thought you knew. You and your husband invited me to your little party. Or should I say, the dowager Duchess of Marlow invited me. Suffice it to say if he realized who I was and what I had done, your husband could cause a great deal of unpleasantness for my very dear friend." He slipped his right hand into his coat pocket and withdrew a knife. "Not to mention the small fact that he could send me to the gallows for murder. You can see why I needed to eliminate him."

Moonlight glinted on the curved blade of the knife he held. Marisa scrambled to her feet as he stalked her. "You won't get away with this."

"Oh, I believe I will." He waved the blade back and forth as he moved toward her, like a nervous cat swishing its tail. "No one knows who I am. Your husband was the only one who could possibly identify me as a murderer. After you are dead, it will be quite safe for me to finish what needs to be done."

Marisa desperately, searched her mind for a way to escape this man. "Finish what?"

He laughed. "You are a curious little thing. But I am afraid I haven't time to answer all of your questions. Someone might have heard the shot. At any rate, someone in the servants' quarters will soon smell smoke and raise an alarm.''

Marisa screamed as he lunged for her. She turned to run. He grabbed her arm and spun her around to face him.

"I'm not really a murderer at heart. Although I suppose there are those who would disagree, since you will be my fifth victim.

My dear friend was appalled to hear of what I had done, even though I did it for him. But I know he will forgive me, once he realizes all the good I have done.''

Marisa stared at him, stunned by his confession. "Five people?''

"The first was not planned. It was actually an accident, so perhaps she doesn't signify.'' He lifted the blade at his side. "I really do not enjoy this sort of thing. I promise to stop after I have eliminated one more problem.''

Marisa lashed out with her foot, smashing her sole into his shin. He gasped, his grip loosening enough for her to escape. She managed to put several feet between them before he grabbed her from behind. He swung her to the side, throwing her against the thick trunk of an elm tree. The breath jolted from her lungs. Pinpoints of light danced before her eyes. Through the pounding of blood in her ears she heard the quiet anger in his voice.

"You are making this easier, bitch.''

She saw a flicker of moonlight on steel as he raised the blade. "No!'' she shouted, pushing against his chest.

"I really have no—'' His head suddenly snapped to one side. She heard a soft crack, a low sigh; then he fell, crumpling in a heap at her feet.

Marisa glanced up from his still form to the man

standing behind him. Her heart surged against her ribs.
"Clay!"

"Are you all right?" Clayton asked, his voice a
husky whisper.

"I am now." She stepped around the fallen murderer
and threw her arms around her husband. "I thought he
had murdered you."

Clayton's arms closed around her in a weak grip.
"He isn't going to hurt anyone ever again."

"You'd better sit before you collapse," Marisa said,
leading him to a stone bench nearby. He sank to the
bench and pressed his hand against his shoulder. "We
have to stop the bleeding."

"The sheets," he whispered.

She ran to where they had left the makeshift rope.
After gathering the white silk sheets, she raced back to
Clayton.

"Leave them. I'll take care of this," Clayton said,
his voice raw with pain. "You have to warn the servants."

"I will, as soon as I bind this wound. You are in no
shape to do it," she said, struggling with one of the
tight knots he had tied in the silk. When it wouldn't
budge, she remembered the knife. Clayton grabbed her
arm when she started toward the murderer's body.

"Marisa, the servants must be warned. Now, before—" Clayton paused as shouts pierced the night air.
He looked toward the house as a burly footman rushed
across the terrace.

"I think they know," Marisa said, breaking free of
his grasp. She ran the short distance to the murderer.
Steeling herself, she pried the weapon from his lifeless
hand, then returned to her husband and began to slice
the silk into long strips.

The footman skidded to a halt beside Marisa. He

glanced at the knife Marisa held, then turned wide eyes on Clayton. "Are you all right, Major?"

"I will be. Make sure everyone gets out, Denby," Clayton said.

"Holcomb and Bikens are seeing to it, sir. We've sent someone for the brigade."

Clayton grimaced as Marisa pressed a thick pad of silk against the wound in his shoulder. She cringed, feeling awkward and horribly clumsy. "Sorry. I have never done this before."

Clayton smiled at her. "You are doing fine."

She draped one end of a piece of silk over Clayton's shoulder, then pulled it one way across his chest, then the other.

Denby eyed Marisa's bandaging technique with a concerned eye. "Is there anything I can do to help, sir?"

Clayton touched Marisa's shoulder. "Denby has had some experience with bandages. Would you like him to help?"

Marisa nearly collapsed with relief. "Please."

The moon had nearly made its circuit across the sky when Clayton and Marisa arrived at Marlow House, refugees from the fire. Although Clayton insisted Marisa tend to her own needs, she stayed beside him like a mother cat protecting her only kitten while the surgeon removed the ball, cleansed, and rebandaged the wound. When she was certain Clayton was doing well, Marisa allowed Isabel and Sophia to usher her from the room, reluctantly relinquishing Clayton into the hands of his valet, Lindsley.

After his valet tended to the mess that was his master, Clayton lay propped against his pillows, watching Justin pace back and forth across the chamber. "I feel a little like a sailor on a rolling sea. You are making me dizzy."

"Sorry." Justin paused beside the bed and frowned down at his twin. "How are you feeling?"

Clayton tried to ignore the pain throbbing in his shoulder, the blood pounding in his temples. "All things considered, well enough."

Justin rubbed his shoulder as though the pain Clayton felt were centered there. "There is another one out there, looking to nail your hide to a wall."

Clayton smoothed his fingers over the shoulder of his nightshirt, feeling the thick bandage beneath, trying to ease the burning centered in his ragged flesh. "I know."

Justin threw himself into the armchair he had earlier drawn next to the bed. "Who the hell was that bastard?"

Clayton closed his eyes, surrendering to the weight tugging on his lids. Although he had refused laudanum, his body demanded rest. "According to Marisa, he was one of the men we invited to the party. I'll have Newberry investigate. It shouldn't be difficult to determine who he was."

"You didn't recognize him?"

"No." Still, Clayton had heard most of what the bastard had said to Marisa. Marisa could supply the rest. Perhaps when they filled in the missing pieces, they could solve the puzzle.

Justin squeezed Clayton's arm. "I'd better let you get some sleep."

Clayton pried open his eyes and smiled at his brother. "That sounds like a good idea."

Soon after Justin left, Marisa entered the room. Clayton smiled at her. She had bathed and washed her hair, coming to him before the heavy mass was dry. Damp waves fell around the dark blue dressing gown Sophia had supplied his wife. As Marisa walked toward him, prim white linen peeked from the front opening of the wrapper. "I see Sophia and Isabel have managed to put you back in order."

"I'm surprised I didn't send poor Perceval fleeing into the night when he saw me." She paused beside the bed and took Clayton's hand in a warm grasp. "You are looking much better than you did when I left."

"I wonder if Lindsley will leave me after this?" Clayton thought of his valet, dealing with all the blood and soot that had covered his master. "He kept shaking his head as he dealt with the mess."

"He told me he was thankful you had survived. I got the impression he was interested in keeping you around awhile." Marisa smoothed the hair back from his brow, the wide silk cuff of her dressing gown brushing his cheek. "Come to think of it, so am I."

Clayton's insides tightened when he thought of how close he had come to losing her. He tugged on her dressing gown, coaxing her toward him. "Come to bed. I want to hold you."

"Your wound. I thought it might be best if I slept on the chaise," she said, glancing toward the Grecian chaise longue by the hearth.

"You thought wrong." He took her hand and drew her down onto the bed beside him. "I have grown accustomed to feeling you beside me each night. Even if you do claim more than your fair share of the bed."

She lifted her brows in mock indignation. "Are you saying I do not share well?"

"I am saying I want you beside me."

She smiled, all the warmth of her love shimmering

in her eyes. "I could hurt you somehow, throw my arm around you, jostle your wound."

"I will take the chance." He realized he would take any chance to hold her. He lifted her hand and touched his lips to her smooth skin. The scent of lilies after rain flooded his senses. Her warmth radiated against his cheek. "Come, lie beside me."

She slipped off her dressing gown, draped it over a chair near the bed, then extinguished the candles. The soft light of dawn filtered into the room through the windows. "Do you want the drapes closed?"

"No. I love your face in the first light of dawn."

She smiled, her entire face glowing from an inner light born of happiness. She climbed into bed beside him and rested her head on his unharmed shoulder. Her warmth radiated against him, kindling embers deep inside him. He closed his eyes and drifted into a pleasant slumber, his dreams filled with a beguiling temptress.

Later that day, Clayton lay propped against his pillows discussing the events of the previous evening with his brother. Rain tapped against the windows, gray clouds filling the early afternoon sky. Clayton had fitted together all of what Marisa could remember of the night before with his own recollections. And still the solution to the puzzle eluded him.

Justin rested his shoulder against a thick post at the foot of Clayton's bed. "Newberry identified the blackguard as David Renwick, youngest son of Sir Edward Renwick."

"The name means nothing to me." What was it? Something hovered just beyond his reach, a question, an answer, lurking in the shadows. Each time Clayton drew near, it darted away from him.

"Last night, did Renwick say anything that might point us toward his accomplice?"

"I have told you everything he said."

"Think, Clay." Justin rubbed his shoulder absently. "There must be something we are missing."

Clayton went over it again, reiterating everything he had heard, forcing a brain dulled by pain to function with all the clarity he could manage. This time, as he mulled over the words of the murderer, a glimmer of light flickered in the shadows of his brain. "He said I could send him to the gallows as a murderer, and cause a great deal of trouble for his dear friend."

Justin's brows lifted. "He obviously thought you could connect him with one of the murders he had committed."

"Yes. He did." Realization slowly trickled through Clayton. He stared at his brother, the pieces of the puzzle falling into place. "I kept thinking it must have been something that happened in England. That's what threw me off the scent."

Justin frowned. "You have an idea of what is behind this."

"I might. Fortunately, I haven't been involved with many murders. I can think of only one."

Justin stared at his twin, understanding dawning in his eyes. "Harry?"

"The man I glimpsed in the hall in Paris before I found Harry. Although I didn't get a good look at his face, he was a slender young man with fair hair. It's possible he thought I could identify him."

"I thought it was robbery," Justin said.

"Perhaps it wasn't."

"Why the devil would David Renwick want to murder Harry?" Justin demanded.

"Two men, involved in murder." Clayton rubbed

his injured shoulder, trying to ease the ache burning there. "The reason behind the murders is the key."

Justin frowned. "Why does a man commit murder?"

Clayton stared at the gold dragons splashed across the emerald silk spilling down the carved bedpost beside Justin. "Jealousy. Greed. Hatred."

"I doubt this had anything to do with hatred or jealousy. Greed would be my wager. It brings us back to the connection between David Renwick and Harry Fitzwilliam." Justin rubbed his shoulder, grimacing as though it pained him. "How would Renwick have benefited from murdering Harry?"

"Maybe Harry was just a stepping-stone. The man had murdered three people before last night. Harry was only one of them. And, after eliminating Marisa and me, he had one more to complete before he was finished. One last obstacle to his goal." Clayton stabbed his fingers at the counterpane lying at his side. "What if that goal was a sizable fortune and a respected title to go along with it?"

Justin looked at Clayton, the muscles in his face tense. More words were not necessary. Clayton could see that his brother was on the same path he was. "You realize what you are saying."

"I don't like it any more than you do, but it makes sense."

Justin nodded. "We have no proof. We have to find a way to connect him with Renwick."

Clayton stretched his hand wide against the counterpane. "As far as he knows, Renwick could have told me everything before he died. Perhaps we can coax him into confessing."

Justin smiled, an icy look entering his eyes. "I think it's time I pay a visit to an old acquaintance."

Clayton grinned. "Give him my regards."

Soon after Justin left, the door opened. Clayton expected Marisa to enter the room, carrying a book to read to him. Instead, Gregory Stanwood strode into the room. The door closed with a soft click behind him. Before Clayton could utter a word, Gregory pulled a pistol from his coat pocket and aimed it straight at him.

"I don't want to shoot you."

"That's good." Clayton held Gregory's gaze, seeing the desperation in his eyes. "Shooting me won't gain you anything. Bow Street already knows about your involvement with David Renwick. At the moment they think he committed the murders. You might actually avoid the gallows."

"I didn't murder anyone—you must believe me. I never wanted to murder anyone." Gregory crossed the room, creeping toward the bed. "It was David."

Clayton thought of the pistol lying in the drawer of the table beside the bed. "When did it start? With your wife?"

"It was an accident. She came in . . ." Gregory paused at the foot of the bed, the pistol trembling in his hand. "She found us together. She went mad, throwing things, screaming. She said she would have the marriage annulled. David meant only to calm her. He grabbed her, but she pulled away. She fell and hit her head on the hearth."

"Was it David's idea to clear the way between you and the Ashbourne fortune?" Clayton inched his hand toward the beside table.

"What are you doing?" Gregory wagged the pistol at Clayton. "Keep your hands where I can see them. Put them on top of the counterpane."

Clayton clenched his jaw and did as Gregory demanded. "You said you haven't murdered anyone. Do you want to start?"

"No. But I don't want to go to prison, and you can send me there." Gregory shook his head. "Gad, what a tangle."

"If it was all David's idea, you don't have anything to worry about."

"It was his idea. David said I wouldn't need to marry again once I was Earl of Ashbourne. We would have all the money we needed." Gregory flicked his tongue over his lips. "I told him I couldn't do it. But he didn't listen. He killed my uncle and made it look like an accident. I didn't realize what he had done until after he killed Harry."

"That was when he decided he needed to eliminate me."

Gregory nodded. "He was going to murder you, then Braden. I didn't know what to do. He said I was in as deeply as he was. He was afraid you would recognize him. He said if he went to the gallows, I would hang beside him."

Clayton had known Gregory Stanwood most of his life. Even if he hadn't heard Renwick mention how appalled his dear friend had been at the murders, Clayton would have believed Gregory. He didn't have the stomach or the nerve for murder. "Put the pistol down, Gregory. Before it goes off by accident."

Gregory clutched the pistol with both hands, keeping it pointed straight at Clayton's heart. "I cannot go to Newgate. I would rather die. You have to tell them I had nothing to do with the murders."

Gregory was just nervous enough to pull the trigger by accident. "Gregory, I shall—"

The crack of a gunshot ripped through the room. Clayton flinched, his body tensing with the expectation of the impact of a bullet. He heard a groan, and realized it came from the foot of the bed. The pistol fell from

Gregory's limp hand. He fell against the bedpost, clutching his arm, moaning, staring in horror toward the door. Clayton followed his stare and found Marisa moving toward the bed, holding a small pistol trained on Stanwood, an avenging angel dressed entirely in white.

Marisa paused beside the bed, her worried gaze flitting over Clayton. "Are you all right?"

Clayton lifted his brows. "How long have you been walking about carrying a pistol?"

Marisa smiled down at the short-barreled pistol. "This morning I decided to slip this into my bodice."

Clayton eyed her neckline. "I suppose I should be prepared for anything with you."

Gregory moaned. "I'm bleeding to death."

Marisa stared at him, her eyes narrowed like a cat about to strike. "Tell me, Mr. Stanwood. Why the devil should I care?"

Clayton touched her arm. "He will bleed all over the carpet, my darling. Sophia will not be pleased."

Marisa frowned. "Very well, I shall see to it."

Moonlight spilled through the windowpanes, streaming like cream over the emerald and gold swirls in the carpet of Clayton's bedchamber, as though seeking the man lying beside her. Marisa lay propped on her arm, looking down at her husband. "You and Braden are much too kind." She smoothed the soft black waves back from his brow. "I still cannot believe you are going to allow Gregory Stanwood to walk away from this without any punishment at all."

Clayton grinned. "You did shoot him."

Marisa plucked at the sleeve of his nightshirt. "He might have murdered you."

"Gregory is not a murderer. You heard Renwick;

his dear friend was appalled at what he had done."
Clayton lifted a lock of hair that had tumbled over his
chest. Slowly he slid the strands back and forth between his fingers as though he loved the feel of her
hair. "He came here because he was frightened and
had no idea what he should do next. He hoped only to
convince me to testify on his behalf."

"With a pistol?"

Clayton smiled. "I told you he was desperate."

"You honestly believe this was entirely David Renwick's idea?"

"I have known Gregory Stanwood most of my life.
He would never have thought of anything so diabolical.
Braden agrees."

Marisa pursed her lips, acknowledging her own
doubts about Gregory's ability to murder anyone.
"Gregory could have warned you."

"He was too frightened to warn me, too interested
in saving his own neck. He did tell me I should leave
town until all the trouble had passed."

"His cowardice caused a great deal of trouble."

"It did. But I was thinking this afternoon, if you
hadn't overheard Renwick and Gregory, we might
never have found our way back to each other." Clayton
slid his fingers over the curve of her jaw. "I am thankful at least some good came out of all this tragedy."

"I wasn't certain what I would do when I heard you
were going to take a wife this Season. I like to think I
would have found a way to upset your plans."

"Would you have fought for me, my love?"

She smoothed her hand over his chest. "With every
tactic imaginable."

He laughed, a soft sound that wrapped around her in
a warm caress. "I love you, Mari."

The sweetness of those words curled around her

heart. "I have waited a very long time to hear you say that again."

"Too long." He eased the gold chain over his head. The ring gathered the moonlight and delivered sparkling shards of color in return. He grimaced, his fingers clumsy as he worked the clasp and removed the ring from the chain. Marisa resisted the urge to help him. She sensed this was something he needed to do alone.

He stared down at the ring as he spoke. "We were both too young to understand everything we shared the first time I gave you this. I want you to know there are no doubts in my heart, Mari."

Tears welled in her eyes, tears of joy she could not contain. "No doubts."

"I love you." Clayton looked up at her, all the truth of his words in his eyes. "I thank the Almighty you waited for me to come back to you."

"How could I not wait for you? I love you," she whispered. "I always have."

Her hand trembled as she held it for him to slip the ring onto her finger. When the ring was once more where it belonged, he lifted her hand and touched his lips to her skin. "Now and forever, my love."

Marisa brushed her lips over his. "Now and forever."

Epilogue

London, 1823

Clayton stood beside his wife's bed, staring in awe at the woman who cradled his daughter in her arms. Marisa's hair spilled in thick black waves over her pillow. Candlelight glowed upon her face, illuminating the curve of her smile. She could still set his pulse racing with a smile. "Are you certain you are feeling all right?"

"A little tired, but fine." Marisa gripped his hand. "Come lie beside us. I want your arms around me."

Clayton eased onto the mattress beside her and slipped his arm around her shoulders. Marisa turned her head against his shoulder and sighed. "She is beautiful."

"Like her mother." Clayton touched his daughter's hand, smiling as the baby gripped his finger in her small fist. Sophia crinkled her tiny nose, staring with

392

unfocused eyes up at her papa. She was their third child, their first daughter. Still, he knew he would never get over the wonder, the complete miracle of birth, or the fear he felt each time his wife went through the pain of bringing life into this world.

"Stay with me," Marisa said in a sleepy whisper.

Clayton brushed his lips against her brow and silently gave thanks for all of the gifts he had been given. "Always."

AUTHOR'S NOTE

I hope you enjoyed spending time with Clayton and Marisa. When writing a sequel or a book in a series, a writer is presented with the peculiar challenge of making each book capable of standing on its own. In this case, several areas of the book actually overlap my previous release, *Devil's Honor*, which made it an interesting balancing act. I always love a challenge.

If you are wondering how Isabel managed to tame Clayton's wicked brother, Justin, their story is brought to life in *Devil's Honor*.

For excerpts from my books, a glimpse at my current project, and a little about me, visit my web site at: www.tlt.com/authors/ddier.htm. You can also send me E-mail at: DebraDier@aol.com.

I love to hear from readers. Please enclose a self-addressed, stamped envelope with your letter. You can reach me at: P.O. Box 4147, Hazelwood, MO 63042-0747.

Lady of the Night — Cordia Byers

Manacled to a stone wall is not the way Katharina Fergersen planned to spend her vacation. But a wrong turn in the right place and the haunted English castle she is touring is suddenly full of life—and so is the man who is bathing before her. As the frosty winter days melt into hot passionate nights, she realizes that there is more to Kane than just a well-filled pair of breeches. Katharina is determined not to let this man who has touched her soul escape her, even if it means giving up all to remain Sedgewick's lady of the night.

___4404-8 $5.99 US/$6.99 CAN

Dorchester Publishing Co., Inc.
P.O. Box 6640
Wayne, PA 19087-8640

Please add $1.75 for shipping and handling for the first book and $.50 for each book thereafter. NY, NYC, and PA residents, please add appropriate sales tax. No cash, stamps, or C.O.D.s. All orders shipped within 6 weeks via postal service book rate. Canadian orders require $2.00 extra postage and must be paid in U.S. dollars through a U.S. banking facility.

Name_____

Address_____

City_____State_____Zip_____

I have enclosed $_____ in payment for the checked book(s).

Payment <u>must</u> accompany all orders. ❑ Please send a free catalog.

CHECK OUT OUR WEBSITE! www.dorchesterpub.com

DEBRA DIER

DEVIL'S HONOR

Known as the Devil of Dartmoor—the most dangerous man in London—Justin Trevelyan prefers the company of widows and prostitutes to the charms of innocents. The last thing he needs is an impertinent maiden and her two young sisters under his wardship. Yet from the moment he lays eyes on Isabel, he is captivated by her sweet beauty and somehow needs to protect her as well as possess her. But before he can gain an angel's trust, he has to prove his devil's honor.

___4362-9 $5.99 US/$6.99 CAN

Dorchester Publishing Co., Inc.
P.O. Box 6640
Wayne, PA 19087-8640

Please add $1.75 for shipping and handling for the first book and $.50 for each book thereafter. NY, NYC, and PA residents, please add appropriate sales tax. No cash, stamps, or C.O.D.s. All orders shipped within 6 weeks via postal service book rate. Canadian orders require $2.00 extra postage and must be paid in U.S. dollars through a U.S. banking facility.

Name_____
Address_____
City_____State_____Zip_____
I have enclosed $_____ in payment for the checked book(s).
Payment <u>must</u> accompany all orders. ❑ Please send a free catalog.

ATTENTION ROMANCE CUSTOMERS!

SPECIAL TOLL-FREE NUMBER
1-800-481-9191

Call Monday through Friday
10 a.m. to 9 p.m.
Eastern Time
Get a free catalogue,
join the Romance Book Club,
and order books using your
Visa, MasterCard,
or Discover®

Leisure
Books

LOVE SPELL

GO ONLINE WITH US AT DORCHESTERPUB.COM